Penguin Books
Greenvoe

George Mackay Brown was born in Stromness, Orkney,
(the 'Hamnavoe' of his stories and poems) in 1921 and
was educated at Newbattle Abbey, when Edwin Muir was
Warden there. He read English at Edinburgh University
and undertook post-graduate work on Gerard Manley
Hopkins. He now lives and works in Orkney.

Mr Brown was awarded an Arts Council grant for poetry
in 1965, the Society of Authors Travel Award in 1968,
which he used to travel in Eire, and the Scottish
Arts Council Literature Prize in 1969 (for *A Time to Keep*)
as well as the 1971 Katherine Mansfield Menton short-
story prize for the title story in his *A Time to Keep*
volume.

A prolific writer, his books of poetry include *Loaves and
Fishes*, *The Year of the Whale*, *Fishermen with Ploughs*
and *Poems New and Selected*. He has also published three
collections of short stories: *A Calendar of Love*, *A Time
to Keep* and *Hawkfall*; a non-fiction work, *Orkney
Tapestry*, *A Spell for Green Corn*, a chronicle of six
scenes. *Greenvoe* was his first novel and his second,
Magnus, appeared in 1973. His latest publications are *The Sun's
Net*, a collection of short stories (1976) and *Winterfield*, a collection
of his poetry (1976). He was awarded the O.B.E. in 1974.

George Mackay Brown

GREENVOE

Penguin Books

Penguin Books Ltd,
Harmondsworth, Middlesex, England
Penguin Books, 625 Madison Avenue,
New York, New York 10022, U.S.A.
Penguin Books Australia Ltd,
Ringwood, Victoria, Australia
Penguin Books Canada Ltd,
41 Steelcase Road West, Markham, Ontario, Canada
Penguin Books (N.Z.) Ltd,
182–190 Wairau Road, Auckland 10, New Zealand

First published by The Hogarth Press 1972
Published in Penguin Books 1976
Reprinted 1976
Copyright © George Mackay Brown, 1972

Made and printed in Great Britain by
Cox & Wyman Ltd, London, Reading and Fakenham
Set in Linotype Juliana

Contents

ONE

Slowly the night shadow passed from the island and the Sound. In the village of Greenvoe lights burned in the windows of three fishermen's cottages above the pier.

A small dark knotted man came out of one of the doors. He picked up a half-dozen lobster creels from the white wall and carried them across to the pier and down a few stone steps. A motorboat called the *Ellen* was tied up there. Bert Kerston stowed his creels on board. He untied the *Ellen* and pushed off. He swung the starting handle. The *Ellen* kicked and coughed into life. Her bow tore the quiet water apart.

From the second open door came a mild chant. Samuel Whaness the fisherman was reading scripture with his wife Rachel. 'He maketh the deep to boil as a pot: he maketh the sea like a pot of ointment. He maketh a path to shine after him; one would think the deep to be hoary. Upon earth there is not his like, who is made without fear. He beholdeth all high things: he is a king over all the children of pride' ... They knelt down together. 'Lord,' said Samuel Whaness earnestly, 'protect us in our goings this day and always, and be thou merciful unto us. Amen.'

'Amen,' said Rachel.

Samuel Whaness stood at the door in a thick grey jersey and rubber boots. Gravely he and Rachel saluted each other, their necks intersecting, a Hebraic farewell. Then he crossed over to the pier, went down the stone steps, rowed out in his dinghy to the moored motor-boat, started up the engine, and steered the *Siloam* the opposite way to the *Ellen*, into the open Atlantic.

There was a stirring in the third fisherman's house. The door opened very slowly. A thin face with huge glinting rounds in it peered out. A long finger was licked and held up to the sky. The head shook. 'No,' said The Skarf, 'not this morning. I was out all

Saturday for one lobster and two crabs. I might make a start on the history. Joseph Evie will sign the unemployment paper. Anyway, I haven't got any petrol.' He closed his door. Smoke rose presently from his chimney. Anyone looking in through his webbed window could see The Skarf moving between boxes of books and a table covered with writing paraphernalia. He read all morning from a spread of books on the table; his face hopped from one to the other like a bird. Occasionally he would make a note in an old cash-book that Joseph Evie the merchant had thrown out and that Timmy Folster the beachcomber had found on the shore. At his desk he still wore his oilskin and thigh-boots.

A door in a small cottage at the other end of the village opened. Isabella Budge threw oats and bits of bread from the bowl she carried to a white flurry of chickens. 'Cluck cluck cluck,' said the old woman. 'Kitty kitty kitty. Kitty cluck kit.'

'Bella,' shouted a voice from inside. It was not entirely a local voice; it was the voice of an old seaman who had been sailing all his life; it was seasoned with Geordie and Scouse and Cockney and Clydeside; a voice that belonged to the brotherhood of the sea.

'What ails thee, Ben?' said Bella. 'Cluck kit.'

'Make less goddam noise,' roared Ben. 'You make more row than the Calcutta bazaar.'

'Kitty cluck. Kitty cluck,' said Bella among the chickens.

'Bella,' shouted Ben.

'Kitty,' whispered Bella.

'Come in and light the fire,' said Ben. 'It's cold. I want my goddam breakfast.'

Mr Joseph Evie, postmaster, merchant, county councillor, justice of the peace, took the wooden shutters from the window of his general merchant's store. The first bluebottles rose from the slices of melon and boxes of liquorice-allsorts inside. They bounced and droned on the pane. Mrs Olive Evie stood in the door that led from kitchen to shop; her eyes took in the wakening village in one caustic probe. Ivan Westray the ferryman was the first customer. He wanted his can filled with petrol. Mr Joseph Evie went out to the tank to fill the can.

'Twenty Woodbines,' said Ivan Westray to Mrs Olive Evie.

'She's a well-like lass,' said Mrs Olive Evie.

'Who?' said Ivan Westray.

'Miss Inverary the new school-teacher,' said Mrs Olive Evie.

'Is she?' said Ivan Westray.

'Who's crossing over today?' said Mrs Olive Evie. 'The ferry's early.'

'President Nixon and Mao Tse-tung,' said Ivan Westray. He paid for his cigarettes, then went out to get his can of petrol from Mr Joseph Evie at the pump.

Bella Budge came into the shop for a quarter-pound of bacon for Ben's breakfast.

'What way is your brother?' said Mrs Olive Evie.

'Lean bacon,' said Bella. 'The last bacon was nothing but fat. He's fine.'

'Watch him,' said Mrs Olive Evie. 'Watch an old man when he starts to shout for food. They get ravenous in the end. The death hunger.'

'My brother Benjamin Andrew James is quite well,' said Bella. 'A writing pad with lines. After he gets his breakfast he's going to write a letter to Tom in Canada, our nephew. Tom has a very good job in Vancouver, B.C. A box of matches.'

Mr Joseph Evie came back into the shop, smelling of petrol.

Bella gathered her errands under her shawl and slipped out past him.

The sun was brimming all the eastern windows of Greenvoe now with cold fire.

'You know this, Mr Evie,' said Mrs Olive Evie to her husband. 'You know why Ivan Westray's up so early. The laird's grand-daughter is coming for the summer. From that boarding-school in England. She'll have been biding in a hotel in Kirkwall all night. So she's crossing over to Hellya today. That's what it is. Dear me. A young girl like her won't find much to set her up in Greenvoe. That Voar woman with a new illegitimate bairn. Scorradale the publican open every weekend till four in the morning. The Skarf preaching socialism and atheism to all the young folk as hard as he can. Some place to come to!'

'It is a lovely morning, Mrs Evie,' said Mr Joseph Evie.

'There's something not right going on up at the manse,' said Mrs Olive Evie. 'I didn't see the minister's old mother all day yesterday. There's something very queer about that woman, more queer even than ever I thought.'

'The lupins are up early,' said Mr Joseph Evie.

'That new school-teacher would give anything for a man,' said Mrs Olive Evie.

'We're out of fisherman's stockings, I see,' said Mr Joseph Evie.

Miss Margaret Inverary appeared at the school door and agitated a handbell. The clangour rolled from end to end of the village. From the Kerston door Tom and Ernie and Judy ran to school. A dozen children from the farms and crofts of Hellya ran helter-skelter down the brae. From the house of Alice Voar at the back of the village five children straggled, some of them cramming their mouths with bread and jam and dry cornflakes. The youngest one had nothing on but a vest.

'Run, Sidney,' cried Alice Voar, herding them along the road. 'Sophie, you'll be late. Now, Sander, hurry. The clever peedie Shirley, on with you. Sam, the teacher has a strap. No, peedie Skarf, you can't go to the school till you're a big boy – run in, see if the bairn's sleeping, Skarf ... The learning's a grand thing,' Alice Voar remarked through the shop door to Mr Joseph Evie and Mrs Olive Evie; then she took peedie Skarf by the hand and led him back to the cottage and put his trousers on at the doorstep.

'Seven children,' said Mrs Olive Evie, 'all to different fathers. Fancy.'

'I think we will have a week of fine weather,' said Mr Joseph Evie.

The Skarf, in his oilskin and sea-boots, pushed the door of the shop open.

'You're not at the fishing today, I see,' said Mrs Olive Evie. 'That was the worst thing you ever did, Skarf, going to work with your old uncle at the lobsters. You with all that brains. You should have gone on to the school, then the university. There were plenty of bursaries going, goodness knows. You'd have been a high-up man now, a professor maybe.'

'The Lord works in a mysterious way, his wonders to perform,' said The Skarf.

'Morning,' said Mr Joseph Evie to The Skarf, not cordially.

'Loaf, gallon of paraffin, four candles, half pound margarine, two clothes pegs, a black ball-point,' said The Skarf. 'I'll pay on Saturday. And I need my unemployment paper signed.'

Mr Joseph Evie took a ledger from his desk. He opened it and ran his finger down the items. 'I find you owe three pounds eight and threepence,' he said.

'All will be paid,' said The Skarf patiently.

'I can't extend credit indefinitely,' said Mr Joseph Evie.

'No,' said The Skarf, 'and the hawks don't fly south in the winter either. I'll take the ninepenny biro now.'

A singing lesson was proceeding in the school. Miss Inverary thumped the piano. A score of faces had lost all human expression and were caught up in one cold seraphic trance. The mouths opened and shut.

> Speed, bonny boat, like a bird on the wing
> 'Onward,' the sailors cry.
> 'Carry the lad that's born to be king
> Over the sea to Skye.'

'That was *nice*,' said Miss Inverary. 'Ernie Kerston, take your finger out of your nose. Now I'm going to write the next verse on the blackboard. Those who can write, copy it down in your exercise books, neatly. Now tell me, who has a boat like the boat in the song? Think hard. Hands up.'

'My dad,' said Ernie Kerston, and drew a long pale worm out of his left nostril with the nail of his right forefinger.

'No, Ernie,' said Miss Inverary, 'your father has a fishing boat, but it isn't exactly like a bird on the wing, is it? Think hard.'

'Ivan Westray,' said a boy from the farms whose jacket smelt of peats.

'Very good, John Corrigall,' said Miss Inverary.

*

There was one cottage in Greenvoe that had a charred façade, as if it had been built on the lip of a volcano. There was nothing quite so terrible in its situation. But three years before, the occupant, Timmy Folster, had overset the primus stove when he was frying onions for his supper. The curtain had never been renewed – a scorched rag still hung at the window. The fire had burst out three panes, which had been replaced with cardboard squares. In place of the door was a sheet of corrugated iron held in place with a huge stone at the base and two crossed slats of wood higher up. Timmy Folster emerged, as he always did since the burning, through the window. He ambled towards the pier. He bent down and picked up a cigarette end that Ivan Westray had dropped and put it in his pocket. He sat down on a soap box outside the general store and poked the tobacco from three cigarette ends into a pipe. He spoke to himself amiably all the time. 'Timmy's a good boy. Timmy never did harm to a living soul. They can't put Timmy in the poorhouse. Timmy can look after himself. Timmy's no fool. Timmy knows a thing or two. He does so.'

He took his national assistance order book carefully from his inside pocket. He studied the amount due, and his signature. He went into the shop.

'Well, Timmy,' said Mr Joseph Evie.

'National assistance day, Mr Evie,' said Timmy. 'I see this is the last order in the book. I hope you have a new book for me.'

Mr Joseph Evie stamped the order book and opened the tin box where he kept the Post Office money. 'Four pounds six shillings and sixpence, Timmy,' he said.

'Timmy requires a loaf and a pound pot of raspberry jam, a half pound of margarine, three tins cat food, a bottle of methylated spirits.'

'Now, Timmy, I'm going to speak seriously to you,' said Mr Joseph Evie. 'You always sign a declaration in my book that the meth you buy is for your primus stove.'

'And my tilley lamp,' said Timmy.

'Well, Timmy, now,' said Mr Joseph Evie, 'see that you use it for that purpose only.'

'Of course, Mr Evie,' said Timmy. 'What else?'

*

Greenvoe was suddenly shaken out of its dream. People appeared at every door. A car coughed and rattled at the end of the village. It approached in a cloud of dust and fumes. It entered the village and stopped at the pier, shuddering. It was a very old car with a canvas hood and brass headlamps belted on to it. Colonel Fortin-Bell the laird got out and opened the other door for his niece, Miss Agatha Fortin-Bell.

'A simply lovely morning,' announced Miss Fortin-Bell. 'She's coming. That must be her now.' She spoke as if she were shouting into a gale. (The islanders could never understand why the gentry spoke in such heroic voices – their own speech was slow and wondering, like water lapping among stones.) Miss Fortin-Bell faced seawards. The ferry-boat *Skua* entered the bay in a wide curve and glided towards the pier with shut-off engine. Ivan Westray stood at the wheel. A young girl waved from the stern, a little white flutter of hand, and smiled, and stroked down her dark windblown hair. 'Welcome to the island, darling,' shouted Miss Fortin-Bell. 'Isn't this lovely, all the village has come out to welcome you . . .'

Ivan Westray leapt ashore and handed Miss Inga Fortin-Bell on to the steps.

The village watched with sardonic awe as the grand folk greeted each other with shouts and kisses. (Their own greeting, even after a decade of absence, was a murmur and a dropping of eyes.)

Ivan Westray passed from boat to pier Inga's trunk and cases and coat; a flaccid mail-bag; a box marked *School Books – With Care*; and a tea-box full of new loaves from the town, a faint incense wafting from it.

'Fifteen bob,' said Ivan Westray to Inga.

Inga laid down her paperback copy of *Women In Love* on the sea wall and took her purse out of her skirt pocket.

'You must be utterly worn out, you poor darling,' shouted Miss Fortin-Bell. Then she turned to the villagers. 'Thank you, one and all, for turning out to welcome Inga. It was jolly nice.'

The school rushed out for dinner with a medley of cries. Then the children were suddenly silent. They stood around the gentry like pigeons round a crushed cake, making little astonished noises and silences through rounded lips.

'Bloody parasites,' said The Skarf, and went back to his desk.

'Thank you very much, boatman,' said Inga. Ivan Westray looked at the small sweet hidden curves under her sweater, and nodded. She smiled back at him. He nodded again, unsmiling.

Miss Fortin-Bell pushed the girl into the back of the car. Mr Joseph Evie stowed the trunk and cases on to the back rack and lashed them down with a piece of rope from the store. Colonel Fortin-Bell flung the handle round and the car racketed and shuddered. The colonel got back in. The car jerked forward. A dozen hands fluttered. Inga looked back at Ivan Westray until the car turned the corner of the general store.

Mr Joseph Evie picked up the mail and took it into the shop.

Timmy Folster went into the stone latrine. He took the blue bottle out of his coat pocket and uncorked it. Then he remembered Mr Joseph Evie's stern warning. He corked the bottle again. He put it back in his pocket. 'Timmy must try to be good,' he said. 'They'll stop his money if he isn't. They will.'

Alice Voar's children and Ellen Kerston's drifted indoors for their dinner. The children from the farms ate their pieces sitting on the sea wall. Gino Manson ate a scone by himself, on Bella Budge's doorstep.

The excitement was over.

The laird's car stuttered distantly among the hills of Hellya.

In the following silence Miss Inverary crossed the road from the schoolhouse and entered the shop. She rapped on the counter. Mrs Olive Evie appeared at the between-door with a steaming soup ladle in her hand. Miss Inverary asked Mrs Evie for a pound of eating apples. Mrs Evie selected the best apples from a hoard that was beginning to fester slowly in the barrel, and said, 'The Westrays were never right in the head. Clever but tainted. His uncle and grandfather died in the Edinburgh asylum. Evelyn Westray committed suicide in the quarry, a girl of seventeen. She was his cousin . . .' Miss Inverary stroked the black cat that was curled on top of the counter.

Afternoon was always the quietest time in the village. The fishermen were still at sea. The crofters had not yet unyoked. There was little sound in Greenvoe on a summer afternoon but the murmur of multiplication tables through the tall school window, and the drone of bluebottles among Mr Joseph Evie's confectionery, and the lapping of water against the pier.

In the manse parlour old Mrs McKee knew without a shadow of a doubt that with her it was once more the season of assize. On every bright and dark wind they came, her accusers, four times a year; they gathered in the manse of Hellya to inquire into certain hidden events of her life. The assize lasted for many days and generally covered the same ground, though occasionally new material would be led that she had entirely forgotten about. All the counts in the indictment had to be answered in some way or other. This was the summer assize; it was a shame that all these beautiful days (not that she ever went out much to enjoy the weather) must be wasted with charge and objection and cross-examination. Moreover, the tribunal was secret; nobody in the village or island knew about it but herself, not even her son Simon who was the parish minister; though Simon shrewdly guessed, she felt sure, that something preoccupied his mother sorely on such occasions; and moreover – this was very strange – the assize usually assembled when Simon was bearing or was about to bear his own little private cross. For a few days, sometimes for as long as a week, the manse was an abode of secret suffering. It should not be supposed, though, that for the prisoner it was all un-mitigated pain. In a strange way Mrs Elizabeth McKee actually looked forward to her sequence of trials; she enjoyed the vivid resurrection of the past, however painful. There was a whole team of accusers, and it gave her pleasure to recognize their distinctive turns of phrase and the rhythms of their speaking (though some of them no doubt were very unpleasant dangerous persons indeed). It was all too plain what their purpose was: they wished to nip her as soon as possible from the tree of living, to gather her for good and all among ancient shadows and memories; and she was equally determined not to go until such time as the finger of God stroked her leaf from the branch. Beyond tacitly recognizing that she was their prisoner she refused to have any part in their proceedings; would not say she was guilty or not guilty; would not even start to her feet when some damnable untruth was being uttered concerning her. She knew this: as soon as she involved herself actively in the series of trials that was mounted against her again and again, that would be the hour of her shame, she would be exposed to the whole world as a wicked woman. Then her substance would crumble into shadow; but not like those dear dead ones, a fragrant shadow; no, a cursed shadow that could only be lifted from the gates with the candles and waters of exorcism.

Mrs McKee sat in the parlour rocking chair that was now, for a week or so, to be her prisoner's dock. The curtained room was all a crepitation: whispering, rustling of papers, shuffle of feet. Who would today's prosecutor be? She waited. A voice at the edge of the shadows began to speak. It was the advocate with the thin precise gnat-like voice who invariably dealt with her financial and other material misdemeanours. She did not like him, he was mean and trivial. She prepared herself for a rather wearisome afternoon.

'I think it might be interesting,' said the voice, 'if we were to consider this afternoon a china teapot with a willow pattern design in blue upon it. Mrs Elizabeth McKee, or Alder, keeps it at present on the top shelf of her china cabinet, in quite a prominent position. As I hope to show you, that teapot belonged originally to Mrs McKee's aunt, a Miss Annabella Chisholm, who at the time of her decease resided in the town of Perth, Scotland. By the terms of Miss Chisholm's will (which I intend to read to you presently) all her moveable possessions – I repeat, all of them – were bequeathed to Mrs McKee's younger sister Flora – Miss Flora Alder, lately resident at number two Marchmont Square, Edinburgh, Scotland. Mrs McKee was remembered financially, in a modest way, in the same will. Now, then . . .'

The tribunal was well and truly in session. The thin voice scratched on and on as if it scurried over a disc of worn ancient wax. Mrs McKee turned round once and looked in the direction of the china cabinet. Yes, there it stood, Flora's china teapot that had somehow got mixed up with her own furniture the time they moved north four years ago. It was a beautiful object, but now it began to glow like a lamp of evil in the shadows. (She had always thought somehow that Flora had *given* her the teapot.) It was the first time it had ever been brought up in the tribunal. It might prove to be a rather interesting afternoon.

Ben Budge sat at the scrubbed table and wrote on a blue-lined writing pad with a stub of pencil. 'The Biggings, Greenvoe, Isle of Hellya, Orkney. Monday. Dear Tom, I take pen in hand to acquaint you with our news. Here we are much as usual. Not a thing happens in this place. Your aunt and I are as well as can be expected considering our age. We would like it if you came home for a spell. You aunt is worried about you. Eddie Ainslie from Quoylay came back from a Pacific trip last week and he blazed it all over Greenvoe that you are down and out in Vancouver, B.C. A real wharf side bum, that's what he called you – Tom Groat is walking on his uppers, he said to everybody in the pub. It soon came round to your Aunt Bella's ears, she hears every cat's fart of news. Now, Tom, we know Eddie Ainslie is if not a liar exactly, a gross exaggerator, but there's no smoke without fire and it could be that you are hard up and out of work for the time being. Just write and let us know. Your Aunt Bella and I are not barehanded, we could send you your passage money, we get the pension every week and we put it by as our needs are not great and we can live fine off the egg money and as you know all we have will be yours after we are gone. Now for the village news. The laird's granddaughter came on holiday today from England where she is at school. She doesn't usually come till the middle of August to be in time for the regatta and agricultural show. Miss Fortin-Bell, old Horse Face, likes us more than ever. She was gushing all over the village like a broken jar of syrup. A new school-teacher came at the beginning of May, a Miss Inverary from Edinburgh, a prim prissy bit of a thing but Ivan Westray the ferryman is casting his eyes on her and if he does to her what he did to the croft lasses at the other end of the island I guess we'll soon stand in need of a new school-mistress. Timmy Folster has been off the meth for a week or two, I hope he keeps that way, the poor thing that he is. I reckon old Evie in the store knows Timmy drinks the meth he supplies, a bloody shame, and Evie a kirk elder too. Ellen Kerston is expecting her sixth any day now. Maybe you don't know her, a Quoylay girl, she's married to Bert Kerston the fisherman, a little runt of a man, a damned awkward thing in drink, you wouldn't think he had it in him. Well, Tom, that's all for today. I am feeling a bit tired. I'll write with more news tomorrow. The rain came pissing down at the weekend and our thatch is leaking.'

'I'm not writing any goddam more today, Bella,' said Ben. 'My wrist is sore and the goddam words are swimming in front of my eyes. What about some dinner?'

'My, you write a good letter, Ben,' said Bella.

An immense woman crossed over from the Kerston house to the shop.

'A pound of raisins when you're ready,' she said to Mrs Olive Evie, 'and twenty Woodbines for Bert Kerston.'

Mrs Olive Evie paid no attention to Ellen Kerston until she had finished telling Rachel Whaness, who was already in the shop, that it was high time Timmy Folster was put in the County Home for good and all, she had seen a louse crawling up his coat when he was in for his assistance money.

Alice Voar came in with young Skarf clutching her apron and whining for sweeties like a sick dove.

'Rachel,' said Ellen.

'Ellen,' said Rachel.

'I'm sorry,' said Ellen, 'for what Bert Kerston called you and Samuel on Saturday night when he was drunk.'

'It's all right, Ellen,' said Rachel.

' "Whited sepulchres",' said Ellen. 'He was drunk at the time!'

'Never mind, Ellen,' said Rachel.

'It was the drink speaking,' said Ellen. 'You're not a whited sepulchre anyway, Rachel.'

'Don't worry about it, Ellen,' said Rachel.

'I just thought I would apologize,' said Ellen. 'He doesn't know what he says when he has a fill of drink. Whited sepulchres – I gave him whited sepulchres when he got home.'

'He called me a whore the same night,' said Alice Voar mildly. 'I never took a ha'penny from a man in my life.'

'I'm sorry, Alice,' said Ellen.

'When is your time?' said Mrs Olive Evie to Ellen Kerston. 'It's not good for you, having all them bairns. One every year. It'll kill you. I'm telling you that as a medical woman. I was a nurse and a midwife before I married Mr Evie. What is it you want?'

'Peedie Skarf wants a liquorice strap,' said Alice Voar, 'when you're ready. Serve Ellen first.'

Mr Joseph Evie sorted the mail at his desk: a new national assistance book for Timothy John Foster; *British Weekly* for Rev. Simon McKee; a long plain sealed envelope for Ivan Westray; four letters for Colonel Fortin-Bell, also *Punch* and *Illustrated London News*; a brewer's account for Mr William Scorradale; a letter from Edinburgh for Miss Margaret Inverary; *New Prophecy* for Mr Samuel Whaness; a parcel of books from the County Library for Jeremias Jonathan Skarf, Esq.

'What's in the mail?' said Mrs Olive Evie when the shop was empty once more.

Mr Joseph Evie put the mail inside his desk. 'Nothing,' he said.

The school came out at four o'clock. The pupils whirled like a flock of starlings round Miss Inverary and then darted in every direction across the playground. They yelled and screamed. They jostled at the gate of the playground. Judy Kerston was crying. Sander Voar fell. Charlie Brown from the Glebe hit Johnny Corrigall from Skaill on the cheekbone, and Johnny Corrigall looked back at him with quivering lips, then laughed uncertainly. Simon Anderson from The Bu studied a scraped bleeding knee. At the blank wall of the shop Sophie Voar and Shirley Voar and Lila Corrigall from Skaill lined up and held their clenched fists straight out in front of them. Maggie-Ann Anderson from The Bu faced them; she used her two fists like hammers and knocked their fists down, chanting ritually:

> Ickle ockle black bottle
> Ickle ockle out
> Tea and sugar is my delight
> And O—U—T spells out.

At every chanted syllable she struck down a fist with her own fist. Ola Corrigall's left fist was the last fist to be struck down. The final blow, the last chanted syllable, ennobled her. At once she was invested as queen, but queen of a rebellious and broken kingdom. Her faithless handmaidens led her to the wall and left her there with her face hidden on her forearm, a grieving statue. Yet the lips fluttered, they began to count rapidly and secretly up to a hundred, as if she was summoning her scattered troops to restore order and harmony. Shirley and Sophie and Maggie-Ann ran and hid themselves. Other children joined in the game. They scattered silently in all directions. They melted like shadows. They hid under boats, in Timmy Folster's tin door, in the long grass of the manse garden, behind the latrine, and in the many windows of the hotel. Ola Corrigall breathed the magic number from the wall; then 'Leave-o' she shouted, turning round swiftly. The clarion call was a proclamation, a summons, a warning. She began cautiously to hunt them down, taking care to stand between the hidden traitorous ones and the wall, lest one rush past her and touch the sacred stone and so gain his freedom.

Only Gino Manson, who was simple-minded, took no part in the game. He played with the Kerston dog, Laddie, in the middle of the road. The dog barked and leapt up at him. Gino kissed him on his cold nose. The dog and the boy laughed together.

Ivan Westray set down the box of books on the parlour floor of the schoolhouse. 'Three shillings,' he said.

'The Education Committee pays,' said Miss Margaret Inverary. 'I've just put on a pot of coffee. I'll set out another cup. Sit over beside the fire.'

'I'd rather have a dram,' said Ivan Westray.

She brought out the whisky decanter and a heavy crystal glass.

'Well then,' said Ivan Westray. 'Have you thought about it? Have you made up your mind?'

The bowl on the sideboard was loaded with apples. One had a wrinkled yellow skin, one had a patch of softness on it. They glowed in the stillness. They tumbled inexorably and silently out of the region of ripeness. They shone and rotted slowly.

Miss Inverary said nothing.

'Because I'm not going to hang on for ever,' said Ivan Westray. 'What do you take me for? Some bloody kind of a statue?'

Miss Inverary stirred her coffee slowly.

'When was it we first met?' said Ivan Westray. 'It was a long time ago.'

'It was at the dance in the community centre,' said Miss Inverary. She smiled. 'It was the second Friday in May. It was just after I came to the island.'

'A long time,' said Ivan Westray. 'Seven weeks. I have this hurt and this hunger inside me. You put it there.'

Her silver spoon chinked in the china saucer.

'I want to know,' said Ivan Westray, 'what are you going to do about it?'

'I'm sorry,' said Miss Inverary.

Ivan Westray put down the empty whisky glass and stood up.

'I'm truly sorry,' she said.

Ivan Westray stood in the door, a flushed statue.

'Light that green lamp and set it in your window upstairs at ten o'clock,' said Ivan Westray. 'Then I'll know I can come. That was the arrangement.'

He put his seaman's cap on in the door.

'Good-bye for now,' she said.

He left without another word. He closed the front door so hard that the top apple trembled in the bowl.

Miss Inverary sat down again and poured herself another cup of coffee.

There was a gentle tap on the door.

It was Johnny Corrigall from Skaill. 'Please, miss,' he said, 'Charlie Brown struck me in the playground.'

'Did he now?' said Miss Inverary. 'Everybody gets hurt one time or another. We must just be patient. I'll speak to Charles Brown in the morning.'

She gave Johnny Corrigall a yellow apple from the bowl on the sideboard.

*

The bar of the Greenvoe Hotel only opened in the evenings. Four generations of country mud had been beaten on to the original flagstones of the floor. The single window was never cleaned but by rain; the drinkers moved about like ghosts in a meagre light. On the gantry stood a bottle of whisky and a bottle of rum. Beer snorted and spat and vomited out of the barrel whenever the wooden tap was turned. The dominant colours were grey and brown, a dingy dapple that met and merged and disagreed everywhere. The landlord fitted well into the setting; Mr William Scorradale was like a toby jug came to life. The prime piece in his livery was a leather apron that gleamed like a dark mirror with a lifetime of grease and unction.

Beyond the bar was the billiard-room. No one had played billiards there within living memory. Occasionally the agricultural society met there in winter, or the district council. Mr Joseph Evie would put his head round the bar door three or four times a year. 'A fire tonight, if you please, William.' This meant that the district council would require the billiard-room for a meeting.

Upstairs were half a dozen guest rooms. People had been known to stay there for one night – bird watchers, American tourists, folk-lorists – but never for more than one night. Bill Scorradale was very pleased and self-important whenever he had a guest. 'Just be quiet tonight,' he would say to the silent draughts-players. 'Tone it down, no singing, no shouting. There's a guest upstairs.' Bill Scorradale, besides being the host, was cook, porter, chambermaid, and waiter to the guests. One rather busy summer nine years ago he had employed Alice Voar.

It was now seven o'clock and the only drinker at the bar was Ivan Westray. Passing six, Bert Kerston the fisherman carrying a live lobster had attempted to gain entry but had been intercepted at the porch by Ellen Kerston. 'Where do you think you're going?' said Ellen Kerston.

'Bill Scorradale wants to buy a lobster,' said Bert Kerston. 'He has a guest coming to the hotel tomorrow.'

'Does he?' said Ellen Kerston. 'Is there? Mr Scorradale can buy his lobsters from the Fishermen's Society in the ordinary way of business. I'll tell you exactly what you're going to do, Bert Kerston. You're coming with me to the phone box and you're going to phone the Fishermen's Society stating that you have five two-pounders – no, six, take that other one out of your oilskin pocket – and you'll ask what the current price is. And tell them to address their cheque to Mistress Helen Kerston, enemy of ale-houses, Greenvoe, Hellya, Orkney.'

Ivan Westray stood in the door with his pint, watching the Kerstons in the phone box.

'Did you ever see an elephant and a mouse caught in a red trap?' he said.

The Skarf came into the pub, carrying his manuscript book.

Samuel Whiness laid a basket of haddocks at his threshold.

'The Lord has blessed us with beautiful fish today, Rachel,' he said.

'Praise be, Samuel,' said Rachel.

Rachel laid the haddocks on the outside wall and strung the jaws of three together. Samuel sat in the doorstep and gravely removed his rubber boots.

Rachel returned from putting a haddock through Timmy Folster's window.

Samuel dipped his hands into the water bowl as though it was a sacramental act.

Rachel stood in Alice Voar's open door. 'A haddock for the bairns' supper,' she said.

'Very kind of you, Rachel,' said Alice Voar, and held the bunch of three up by the string. The glancing underwater quicksilver was leaving them; they were touched with the tarnish of death; soon they would be grey stiff headless gutted shapes on a big blue plate. 'You're kind, Rachel,' said Alice Voar.

'No,' said Rachel, 'for we own nothing, do we? The Lord gives us this and that, but then we must imitate him and divide out what's left among other folk, so there's nobody that won't have a little.'

Samuel was laying salt in their own split gutted haddocks when Rachel came back.

'That isn't business, Rachel,' he said in a tone of mild reproach, 'giving our hard-earned goods away to the idle and the improvident.'

'The miracle of the loaves and fishes is never finished, Samuel,' said Rachel.

The Skarf, perched on the high stool in the corner of the bar with a half-pint on the counter in front of him, was reading aloud from his manuscript:

'Darkness and silence, darkness and silence. The light of the intellect had not yet touched the island. From the summit of Korsfea to the sea-banks of the Taing a weave of dense heather. But the animals abounded, the animals and the birds and the fish, they were everywhere, they made their swift instinctive circuits and died, and again and again with the renewing sun the hills and waters of the island swarmed. Instinctive thrusts at the light, withdrawals into darkness. Hawk fell on rabbit. Whale sieved plankton, millions by millions, through the combs of his teeth. Vole nibbled quick roots. Yet all was a ritual of darkness. The bone of the whale lay high on the beaches that knew as yet no footprint of man.

'Darkness over all; these gleams of instinct are not light, the quick thrustings at the sun; the sun itself is a darkness until the mind of man is there to take cognizance. For a million years there was no man to observe, there was darkness, the islands lay on the water like black lumps, the wind was darkness, the blind sun rose and set in a blank sky.

'Somewhere, somehow, sometime, a boat blundered on the beach at Keelyfaa, a frail skin boat; men stepped on to the rock, creatures clothed in the brightness and sweetness of flesh. Light came to the island, but a feeble glow-worm light, for they were children of darkness, these first-comers; the grave was their kingdom. How did they live? How did they speak? How did they think? No one can tell. But in what manner they were borne into the kingdom of death, that we know well; for to the kingdom of death they paid mighty rents, there they lavished much wealth and skill. In the meadow of the farm of Isbister, three summers ago, a cow put her hoof through a hole in the ground. For five weeks the spades of archaeologists deepened and widened the hole, scraped against stonework, discovered the shape of a wall, a chamber, a long barrow corbelled with some skill that opened out into minor chambers on each side, a dozen of them, radiating from the central barrow like rays of a dark sun. The spades of the excavators were bright with their probing. And found what? Bones; in every little chamber skeletons laid out in the triumph and finality of death. Skeletons of two old men, their finger-bones contorted with arthritis; a skeleton of a young man with a smashed rib where the spear had gone into his heart; three skeletons of women (the neck-bones of the two young women were wrenched as though they had been ritually strangled, but beside the old woman was a thick red jar). The remaining six skeletons were of children ranging in age from two to twelve, the manner of their death uncertain, but beside the twelve-year-old were skeletons of a young horse and a hound and many bone beads (no doubt but death had untimely come to the young son of a chieftain).

'And this is all we know about the first dwellers in the island: the solemn state in which they passed into the kingdom of death, as if life was a shadow and death the hard reality. Of the villages where they passed their days nothing remains.

'A merry race came, after thousands of years – a merry bustling aggressive race. From the Mediterranean coasts they set out in their wooden ships, men and women and dogs and horses and children and (very precious – guard it, watchman, with your life, for it is life and the promise of life) the jar of seed corn. Away it sallied, from a coast grown eroded or effete or anarchic or pestilential, out first to the fruitful Atlantic coasts of France; but could not long bide there, for hunger and lust are not welcome at ordered tables and lawful bedchambers, and there were spear-showers in the harbours. An urge, a powerful thrust, took them west and north, past Scilly and Anglesea and Man. In Jura a great stag stood on the horizon. Not here, not here the place, among rock and marsh, but steer always northwards, into the growing light of summer. They found one morning the place, a cluster of islands in the opening oyster of dawn. Carefully they carried ashore the cow, and cheerfully the sheep, and with gaiety the horse, and with gaiety and lewd whispers the nubile girl, and with reverence the jar of seed corn (the most powerful swimmer bore it on his shoulder). And finally the men of the tribe, the seamen, the adventurers, the fighters, themselves stood on the beach at Keelyfaa, glistening with sea-water from throat to ankle.

'They drove the people of the dark kingdom from their little pastures and fishing grounds, they scattered them among the barren hillsides and the interior marshes. And they piled together mounds of building stone from the beach, and tore away the tough skin of heather, and dug flagstones and sandstone out of new quarries. They prepared to build. Not perpetual cities of death under the hill. They built near their landfall a thick high fort, a keep, a primitive castle with a moat. And a great width of marshland was drained round about, and the ox was yoked, and the wooden plough stottered after it through tough fibred virgin soil. The cow, the butterkirn, the cheese-press, the beef board, made one circle of life. The sheep, the spinning wheel, the harmonious loom, the mutton trencher, made a circle of life for these gay people. The boat, the net, the fish, the bone needle, the oil lamp, made a third circle of life. The ox, the plough, the seedjar, the harrow, the sickle, the flail, the quern, the oven, made a great circle of fruition, as if the round life-giving sun had smitten the earth with its own burgeoning image.

'But the keep, the fort, the "broch" (as we call it) – what does it signify, standing above the seabanks? It is the guardian of the tribe. At night the dark death-people come out of the bog and hill with their nooses and their stone knives, and they kill the new lambs and put torches into the haystack. But that is nothing; that can be contained. There are other hungry restless tribes on the sea, thrusting northwards, their own cousins, and these wayfarers must be given a hard door. There are three ships on the horizon. Into the round open courtyard of the broch with everything: women, children, cattle, pigs, sheep, nets, chattels, bread, beer, the sacred seed-jar. The last man slid the bolt in the single low narrow door. The broch was impregnable then. Everywhere it presented a high blank circular wall. The men climbed up the interior spiral stairway that knit the double walls together, up and up to the battlement, with their huge stones and their arrows and their torches greased for flame. "Come, cousins from the south coast, you are very welcome. We trust your health will benefit from the clear air. We have nothing to give you, not an acre, our barley and our beef will see us through the coming winter, no more. If you come too close, if you make scratches on our wall, we have some fire that we can let you have, also some rib-cracking boulders. You are our cousins from Corsica and Biscay and Brittany, so we'll tell you a thing to your advantage: to the north are other islands, Shetland, Faroe, Iceland."

'After a hungry impotent day or two, the besiegers sailed on north. And the cheerful tribe, the light-worshippers, emerged from the narrow circle of their broch to resume the wide fecund cycles of their existence.

'The Broch of Ingarth is still there, though the wave of time has gone over it and drowned it utterly. All that is left is a green mound, a few stumps and stobs of stone.

'They vanished in their turn, the broch-builders.

'Came from east-over-sea, from Norway, a tall blond people, in beautiful curving ships with dragon-prows. Across an empty sea they sailed, into the sunset. Two days out at sea they took a starved raven out of its cage. The raven stood above the mast, and stepped higher, and swung its eye round the horizon, and mounted again till it was only a quivering black dot and then it fell suddenly into the west; for from its sky tower it had seen (what they could not see) land in the west, the Orkneys. Two days still they sailed, through drenches of spindrift, following the vanished raven. They landed, ship after ship after ship, on the unsuspecting islands. They took their axes from their belts.

'In all the confusion of anabasis, domination, settlement that followed, only one clear fact is stated concerning Hellya. It is recorded in the saga: "Sigurd the first earl of the Orkneys gave the island of Hellya to Thorvald Gormson, who was usually at home in Hardanger. He was a good farmer and he was given the name Thorvald Harvest-Happy out west in Orkney" . . .'

The Skarf closed his manuscript book and took a long meditative sip at his beer.

'Well now,' said Bill Scorradale, 'I had no idea all them things happened here in Hellya.'

'Give The Skarf a pint,' said Ivan Westray. He moved over to the pub door and looked up at the schoolhouse. There was no lamp in the high window.

'It's ten o'clock,' said Bill Scorradale. 'Closing time.'

Ivan Westray wandered back into the bar.

'All the best,' said The Skarf. 'Skol.' He put the new pint to his lips and slowly raised it till it was at right angles to his recumbent labouring throat.

'It's after closing time,' said Bill Scorradale. 'Will you drink up, please, gentlemen. Oh, and Ivan, I'm expecting a guest tomorrow. He'll be taking your boat from the town. I want you boys to try and make less noise than usual while the guest is in residence. Come on now, drink up.'

'I'll have a double whisky,' said Ivan Westray. 'Give the historian another pint.'

At midnight they were still drinking.

The lights went out in the Kerston house, then in Alice Voar's house. The lights had been out for some time in the manse and in the Whaness house. The light had never been on in Timmy Folster's. One by one the lights went out in the room above the store and in the Biggings and in the schoolhouse kitchen. Greenvoe was wrapped in night and silence. About half-past eleven, Timmy Folster began to sing under the pile of coats that was his bed.

> *Romona, I hear the mission bells above,*
> *Romona, they're pealing out our song of love.*

Bert Kerston opened his bedroom window and shouted, 'Be quiet, you bloody weed! I have to be at the creels in an hour.'

Timmy Folster sank into a blue sleep again. One of Alice Voar's little ones whimpered in its cradle. Then the village was silent again.

Inside the stable of The Bu farm three miles away, Tammag Brown of the Glebe and Leonard Isbister of Isbister pushed the great door shut and bolted it. Dod Corrigall of Skaill and Andrew Hoy of Rossiter were helping young Hector Anderson off with his jacket. 'I bet,' said Dod Corrigall of Skaill, 'thu would rather be having a bonny lass to take thee claes off.' Andrew Hoy laughed. Sandy

Manson of Blinkbonny opened a battered brown suitcase and took out a parchment, a horse-shoe, a black blindfold, a lantern, a half-dozen sackcloth sashes and a long apron. He hung the horse-shoe on a nail at the east wall of the barn.

Tammag of the Glebe slid a half-bottle of whisky out of his hip pocket and uncorked it. 'Put that away!' cried old Mansie Anderson of The Bu. 'Hide it out of sight. There'll be no drink taken this night or any night till the ceremony's finished. If thu'd so much as put it to thee mouth, thu'd have spoiled everything. I'm surprised at thee, Tammag Broon.'

Tammag flushed and put the flask back in his pocket.

'I'll thank you all,' said the old man, 'to behave as solemn as if you were in a kirk.' He spread over a stall the master's regalia – an apron crudely stitched with yellow wool in the form of a blazing sun. The other men put their sashes on; a more modest decoration, plough and sickle and quern stitched with black and grey wool. The boy stood in trousers and grey shirt, sweating slightly. 'It's all right,' whispered Leonard Isbister to him, 'nothing'll come at thee.'

Tammag of the Glebe struck a match and lit the candle in the stable lantern. Old Mansie took up the parchment. He was now the Lord of the Harvest. He kissed the horse-shoe nailed to the wall.

The first of six initiation rites into the Ancient Mystery of The Horsemen began.

LORD OF THE HARVEST: Here is the first station, THE PLOUGH. What are you seeking here, man, among the master horsemen?
NOVICE: A kingdom.
THE HARVEST LORD: The lad that mucks out stable and byre – that's what you are – what kens he of any kingdom?
NOVICE: Once I lived there. Now I'm an outcast. I desire to return.
THE HARVEST LORD: What hinders you from the place?
      (One of the Master Horsemen extinguishes the lantern.)
NOVICE: Darkness.
THE HARVEST LORD: In a deeper darkness you must seek it

again. (*One of the Master Horsemen blindfolds him.*) There are many stopping places along the road. What estate do you first desire to enter?

NOVICE: The ploughman's estate.

THE HARVEST LORD: Are you prepared therefore to undergo a terrible thing, the three-fold darkness, to arrive at this state?

The Novice does not answer.

THE MASTER HORSEMEN (together): Answer. Answer.

NOVICE: I am willing.

THE HARVEST LORD: Kneel down.

The Novice kneels on the floor, or rather, he is ritually thrust to his knees by the Master Horsemen. The horse-shoe is taken from the wall and put into his hand.

THE HARVEST LORD: Take the sign of the horse with thee in all thy goings. Here is the door. Knock, Ploughman.

The Novice knocks on the floor with the horse-shoe three times. The Master Horsemen raise a flagstone. The Novice hangs over a dark opening.

TWO

In the endless bestiary of the weather the unicorns of cloud are littered far west in the Atlantic; the sun their sire, the sea their dame. Swiftly they hatch and flourish. They travel eastwards, a grey silent stampeding herd. Their shining hooves beat over the Orkneys and on out into the North Sea. Sometimes it takes days for that migration to pass. But many are torn on the crags and hills, and spill their precious ichor on the farm-lands. Crofters wake to cornfields and pastures extravagantly jewelled.

Bert Kerston was awakened by a steady tap on the ben window. He rose at once and pulled on his trousers. He left the warm snoring hulk at his side. He groped his way through a scatter of sweetly breathing cribs and cradles. He took a black oilskin from the hook on the wall and put it on. His thigh-boots stood in the corner, long collapsed tubes; he eased his legs into them.

Bert Kerston boiled the kettle on the primus stove and made himself a pot of tea. The rain lashed against the window. He spread a barley scone first with butter and then with rhubarb jam. The tea in the pint mug was too hot; he slopped some over into a saucer. Tom turned over in his bed and threw his arm over Ernie and sighed once and breathed regularly and slowly again. Bert Kerston sucked the last drops of tea out of his moustache. He passed out into the pouring morning.

Samuel Whaness in his oilskin passed, going down to the *Siloam*. The two fishermen met outside Timmy Folster's burnt window. 'To think,' said Bert Kerston to Samuel Whaness, 'that we have to slave our guts out in every kind of weather, and pay national insurance, to keep bloody scum like that! I could hardly get a wink of sleep for him all night.'

Samuel Whaness, his mouth holy from praise and scripture, passed on without a word down to his boat.

Bert Kerston stood against the latrine wall and added his bladder trickle to the steaming surging pier.

Samuel Whaness's engine started up.

The Skarf woke with a dry throat. (How many pints had Ivan Westray given him in Scorradale's last night? Six, maybe seven.) He rose in his shirt and drawers and poured himself a cup of water from the jug and went back to bed. Well, it wasn't weather to fish, that was one thing sure. A name emerged from his ruck of half-awakened perceptions: Thorvald Harvest-Happy. About this man nothing was known. Thorvald Harvest-Happy got one sentence in the saga. But there was an indwelling image; it stepped out of the name and drew other images about itself: a glebe, a great barn, a host of labourers, seedtime and harvest, snow and sun, a sprinkling with water, a kiss, a death-sweat. And a rhythm smote upon the host of images, pulsed through them, and gave them an ordering in time, so that they were gathered into a single dance.

The Skarf flung the blankets from him and dragged on trousers and jersey. He sat down between his tea-boxes of books. He took up his ball-point and opened the old cash-book on his desk.

It is going to be a long session today, Mrs McKee thought, putting the lid back on the marmalade. Already the black shapes were astir at the edge of her consciousness, there were whispers, scurries, consultations. Normally the trial began in the early afternoon, once the last soup plate was back on the dresser rack and Simon had gone into his study. Well, there was nothing else for it; if she was summoned she was summoned, she would have to hear them out, that was all. She had so much wanted that morning to visit Mr Budge the old sailor, who was quite ill, she had heard him coughing terribly all night. He swore a great deal, but that was just the way of sailors, he was a very nice old man for all that, and his sister was just delightful, the way she spoke to the hens and everything.

'All right, old bird?' said Rev. Simon McKee.

'I'm perfectly all right, Simon,' said Mrs McKee.

'It was a silent breakfast,' said the minister. 'I don't think you answered me once since the grace and the porridge.'

'Well, dear,' said Mrs McKee, 'I expect it's the weather. Such a day of rain. I'll cheer up as the day goes on. One's a wish – where did you pick up that sneeze? It's yourself you should be worrying about.'

'You spoke two words to your poached egg,' said Simon. 'Love. Infidelity.'

'Did I, dear?' said Mrs McKee. 'I expect it's that novel of Winnie's I'm trying to read.'

'I'll get me into the study then,' said Simon, and sneezed twice into his paper napkin.

'Yes, dear, do,' said Mrs McKee. 'I'm going to be quite busy this morning. Don't sit in a draught. Close the window next the sea.'

One of the team of prosecutors was on his feet and shuffling his papers behind the curtains in the next room, waiting for Simon to leave.

The tolling of the school bell woke Ivan Westray in the cabin of the *Skua*. He threw the blanket off and splashed his face in a bucket of sea water. 'The bloody bitch,' he said, shuddering into the towel. 'She should have her knees chained and padlocked.'

He put the two books he had been reading the night before back on the shelf, *The Orkneyinga Saga, On Love Carnal and Divine*.

The first thing he had to do was collect the mail from the shop. Also Bert Kerston had a box of lobsters for the depot in Hamnavoe. Scorradale had said something last night about collecting a guest from the town, as well as a case of gin and three canisters of beer. He had plenty of petrol. He would need another twenty packet of Woodbines. That was not a bad-looking bird that he had ferried across yesterday, the young thing with the posh accent, the Fortin-Bell. A schoolgirl in a sweater. Maybe next summer. By next summer she should certainly be ready for it. Oh, but that bitch up in the schoolhouse!

He munched an apple for his breakfast.

It was a very bleak morning in the Greenvoe school. They had hardly entered the classroom and hung up their coats and said 'Our Father' together when Miss Inverary announced, 'I find we're very far behind in arithmetic. Tom Kerston, what is nine times four?'

'365, miss,' said Tom Kerston after a long pause.

'That's what I mean,' said Miss Inverary. 'I've been far too lenient with you this term. There has been too much singing and story-telling. You'll find, when you leave school, that life does not consist of singing and story-telling. Then we will have to work, and plan and calculate. There will be measurements to be made every day, bills to be paid, such things as insurance and mortgages to be calculated, all that kind of thing. And so, today, we are going to make up lost time, we are going to have two full periods of arithmetic. Oh, I know some of you will think that this is not so pleasant as hearing all about Robinson Crusoe and – who, Sander Voar?'

'Man Friday,' said Sander Voar.

' – and Man Friday,' said Miss Inverary. 'Maybe it is more fun to sing about Bonnie Prince Charlie and the golden apples of the sun. We all like to work on the wall picture of Saint Magnus. But the sooner you realize that life is not all sport and pleasure, but hard duty, the better it will be for all of us.'

And so all morning while the rain swept and susurrated against the tall school windows, they did multiplication tables. Miss Inverary wrote the tables on the blackboard, so swiftly and fiercely that she broke three new pieces of chalk and the sleeve of her nice blue apron was grey with fine dust. Then she took up her long pointer and the chant began:

> Six times one is six
> Six times two is twelve
> Six times three is eighteen
> Six times four is twenty-four ...

The little ones who had just begun school that term sat with a heap of dried oats and melon seeds and made patterns on their slates. Big Gino Manson of Blinkbonny who was not quite right in the head squatted beside the fire and played with pictures cut out of magazines. A little steam rose from his wet clothes. Now and then Gino poked the fire gently; he would make a red chasm among the caked coal and then fill the chasm with a few fresh lumps. This was his task every day that the fire had to be lit.

> *Nine times seven is sixty-three*
> *Nine times eight is seventy-two*
> *Nine times nine is eighty-one*
> *Nine times ten is ninety ...*

Relentlessly the pointer beat on the blackboard.

Inga Fortin-Bell left the road above the farm of Isbister. She had to begin walking in wet heather then. The land rose slowly. Her waterproof was buttoned to the throat but still a little trickle of water oozed into the cavity between her collar bones. She went from rock to heather clump to clay fissure, on and on and up the side of The Knap, more and more slowly as the slope grew steeper, and stopping breathless every now and again to get relief from the steady onset of the rain against her face. Down below she saw, in miniature, the whole farm of Isbister, the house and steading among its squares of pasture and cultivation. A dozen Ayrshires were huddled together in one field against the rain. The sheep seemed not to care for the weather; grey blurs, they were scattered all over the lower hill. A black collie leapt over the ditch and barked twice, faint and sharp, and flowed through the open door of Isbister. Beyond Isbister was the farm of the Glebe; and how a man and wife and five children could wring a living from such a small patchwork of fields Inga would never know. And yet when Inga had passed the grocery van on the road twenty minutes before, there was Jessie of the Glebe laughing with the van-man, her cheeks polished like apples; and when she had noticed Inga passing she bent a mute obsequious face. She had been a servant up at the Hall when Inga was a child.

Inga turned and climbed higher. She found a narrow sheeptrack and moved faster then, her body thrust forward from the hips. The cold rain dribbled from her saturated hair (what wasn't covered by the plastic hood) and coursed thinly between her shoulder blades. Behind a rock a dead sheep festered, half-way to a skeleton. A kestrel swung in a wide arc under the pealing rain and faded into the darker hill beyond. Inga turned again. There it was, the Hall, and all the farms and crofts of Hellya gathered round it like serfs about a master. But something had happened: the grey baronial edifice, built in imitation of Balmoral, stood gaunt and patched in a wilderness of weeds. The former serfs had encroached, they had taken over the fertile summer fields of the laird, and it seemed from this altitude had turned their backs on their former master and were flourishing by their anarchy.

The village was hidden by a sloping buttress of hill.

Inga turned and climbed higher. The sheeptrack gave out. She put her foot into a sudden patch of bog. She was wearing rubber over-shoes; incredibly cold water saturated her foot in an instant. She dragged her foot out with a suck and a plop. Far in front and below, out of sight, came a broken thunder of sea. She climbed higher, and found herself on the summit of The Knap. But this was only a buttress of the main hill, called Korsfea. Between The Knap and the scarred head of Korsfea lay a shallow scoop of valley. She paused to get her breath and dry her surging face.

'A terrible day, my girl,' grandfather had said, coming into the cold dining-room. He bent and kissed her on the brow, then helped himself to a kipper from under the grill. 'Not weather for a dog. Just you go back to bed, my dear, cover up with a hot-water bottle and have a good read. *The Illustrated London News* and *Punch* came yesterday. That's what I would do.'

'Inga has other plans,' said Aunt Agatha, pouring out the colonel's coffee. 'We're going to arrange the welfare clothes for the children. We were just speaking about it when you came in. That'll take most of the morning, I should think. Then there's the garden. And there's Thunder to groom.'

Inga had left her second cup of coffee half drunk, and put on her waterproof things in the hall, and gone out into the down-pour ...

She leaned along a crest now and an assault of wind nearly thrust her down again. A deluge of rain broke up her vision. She snuggled her chin into her coat and inclined her head, then struggled a score of precarious steps to the summit of Korsfea. She picked up a small stone and added it to the cairn – that had to be done by every visitor. Then she leaned against the cairn's sheltered side and looked down. The whole of Hellya was spread beneath her, every farm and field and howe and lochan and dyke and telegraph pole – except for the moorland to the north-west – it was cut off by another shoulder of hill called Ernefea. She faced once more into the wind and rain. Down below, it was a slope of moor and a sheer cliff-fall to the Atlantic Ocean. But today the sea was a drabness that met the farther sky in a blurred horizon. Three miles out, the Skerries lighthouse stood in shifting veils of rain. Other islands – Quoylay, Hrossey, Norday – lay like ghosts athwart the murk. And there right beneath her was Greenvoe with its pier and beach and houses and church and shop, as neat as if a child had composed it with wooden bricks in his nursery – the centre of this beautiful island that she loved with all her heart. She lay against the cairn and hunched her shoulders. The coldness and the wet were a sensuous delight.

And there, very faint and far and blurred, Inga saw the ferry-boat. It was turning the point of Skar Head in Hrossey into the Sound of Quoylay, slowly edging into the tiderace. She scooped the rain out of her eyes. There was nothing to be seen – the ferryman and his passenger were inside the cabin. Inga looked very thoughtfully at the boat as, entering the stream, it swung round and came in rapidly towards the still distant harbour of Greenvoe.

Farther out, a blue fishing boat veered towards the shelter of Sutbreck in Hrossey.

'A bastard of a day,' said Bert Kerston at the bar counter of Sutbreck Hotel in the island of Hrossey, and set down his basket of crabs.

'What can I do for you?' said Mr Selfridge the English proprietor, reaching for a pint glass.

'Nothing,' said Bert Kerston. 'I have no money. I've just come in for some shelter.'

'Have the crabs come in for a rest too?' said Mr Selfridge.

'You vagabond,' said Bert Kerston. 'You blackguard. I'll have a glass of whisky and a pint of heavy to start with.'

In the end Mr Selfridge agreed to buy the basket of crabs for a pound; but only after much friendly wrangling, only after Bert Kerston had downed his third glass of malt.

'I draw your attention,' said the prosecutor, 'to a copy of *The Lowland Courier* dated 3rd May 1916, page four, column dealing with Births, Marriages, Deaths, etc. Under the heading "Engagements" appears among others the following item: "The engagement is announced between Alan McKee, fourth son of Mr and Mrs John McKee, 5 Rural Place, Tirfals, and Elizabeth Alder, elder daughter of the late Mr Thomas Alder and of Mrs Alder, 23A The Meadows, Edinburgh" ...'

Mrs McKee had had experience of this inquisitor before, of course, many times, and she rather liked him. She couldn't see him, that was true; he stood like the others at the edge of the shadow; but he had a pleasant rather roguish voice, as if he knew the things that happen under the sun and wasn't too put out about them; but still he had this job to do and here he was doing it. Mrs McKee imagined a stoutish young lawyer with a handsome full-complexioned face, and fine blue eyes and a shapely mouth. He had appeared against her a score of times, and never with venom or vindictiveness, though the charge was serious enough, in all conscience.

'Now I want to show you a piece of film concerning this same Miss Elizabeth Alder, at a time only five weeks subsequent to the announcement in the press; on, in fact, the tenth day of June 1916. I apologize for the quality of the film; you will realize that this art was then in its infancy. The reel I am going to show you is full of flickers and jerks, but I think you will be able to follow fairly clearly the gist of it. Would the operator begin now, please. Yes. Here then you see Miss Elizabeth Alder on her way to a party given for a friend of hers, Miss Millicent Brae, at the home of Miss Brae's parents at 359 Melbourne Street, Leith. The occasion is Millicent Brae's twenty-first birthday. Here you see the house 359 Melbourne Street . . .'

Mrs McKee closed her eyes; not that she could see any screen, or hear the whirr of a projector, but she knew all too vividly what was about to unfold.

Millicent's twenty-first had been simply the nicest evening since the war started. Yes, it had. Mrs Brae, and Maisie and Wendy her two servant maids, and Mrs McKenzie the hired cook, had gone to no end of trouble to see that everything was just first-rate. The parents were there, of course – Mr and Mrs Brae – but they kept discreetly in the background. Mr Brae only appeared twice in the course of the evening, once with a box of cigars after dinner for the men; and again just after eleven o'clock when the whisky gave out and Millicent cried, 'O poor Gussy Park, how will you get home if you don't have one for the road? . . .' Then Mr Brae had appeared as if by magic – such a distinguished-looking man, even among chartered accountants, with his silver hair and dark moustache – bearing in, smiling, a new bottle of whisky, and what was more, for the ladies simply the biggest box of chocolates that she had ever seen. And 'O daddy, you're a *darling!*' Millicent had cried, throwing her arms around him.

And oh, the presents – the oak table in the parlour was simply covered with them! There was a zither from Fred Somerville, and a portable Corona typewriter from Mrs Brae, and a canary in a cage (a wonderful singer) from Gus Park, and an evening dress in satin from this aunt in Morningside, and a set of bone decorative boomerangs from some cousin in New Zealand, and a postcard album bound in silk from Pussy, Millicent's young sister, and goodness knows what other lovely things. (She herself had given her best chum the *Complete Works of Lord Tennyson.*) Crowning the hoard, and fluttering in every draught like a bird – whenever the door opened, and that was a hundred times – was a cheque for one hundred pounds from Mr Brae himself. (And 'Do be careful with that cheque,' said Mrs Brae time and again, as she came in with a tray of trifle or a bowl of nougats and peppermints – 'Do be careful.

If somebody opens the front door it'll fly out through the window ...') Finally Bongo, Millicent's big brother, had put the cheque in his wallet for safe keeping.

Words failed Mrs McKee when she pictured – only too vividly – that loveliest of dinners. First the sherry in the parlour that made her feel slightly wicked (she was glad her mother wasn't there, and she hoped nobody would ever tell her); then the soup, turtle with cream in it; then the smoked salmon; then the roast turkey, with stuffing and all kinds of delicious accessories; then the roly-poly with custard ('Oh, I'll burst!' Millicent had cried when Wendy set that on the table); and finally the coffee and sweet biscuits ... She had sat between Bongo Brae and Fred Somerville, and they had been very attentive to her throughout, especially Bongo who was home on furlough from the Transvaal. In fact the evening would have been perfect if only her Alan had been there. But Second Lieutenant Alan McKee had been in France since the middle of May. Instead she had to talk to Bongo, who wasn't a brilliant conversationalist though a very nice fellow, and Fred Somerville. Once Fred Somerville, passing the sugar, had held her fingers in his for fully five seconds. She had let on never to notice.

Afterwards the men separated from the girls for an hour; and that was very nice, standing round the fire in the sitting-room, except that Millicent had suddenly begun to cry because (as she said) 'I'll never be sweet-and-twenty again.' They all kissed her, and she soon cheered up, and just before they went back to rejoin the men in the lounge Millicent said to her, 'Do you know this, that Freddy Somerville has his eye on you'. And Pussy said yes, that was right, she had noticed it too.

So after that she had taken care not to sit beside Fred Somerville in the lounge during the musical part of the evening; though she was feeling happy and rather reckless in a way after that post-prandial glass of chartreuse.

When she came back from viewing the presents with Mrs Brae and Millicent (who was now quite recovered, and reconciled to being twenty-one, and ready to face anything the world had to confront her with) the lounge was surging with a polka ... Sur-prise after surprise – they were not dancing to the piano only, but

Mr Brae had hired a violinist, a foreign-looking middle-aged man with a waxed moustache and tails. The polka ended with a scamper and a swish. She had sat down, rather vacantly, on a chair against the wall, half-aware that Gerry Monteith had announced a waltz and that violin and piano were striking up the opening, when a shadow fell across her and she looked up into the quite good-looking face of Fred Somerville. 'Please, Miss Elizabeth,' he said.

Well she could hardly refuse. And he was really a very good dancer. And he spoke quite pleasantly to her. She knew vaguely about him. He had been a journalist but had always been mad about things mechanical, and soon after he had been called up in the Army he had got a transfer to the Royal Flying Corps. He and Bongo had been at Watson's College together. And here he was, home on leave. She swayed with him like blossom on branch, it was most exhilarating. Only – just after the pause at mid-dance, he had laid his hand on her bare shoulder, and his fingers had hurt, and then he had bent down and put his mouth to her throat. She could not speak, she was so taken aback. Then once more the floor was one melodious whirl, into which she and Fred Sommerville were gathered. The music ended. He bowed to her, frowned in a hurt kind of way, and returned to the sideboard where the men were smoking and drinking. Blushing like a rose, she said to Millicent and Audry Wetherspoon, 'Your precious Mr Somerville, I will never dance, no nor speak with that man again, so long as I live . . .' Of course the girls had wanted to know the reason, but she hadn't told them.

It was such a lovely party that she soon forgot the incident. There was the sherry-flavoured trifle, and Bongo's imitation of a Zulu dance – that brought the house down – and the eightsome reel, and the Italian violinist's simply perfect rendition of Dvorak's *Humoreske*. There was one small contretemps: Gus Park fell on the floor beside the bookcase and had to be helped outside. 'Poor Parkers,' said Pussy, 'he always gets drunk . . .' But she never encountered Fred Somerville again. Once she thought he was crossing the floor to take her up in the Eva Three Step. She turned and pushed herself into the arms of Theodore McCuish, a shy medical student . . .

What had been a wonderful evening finished at midnight. They all stood around Millicent and sang 'For She's a Jolly good Fellow' – even Gussy Park had recovered sufficiently to join in – and she thought for a moment Millicent was going to cry again; but Millicent, after gnawing her lip and gazing in anguish at the floor, laughed during the last chorus and flung herself into the arms of Hamish Tosh with a shriek.

Then it was 'Coats, ladies,' and cries at the outside door for cabs. Elizabeth, in Pussy's gas-lit bedroom, was struggling into first her coat and then her outdoor shoes, when Wendy put her head in and cried, 'O Miss Alder, you'll need to hurry up, the last of the cabs is leaving . . .' She got her hat on somehow, and found her bag under Pussy's pillow, and flung through the hall with a hurried 'Thank you so much!' to Mr and Mrs Brae, and 'Bless you, dear friend' (with a kiss) to Millicent; and out through the door with her and down the steps and into – if you please – a motor car with engine running. Bongo, standing on the pavement, clashed the door behind her and said 'Tootle-oo!' The car jerked off. 'To The Meadows, is it?' said Fred Somerville. 'Just lean back, make yourself comfy. We'll be there in ten minutes . . .' And really, all the way, he was very nice. He never said or did one thing wrong or out of place. He just spoke pleasantly about poor old Parkers, and how much he had enjoyed himself. 'It's grand to be home, out of that inferno over there, in France, for a few days,' he said. Then they were outside the gate of 23 The Meadows. Fred got out of the car and opened the door for her . . .

'I want you now,' said the prosecutor, 'to take special note of this embrace. There they are standing outside a respectable middle-class home in the city of Edinburgh. It is not the man who is kissing the woman, is it? I think not. The behaviour of this Air Corps officer is quite impeccable, isn't it? I am going to ask for this part of the film to be played over now in slow motion. Observe: it is the woman who is kissing the man. And it is not just a good-night kiss, a formal salute on the cheek. No – both her arms are about him, and she is standing on tiptoe, and under the street lamp her mouth is searching for his mouth. The ensuing kiss is what I would call one of utter voluptuousness, and it lingers – how should we put it – for as long as the butterfly clings to the blossom . . .

'This is the same girl, remember, whose name, some five weeks previously, was publicly announced as being betrothed to another man; to a young soldier who, at that very moment, for aught she knew, might have been lying dead in some shell-crater of the Somme.'

Mrs McKee put her handkerchief to her quivering mouth. Outside the rain plucked and spat and drummed on the windows.

The stranger walked from the ferry-boat to the hotel. His coat lapels were drawn to his nostrils against the rain, his hat pulled well down. Ivan Westray followed in a yellow oilskin, carrying a suitcase, a brief-case, a typewriter and a tape recorder. In the hotel porch William Scorradale received his dripping guest, with the usual remarks about the weather, and he hoped the gentleman hadn't been sick on the crossing; nodding and scraping his feet all the time and rubbing his hands on his leather apron. Then he led him up two flights of linoed stairs and one flight of bare wood, chattering like a machine-gun – about Greenvoe being a remote but a humble hard-working honest community. The trout fishing on Warston Loch was said to be good this year. Would the gentleman like ham-and-eggs for his tea? – nearly everybody liked ham-and-eggs for their tea. The guest went into his room and shut the door.

Ivan Westray left the guest's luggage in the porch and went back to the pier.

William Scorradale stood half-way down the stairs for a good five minutes; listening and blinking and shaking his head. The man, he concluded, must be a deaf-mute. It was strange altogether.

Later that evening he went to the guest-book to find the man's name. Something was written there indeed. He put on his steel spectacles. It was not a name, it was more a strange involuted squiggle, a sign or a hieroglyph out of the remote past or the remote future.

'Timmy me boy,' said Ben Budge, 'you want to quit drinking that goddam meth. It'll rot your guts.'

'Timmy would never do that,' said Timmy. 'No. Never.'

'You were seen coming out of Evie's emporium yesterday morning with a bottle of the goddam stuff sticking out of your pocket,' said Ben.

'For the primus stove,' said Timmy, 'and for the tilley.'

'I seen two wharfside bums in Poplar on the Thames,' said Ben. 'They were blind as goddam moles. They'd been drinking the stuff for years.'

'Never Timmy. He wouldn't,' said Timmy.

'Timmy, you're a goddamn liar,' said Ben. 'I went into the piss-house at the pier one day last month and I met you wallowing against the wall with your legs like rubber. The smell from that piss-house wall – it was like a thousand tomcats had been shut in the place all goddam night.'

Bella came in with her aluminium bowl full of eggs. 'Fifteen,' she said. 'There's two for you, Timmy.'

Timmy Folster took a warm egg in each of his trembling palms. 'Thank you, Miss Budge,' he said.

'Down the gangway, Timmy,' said Ben. 'Bugger off, I'm in the middle of writing a letter to Tom in Vancouver.'

'Stick to tea, Timmy,' said Bella. 'Tea warms you in the cold weather and cools you in the summer. That's a good boy.'

'I've known bums that drank brasso and eau-de-cologne,' said Ben. 'There was a Glasgow man I was shipmates with that would buy a half-pint of milk from the corner shop. When he was in dry-dock, when his money was gone. He would get a piece of rubber tubing and fix it to the gas bracket in the tenement stair-head. He would bubble the gas through the milk for half-a-minute.'

'Mercy,' said Bella.

'Then he would drink the goddam mixture,' said Ben. 'He would be drunk as a monkey all day.'

'Timmy would never do a thing like that,' said Timmy.

'No,' said Ben, 'because there's no goddam gasworks in Green-voe. Off the ship, Folster. I aim to be busy.' Timmy Folster went away, virtuous and smiling.

'Too goddam true it's leaking,' said Ben. 'There's damp all over the writing pad. I reckon Noah's Ark was a tighter ship than this. Is there any news in the village I can tell Tom?'

He was seized with such a violent spasm of coughing that the pen fell out of his hand.

There was very little news in the village, on account of the weather. The shop was as quiet as a mousehole all morning and afternoon. Alice Voar came in for a twopenny candle, with peedie Skarf half-draggled among her skirts. Ellen Kerston came in just on the dinner closing-hour for a half-pound of tea and a pound of margarine: to be paid for on Saturday. In the afternoon Ivan Westray deposited on the floor a flaccid mail-bag, a carton of tomato sauce, a carton of detergents, and a box of new bread still fragrantly smoking. Mr Joseph Evie sat at his desk between the sack of potatoes and the column of plastic buckets and wrote out the minutes of the district council meeting. Mrs Olive Evie stood at the kitchen table with her spectacles at the end of her nose and a flat-iron in her fist. The mince pot and the potato pot and the cabbage pot bubbled on the moons of the stove. Mrs Olive Evie finished ironing the last pillowcase, a warm immaculate rectangle, and added it to the snowy strata at the end of the table. Then she clashed down the flat-iron on the fender and sent her voice echoing the length of the corridor.

'Are you coming for your tea, Mr Evie?' she shouted.

In the Bay of Seatter Samuel Whaness took four lobsters, smallish ones, up to a pound in weight. They scrabbled and slithered on the bottom-board of the *Siloam* until Samuel put elastic bands on their claws and stowed them in the box. The rain was constant all the time but the bay was sheltered from the wind. Samuel turned the *Siloam* round and made along the north shore of the bay. He had set a score of creels under the Red Head the day before yesterday. Beyond the Ness the wind struck him. The *Siloam* lost her rhythm and jigged and slithered among broken waves. Samuel debated whether it would be wise to make for the Red Head. He had been out in many a worse day but he didn't like it. Ten years ago he wouldn't have thought twice about running under the crags there and hauling his creels. The *Siloam* nosed and ettled into the grey sprawl of waves and sent up arcs of swift stinging spray. The Red Head loomed out of the murk to the north. Samuel held his course. The thing was – if the bad weather went on he was liable to lose all his creels. He had to keep fairly close inshore under the rising crags because the ebb in the Sound was at the top of its strength. Yet hugging the coast was dangerous too; the heavier land swell could throw you against the cliff barrier. You had to be very careful. For two hours yet the ebb would be rampant, draining the sea out of the Sound, leaving tooths of rock exposed, barely keeping covered reefs that the eye couldn't see. It was round about here that the hidden reef of Kellyan was. Samuel noted two landmarks, the cave mouth called Thorlak's Hole and the deserted croft of Anders that lay in a steep valley between two cliffs. He set his course and went in there, turned the *Siloam* to port as soon as Thorlak's Hole shut like an eye. 'I think now,' said Samuel, 'I did that fairly well.' He had slipped through by ten or a dozen feet; you couldn't see the reef-flurried water until you were right on top of it. In Samuel's time two trawlers – a Grimsbyman and an Aberdonian – and a Norwegian shark-boat had ended there. The sandstone crags reared alongside him, shutting out half the sky, rising higher and higher until they culminated a mile farther on in the buttress of the Red Head. Kittiwakes and cormorants looked at him from their ledges. He could hear under the noise of the wind a continuous roll and rasp as the ebb sucked at the round boulders under the crag, and the waves threw them back. Beyond Thorlak's Hole he found his first cluster of floats. There were lobsters in two creels, a small thing and a two-pounder that clashed blue armour at him until Samuel pinioned it with elastic bands. Three creels had been smashed. Samuel stowed the last of the creels in the bow. There were two more lots of creels a half-mile farther on. A grey beetling comber, an undulation fetched from the floor of the ocean – one of those freaks that fishermen call, with awe, a 'mother wave' – took the *Siloam* and raised her level with the indifferent gallery of kittiwakes and balanced her there and toppled her slowly against the looming fissures. Samuel could see the small reticulations in the face of the Red Head, barnacles and plasters of seaweed, even a brave knot of seapinks. He clung on to the tiller. The wave collapsed in ruin all about him. The boat surged high and buoyant. Samuel swung the tiller and, half blind with deluges of spray, took the *Siloam* swiftly out into the open sea.

> *... Twelve times eight is ninety-six*
> *Twelve times nine is one hundred and eight*
> *Twelve times ten is one hundred and twenty*
> *Twelve times eleven is one hundred and thirty-two*
> *Twelve times twelve is one hundred and forty-four*

It had continued long into the afternoon, the mouths opening and shutting, the measured treble chant, the pointer thwacking the blackboard, the eyes veiled with increasing boredom and resentment. When the clock stood at twenty past three Tom Kerston's blond head nodded on his chest. 'Thomas Kerston,' said Miss Inverary quietly, 'what is nine times seven?' The silence startled Tom Kerston awake. He opened his eyes like a wary animal. Everybody was looking at him. He was caught in a trap.

'Rio de Janeiro,' said Tom Kerston. They sniggered all round him.

'Be quiet,' cried Miss Inverary. 'How dare you laugh? This is a very serious matter. Thomas Kerston, come out to the floor.'

Tom Kerston trudged between the desks to the blackboard.

'This school is not a dormitory,' said Miss Inverary. 'Go and stand in that corner till four o'clock.'

The chant was resumed.

> *... Three times three is nine*
> *Three times four is twelve ...*

Gino Manson placed a cut-out photograph of a lion next to a cut-out print of the Eiffel Tower, and at the other side placed a cut-out coloured clown. This juxtaposition pleased him very much. He smiled gently in every direction but his felicity was private. The desks were smitten with the same chant that had gone on all day, over and over again. Like the sea on the Red Head, like the beating of flails in a barn. Gino Manson smiled at Tom Kerston in his corner, but Tom Kerston was too preoccupied with his own misery; he sniffled and gulped and hung his head. Gino Manson smiled and raked the fire and added two lumps of coal. The melon seeds and oats trickled through the fingers of the three smallest ones, like water or sunlight. Hamish Anderson of The Bu carefully gathered a handful of oats again. He closed his fist on them, then slowly opened his fingers. Oats filtered out. They were coins. 'I'm the richest man in the world,' whispered Hamish Anderson to Judy Kerston. He opened his hand. The oats showered on the desk, a torrent of gold.

Miss Inverary beat out the five times table and raised her pointer to the column of sixes. The pupils were all looking at the clock and nodding and whispering; looking and nodding from Miss Inverary to the hands of the clock, which stood at two minutes past four. 'Very well,' said Miss Inverary, 'that's all for today. Tom Kerston, see that you go to bed earlier at night. Gino, put the pictures back in the box, that's a good boy, then place the guard over the fire. Infants, seeds in tin, slates in slots. There. It's still raining. You will put on your coats and caps in the lobby before you go out. Bigger ones help the younger ones. Gino, tell your daddy that he *must* get you a coat for rainy days . . .'

Outside, in the school playground, they opened themselves to the rain, like animals that had been for a long time in a place of bones. They turned their faces to the sky. Their faces shone and streamed. They ran here and there through ditches and puddles. They were like young animals after the restriction and goading of the long dark day in school. They circled and gathered together, like a pack looking for some victim to glut their anger on. They found their victim. They found Gino Manson who was half a tinker and simple-minded and who had no coat. He stood at the corner of the school, alone, smiling in the rain. First Tom Kerston grabbed him by the arm; then they were all round him. Hands tore at his scruff and sleeve and trouser-leg. They jostled him slowly across the road. Behind the hotel a pool had formed. They forced Gino to walk through the water. Gino never said a word; they often played games like this with him. They pushed him to his knees. Tom Kerston stood behind Gino and put his arm round his throat and lowered him on his back into the deepest part of the pool. They scooped up filthy water while Tom Kerston held Gino down and showered it over his eyes and throat. They kicked mud at him. A black star filthied his cheek. Gino felt their hatred then; and he cried out, a single sweet gentle plaint. As if they were waiting for just that acknowledgement of their power they scattered and fled in all directions, round the hotel and into the store and down the long pier and across the shining beach. They were children again, miserable because they were hungry and it was raining and school all day had been a burden not to be borne.

Gino Manson, a sodden scarecrow, limped on home along the country road towards the gentler animals of Blinkbonny.

'The Lord was with me,' said Samuel Whaness. 'The Lord bestrode the waters.'

'To be sure he did,' said Rachel, and thumped the bellows into a setting of black peats.

'I could see the seapinks in the face of the Red Head,' said Samuel. 'I saw three seapinks growing out of a crack in the sheer face.'

'Take off everything,' said Rachel. 'I must get the salt out of that jersey and trousers right away.'

The fire covered Samuel's naked body with shadows and shifting silent golden lights.

'It's come to this,' said Samuel, 'I no longer like the sea or the things of the sea.'

'I thought you knew better than to go under them crags in a westerly swell,' said Rachel. 'A man of your age. Your clean clothes'll be aired in five minutes.'

'I'm very hungry, Rachel,' said Samuel.

'The broth's on the boil now,' said Rachel. She held a clean flannel shirt out to the fire, first the front, then the back. 'Tell me this, Samuel, were you not disappointed? You might have been walking this instant beside the rivers of heaven.'

Samuel's huge eyes brooded upon the fire.

'No,' he said, 'I'm glad to be where I am, woman.'

After their supper, and before they went to bed, Samuel read aloud to Rachel, as he did every night, a chapter from one of the books in the window ledge: Foxe's Book of Martyrs, Grace Abiding, Meditations Among the Tombs, The Pilgrim's Progress.

*

Ellen Kerston stood waiting in the rain at the pier till Bert Kerston had finished tying up the boat. ('And a poor job he's making of it,' she thought.)

'How many?' she said.

'Not one,' said Bert Kerston, his cheeks like two rumps of beet-root. 'Not one bloody lobster. Not even a crab.'

'I wasn't asking that,' said Ellen, 'I can see that you have no lobsters nor crabs. I was wondering how many glasses of whisky you've put down your throat since breakfast time in the Sutbreck Hotel.'

'I've been fishing all day,' said Bert Kerston.

Ellen Kerston turned and walked up the pier through the rain to her house. The children were scattered through the room, eating their supper, bowls of porridge and milk. Some were sitting beside the fire. Willie, the oldest boy, was pulling a comb through his black oiled hair. He was going to visit his girl at the Glebe on his pushbike, rain or no rain.

'Your father has been to the fishing and yet he has not been to the fishing,' said Ellen Kerston.

'I wish our dad would catch a whale,' said Ernie. 'I wish he owned all the fish in the sea.'

'Your father doesn't care about fish,' said Ellen. 'He is a fisher-man and yet he doesn't care about fish. He is your father and yet he doesn't care about you or about me. We can starve. I'll tell you what your father cares about: publicans. Your father's pleased so long as he can make the brewers live and die like lords.'

Bert Kerston stood in the open door. 'You're trying to set the bairns against me now,' he said. 'Pay no attention to her. Never fear. Your father has had a poor day at sea but your father'll keep a tight roof over your heads.'

Seven white faces looked round at him.

'I am not going to say anything tonight,' said Ellen Kerston, 'I will not say a word. "Never speak to a drunk man," my mother that's dead and gone used to say. "Wait till he's sober." So I'm saying nothing. Not tonight. I'm saving up what I have to say till tomorrow. I will have a few things to say to you in the morning, mister.'

Bert Kerston turned round and shut the door behind him. They heard the plop and splash of his rubber boots wandering across the road.

'Is our father a bad man?' said Judy.

'No,' said Ellen, 'because he can't in the first place be said to be a man at all.'

'I'll tell you something, mam,' said Tom Kerston, licking his spoon beside the fire.

'What's that, Tommy?' said Ellen Kerston.

'Six times ten is sixty,' said Tom. 'Six times eleven is sixty-six.'

'Bed-time,' said Ellen placidly. 'Come on now, off clothes.'

Alice Voar's children had been in bed for half-an-hour. They had knelt in shirts and vests all over the house and chanted mildy:

> God bless Sidney
> God bless Sophie
> God bless Sander
> God bless Shirley
> God bless Sam
> God bless Skarf
> God bless peedie Sigrid
> God bless Mother. Amen.

Then they chanted:

> Now I lay me down to sleep
> I pray thee, Lord, my soul to keep.
> Four angels round my bed,
> One at the foot, one at the head.
> If I should die ere break of day,
> Two to carry my soul away. Amen.

The children climbed into bed and covered themselves up.

Alice kissed them, one after the other, and lowered the flame of the paraffin lamp.

'Thorvald Gormson became a great chieftain in the west. He had eight sons and seven daughters. One of his sons, called Sven, was a monk in Birsay. Later he became abbot in Eynhallow. His name in *religion was Serenus. He was a truly pious man. The third daughter of Thorvald Gormson was called Ingibiorg. She was the most beautiful of women. Thorvald Gormson died at his estate in Hellya during Lent, in the seventy-eighth year of his age ... This* – I have quoted from the saga – is all that we know of Thorvald Gormson, the first laird of Hellya.'

The Skarf sat on his high stool at the bar counter and read what he had written that day in the cash-book.

'We have passed beyond the age of anonymity now. Here at last is a man with a name. He has sons and daughters, fifteen of them. Of thirteen nothing has been said. They are faceless nameless ones; the time has not yet come for all men, however ordinary, to have their names emblazoned on time. Only the clever one, Sven, and the beautiful one, Ingibiorg, are glimpsed for a moment before they too are out of the story: the wise ghost and the fragrant ghost.'

Bert Kerston came in and ordered a pint of beer. 'They can say what they like,' he murmured, 'I've been a good provider to them.'

'But I do not think a ghost when I think of Thorvald Gormson, whom men called Harvest-Happy. I see in the dawning of our history an immense jovial man. He is entering his new hall in Hellya from supervising the spring labour. In the field between hall and shore a team of oxen is dragging a wooden plough. The whip of the ploughman snakes over their black steaming flanks. This is the second year that this side of the hill has been ploughed. Often the ploughman, with wrenched arms, has to cry "whoa!" and drag an obstruction from the share, for there are still stones and deep roots in the field, bits of primeval stubborn darkness.'

Ivan Westray came in. He ordered a double whisky and leaned against the bar, sipping moodily from time to time.

'Thorvald Gormson enters the hall. He claps his fat brisk hands. The maid who has been stroking the hound's head runs to throw peat and driftwood on the fire. From the kitchen a sudden clatter of pans and chains; the food, boiled and grilled, is being taken from the fires. There enter from the rooms beyond, demurely, the nameless daughters, wisps of wool still on them from the embroidery frames. They bow to their father, then sit along one side of the bench. There enter one by one from sheepfold and smithy and boatshed the surly nameless brothers; they nod in their father's direction; they stand here and there about the fire; one kneels and warms his hands. There enters another nameless one, Thorvald's wife, wan and wasted as a summer moon from childbearing. The sons turn ceremonially to her. The daughters rise from the bench and bow. The mother takes her place at the far end of the table. There enters a young man with an open psalter bound in calfskin; he sets it on the table before sitting down; the capital letters shine out like flowers among the dark ruck of the script. This is Sven, the clever one. The mother smiles at him, wanly. The seated sisters smile. The brothers glower from their various stances about the central hearth. Now servants issue one after another from the kitchen, a woman bearing a wooden platter with two boiled cod smoking on it; a man with a pig's head on a trencher; a boy with a skewer and a carver newly sharpened; a girl with her arms full of drinking horns, who takes her place beside the ale-barrel. The working brothers sit down one after another. All is ready; what hinders them from making a start? The sisters whisper agitatedly among themselves. The mother folds her hands patiently. The blacksmith brother mutters that the fish is growing cold, and what in hell's name is the use of a cold fish to a working man? . . . There is a stir at the far end of the hall. A door opens. A girl enters, smiling, conscious that all eyes are on her, she walks the length of the hall to where her father is standing with his back to the fire, warming his hands. She goes up to him with grace and confidence, and takes a great fat hand in hers and kisses it. And says Thorvald her father in tones of gentle reproof, "Ingi, you must not keep your brothers and sisters and your mother waiting at meal-times." She takes her seat, the beautiful one, among her sisters; they turn their faces from her, they arrange their plates and busy themselves with their napkins. The white-faced son reads aloud from the psalter: *Happy are you who fear the Lord, who walk in his ways! For you shall eat the fruit of your hand-*

work, happy shall you be and favoured. Your wife shall be like a
fruitful vine in the recesses of your own home, your children like
olive plants around your table. Behold, thus is the man blessed
who fears the Lord.'

'A better father nobody ever had,' said Bert Kerston to his beer
mug.

'Then Thorvald Harvest-Happy takes his place at the head of
the table. "Eat," he says in a loud careless voice. "Put in your
hands, fill your bellies." His presence at the table transforms everyone. His face is like the sun, fringed with the radiant circle of his
hair and beard. "Eat till your jaws are tired," he shouts. All along
the table are laughter and good fellowship. Even the worn-out
mother shines in his life-giving presence; her face is full of the
smiling reflections of his great laughter. The codfish are broken and
the bones sucked clean. The shepherd brother empties his ale-horn
at one gulp and hands it back to the keeper of the barrel for replen-
ishment. They laugh and chatter among themselves. The girls pre-
tend to steal bits off each other's plates. The brothers boast about
their capacity for ale. And "Pass the swine's head now," comes the
golden trumpet of a voice from the head of the table, "till I carve
him up." And the mother murmurs gently for him to be careful
with the carver – it has been newly sharpened that morning.
  'Only two in all that company are silent – Ingibiorg imprisoned
in her mirror of beauty; and Sven who is seeking to pass beyond
all appearances and shadows and illusions to the light that never
was.
  'The pigs ear flutters on the table . . .'

'I like that bit,' said Ivan Westray. 'Give The Skarf a pint.'
  A man in a black cap stood in the outside door of the bar, his
back turned, an umbrella over his head like a bat rampant. He
looked right and left, then quickly furled his umbrella and turned
and came into the bar. It was the minister. He made a row of dark
shoe-prints all the way to the counter.
  'Are you there, Mr Scorradale?' said Rev. Simon McKee.
  'Yes, Mr McKee,' said Bill Scorradale, 'I'm always here.'

'It's so dark,' said Mr McKee. 'Is that you, Bert Kerston? How about one of your fat crabs some night for my supper? ... Well, Westray, and how are the girls in Quoylay this weather? ...'

The drinkers grunted with embarrassment all about him.

'What can I do for you, Mr McKee?' said Bill Scorradale.

'It's my mother,' said Mr McKee.

'O yes,' said Bill Scorradale.

'Taken another cold,' said Mr McKee. 'The changeable weather.'

'Dry one day, wet the next,' said Bill Scorradale.

'Exactly,' said Mr McKee. 'The cough mixture she got at the store doesn't seem to help.'

'It doesn't always work,' said Bill Scorradale.

'She coughs a lot in bed, at night,' said Mr McKee.

'That's very annoying,' said Bill Scorradale.

'Yes, when you can't sleep,' said Mr McKee. 'She just suddenly said, at breakfast-time, when she was having her toast, *toddy*.'

'Toddy,' said Bill Scorradale.

'Yes,' said Mr McKee. 'She remembered that from her childhood. Apparently her mother used to give it to her whenever she had a bad cough.'

'One glass of whisky to an equal quantity hot water, add sugar or honey to taste, drink before retiring,' said Bill Scorradale. 'You can't beat that for a cold.'

'So it appears, Mr Scorradale,' said Mr McKee. 'You know your trade.'

The minister gave the publican a prolonged bitter wink.

'Well, then, sir,' said Bill Scorradale, 'I don't keep hot water, nor sugar or honey, but I could supply the other ingredient at fifteen shillings and twopence a quarter bottle.'

Mr McKee leaned his umbrella against the bar counter and took out his wallet. 'Shall we say,' he said, 'a *full* bottle.'

Bill Scorradale bent down and took a bottle of whisky from a shelf under the counter. 'Two pounds eighteen and sixpence,' he said.

'A summer cold is bad to shift,' said Mr McKee.

'The very worst,' said Bill Scorradale.

'Two bottles therefore,' said Mr McKee, 'and put brown paper round them, if you please, in case Mrs Evie is looking through her kitchen window.'

He went then, with a 'Goodnight, men,' and 'Much obliged, Mr Scorradale,' and a wink and a touch to the rim of his black cap. In the doorway he unfurled his umbrella, and leaned into the sloping sopping slappering downpour.

'Go on,' said Ivan Westray to The Skarf. 'You haven't finished yet.'

'It needs must be that there are occasional interruptions,' said The Skarf, examining the fleece of froth on the side of his empty mug. 'Incursions from the realm of superstition and obscurantism.'

'Driven from my own hearth and home,' said Bert Kerston, his nostrils wincing with emotion.

'Keep your voices down,' said Bill Scorradale, and pointed to the ceiling. 'The guest.'

'A pint for me and a pint for The Skarf,' said Ivan Westray. 'And you might as well give Kerston one to cheer him up. I didn't care for the look of that man I ferried across today. That guest of yours. I didn't care for him one little grain.'

The Skarf, having rubbed his spectacles with a corner torn out of *The Orcadian*, put them back on his face. He focused into the cash-book. He resumed.

'Thorvald Harvest-Happy: a golden mask of fertility looks at us down the long corridor of history. Somewhere in this island, among cornfields, a skull is buried. Of the flowering wilting flesh between mask and skull nothing is left but a pinch of fragrant dust.

' "He died," says the sagaman, "in the season of Lent."

'I delight to imagine the death of this fat merry man in that hungry time of the year. He was then seventy-eight years of age. The ploughman unyoked his team; the sower scattered his seed; the shepherd wandered among small new fluttering bleats on the hill. For nineteen days after Ash Wednesday, obedient to the laws of the church, Thorvald Harvest-Happy ate smoked sillocks and drank well water. He knelt alone for an hour, morning and evening, by candle-light, in his cold chapel. One evening when he was listening to compline, devoutly, but with a hollow belly, he heard a distant cry of "Whales!" and a flurry and scurry and a shouting down at the beach. Then he turned his attention once more to the penitential psalm that the chaplain was intoning.

'That night a dozen whales were driven on to the beach at Keelyfa. His son who had charge of the fishing boats told him the news at breakfast-time next morning. (Breakfast was a square of hard bannock and a horn of cold water.)

'All that morning Thorvald Gormson seemed very preoccupied. He sat at the hearth, occasionally kicking a smouldering log back into the heart of the fire.

'Down at the beach they were flensing the whales and running off the grey oil into barrels and dragging huge red steaks through a drift of salt. The whole island of Hellya was there.

'At noon Thorvald sent for his chaplain, Father Erling. "Tell me, Father," said he, "is a whale a fish or isn't it?"

' "A whale in my opinion is a fish," said Father Erling.

' "I'm very pleased to hear it," said Thorvald. "Then it is permissible to eat a whale in Lent."

'Father Erling was not quite so sure about that. He hummed and he hawed. "The flesh of a whale," he said, "is red like butcher-meat. Yet whales swim in the sea like fish. I really know very little about it. I am only a curate. I will send word to the canon – he will know for sure."

'They ate dinner in the Hall, a few boiled crabs and cups of milk. It was not a cheerful meal.

'The canon arrived on horseback in the middle of the afternoon. "A whale is a fish and yet it is an animal," said the canon pedantically. "Does not the female give suck? On the whole I would say a whale is a beast, a salt-water ox, that feeds on the pastures of the sea. Yet it is in many ways a fish too. We are told in holy writ that the Lord prepared a great fish to swallow the prophet Jonah. Though it nowhere categorically states in the scripture that this great fish was a whale, yet tradition leads us strongly to assume that indeed it was a whale that was meant. So, in that sense, a whale is a fish."

' "A whale is a fish," said Thorvald, "and therefore may be eaten in Lent."

' "It is not as simple as that," said the canon. "That I would not

57

go so far as to say. We may observe, here and there in the scheme of creation, a confusion, a blurring of boundaries, a kind of divine joke, an equivocation. What is a jellyfish, a fish on the fiercely concentrated essence of salt water? There is a creature in Africa that is winged and goes on two legs and lays eggs, yet it cannot fly – is it a bird or a beast? I have heard butterflies described as flying blossoms. The whole question is encompassed with difficulty. Why do you not consult your son who is the abbot in Eynhallow? He is a far more learned man than me. He would be able to tell you for sure."

'So Thorvald sat down the same evening and got his scribe to write a letter on parchment: "To Serenus, Abbot of the monastery in Eynhallow. Your father according to the flesh sends word to acquaint you with the news that all is not well with him. He is fallen into a melancholy. There is little laughter any more in the long hall of Hellya. He feels that all might be well with him yet if he could fill his belly with good food. They give him dribs and drabs to eat. They give him roots and husks and buttermilk. One day for his dinner they put *stewed seaweed* in front of him. He prays often but his mouth is cold and fervourless. O Sven, my boy, I was a good father to you in the days when you were small and helpless and were afraid of the shining eye of the rat in the barn. And I pray you therefore to tell me one thing, Sven my dear son, without any more equivocations or vain circlings about the matter: is not a whale that lives in the sea a fish? . . ."

'The letter was given to Arkol the boatman to take to the monastery in Eynhallow.

'For supper that night there was a boiling of whelks and the third ale to be taken off the malt, a kind of thin barley water.

'The next morning Thorvald was unwell. He was unable to rise from his bed. His daughters were frightened when they saw his flushed cheeks, and how his hair was curled with sweat and clung to his brow, and how his urine had a purplish glow like bog water.

' "Word has not yet come from our brother Sven, the abbot in Eynhallow," said his eldest son, the factor.

' "Who?" said the old man. "What word? I never spoke to an abbot in my life. Where is Ingibiorg, where is my little dove and my jewel?"

' "Our sister Ingibiorg has been married these ten years and more in Ireland," said Helga the eldest daughter. "She is the wife of Solmund of Antrim in Ulster."

'Thorvald Harvest-Happy wept when he understood that he could not see his beautiful daughter Ingibiorg. That frightened them more than ever; they had never seen tears in his eyes before.

' "Where is my wife?" said Thorvald Harvest-Happy. "I did not love her but she brought me a good dowry. She has a sweet nature and I got to like her well enough after a time. I want to see her now."

'Three of the daughters began to sob.

' "Our mother is in her grave these seven years past," said one of the sons.

' "Is she?" said Thorvald Harvest-Happy. "In her grave. It is after all the happiest place for any person to be. I am very tired. I have a pain that is like two millstones grinding together in my breast."

'He had never said a stranger thing. The son who was the blacksmith turned away and kneaded his cheek with a huge smoky fist.

' "Father," said the daughter Gudrun who was in charge of the kitchens, "I will prepare a lobster with an oil dressing. That always cheered you up in Lent. It is a small sweet lobster that Ubi caught. It will put new strength into you."

' "No, child," said Thorvald Harvest-Happy, "I have no relish for food any more. One Yule I ate the whole side of a sheep. In the Seal Holm two days later a family were found dead of starvation behind their shutters. That troubles me now."

'Then he fell into a light sleep.

'Towards noon Father Erling came with the sacring oils and a consecrated Host in a pyx and a parchment of scripture. The sun shone on the brilliantly dyed initial letters. Father Erling shepherded the sniffles and the washed eyes and gulping throats and wringing hands out into the corridor.

' "Who's there?" said Thorvald Harvest-Happy. "I can't see. It's very dark."

' "It's me, Father Erling, your chaplain," said Father Erling. "I think it is time for me to read you a piece of holy scripture."

' "Yes," said Thorvald Harvest-Happy, "very good. Read me *The Lay of the Jomsvikings*, the piece where Sigurd is to have his head cut off and the executioner's assistant stands before him and winds his hands through Sigurd's long hair. Read me that."

'*Go thy way, eat thy bread with joy, and drink thy wine with a merry heart*, Father Erling read from his parchment, *for God now accepteth thy works. Let thy garments be always white, and let thy head lack no ointment. Live joyfully with the wife whom thou lovest all the days of the life of thy vanity, for that is thy portion in this life, and in thy labour which thou takest under the sun.*

' "That was beautiful," said Thorvald Harvest-Happy. Then after a minute he said, "It gets dark early in winter. Light the torches."

'Father Erling's acolyte, a herdboy called Ljot, lit a blessed candle and set it at Thorvald Harvest-Happy's bed-post. The thin flame was lost in the sun through the window. "That's better," said Thorvald. "It's bright now."

'There was a steady groundswell of sobbing and wailing from the corridor outside. All the household were gathered there: the sons, the daughters, the cook, the butler, ploughmen and cattle-men and fishermen, maidservants, herdboys, wives, widows, children. A tramp had even wandered in from the road. They understood that Thorvald Harvest-Happy was about to set out on the longest voyage.

'Father Erling touched the holy oil to Thorvald's eyes and lips and ears and nostrils and hands: the five portals through which evil enters to stain the Christ-destined soul. And as he did so he murmured the words of absolution.

'Arkol the boatman had come back from Eynhallow. The congregated mourners heard the scrape of his keel over the stones. Nobody was interested in him or his message. He stood at the door of the boatshed most of the afternoon, scratching his head.

'An hour before sunset Thorvald Harvest-Happy had much difficulty with his breathing. Two sons, the factor and the viking skipper, heaved him up on his pillow; then groped out of the chamber again, wet fingers over wet eyes.

' "I've been hungry all my life," said Thorvald: "I had the wolf continually in my belly. I thought about roast beef and ale more than anything."

'Father Erling took the consecrated Host out of the pyx and made the sign of the cross with it over the luminous face on the bolster. "This banishes the wolf," he said. "You will never be hungry again. Here is the food of the dwellers in heaven, *panis angelicus*." He put the wafer on the tongue of the dying man. And Thorvald Harvest-Happy ate it with devotion and wonderment.

'In the courtyard the son who was the falconer fixed an ebony ring to the leg of the pigeon that Solmund had brought from Ireland for Ingibiorg. The bird flew out of his hands and circled twice and hovered for a moment and flew straight into the southwest.

'A minute after the dove had dwindled to a quivering dot and disappeared under the horizon, Thorvald Gormson, called Harvest-Happy, died. Father Erling held the feather to his lips; it did not stir. The herdboy lit another candle.

'When the lamentation in courtyard and corridor had subsided somewhat, the eldest son – the new laird – took the wallet from Arkol the boatman. He opened it and read the message from the Abbot of Eynhallow. It set forth twenty good reasons why the whale might be considered a fish, and as many equally cogent for thinking that it was an animal. The letter conceded that the question was one of the utmost subtlety, which no bishop or abbot would dare to answer without collegiate discussion; therefore the writer proposed to put the matter before his grace the Bishop of Nidaros in Norway when next they met, which might be next year or in a dozen years' time, or might indeed be only in heaven, so tinctured with vanity are all our desires and aspirations and plans. Also he would raise the matter with his grace the Archbishop of Saint Andrews in Scotland. Not that the concurring opinion of even three such reverences was conclusive; it might have to go to a council of the entire Church, when next such a council met, perhaps after two centuries or twelve centuries (councils were a most rare occurrence); it might have to be laid before the Chair of Saint Peter itself, but then the Successor of the Fisherman might not consider the matter worth pronouncing upon. The writer thanked his father-in-the-flesh for his prayers. The abbot likewise sent his blessings to his ghostly son the laird of the island of Hellya. The abbot was glad indeed that the laird was taken up with such interesting speculations, which though natural had metaphysical overtones; it could therefore be considered a sign of grace in him. He hoped however with all his heart that the laird of Hellya did not seriously consider the devouring of whale-meat in the season of Lent . . .

'Down on the beach they began to prepare a great pyre.'

'Give The Skarf another pint,' said Ivan Westray. He strolled to the door and looked out into the dark wavering slurping downpour. There was only one light in the village, from the attic at the top of the hotel; the guest was working late. The schoolhouse was in darkness. Ivan Westray came back to the bar and studied the whisky in the bottom of his glass.

Bert Kerston raised his head from his arm. 'The bitch!' he shouted suddenly and brought his fist down on the counter with a crash. Glasses and water-jugs rattled.

'Any more of that,' said Bill Scorradale to Bert Kerston, 'any more of that, my boy, look here, and you'll be out on your neck. I have a guest . . .' To The Skarf he said, 'I had no idea things like that ever happened in Hellya, Skarf.'

'You've heard nothing yet,' said The Skarf. 'The best is still to come.'

The stable at The Bu farm.

> *The Lord of the Harvest. The Master Horsemen. The novice who has obtained the degree of Ploughman; he is blindfolded; he carries the horse-shoe.*

THE LORD OF THE HARVEST: We have come to the station of THE SEED. What are you seeking here, Ploughman, among the master horsemen?

THE PLOUGHMAN: A kingdom.

> *The mockery of the Master Horsemen.*

THE LORD OF THE HARVEST: The man with a new bride, who has ploughed a field in March, what does he know of kingdoms?

THE PLOUGHMAN: Beyond the blood of beasts, further than axe and fire, there it lieth well, in the light, a kingdom.

THE LORD OF THE HARVEST: What hinders you from this kingdom?

THE PLOUGHMAN: Blindness. And it is a long road through the new furrows.

THE LORD OF THE HARVEST: Are you willing to enter the earth womb? Can you suffer the passion of the seed?

THE PLOUGHMAN: (*Does not answer.*)

THE MASTER HORSEMEN: Answer. Answer.

THE PLOUGHMAN: I am willing.

> *The Master Horsemen stretch the Ploughman supine on the floor. They lay a straw-woven seed-basket on his chest. They lift his knees and shoulders. They lower him through the opening in the floor. They stand like mourners about a grave.*

THE LORD OF THE HARVEST: Take him, earth. Receive the Sower.

The rain slanted across the island, a dark lustration upon the suffering and the unborn; but especially it filled the water-barrels under the eaves, and further rotted the woodwork of Timmy Folster's window, and put silk and sap in the ripening Hellya corn.

THREE

Mrs Learmonth's hotel,
Hamnavoe

My Dear Uncle Pannadas,

As you have commanded me, so I have obeyed: namely, the day before yesterday (Wednesday) by crossing over by ferry-boat to the island of Hellya with a full bag of assorted draperies and fancy goods, of a gaudiness and general shining quality to take the eye of the ladies. As you further commended me, dear Uncle, so now I write. 'Be brief, succinct,' you said. This I will attempt, though it may prove difficult in one whom you have so often rebuked for discursiveness.

At the wheel of the boat, as last year, was the ferryman Westray, the silent bright-headed one. You remember how last year I called him in joke 'the bringer of warriors and heroes to Valhalla'. At once he set a black look on us, but proved subsequently to be friendly in a brusque laconic way, and charged twelve shillings and sixpence for each crossing.

Just so it turned out today, one year later, with one serious exception, that is, that the fare was higher.

– Please, how much? I inquire on the slipway at Greenvoe.

– Fifteen bob, he replies.

– Fifteen shillings! I state. This is most expensive.

– And fifteen bob return. One pound ten shillings. What time are you wanting to go back? he says, unmoved.

– I cannot pay such ransom money, I exclaim. O no.

– I'll tell you what I'm going to do then, says this Westray. I'm going into that phone box up there and I'm going to ring the police station in Kirkwall and the sergeant will be meeting you at Kirkwall pier with handcuffs.

All the while he is coiling a rope.

– Let us please be reasonable people, I say.

– Your move, Johnny, he says.

– The perfect solution has occurred to me, I say. Wait. Is not this good?

Thereupon I kneel down and remove the leather strap from my case and open it and lift out an art silk scarf or cravat, black and white dots upon a scarlet ground, and make a heavenly bridge with it over my two extended arms.

– This silk scarf, I say, is value two pounds. I will give you this. This pays for the ferry, eh?

– No, he says.

– But surely, I say. Such a bargain.

– I never wear a scarf, he says.

Whereupon I make deeper delvings into the case.

– Here are socks, I say, black silk. Box of handkerchiefs, initialled. A necktie. One suit pyjamas, Paisley pattern, so lovely.

– I sleep naked, he says. What's that?

– That is headsquare, I say, silken, for ladies, twelve shillings.

– That will do, he says.

– Is for ladies, I say.

– I'll take it, he makes swift answer. That's you and me square, Johnny.

So, my dear uncle, this turned out most satisfactory. I trust you will approve my acumen.

I fasten my case. The ferryman is attaching his boat by a rope to an iron bolt in the face of the pier.

– We are good friends, no? I say.

– Same as always, he answers.

Whereupon we shake hands.

– Where is old Abdul the Damned this year? he says. (My dear uncle, I trust you will not take it amiss, he was referring, in joke, to you. I explain that you are incapacitated temporarily by reason of very painful arthritis in your knee.)

– Poor old bastard, he answers. (Please, Uncle, not to take this amiss; it came out of a rough kindliness.)

– These bargainings between us at the pier of Greenvoe, pedlar and boatman, I say, are always so very keen. I laugh to remember them afterwards.

We part most good friends.

Thereupon I made a circuit of village and island with my merchandise. The bag was very heavy. I fear, by the time this summer is over, my right shoulder will be nearer Leith Street by six inches than my left.

I came first to the burnt house whose door was of undulating iron, as last year, only more rusted. No steps had been attempted towards repair.

– Ah, my good friend, I call in at the window, are you in there? Are you at home?

– Timmy is in residence, comes the answer.

– Here I have many silken articles for you, I say.

– Timmy is impecunious.

I heave my bag in through the window and climb in after it. Such is the only mode of entry into this house. This Timmy is lying on his bed, if such it can be called by western standards, being the floor, and he is covered with a drift of ancient coats. It is a house of the utmost gloom. I perceive a table with a tin of cat-food on it, and a half loaf of bread, and a sculpted slab of margarine. Dominant upon the table, like a king in an evil purple robe, is an almost full bottle of meth. There is a spirit stove under the table. No brush has kissed that floor for many a month past. There is an odour of ancient rot everywhere. It is a kingdom for spiders. Beside Timmy's bed is a zinc pail with a quantity of stale urine in it. The curtains are as they were last year, abbreviated and scorched.

Yet Timmy from his litter of coats gives me a cheerful welcome.

– Timmy is pleased to see you again. Timmy has no colour prejudice. All men are equal to Timmy.

He then quotes the poet Burns on this subject: 'Man to man, the warld o'er/Shall brithers be, for a' that.'

My dear Uncle, you must forgive me for wasting a half-hour in such a place of unpromising business. I confess that I stayed in this cold oven of a dwelling for a full half-hour. I sat down on the floor beside the bed. I opened my packet of cigarettes, and Timmy and I smoked together in friendly silence. He tapped out the ash in the pail of urine. But first I entered upon the jargon of business, more in the fashion of a game than of any serious attempt at negotiation.

– How good that I have come! You have burned your curtains, therefore I have a length of satin to fit your window exquisitely.

66

– You'll find a box of matches in the jacket pocket, over there, hanging on the chair. Timmy is much obliged for this cigarette.

It was so gloomy. The flame hung between us for a moment, a tranquil ruby.

– What will transform your room, I say, is a bedspread in spun rayon, golden and scarlet flowers upon a blue ground. This will render your house gay, in winter especially.

Timmy did not reply. I feared to have hurt him, taunting his poverty with an image of unattainable opulence, but he smiled at me through a veil of tobacco smoke.

And so we sat in tranquillity until our cigarettes were smoked. First Timmy and then I threw the burning ends into the urine pail; they each expired with a brief hiss.

I get to my feet then.

– Blessings on this house, I say. May the creature fire, that broke loose with rage and destruction the winter before last, now be forever the friend in the hearth.

– I hope you do good trading, says Timmy with the utmost sincerity.

Whereupon (forgive me, Uncle) I place a further tipped cigarette on the coat that serves as his upper blanket.

Outside on the road, after that fetor, was such a good mingling of smells, seaweed and cowdung and wild white clover. I drank it like a rare wine.

It will not be lost to your remembrance, the village shop where the glinting woman probes always deep among our origins and circumstances and beliefs. I approached that place with much trepidation. I put my head in at the door, a tentative insertion, and observed with joy that only the careful old man was on the premises. Thereupon I entered at once.

– Nothing doing, says Mr Evie.

After adumbrating upon the weather, and how pleasant a day it was, mild if cloudy, and so agreeable after the incessant rain of yesterday; and moving on then to the political situation, especially the dock strikes (which shopkeepers in general abhor) and the rising cost of living, the ever-upward tendency of the graph (a most telling counter with everyone, in particular housewives and retailers); I then – as you have well trained me to do Uncle – heaved my bag upon the counter with this remark, 'But you will be glad to learn, however, that the price of these articles has not gone up, indeed they have decreased since I was here last year...'

– I need nothing, says the shopkeeper. I want nothing.

Nevertheless, I swiftly unlocked the case and threw the lid open and presently my hands were brimming with stockings, brassières, tablecloths, runners, chair covers, nightgowns, handkerchiefs. The praise of this lovely soft cascade flowed from my lips, an urgent beautiful poem.

All was wasted upon the desert air. At the conclusion the shop-keeper said nothing, but indicated with his finger certain articles that hung diagonally across the ceiling of his premises on a string. These were: two print cotton aprons, a grey woollen jersey, a grey cardigan with a meagre pattern of Fair Isle at yoke and cuffs, cotton stockings for small boys, four black berets, three pairs cor-duroy trousers, a spread of ladies' knickers and men's winter drawers, fishermen's thick white stockings.

The shopkeeper pointed for half-a-minute at this utilitarian dis-play.

– But compare, I say, contrast, match one class of goods with another. Your stock is worthy enough, your stock is for peasants and fishermen, very good, but these in my case are the very trap-pings and appurtenances of paradise.

And I slid a lady's yellow silk camisole through my fingers. It fell back into the case with a voluptuous whisper. (Well have you trained this nephew!)

The old block of stubbornness sat looking at me with a fixed smile of denial on his face.

And with that the door at the back of the shop burst open and the terrible woman appeared, her spectacles glinting and her artificial teeth knocking like castanets with the volubility of her speech.

I hastened to fold and depart but she detained me with her ancient mariner eye.

Had she not seen me before? Was I not here last year at this very time with another older man? She was sure of it. And had I got married in the meantime? What a wonder, a young well-set-up young man like me. How many wives was I permitted to marry in all? Was that so? Well, then, and I was still at the university, in Edinburgh. What stage in my studies had I reached now? It was medicine, was it not? Oh, English literature. And what good, she would like to know, would knowledge of poems and novels do out there in India? Would that help the darkies in any way? Would that keep them from starving? Would that deliver them from the worship of idols? She didn't see it herself. But still, education was a grand thing. She urged me to stick well to my books. Did I have a girl back in Kashmir? She bade me for God's sake to watch out for some of the women in the cities, particularly Leith Street in Edinburgh. And there was no need either to go as far as the cities, certain characters in this island were as bad as any of the Leith tarts. Not that she was mentioning any names. But just that I should beware.

The shopkeeper remarked that, since yesterday's solid downpour, the lupins at his front door were an inch taller.

The harridan then turned her attention to my stock. Under the strait compulsion of her gaze I was driven to open up again. She was then like a goddess at the sundering of souls, praising this and condemning that. She approved and examined all with her fingers. There was not one single square inch that she did not probe and paw, and even subject to her olfactory sense, passing it under her nose and sniffing. She rooted everywhere in my case like a pie-dog. (Lovingly however had I interlaid each layer, before setting out, with sweet orient herbs.)

After such mountainous labour a mouse was born. She selected a head square such as young girls wear: a rash of scarlet poppies upon a yellow ground.

– Yes, she says, this scarf will do for the agricultural show in August. It matches my blue coat. How much?

– One half-guinea, I say. (This, you have always taught me, Uncle, is much more acceptable to the emptor than ten-and-six.)

She vents a black laugh. Mr Evie is reading a newspaper a month old.

– There is such a thing, young man, she says, as the Prices and

Incomes Board. I know one of the men who works in it, he comes here in the summertime to fish. Five shillings, not a penny more.

– Eight-and-six, I say patiently.

Whereupon the game works out to a foreseen conclusion: seven shillings.

– Give me seven shillings, says Mrs Evie to Mr Evie.

Mr Evie puts down his newspaper. He closes the drawer of the till, then turns the key and puts it in his pocket.

– I see, he says, Ghana is to have the atom bomb by 1977.

Mrs Evie killed Mr Evie with her eye. She flip-flapped into the inner room. She returned at once. She snapped open the mouth of her purse. Her fingers probed and pulled three florins out, one after the other, and set them on the counter.

– There you are, she says, six shillings.

Seven shillings had been the agreed sum. Yet I took the six shillings without further argument, being anxious to set myself beyond the knives of the woman.

– Good morning, I say to both, turning for the last time on the threshold.

Mrs Evie is holding up the headsquare, her head aslant with rapture. It is an article of great ugliness.

– Silk and scarlet, remarks Mr Evie, not looking up from his newspaper, covers many a harlot.

I am on the road outside.

A clatter of hidden hooves on tarmac, an excited snicker and whinny, and round the corner of the hotel comes a young horse-woman. She is such a beautiful girl, in cap and jodhpurs. The horse is a chestnut with a white blaze. I have not seen this girl in the island before.

– Bargains for you, nice girl, I say, venturing into the middle of the road.

She urged the horse forward in a shower of stars and stones, urgent, leaning forward on his neck, spurring him on between the shop and the fishermen's houses to the seafront. The cobbles clattered as down the long pier the hooves hesitated. The girl gestured with her whip. She called. Her voice is not like the voice of the islanders, it is more like the loud imperiousness of our former administrators and civil servants, a sequence of brassy shouts.

The ferryman turns. He is stowing aboard the *Skua* a mail sack, several empty portable gas cylinders, a wire netted cage with a silent cockerel inside.

The horsewoman dismounts. She holds the rein lightly in her fingers and speaks to the ferryman. Ivan Westray does not answer until the last cylinder is safely stowed and the cockerel begins to rage from the stern. Then he gives his attention to this most attractive girl with the unpleasant voice; who, however, is all awkwardness and hesitancy now; her arm round the gently smoking neck of the pony, her eyes moving between the sea and the houses, anywhere but on the ferryman with whom she has agreeable but difficult business. She rubs one knee nervously on the other.

Westray lights a cigarette. He moves closer. He points out to sea, to the lighthouse. Her eye follows his finger.

Ferryman and horsewoman look at one another. Their mouths move. There is a quickening in the air between them. I imagine a rose straining to open in an evil summer: fog, rot, tempest. I turn away.

Uncle, you must remember the little cluster of fishermen's houses – four of them – on the terrace above the pier, where we are so variously received year after year.

There I next turned my steps. The fat woman (who is fatter than ever, burdened with new imminent wombfruit) was in a rage of heroic dimensions, like a trumpet pealing. The impressive anger was not, I say with gladness, directed at me, but at a motionless shape on the bed.

– Look here, Johnny, she cries (as soon as I am seated on her couch), look at that object under the blankets, it is supposed to be a fisherman, it is supposed to feed and clothe and house its children, and there it lies, a bloody drunken hulk, and the sea full of fish! ... O Johnny, that's a lovely blouse, right bonny, I wish to God I had the wherewithal to buy it ... The thing came to our farm, after me, wanting to marry me, fifteen years ago, and it was full of the grandest talk you ever heard. No crab fishing for him. O no, he was going to get a government grant, he was going to have a seine-netter built to his specifications, if you please, he was going after halibut and cod, he would have a crew of six men under him, they would fish half-way between here and Norway. 'And as for you,' says he to me, 'you're not biding another winter in this croft, in all the cow-shit and gutter. I'm going to take you to a fine big house with two storeys on a Hamnavoe pier, and when you want eggs in future,' says he, 'or cheese, you'll order them from a shop, and you'll say to the shopkeeper, *Put it down to Mr R. Kerston's account* ... Johnny, I would give my right hand for a dressing-gown like this. Lord, what bonny! Look at the way it changes in the light, shot silk, now dark and now shining ... Well, that was fifteen years ago. And I wish to God I was back among my dad's beasts, at Vertafiold in Quoylay. I do that. I wish I was going to milk the kye on a winter's morning with a lantern in my fist, and having to shovel and scrape the snow away before I could get the byre door open. I would go back like a shot – and my brother-in-law would have me too – if it wasn't for the bairns ... Johnny dear, you shouldn't have opened your pack, it makes my heart sore to look at all them lovely things ... Well, but listen, this beats all. Yesterday the thing sets off in the morning in his old tub – no word of the seine-net boat after he first filled me and then married me, not a word, not a mouse's weisk – away he sails in the rain, a fine day for haddocks, Samuel Whaness said the west was swarming with them – out he sallies, as I say, early. And home come the bairns from the school, for their dinner. The father, the provider, has not returned. Bannocks and margarine and milk the bairns got for their dinner instead of baked haddocks, then away back to school with them. 'By God,' says I to Rachel Whaness and Alice Voar in the shop in the afternoon, 'by God, Kerston's getting himself some catch today out beyond the Red Head, haddocks enough to see us through the winter (salted).' But of course I was saying it to keep my heart up, because I had been through all this performance before. Still no Mister Kerston at four o'clock when the school bell rang. The kids ate syrup and bread to their tea. 'The great skipper is still at the dragging-in of his burdened nets,' I said to them as they sat about the fire drying their wet jerseys. And with that the door opens and it stands in threshold, reeking with whisky as if it had been steeped in a hogshead in a distillery for a year and a day. Fishless it stood in the door ... Johnny, I just can't resist them peedie white socks with the blue ring round the tops. If I should die in the poor-house I'll get a pair each for Judy and peedie Maud. Only five bob? For the two pair? I'll tell you this, Johnny, you've fairly cheered me up, and I'm right glad you've come. How much is that silk tie? Willie, you see, the oldest boy, he's courting one of the lasses at the Glebe – he would just love the like of that. God knows, they need some comforts with the kind of object they have for a father ...

Thereupon Mrs Kerston went and stood over the grey-blanketed twist on the bed, and she stabbed him several times with her tongue: waster, object, drunkard, liar, bed-fart, seducer – and during these thunders and lightnings I judged it expedient to close my case and tiptoe to the door and make an unceremonious exit.

– Please, Ellen, leave me alone, I'm feeling ill, came a thin pleep from the bed.

– Ill, cried she, I wish you were dead, and a headstone over you. I wish I was a widow.

I knocked at the door of Mrs Whaness.

It is as last year, she will buy nothing. She is kind. She puts me in the chair beside the fire. No, I must on no account spread my goods on the table. She raises her hands in an access of gentle horror – it is as though my bag is stuffed with all harlotry and vanity and incensed hell-bait. I open the lid six inches. She shuts her eyes. And truly in such a plain little room – scrubbed table, blue stone floor, black stove with a decent twinkle of fire in it, plain walls, scoured windows – our splendour would, I know it, offend the simple harmony. She gives me two pamphlets. We part peaceably.

The titles of the tracts are as follows, respectively: *How a Child led me from the Hell of Drink,* with a drawing of a boy in a bed of sickness who looks angelically at a scarecrow with a bottle; and *The Scarlet Woman – The Menace of Popery,* depicting the Servant of the servants of God in his triple tiara, who however is made to cringe and cower under a great open shining book entitled 'Revelation'; a section of the type is underlined in red.

I gave these writings to the wind. They fluttered like two white butterflies into the ditch. There they drowned.

You remember certainly the fisherman who does not fish. Today a marvel has taken place. He is in his boat. So I am informed after I have knocked at his door three times, by a small boy who pipes up at me from the end of the house, a few frail bird-cries.

– The Skarf is down at his boat.

– What is your name? I ask.

He moons against the wall. He twists himself. He lays his brow against a stone in the wall. He is shy. He will not answer.

– In what house do you live? I say.

He studies the cement between the stones with the utmost concentration. One hand flutters free. A finger points crookedly. I should have known. He lives in the house of the passionate dove. He lives in the house whose door is shut on me for ever; such is your command; I bow and obey. He lives in the house of roses.

– I will give you one whole sixpence for yourself, I say seriously, if only you will tell me your name.

This woman's children have all different names. She is very desirable. We know that. My hand trembles; observe the havoc in the handwriting.

But no. He will not tell. I have the impression that wild horses will not drag the name from him, yet he looks at the offered coin with immense Alice-like eyes.

Now he is going to tell me.

He whispers. It is something about an engine. The engine wouldn't start.

I turn the silver into the light till it glints.

– The name, I say. Please. What your brothers and sisters call you.

The lips flutter open and shut. Petrol. There was no petrol to put in the engine.

The sixpence shines like a star. He is sick with desire for it.

– Skarf, he says after a time.

– And still I wait for the revelation of the name, I say, shaking my head sorrowfully.

I am overshadowed. I am breathed upon. I turn and that long creature, The Skarf, is hanging over me like a question mark. He has come upon me so suddenly in his rubber boots that I have not heard him.

– Johnny, says he. You're late this year.

– Not so, I say. Generally it is the beginning of August. I come alone. Unfortunately my uncle is sick.

– I have something I want you to hear, he says.

He lollops inside the house and returns at once with an account book, very bleached and stained.

He sat on the wooden bench beside his door and stretched out his long rubber legs into the grass.

– No petrol, he said. So I couldn't go. The old yawl coughed twice and then she died on me. Thank God for National Assistance. The sun of socialism warms me, however feebly. I'm not complaining. I can smoke. I can eat potatoes and margarine. I have leisure to write.

The nameless child fluttered and eddied on the cobbles.

– Go home to your mammy, says The Skarf. Be quiet. I have business with this Indian gentleman, my friend.

– This dancing one will not tell me his name, I say.

– He is called Skarf, said The Skarf. I'm his father.

They looked at each other. A likeness trembled between their faces at once, as if The Skarf glanced momently into a mirror of innocence; and as if the child gazed with much earnestness at an inauspicious destiny.

– My name is Skarf, he chirruped. I told you. Skarf, Skarf.

And he fell on the sixpence like a seagull snapping up a crust. And bore it off, shouting, to the shop window. And there furled his feet and gazed for a long time, wondering, at black-striped balls and fudge and liquorice. He was lost in a dream of sweetness.

The Skarf opened a tobacco tin and rolled a cigarette between his fingers; then offered the tin to me.

– I have a tale to unfold, he said, that will harrow your blood.

He opened his MS book and began to read in a slow chant:

'For several centuries after the death of Thorvald Harvest-Happy the island of Hellya drops out of history; all records are lost; not even a ballad survives to give us a glimpse of the life of the people.

'We know, of course, that in Orkney important changes were taking place. The kingdom of Scotland slowly wrested the islands from the grip of Norway. Without a doubt Hellya men sailed in King Haakon's forlorn expedition that ended disastrously at Largs in 1263. But two centuries went by before Orkney passed into the keeping of Scotland. The glory of the Norse earldom, which boasted such names as Thorfinn the Mighty, Magnus the Martyr, Rognvald Kolson (earl, poet, courtier, adventurer, saint), Sweyn Asleifson, was shorn away. The new Scottish earls were incomers; they looked on the islands as a mine with thin veins of gold branching through it. The islanders, so that a planned spoliation could take place, were degraded to the status of beasts of burden.

'The worst of all these predatory Scottish earls was Robert Stewart, a bastard half-brother of Mary Queen of Scots. He was the complete Renaissance nobleman. He had an exquisite appreciation of the arts, especially architecture. Palaces were built for him all over the islands, in Birsay, Kirkwall, Scalloway, Hellya. An architect of genius planned these places. There were round turrets where the ladies sat with their embroidery; they looked out over a green courtyard where the earl's men vied at archery and wrestling. A whole ox could be roasted in the fireplace. There was a vomitorium where you tickled your throat with a feather to spew up the baked trout so that there would be belly-room for the next item on the menu, roasted swan stuffed with larks. Great stone jars of claret stood on the tables. There were flutes, fiddles, pavanes on the long summer evenings.

'It was well in Hellya, in the days of Robert Stewart, to be born strong if you were a man and ugly if you were a woman. For it was the naked shoulders of the men who quarried and set the stones for the earl's palace. And it was this beautiful girl or that who was coldly summoned by a horseman to comfort his lordship on a winter night. Every bride, ugly or beautiful, yielded her virginity to the earl before her husband was allowed to touch her. (The accomplished architect has allowed for a dungeon between the foundation and the cellar, fitted with the latest instruments of torture: the boot, thumb-screw, rack, grill, flogging-block. There islanders who had incurred the earl's displeasure suffered correction – a protesting bridegroom say, a reluctant tax-payer, an uncooperative concubine. The earl's palace stood there like a kind of blashphemous parody of the divine cosmos, with shrieks and fire underground, and banqueting and love on top, and in between the hosts of servants, the milk-maids, sty-keepers, cooks, brewers, who bore unquestioningly the burden of humanity. There was no sign of a Christian chapel in all these ordered exquisite harmonious damned stones.)

'This is all we know of Hellya in the early seventeenth century; peasants' hovels everywhere scattered about a heraldic shield of gules and beasts rampant.

'The people suffered and were silent . . .'

The Skarf closed his manuscript book.

The boy whirled past us, bearing an iced lolly, a rigid orange tongue.

I thanked The Skarf for the entertainment. I went on to say that it bore as much resemblance to the truth as a cinder to a diamond: for the flame of prejudice had shrivelled it.

An enchantment possesses the morning.

She is standing in her threshold. I know it. I will not look. I tremble where I sit. Much trouble you had last summer, uncle, to drag me from that seductiveness. She had set a jam-jar in her window with a rose in it. Much trouble you had after sunset to keep your lascivious nephew from that unfolding and petal-fall.

The Skarf got to his feet and clapped me on the shoulder.

– Darkness, he says kindly, go away. You're wasting your time. I have a lot of work to do this morning.

He goes indoors.

I am up and away quickly. I turn my back on that house at whose threshold you have set on guard a stern angel. I lurch, weighed down with my cargo, from the siren-song. And quickly turn the corner into a rout of school children, released for dinner.

> Chin chin Chinaman
> Slanty eyes

> *Come out of your wash house*
> *I'll give you a surprise.*

– Such beautiful voices, I say. Really you sing so well. It is of me you are singing, no? I am not a Chinaman, I am just a poor Indian pedlar. My name is Johnny.

> *Chin chin Chinaman*
> *Yellow skin*
> *Kiss me in the moonlight*
> *Run away in.*

– Alas, I say, I am not so fortunate. What troubles I have to sell my few nice articles to your mothers. It is true. From house to house I go. But now this Johnny can get to no more houses because he is held back. Very many joyous children keep me from my work.

Hands fluttering, merry mouths.

Eyes with the look of the fisherman's fat wife stare at me hard and remote and brazen, the fingers of this one pluck at my bag, with a sucking in of cheeks and a writhe of lips he gathers spittle in his mouth. This must be stopped. Children can pass so quickly from poetry to hostility. He balances the spit on his tongue. I reach deep in my coat pocket. A yellow Orlon handkerchief flutters in my hand above the now veering, jeering, dangerous faces.

– This handkerchief is for you, I say. It is a prize. It is for running a race.

They look with wonderment at this bunch of sunlight. The pack leader swallows his spittle.

– For the boy or girl who runs best to the boat *Engels* at the pier and back to this telegraph pole. That will be good, eh?

They laugh and cheer and champ to be gone.

– No cheating, I say earnestly. Whoever cheats will suffer disqualification.

The vicious boy is off at a canter.

– Come back, I say. The starting signal has not been given. All runners must touch the boat with their hands. I have made that rule.

They range themselves into a ragged line. Each finds a place with jostling elbows. There are protests, snarls, whimpers.

– Another matter, I say, since you are all of different sizes and therefore speeds. The prize will not necessarily be given to the swiftest, O no, it will be given to him or her who runs most beautifully. Is that clear? Very well. One, Two. *Three.*

They are off like a whirl and undulation of starlings, all but one little girl with Alice-eyes; she also. This one hops a few steps after the others. She stands and watches them. She is not interested in races. She whirls about. She meanders to the ditch, plucks a buttercup. She sniffs it, throws it from her. She circles across to the other side of the road, jumps once up and down, inserts herself half into the fence, bleats high and plaintive to a munching sheep on the other side, unfurls a finger in her mouth, and tilts her head, examining nothing, quizzing the huge luminous pearl of the sky. There she stands. She has gathered all her movements into a stillness and a silence.

– What is your name? I say.

There is much shrieking about the boat. There is a cry of pain and rage. Someone has fallen.

She turns and looks at me. Those eyes.

– Shirley Voar, she says.

– There is no doubt of it, I say. You are the most beautiful dancer in the island of Hellya. Here is your prize.

I give her the yellow handkerchief and hurry away before the wave of vengeance recoils on me from the boat *Engels*; up a cement path to a steeple-shadowed door. Resoundingly I swing the brass knocker.

A throng of brazen echoes inside, silence, a slow whisper of feet. The door knob turns.

A gentleness stands there, so gently, a gentle old suffering face glimmers out of the gloom of the hallway. The light of day makes her squinny. She shades her brow with her hand.

– Good afternoon, I say. I have today such beautiful things here in my bag for you.

Round the finishing post the school children scream with rage. I am glad of the sycamore tree in the manse garden. It hides me.

– There are people inside, says the old mouth that resembles a few shadows sewn together. I need absolutely nothing from your pack. We are going rather deeply into private affairs. Millicent Brae is inside – of course you don't know her – my very best friend, and Dr Niall Keir, and the Swiss doctor who attended Millicent in her illness. That was at Davos, in Switzerland, it must be nearly forty years ago now. They are all waiting. It is a difficult case – to tell the truth, an inquiry into the origins of Millicent's illness. Speaking for myself, I'm sure I have nothing to reproach myself with, but the prosecutor seems to think otherwise ... I don't know why I'm telling you all this, a stranger like you.

Her face is an assize of suffering.

– Alas, I say, another year must pass before I come this way again. Please just to look once.

Her face softens and smiles in the sky-lustre. Millicent Brae and Dr Keir and the chest specialist and prosecutor and jurymen are inside, they are waiting, but cannot proceed with their business until the main person, who is this old lady, is present. She smiles. She nods her head resolutely. Let them wait for five minutes. She is not exactly their slave.

– Well, she says, it is a very hard thing if you have come all this way from India to my door in Hellya for nothing. A very hard thing. Perhaps if I could have just the teeniest peek at your stock. Mind, I can promise to buy nothing really expensive. Please understand that. I need nothing new. I have a lifetime of clothes in my trunk under the bed.

I lay the case on the doorstep. I unstrap it. I slide the double locks. Meantime the burdened voice goes on and on, a gentle insistent overflow: Millicent, Davos, Alan, the first of May, a bad cold, Arthur's Seat, the rain ... 'I never saw such rain as that morning. We got soaked, all three. Millicent, she had to go back to bed as soon as we got home. That was the start of her trouble ...' A new name, which proves to be the most important of all, enters her monologue: Simon. Simon, it seems, is her son. He has gone visiting among the farms. He is not so well today, he shouldn't really be out at all. Simon is the parish minister. Simon rides on a bicycle to the farms. They brew such strong ale on the farms. Dear Simon, it is a hard cross he had to bear, but they needn't try to put the blame on her. What she had done she had done all for the best.

I am spreading out ties, handkerchiefs, shirts, cravats, that I hope, in her opinion, will look well on this paragon, this Simon of hers. I might as well have been spreading the invisible clothes of the fabled Emperor.

– Young man, she says, forgive me, how I babble on. I'm sure you're simply dying for a nice cup of tea.

This invitation falls not disagreeably on my ear. A cup of tea and biscuit is generally prelude to a sale of some moment. I follow this old lady into her drawing-room. She ushers me into a chair. She disappears into the scullery, runs water, strikes a match, sighs, opens a biscuit tin. The gas fire rages and blurps. The kettle mutters, falls silent, snores, shrills.

I am left alone in a Victorian chamber burdened with immense articles of furniture. The shadows seem more solid than wardrobe or armchair. A gallery of framed photographs glimmers from every wall. Never have I felt the pressure of so many earth-bound preying ungenerous spirits. The room crepitates with them. They are offended with me – I have disturbed their communion with this gentle frightened old lady.

She comes out of the kitchen, smiling, with a cup of tea and two biscuits frosted over with sugar; the biscuits lie aslant in the saucer. (How the women of Britain assault me with cups of tea and biscuits! This summer a thousand clay hollows with sweet hot 'blended' tea in them have corroded the taste-buds of my mouth and destroyed all memory of the subtle perfumed astringency of Darjeeling. Thus, with self-denial, one pursues one's calling.)

What is required in this room is exorcism. What is needed is some pure blessed deliberate ritual to rid this old woman of her ghosts. They feast on her flesh. They drink her blood, obscenely, like black bats. What can one Indian boy do in ten minutes? I am not a holy man.

I talk about the wild lupins in the island of Quoylay.

– Two days ago, I say, I was in the island of Quoylay. There is a hillside in that island covered with wild lupins. I have walked through them with my pack. The wind fell on the expanse of lupins and for a moment that part of the hillside was a deep thrilling purple.

– That must have been lovely, she says. I rarely go out myself.

– I walked among those lupins, I insist. They reached to my thighs. Fragrance encompassed me.

Her face brightens for a moment. I have hope. But the ghosts are too much for her. Shadows cluster once more about her eyes. The haunted mouth begins its litany.

Her late husband. How dared they say she was ever unfaithful to him? One excited kiss at a party. The willow pattern teapot in the china cabinet over there. She doesn't own it, the teapot is her sister Flora's by rights. There was a little uncertainty about it, as to who should have it. Flora died in Edinburgh eight months ago. What can she do with the teapot now? There is no one she can give it to, for it isn't hers really. She cannot solve the problem by letting it fall and break, can she? The teapot is a burden to her.

– But a teapot, what's a teapot compared to the death of a beautiful young girl? It is Millicent they're on about today. That even I should be suspected of such a thing. Millicent Brae was my very best friend. Tell me, young man – perhaps you can help me – can a person be guilty of causing the death of another person if the first person didn't intend to do it, but only wanted what was good and happy for her?

Through the fog a picture begins to emerge.

Every year, it seems, she had washed her face in the May dew on the side of Arthur's Seat with Millicent and Pussy Brae and, sometimes, Flora. Millicent and Flora were sisters. They were both dead now. Millicent died in a sanatorium in Davos, Switzerland, in the year of the Wall Street crash, 1929. Millicent had been the loveliest girl she had ever seen. She sat on Dapple, Niall Keir's horse, like a young goddess. Millicent had been engaged to Niall, Dr Keir. Well then, this particular May morning it was raining heavily. She was staying for the week-end at the Braes' house in Leith. Millicent was recovering from a cold, she didn't think she ought to climb up Arthur's Seat on such a wet morning. Pussy was in two minds. *Come on, you pair of cowards*, she (Elizabeth Alder) had cried from the lobby, belting her raincoat around her.

Then she and Pussy and Millicent – the latter with the dregs of the cold still on her – went out into the pouring morning ... For hours this very day the prosecutor had been attempting, as he phrased it, 'to build a bridge' between that unhealthy morning and poor Millicent's death some years later. 'She, Elizabeth Alder, is the black keystone in the affair,' he had declared to the jury.

– One should not summon the dead, I say. The present world is full of such beautiful things. For example.

And I put down the empty cup on the floor and throw open my case. The air of this mausoleum is dyed with many brilliant hues. The ghosts shrink back. The room is enriched.

She smiles like a girl in a garden. Many years ago she has been, I know it, a most beautiful girl.

She stoops over the case. Her hands go through the silks and Rayons and Orlons, softness among softness. Her cheeks dimple. Then she goes down (alas, only for a moment) into our pool of brightness. She comes up with a red silk dressing-gown.

– For Simon, she says somewhat breathlessly.

I hasten, before the shadows drag her back to her mildewed mothy memoried chest of old clothes under the bed, to explain that this is indeed the latest fashion for men, to be worn while they are having breakfast, or smoking a cigarette in front of the fire prior to retiring for the night.

Simon, it seems, is going on holiday in the month of August. Brochures have been coming from the travel agency to Simon for weeks and weeks. At the moment Simon is undecided where to go: perhaps Greece, perhaps Majorca, perhaps the Channel Isles. Simon badly needs a change. O, she will manage quite well on her own for a few weeks. She is never a day lonely. Old faces come about her, old voices remind her of things she had almost forgotten ... She would like to buy Simon a suitable present for him to take away on his holiday.

– Nothing, I say, could be more fitting than such a dressing-gown. In hot weather, it cools. Such an article can be worn on the beach even, prior to or subsequent upon sea bathing. Many eyes would admire from sand and rockpool and dune.

She holds a fringe to her face. Her cheek flushes like a withered apple.

– Two pounds five shillings sixpence. For you, dear lady, two pounds two. Two guineas.

The dressing-gown lies across the settee like a great brilliant butterfly.

She opens her purse with brisk intent fingers. A Bank of England pound note. A Royal Bank of Scotland pound note. ('Now I hope you don't think that a counterfeit note. It is perfectly legal tender, a Scottish note.') A shilling. A sixpence. A threepenny piece. Three pennies. My hands brim with treasure. I stow notes into wallet, coins into hip pocket. So the deal is concluded to the satisfaction of both parties.

– It will be a great surprise for Simon, she says.

Her writhen face releases shy roguish laughter. I also laugh. It is like springtime in that Victorian room. The mingled laughter, the spread of scarlet, the promise of flowers.

It will not last. I am sorry to say, it will not last. In a very brief time the squandered shadows will gather themselves, deploy, begin again to feast on the remnants of her life.

Already one has fallen.

– O dear, she says in the door, Simon in Majorca. I know my Simon. I know his little weaknesses. The Spanish wine is very cheap. O well, I am not to blame. They needn't point their fingers at me. It was purely for the boy's own good I did it. He was ill at the time.

Fear and defiance and petulance in her gestures.

– Dear lady, I say, these shadows are unreal. Bid them be gone. Understand what you are, a pilgrim in search of enlightenment.

Shadow by shadow falls about her; they gather; batten on her.

– You have done me a great deal of good today, she says. You have indeed. I am so glad that you came to my door. I will be quite frank with you. I know I must soon be lost among these memories of mine. I long to be with the dead. And yet I confess I am very much afraid.

– Dear lady, I say, unfortunately to be lost in these shadows is not to die. It is to be, for a space, a burdened ghost. One has not found silence, peace, the song of Krishna. The wheel turns. You must suffer it all over again – birth, desire, hunger, remorse, death.

– So, she says sadly.

– Until at last one escapes. Perhaps only after many turnings of the wheel. At last the soul, loving both God and man, will be free. It is lost then in light and silence.

I bid her farewell.

She closes the door. She returns to her ghosts, her shadows, her accusers.

A large forbidding structure confronts me: the hotel.

I enter. Nothing stirs. The door into the bar is locked; the taps do not flow there till evening. I push open another door. This is the kitchen. The floor is littered with potato peelings. A jug of old water festers on the draining board. There is a sheet of newspaper with footprints on it. Beside the door is a saucer of milk; a brindled kitten is nibbling at the edge of that moon.

I call, querying, among stinks of cooking. There is no answer.

Very steep the stair ascends, up to the very summit of the hotel. At this height the linoleum has given way to bare wood. Five doors, two at each side of the sky-lighted corridor, one at the very end. Four doors in turn are locked. Shall I try also the handle at the far end? (Persistence in the face of seemingly hopeless odds is the first virtue of a salesman, as well you instructed me, Uncle.) I knock. No answer. I subtly turn the knob. The door creaks, gives. I see an open case on the floor, a coat slung over the end of a bed. I hear breathing. A guest is in residence.

– Very much excuse me, I cry. So sorry indeed. Inexcusable intrusion.

And I open the door wide.

He is seated at a table in the window. He presents only his back. On the table are a typewriter, a ream of paper, a scatter of notes, a file. It is a businessman.

– I bring success, good fortune, many profits, I say.

He does not turn.

This is strange. I have made several shrill exclamations, he has not turned. I have the impression that even if a bull elephant were to trumpet behind him, still he will not turn. Is it a statue, a simulacrum in stone, that is wedged into that chair? Fingers flick among the papers in the file. I hear an impatient sigh.

– I have here socks in a wide range of styles, also gloves, I say.
We might be living on different continents.

– Please, I am looking for the proprietor, Mr Scorradale.

What are we, a ghost and a man? Who is the ghost? Who is the man? It is a singularly unpleasant thing to experience. I put my finger to the brass knob of the bed, solidity against solidity, to reassure myself. The metal is cold.

He now writes some words in a notebook. He is a journalist; he is intent upon an article.

– This is a most beautiful place indeed, I say in a voice that I feel shakes somewhat. Such colours in the sky. People in the cities will read your account with much joy.

And then, slowly, he turns.

An axe-like profile, then the full face, meagre and puritanical; sieving abstracted eyes behind a thick glimmer of spectacles. The eyes seek athwart and beyond me, quickly, and come to rest at a spot on the wall. I track his gaze. There is a calendar there. This he glimmers at. His lips mould, silently, a sought number. Neck swivels, head turns and droops again over the scatter of papers on the table, the hand holding the pencil makes a mark.

He is a bureaucrat. He is Western Man arrived at a foreseen inevitable end. I see it now. He rules the world with a card index file.

Ghost leaves ghost. I retire silently, silently turn the knob, find myself in the draughty corridor. My lips shake with cold uneven breaths.

This creature and I, indeed we live on different stars. I have known for some time that the mysterious omnipotent life-giving word has grown very old. Yet men must dance to some music, answer to some utterance. For our worship is erected now, all over the world, in place of the Word, the Number. And the belly is filled with uniform increasingly tasteless bread, the hands cannot have enough of possessing, face by face by face comes from the same precise mould and gazes, a rigid numbered unseeing mask, into the golden future. Abstractly I have known this; I have not proved it on my pulses till today. I shake with supernatural dread.

And still, as I descend the stair, trembling somewhat, I have not found the minotaur, Mr Scorradale.

I find him at last at the very bottom of the labyrinth, in the cellar, among barrels and canisters and cases.

For a moment the supernatural dread intensifies, for it is with the landlord as with the bureaucrat in the attic. His back is turned to me, he is not aware of my presence. I haunt the hotel today. I am a ghost. The island is full of ghosts.

Yet quickly I reassure myself. I have simply to say 'Good afternoon' and Mr Scorradale will turn and put his warm-blooded hand into mine, as always (though he will buy nothing, being the soul of parsimony). I forbear to greet him immediately, being curious as to the task upon which he is so intent.

I shall describe his deft operations. He is seated upon a stool in front of a barrel. About his feet are many empty bottles. On the bench at his right hand are several full bottles. One by one he is filling the empty bottles at the barrel, turning on and off a brass tap. He is most impatient if one golden drop is spilt or squandered. At last he has filled every bottle. They glint on the bench, the ranked armies of summer ready to march into the snows and gales for the relief of bewintered man. Now he produces from the drawer of the bench a selection of crudely printed labels. They are labels belonging to various unknown brands of whisky – Wild Heather, Viking, The Old Silver Dirk, Ceileidh, The Percentor, Machair, a little pile of each. He moistens the gum on the back of the labels with his hot blunt tongue, and affixes them at random until all the blank bottles have been given a name, an identity, a pedigree. Yet all these brands have come out of the same barrel.

– Good afternoon, I say. How busy you are.

If my mouth had been a gun, Uncle, and these words bullets, they could hardly have wrought more havoc on Mr Scorradale. Literally he falls off the stool. He gapes at me from the floor. While I look, a circlet of silver grows on his brow, then melts and bedews every furrow of his face with sweat. His face is a glittering mask.

– How long have you been standing there, Johnny? he says at last in a faded voice.

– O my goodness, I say, I have been most interested, a long time. I did not wish to interrupt your important work.

By now he is on his feet, but holding on to the bench like a boxer who has been weakened by a shattering blow to the heart. He dabs at his quicksilver face with a large red handkerchief. He selects a bottle of *Machair* from his newly filled stock, and hesitates, and hands it to me.

– For you, Johnny, he says.

Now it is my turn to almost sink to the floor. Such generosity has never been known in his house before. Yet I conceal my astonishment.

.– You are most kind, I say, but no, I could not.

– You are a very hard man, Johnny, he says.

He selects another bottle from the ruck. This time it is *Viking*. He offers it also.

– For Pannadas, he says, a present.

(Uncle, you will have your arthritic knee well rubbed with Hellya home-distilled whisky very soon after the boat docks at Leith. And perhaps enough left over for hoots, waes-haels, drams, libations. We shall see.)

– I have many beautiful articles in my pack for you, I say.

His face sweats and suffers.

I open my case. He selects in a kind of pleading panic article after article: a red crêpe-de-chine curtain length, two boxes handkerchiefs, three pairs sox, a blue rayon shirt, one art silk table runner, one set cushion covers, a tea cosy with a snake design and a tea cosy with a lotus design (both designs in shot silk stitching). I stow the two bottles of whisky in a corner of my case, securely swathed in silk.

– Eight pounds four and six, I say.

The sweat begins on him again. It darkens the stubble on his jowls, it sets his upper lip in thousands of minutest seed pearls. His eyes are like two fish in a sluggish pool. He extracts from his wallet two five-pound notes.

– With all these acquisitions, I say, your hotel will now be most beautiful. How pleasant for example to sit in your lounge with the red curtains!

– Johnny, he says, we are good friends, eh?

– O yes indeed, I say. Very good friends. Always.

– And you would not wish, he says, to get me into trouble of any kind?

– Indeed no, Mr Scorradale, I say. Such would be my last desire in the world.

He puts the two five-pound notes into my hand, he closes my fist upon them. He looks at me with gratitude and supplication, that is none the less lightly spiced with hatred.

– I do not want any change, he says.

He follows me upstairs from the cellar. He insists on carrying my bag along the narrow corridor, awkwardly, his breath guttering. We pass the ramshackle billiard room. We stand at last in the open door.

– Johnny, he says, you will not tell anyone what you have seen in my cellar today. You will not breathe it to a living soul.

I look at him. I smile. I lift the case from the threshold.

– If you do, I won't so much as buy a pair of sox from you. No, never again. Not a hanky. Not one.

I press his slippery hand.

– You can always be sure of a good drink, Johnny, in this hotel, whenever you come to Greenvoe.

As I turn the corner I wave back to him with my free hand. He sees me and does not see me. He is preoccupied. His hand is a wounded bird. It flutters. It drops.

Following our visit to the hotel, my uncle, you led me then these past three summers to the schoolhouse. This year it will not be possible, the sequence must be altered. Because of the delays – which I have described, I fear, in all too much detail – the teacher's dinner hour is past, when formerly we bargained. I hear through the tall school window the murmuration of many voices. They are engaged upon some repetitive exercise, a thing abhorrent to young children yet necessary if the wisdom of the world is to be ineradicably imprinted on their minds. I listen. They are engaged upon the discipline of history.

> 1066 *Battle of Hastings*
> 1314 *Battle of Bannockburn*
> 1513 *Battle of Flodden*
> 1588 *Spanish Armada*
> 1746 *Battle of Culloden*
> 1805 *Battle of Trafalgar.*

They chant. They touch with innocent mouths a vast unimaginable welter of blood and gules and horror.

1943 Battle of Stalingrad

It will not be possible to see Mr Lomax the teacher until I get back from the farms. Mr Lomax is very pleasant. We discussed literature last year, the dark sonnets of G. M. Hopkins, also inscape and outrides. I look forward to stand at his door at sunset.

The enchantress is standing at the end of her house with a saucer and a small fish. She summons her cat: *Tompuss.*

The small boy is searching in the grass. He suddenly shrills. He throws himself down and disappears in the long stalks. The cat leaps out of a green shimmer on to the stone wall. There it stretches, poised on stiff hind legs, and digs its front claws into the lichen. And gathers itself and stoops delicately and urgently – smelling now the fish – and flows down to the brigstone, to the milk-moon and the silver sillock. The boy sits up in his green sea. Alice has vanished indoors. Her panes glitter, but the inner sill is empty. There is no rose for me today. My heart feels a small wound of disappointment; that I should be so soon forgotten.

A mile away on the beach Timmy Folster is stooping among the rock pools.

Nearby the old henwife is chiding her white flock. I pass her window. She stands at her door with a bowl of oats and bread, held high. The chickens hasten to her from every corner of the little field. They besiege her. They are beside themselves with greed, half insane. One eddies round her knee, a white wild flailing wing. She chides it. She dowers her flock with lavish handfuls. So much manna has fallen they are confused, they make darts and flurries, they do not know where to turn. They dip and dart, dispute.

– Bella, shouts a fierce hidden voice, here's that goddam nigger with his pack.

Bella inverts her bowl. She shakes it. Crumbs fall out.

Uncle, my hand falters. Never have I written such an immense letter. It is long past bedtime in Mrs Learmonth's lodging-house in

Hamnavoe; all lights but mine are extinguished. The grandfather clock in the lobby has struck half-past one. The last drunkard is long home.

I ask myself why I have written you an epistle so vast. Nothing is hidden from you, old wise one. You must know already that it is to delay as long as possible the relation of an event which I both wish and do not wish to relate, it is so compounded of delight and shame. The matter cannot be held back much longer. My hand hastens once more over the paper. I could fill as much space again, and more, with what happened in the farms, but now all rambling disquisition is over, I promise I will write abrupt telegraphese.

Miss Bella Budge: So pretty (*drawing her finger across a table runner*).

Johnny: Calcutta. Hand made.

Mr Benjamin Budge: Calcutta be buggered. Birmingham.

Mr Benjamin Budge is much failed since last summer. A ghost looks out of the bones of his face. Yet, as you see, his language has its wonted energy, between spasms of coughing.

They have bought the table runner, 'for Tom's homecoming', for seventeen six, having coaxed me down from twenty-five shillings.

Mr Benjamin Budge: Bombay is a bloody dump.

When I emerge at last from the Budge household, I see that a window in the village has been signed with a flower. The world is one wild passionate burst.

I turn. I stumble into the interior of the island, towards the farms.

I have met Rev. Simon McKee, the minister, returning from the farms, a half mile outside the village. He is not astride his bike. I would say he is supporting his bike except that it would be truer to say his bike is supporting him. From time to time the front wheel wobbles. I give him good afternoon. There is no reply. His face is a slack bemused mask. Many ghosts will crepitate in the manse tonight.

First, the farm of Glebe. Mr Thomas (Tammag) Brown has three grown daughters. He and his wife are in the peat hill. The daughters rummage delightedly in my pack. Knickers, slips, stockings. One watches at the door for the return of the father. One pays three pounds four and threepence from the housekeeping purse. One pours home-brewed ale for me. I rise at length to go. The watcher in the window kisses me.

Next the farm of Isbister. Mr Leonard Isbister and his excessively puritanical sister. No silks or satins. No home brew. My foot is not suffered to cross the threshold. *I want nothing*, her lips cut me like scissors. The door slams and quivers upon my departing back.

Thirdly, the large farm of The Bu. Mr Magnus (Mansie) Anderson and his apple-cheeked wife and such an immense family of tall shy daughters and shy tall sons and smaller ones and a baby in the cradle – also dogs and cats and a bottle-fed lamb at the door and pigeons and a hutch of rabbits in the yard; besides, beyond, an immense field of Ayrshire cattle.

– Goodness, I say, pardon me greatly, indeed I am sorry, I have come by mistake to Noah's Ark!

There is much laughter. The dogs bark. The home-brewed ale is drawn from a mahogany cask in the corner, and offered to me. But first I have the wisdom to open my case. A flowered apron for apple-cheeks. A child screams for joy at sight of the scarlet ribbons and the blue ribbons. Yellow diaphanous pyjamas – 'light and caressing as a summer air,' I encourage – and a tall girl blushes and fetches a purse from the drawer. The ale sets my backside down in a sudden swoon of well-being on to a straw-back chair. I am at peace with all the world. A kitten stretches himself on a length of silk. I do not care. I left The Bu richer by five pounds five. Silk the road stretches before me.

Beside the bay the farm of Skaill, Mr George (Dod) Corrigall, a man of gentle voice and shy presence. The jug of ale (the flavour varies from farm to farm, here it is imbued with a most delicious creaminess, as if a black cow had browsed all winter among malt in a kiln). My stock is now much diminished. Mrs Corrigall comes in from feeding the hens; who is as loud and cheerful as her man is shy. She inspects my stock. She orders her man out of the room. She buys with dispatch a pair of large red knickers, one pound three six. She puts it in a drawer. She summons her man. Who appears at the door, shy and smiling. How very much I love these people. I belch with joy.

There it stands on the first slope of the hill, the important house of the island, the hall of the laird. Dare I approach it? Last summer the arse was almost torn from my trousers by a dog, a violent deerhound. On the other hand two summers ago, when that dog-loving horse-like woman was on holiday, the laird himself poured out glasses of malt whisky for us (though he bought nothing). I crash down the knocker on the massive oak door. Far and near through the huge house the dogs bark. 'Wolfgang,' shrieks the aged dobbin from within, 'see him off. Enoch, up, boy ...' I am down that long drive on winged feet. I clang the gate behind me. The dogs dance and yelp on the long drive. A weary wisp of a face at the top window: the laird. My feet are on the road. 'Horse-face,' I mouth, between dredgings for breath.

I am gone, my heart fluttering in panic before the teeth of hounds, a mile along the road to the farm of Rossiter, Mr Andrew Hoy. Mr Andrew Hoy is not at home. I shake the door. It is locked.

The hill darkened and rose taller over the island.

I trudged between a peatstack and a garden of gooseberry bushes to the door of the last farm, Blinkbonny, Mr Alexander Manson, Jr. I know you are most anxious of all to hear news of this place. There you went with gladness year by year in the old days, you have often told me, Uncle, to be greeted once more by an old sailor-farmer, and his wife as delicate as porcelain, and a growing goodnatured son. The father had spent his youth in sailing ships. Laughter suffused every word he uttered; he filled an occasional silence with his fiddle. The house was as clean as a sea-washed stone. Brass tongs twinkled at brass candlestick. The china dog on the mantelpiece barked at every visitor brightly and silently. The model ships in their cases sailed over seas of plaster, blue and white and curling waves. The kind hostess would come to you then with her shortbread and rhubarb wine. These things you have told me over and over again, with such delight that I picture the scene vividly.

It has been a bitter bereaved house for seven years past. Between the easy natural deaths of the two old ones, Sandy (the son) came home with a bride, a girl whose grandparents had been tinkers;

who moved vividly and uncertainly between byre and peat-hill and cornfield for a twelve-month (her people never having been bound to the wheel of agriculture), until finally it was plain to all the island that Teresa herself, with her enlarging belly, was part of the fruitfulness of Blinkbonny. The old sailor-fiddler broke his thigh on the peat-hill that summer; he lay in the box-bed a week before he was folded in a last silence and borne to the kirkyard to lie beside his year-dead wife. The time drew on for Teresa's delivery. It proved hard and difficult; her savage cries echoed across the hill. Dr Silver arrived from Quoylay. The child was wedged in her womb, awkwardly poised, reluctant to leave its warm red bourne, it seemed; and in any case the portal into time was unnaturally narrow and constricted. The neighbouring women who had come to help went out of the house one by one, white faced. Dr Silver cursed and shouted for more hot water. He dug in his bag for instruments. The labour had gone on since noon; at sunset Teresa's eyes gave one last dark flash at the door where Sandy stood; and ten minutes later the blind mute bundle was put in the arms of the one remaining parent, the father. So Gino came, motherless and simple-minded, out of the terrible wrenchings of his birth. From that hour the house began to decay. Hens laid eggs under the dresser. The ale-kirn warped in the corner. The fiddle hung at the wall in a tangle of strings. The young widower went to the weekly markets in Kirkwall and Hamnavoe more it was said for the drink than to trade in animals; the boy wandered lonely among the Blinkbonny cows, and spoke seriously to their grave listening faces (but ran in terror from postman and milk officer) and all winter preferred to sleep in the companionable warmth of the byre.

We have hopes, every summer, that Sandy Manson will have found another wife who will make the house a thrift-shrine once more and be a mother to Gino, and set on barn and byre the seal of abundance. But every summer Blinkbonny grows more ramshackle. I have hopes this evening. I cross the quagmire of a yard. There is a broken plate, a dead hen, a sack in the midden.

It seems there is no one at home. I notice that one of the windows is half-shuttered with wood, as if glass had been broken and not replaced.

Yet I am aware of tremulous breath moving about inside.

I try the door. It is locked.

I turn at the peatstack for one last look at this foundering house. A face at the window. Dark eyes flash at me, between fear and wonderment.

I wave to Gino.

The dingy pane frames, momentarily, a sweetness, a shadow falls across it; then it is lost in a web of shadows.

My feet are on the road. I will not look any more.

Hail, old silk-bearded ghost in the corner chair. Farewell, old sea voyager, old fiddler, old ploughman. The ship Blinkbonny is leaking in all her timbers. Her cargo is huge bales of hopelessness, one small casket of innocence, and the ports of the world do not trade in these commodities.

And still this letter grows under my hand, as if I wished to splurge in minutiae and trifles and random impressions for ever. Yet soon now I must make an end.

I returned in late evening to the village, a five-mile walk. My case was almost empty, my wallet was fat with notes. The hill Korsfea in the west was an immense hulk of darkness. My body was drugged with the ale of Hellya; it was the road that came to meet my dreaming feet. Where the shore road intersects with the hill road I encountered them again; the stange lovely girl in her riding habit and Westray the boatman. The pony munched grass at the roadside. She seemed to be pleading with him, her hand lay lightly on his elbow. And he, as always, with the sullen contemptuous look on his face, half turned away, eyes glowering away into the drained dwindled horizon. So the moth troubles the flame; the soft wing threads through and through that yellow eye until at length it lies on the floor, a burnt quivering silent scream.

In the village a kindlier flame burned for me.

Yet I delayed. I called at the schoolhouse. Mr Lomax is not there! He has been transferred to the senior school in Kirkwall. Instead I unfold my pack to a young woman with all the incipient wrinkles and shrillness of spinsterhood on her. Fruitfall, bruising, rottenness. She is courteous, melancholy, a little resentful. She is uncertain whether to invite me indoors (what will the villagers say?) So we bargain on the doorstep. She winces like a puritan when I show her the ladies' garments (a man handling panties and bras!) *Pyjamas,* I say softly, *for your future husband. Paisley pattern.* She shakes her head bitterly. I close the case. I kneel on it. I am about to strap it up. *I will take the Paisley pattern,* she says suddenly. (She will not mention the word pyjamas, because of its connection with bed, therefore sex.) *It is for a present.* Two guineas. She puts a last look on me before she shuts the door: the kind of look that henceforward all men will have from her – hard, hurt, fascinated, baffled. Where will her youth and her beauty be next summer? Ghosts, half forgotten. It has been a day of ghosts. I have been abroad in a haunted island.

The sweetness shakes me again. I will not indulge myself too soon. I cross over to the pub.

The Skarf is reading the fragment that he read to me in the morning to Mr William Scorradale and Bert Kerston and Timmy Folster. They are almost penniless, lector and listeners; they sip half-pints of flat beer. I announce that all the house must be treated to glasses of whisky and bottles of heavy ale at my expense. I produce my wallet. The Skarf pauses and nods acknowledgement, then resumes his arrogant slanted rigmarole. We pledge one another. Westray the boatman comes in, with the smug look on him of a man who has now a woman in his power, though he has not yet made use of his power, so that her need and his power may grow. For him also I buy whisky and beer. We agree about the ferry in the morning, 8.30 a.m. *Where will you sleep all night, Johnny?* says Westray, and winks this. (Uncle, your forgiveness.) The Skarf drones on. Only Scorradale listens with his mouth open. Westray buys pints of beer for all present. The Skarf nods to him, raises his glass, continues with his litany of tyranny and enlightenment. I drink to quell a delight that is now leaping through me like a salmon up a river in spate.

Mrs Learmonth's grandfather clock struck three some time ago. I will be in trouble in the morning for wasting coal and electricity.

Now it can be postponed no longer. Uncle, by many hints inserted into this Everest of a letter it must be plain to you what is to happen to your sister's son, on this occasion when you are far away in Leith suffering with arthritic pains in your knee and therefore unable to check and admonish.

I pass out on to the road.

In the window of the much-loved one the half-deflowered rose hangs in a jar. Sweetly it smoulders in the gathering darkness.

The village is all asleep.

I knock at her door.

In the stable of The Bu the door was bolted and the lantern was hung from the rafters. Six immense shadows gesticulated about one still shadow on the gable wall.

The Lord of the Harvest, The Master Horsemen, The Novice who has attained the degree of Sower – he is blindfolded, and wears a green shirt; he carries the horse-shoe.

LORD OF THE HARVEST: It is the station of THE GREEN CORN. What are you seeking here, Sower, among the master horsemen?

SOWER: A kingdom.

The ritual mockery of the Master Horsemen. They put archaic words on him: Thou root. Thou worm. Thou dung.

LORD OF THE HARVEST: The crofter with hungry wife and bairn, what does he know of any kingdom?

SOWER: An house secure it stands, beyond the hazards of fisherman and hunter.

LORD OF THE HARVEST: What hinders you from this kingdom?

SOWER: I am blind. Sun burns me, rain drowns me, wind shakes me. As any scarecrow I am blind and dumb. I do not know where I shall find the word.

LORD OF THE HARVEST: Are you willing to bear the weight of noon? Can you thole the burden of ripeness? Will you take the mark of the sun on your flesh?

THE SOWER: (*Does not answer.*)

THE MASTER HORSEMEN: Answer. Answer.

SOWER: I am willing.

(*The Master Horsemen take the green shirt from the Sower*

and turn it inside out. The other side is yellow. They put it back on the Sower. The Lord of the Harvest bares the left shoulder. One of the Master Horsemen hands him a sickle.)

LORD OF THE HARVEST: Reaper, of a meikle sharpness is the hook of life. Be cut down as low as to the roots.

(Slowly and deliberately he cuts the flesh. The Reaper bleeds.)

FOUR

All morning the sun had fought with silent blind blunderings of sea fog for possession of the island. Ivan Westray, sitting on the edge of the pier waiting for his passengers to arrive, watched the struggle of the grey ram and the golden god. Within an hour the weather for the day would be decided, one way or the other. The fog leapt forward suddenly, then retreated as a sword of light shore through its outer fleece; then backed about again till The Skarf's fishing boat *Engels* dipped like a ghost at her moorings. Ivan Westray checked that everything was stowed on board: the mail-bag, the boxes of eggs, the empty gas containers, the black calf tied to the handrail. He lit another cigarette. Presently Mr Joseph Evie in his dark Sunday suit emerged out of the swirls, smiling, and climbed carefully down the ladder into the ferry-boat: he was on his way to the county council meeting in the town. 'Half past eight, Ivan,' he said. Ivan Westray cleaned his finger nails with a burnt match. 'We have to wait,' he said, 'till Johnny's had his oats.' The fog staggered silently against the boat and the pier. The Indian packman, Dewas (Johnny) Singh, stood above them, smiling, he lowered his case to Ivan Westray; turned; and climbed down after it into the *Skua*.

'Hurry up, Casanova,' said Ivan Westray. 'We're late. Button your flies.'

Blue chasms of sky appeared over the neighbouring island of Quoylay. The Sound glittered. The sun smote the nearer waters. The fog turned, fled with one great bound into the Atlantic. The sun possessed the morning. The hill and the village were lapped in warm light. It would be a glorious day.

Bands of children roamed here and there over the island. Seeing that it was to be such a lovely day, Miss Inverary decided that the morning should be devoted to nature study. There would be a prize for the pupil who returned with the most interesting item. One troop was despatched to the shore, under Johnny Corrigall, to gather shells, as many different kinds as they could find; some so minute that only the eye of the smallest child could distinguish its whorl among the grains of sand. Gino Manson carried a large Winchester jar for the shells.

Another band of children left the road and climbed the lower slopes of the hill. Their leader was Sidney Voar and they were after wild flowers. A few lingered about the marsh; the ground here was studded with marigolds. Ola Corrigall plucked cotton flowers and said she was going to collect millions of them to make a warm winter coat. Ernie Kerston whirled the tail of his jacket up over his head and careered over the hill, crying like a lap wing.

Sidney Voar and Charlie Brown and Simon Anderson lingered behind the barn of Skaill. They couldn't be bothered wasting a whole morning with them kids. Simon took a charred half-cigarette out of his shirt pocket, and a few matches. They puffed in turn, passing the butt-end around. Simon Anderson's eyes watered; a tobacco strand stuck in his tonsils and slowly poisoned his throat. He coughed and dabbed his eyes.

'I'll take you to a place,' said Charlie Brown.

They followed him across a green field with a few sheep meandering in it, and through a fence. Now they were on the open moor that sloped up, gently at first, to the south shoulder of Korsfea, The Knap. They climbed like goats, Charlie Brown leading them. Finally he stopped, his chest heaving. 'This is the place,' he said.

Grass shone out of the heather, a teeming green trapdoor.

'What is it?' said Sidney Voar.

'A boy is buried here,' said Charlie Brown. 'We are standing on top of the bones of a boy.'

'Was he murdered?' said Simon Anderson.

'You could call it that,' said Charlie. 'It was a Spanish ship that went ashore down there. She struck on the North Head. Oh, a long, long time ago. Before the oldest man in the island was born.

Before Ben Budge's grandfather was born. In the times of Oliver Cromwell. Most of the sailors were drowned trying to get ashore. The Hellya farmers, they went on board and they killed all the rest. Then they broke open the cargo. They turned and they saw a boy wearing a blue silk suit. He had a gold ring on his hand. And there was a girl with him in a blue silk dress. They had got ashore somehow. They were standing high and dry among the rocks at Keelyfa.'

'They must have been the captain's children,' said Sidney Voar.

'More likely the children of the man that owned the ship,' said Charlie Brown. 'The children of the Duke of Something-or-other.'

'I warrant you,' said Sidney Voar.

'There they stood,' said Charlie Brown, 'on the rocks, wet through, and crying, and hand-in-hand.'

'The poor things,' said Simon Anderson.

'No, but listen,' said Charlie Brown. 'The Hellya men had found barrels of Spanish wine, and they were all drunk. They were drunk with the horror of what they had done and they were drunk with the wine. They were in mortal fear of being hung too, if ever they were found out. They threw bales of red silk ashore. They found barrels of oranges. They had never seen oranges before. They kicked the yellow balls about the sloping deck till it was all grey and sticky with the juice. They were drunk with greed.'

'O God,' said Simon Anderson.

'Then they saw this boy and this girl that had got ashore somehow, and they knew the game was up. The boy and the girl would tell the laird. The laird would inform the authorities. They would all be hung in Kirkwall for murder.'

'I warrant you,' said Simon Anderson, 'every man jack of them, like sillocks on a string.'

'So they left the silk and the wine and the oranges,' said Charlie Brown, 'and they went after the Spanish children. They were all rising and falling in the seaweed, they were so drunk. And they chased the boy up the hill. And here on this spot, Simon Anderson, your great-great-great-grandfather killed him with a spade.

Split his skull wide open. But before they buried him they hacked off the finger with the ring on it.'

'I never heard that,' said Simon Anderson.

'It's true,' said Charlie Brown. 'Your great-great-great-grandfather got the ring for killing the boy. Your mother's still wearing it.'

'What about the girl?' said Sidney Voar.

'She escaped,' said Charlie Brown. 'She reached the farm of Skaill. She was very frightened. She couldn't speak any English. The woman of Skaill hid her in the barn there, till the men of the island sobered up. Next day they brought her in to the hearth. They learned her to speak English. They learned her to brew and spin and make cheese. When she grew up she married the eldest son of Skaill. Dod Corrigall of Skaill has Spanish blood in him.'

'Yes,' said Sidney Voar, 'with that dark skin of his.'

'Are you trying to make out,' said Simon Anderson, 'that my people are murderers? The ring on my mother's finger is her wedding ring.'

The younger children came across the hill towards them, wavering and dancing and shouting, their jerseys brimming with wild flowers.

'The truth's the truth,' said Charlie Brown.

The western horizon was overspread with a shimmering silver fleece of sea fog. It diminished. The sun climbed higher.

'We'd better be getting back,' said Sidney Voar. 'Come on, you kids. Make less noise.'

Mr Joseph Evie had removed the wooden shutters from the shop window before he left for the county council meeting, and taken the brass padlock from the shop door. A bee that had wandered into the shop out of Tuesday's rain woke up among the biscuit tins and oranges and Fair Isle jerseys and ball-point pens and probed sonorously around, a strayed reveller from the rosebush at the Voar wall.

'Shoo, get out,' cried Mrs Olive Evie, striking at it with her knitting. The bee throbbed out of the shop into the kitchen.

Mrs Olive Evie brought her knitting to the upturned soap-box outside the shop door, seeing that as yet there were no customers and it was so sunny. The needles clacked in her lap like the beak of an angry bird.

Presently Mrs Ellen Kerston, with peedie Mary at her heels, arrived with an empty paper carrier and her purse in her fist. She required a large amount of groceries. A pound of smoked ham. Two stone of sugar. A packet of flaky biscuits. A drum of salt. A stone of new Prince of Wales potatoes. A jar of hair-cream for Willie and a comb. A lollipop for peedie Mary.

'And pay on Saturday,' said Mrs Olive Evie, her needles clacking. 'Is that it?'

'I have my purse,' said Ellen Kerston. 'And I want a packet of Woodbines for my man.'

Alice Voar crossed the road, yawning.

'A fine morning, Alice,' said Ellen Kerston.

'It is that, Ellen,' said Alice Voar.

The needles clacked slowly and coldly.

Rachel Whaness crossed the road towards the shop, her basket in her arm.

'A fine morning, Rachel,' said Alice Voar and Ellen Kerston, almost together.

'It is that,' said Rachel Whaness.

'If you don't mind waiting a minute,' said Mrs Olive Evie, 'till I turn the heel of this sock. Mr Evie was over twenty pounds down last year, on account of bad debts. I keep having to remind some people of that.'

'I have my purse,' said Ellen Kerston.

The women stood silently in the shop door, in the sun. Thoughts rose in them and faded, unspoken. Sometimes one frowned, another smiled, another uttered a few trite syllables. They had nothing much to say to one another. They kept mute stances about Mrs Olive Evie until she had turned the heel of the stocking she was knitting. They were stone women, statues.

'I thought,' said Alice Voar, 'he would have forgotten about the rose in the window. Last year his wild old uncle came and dragged him away from the supper table. But no, he hadn't forgotten at all, not one thing, that Johnny. His kiss was like eating purple plums.'

'God knows,' said Rachel Whaness, 'I'm anxious about my

Samuel. He has no business going near that Red Head, an old man like him. God knows I have no call to be anxious, for he's a good fisherman and the *Siloam* is a good boat and we're in the hand of God surely, and it's a sin to feel the way I do, but I can't help it, I just want him to sit under the window and make creels all day long and maybe paint the *Siloam* at the end of winter, but I want him never to handle an oar again, for the Lord's been good to us and abundant in his mercies.'

'A man has come to this island,' said Mrs Olive Evie. 'He arrived on Tuesday. He is biding in the hotel. Nobody knows who or what he is. Mr Evie knows who he is, but he won't say. Mr Evie is very discreet. The man is not a tourist. He has never once come out of the hotel with a fishing rod since he arrived. There is something very mysterious about it. Listen. That's his typewriter going now. He is here about secret work of some kind.'

'What I intend to do,' said Mrs Ellen Kerston, 'what I have every intention of doing as soon as this bairn inside me is weaned and walking, I will pack everything I can carry and I will just walk out on him, me and the bairns. That's it. He'll come home some night to an empty house, drunk. And I will be standing with Tom and Ernie and Judy and Mary and the unnamed one at the gate of my father's farm in Quoylay. Won't Glen give glad barks when he hears my knock at the door of Vertafiold!'

'There is nothing so good,' said Alice Voar, 'as love and kisses and children. It was like taking the sun into a winter bed. We were soaked in honey all night long. Yes we were. The rose bled slowly in the window. In between times he kissed me. That was like eating purple plums.'

'I can't tell,' said Rachel Whaness. 'It is hidden from me. The ways of providence are most mysterious. Not that I would murmur against it, not for a moment, but I ask myself, here my Samuel and I have come to a lonely old age with no blessing of children about us; and this fat violent woman who is married to a drunkard, her womb is never empty; and this other girl who I suppose can only be called a loose person, only she wears always the white garb of innocence, every man in Hellya has lain with her, including my Samuel one terrible night seven years ago; and the shopkeeper's wife with the scorpian tongue in her head, even she had the blessing of a son until he fell over the crag at Broganess bird-nesting, and got broken among the rocks. And I, the Lord's chosen, Rachel, I stand guard over an empty womb and an empty grave.'

'If you ask me,' said Mrs Olive Evie, 'it is to clean up this island. That's why he's here. Nothing else. Oh, they know all about us in the south, the authorities. They're not fools. They know what's going on, the drinking and the bad debts and the false tax returns and the unpaid car licences and the malingering and the wrong claims for subsidies. The man is here for no other purpose than to put this island to rights. I know it.'

'There's one day that I can't wait to see,' said Ellen Kerston, 'and it won't be long now. Of course it's nonsense, all that about going back to my father's place, my father is dead and the farm sold a while ago. The day I'm waiting for is this, when Willie grows to his full strength. He had his first shave in April, there are hairs coming on his chest too. Well then, this object comes home drunk, say, and he falls among the cups, then insults me. Willie is reading his history book – no, I forgot, he left the school at Easter – he is knotting his tie to go out courting among the farms. So, then, the thing curses for me. Willie turns and springs at it like a tiger, throws it to the floor, kicks it, shouts to it never to insult Mam again, bangs its head on the floor. And then trembles, for having struck his own father, stands there quivering. And the kids howling all about the village. I straighten Willie's tie and I tell him to forget about it all, go to the women, go on, out, have a good time. Then I pick up Bert Kerston from the floor. I wash the blood from the corner of his mouth. I empty his pockets. I lay him down on top of the bed. I kiss him, my own dear darling Bert Kerston. I loosen his trouser buttons.'

The wool-bird stopped whetting its beak at the centre of the silent meditative ring of women.

'We'll go into the shop then,' said Mrs Olive Evie, 'and I'll get your messages. I want the notice behind the counter to be particularly noted by some people – *Terms Cash. No Tick.*'

'I have my purse,' said Ellen Kerston.

*

Ben Budge had cursed and coughed and spat and cursed and groaned all night. Once before sunrise he whimpered.

Bella Budge came out to feed the hens in the morning.

'Cluck,' she said. 'I haven't the heart to speak to you this morning, hens. Ben has a sore pain in his side. Kitty.'

She scattered oats and bread among the white beseechers.

'You'll have to finish the goddam letter yourself, Bella,' said Ben, his face all silvered with sweat. 'Batten down the hatches. It's blowing up for a gale.'

Bella wiped his brow with a towel.

'I'll phone for the Quoylay doctor,' said Bella. 'Joseph Evie will phone Dr Silver from the shop. It costs fourpence.'

'Keep her headed into the wind,' said Ben. 'I've sprung a leak, Bella. The goddam bed's all wet.'

Ben started to cough again. Then he groaned and held his side. Bella shook her head slowly.

Mrs McKee gathered the cups and plates, the marmalade pot, Simon's quarter-eaten egg, the toast-rack, the butter-dish, the cream-jug, the sugar-bowl, the salt-and-pepper, the teapot, the crusts, on to a tray, and carried it through to the kitchen. She filled the kettle and set it on the gas-ring and struck a match. The assize, of course, was gathering; no doubt but that this would be a weighty session. Let them wait. She wasn't simply at their beck and call. She poured hot water into the plastic basin and squeezed soap liquid into it and stirred it round with a wooden spoon till it foamed up. She lowered the load of crockery and cutlery into the hot water. She washed each article with a cloth, and set it on a red plastic rack. She dried her hands on a worn towel that was kept specially for that purpose; it hung on a hook inside the cupboard door.

Now she must face them.

No, let them wait for ten minutes. Only yesterday she had discovered that, in a certain sense, the tribunal was in her power; she alone decided when each session began and ended. She didn't at all see why she should run after them like a little dog. She found the half-pound of stew that Mr Joseph Evie had set inside the front door at eight o'clock that morning. She unwrapped it. She examined it; it was very fatty; she would get Simon to talk to Mr Evie about that. Such a price it was too.

Unheard voices summoned her.

She took the bread board from the cupboard and spread the meat over it. She cut the meat into pieces with a little plastic-handled serrated knife that had been given away free with the last big packet of soap-powder she had bought. She sprinkled the kitchen table with flour. She rolled each segment of meat in the flour till it was coated white.

It was strange. She was enduring her judgement while she was still alive. She had never heard of such a thing before. Being alive, she still had a certain measure of choice, if it was only to decide the opening time of each session. That Indian lad had been so nice. He had given her the strength to stand up to them, if only to this meagre extent.

She lit the gas-ring again and set the saucepan on top. She cut a yellow corner from her half-pound block of butter into the sauce-pan and let it sizzle. She spread the pieces of meat carefully along the hot bottom of the saucepan, and replaced the lid ... Oh dear, what next. The carrots and the onions. What a handy wee knife, and fancy getting it free! She scraped two carrots under the tap and cut them in to thin red wheels. She sliced the ends from a half-dozen small onions and removed the two tarnished outer coats. That was that. Simon liked stew. If he didn't eat his dinner she would be very very vexed with him. Oh dear, she knew it, she should have been boiling the kettle while she was preparing the vegetables. She put the kettle on the second gas ring to boil. While she was searching the cupboard for the jar of bay leaves, the kettle began to shrill and sing.

The longer you delay. You are just postponing the inevitable; what had been predestined before you were born; for which all the same you must answer. You are simply putting it off.

Not till she had covered the sizzling meat with boiling water; not till she had dropped in the carrots and the onions; not till she had carefully inserted the bay leaf; not till she had put on the lid of the saucepan and lowered the gas flame and the stew began to simmer gently and regularly, did she straighten herself and turn towards the door. And even then she knew she had forgotten something: the seasoning. She turned again to the cupboard and cooker, lifted the lid of the saucepan, sprinkled on salt and herb seasoning. Every prisoner was allowed to eat a hearty dinner, if he or she could.

Now she really must face them.

If only there was somebody in the court to comfort her; somebody like that nice Indian boy who was here yesterday: that would make things much easier to bear. She remembered the red rayon dressing-gown the pedlar had sold her, and smiled. Simon didn't know about that yet. She would give it to him the night before he went on holiday. When Simon was packing the last things into his case she would fetch it from the tallboy drawer in her bedroom and come up silently and lay it among his other holiday clothes in the case. That would be a nice surprise for Simon. The Indian boy had been a wonderful help to her. Really he had. She wasn't quite so afraid now as she had been two days before.

She set her mouth firmly and opened the door into the sitting-room.

The sun dazed her for a moment; three golden squares lay on the carpet, the fourth glittered intolerably out of the wardrobe mirror. She crossed over and drew the heavy red curtain. Then she sat down on her chair.

The court was crowded.

Inga turned over on her belly on the warm rock and cradled her head on her forearms. She would like to be utterly naked under the sun. She remembered the story by D. H. Lawrence called *Sun*. A super story, that. The mindless peasant watching the golden-skinned woman. That was the way Inga would like it to be: summoned by dark gods. If only.

The chug-chug of a motor-boat made her squirm about and sit up suddenly. It was not the ferry-boat. It was a fisherman setting out for his creels in the west. She squinnied at the name on the bow, shading her eyes: *Siloam*. The boat was being borne out fast into the open Atlantic on the retreating waters.

The sea had ebbed far out now. It had dwindled to a curved

gleaming blade between Quoylay and Hellya. Inga saw that the ebb had left, at the far end of the beach, a shallow rock-pool. The sun blazed out of it.

Crossing the rocks, she took care not to set her feet on a cluster of limpets or a frond of slippery tang.

Inga leaned and lowered herself into the rockpool. The water was so cold she almost screamed. She tore the stillness apart; threshing about, gasping, laughing, surrounding herself with showers of spray till blood and salt achieved a balance. Then she turned over on her back and floated in peace, languidly, a long pale flower.

Half-past five in the morning. Would it be possible to get out of the house at half-past five in the morning without Grandpop or Aunt Agatha knowing? If a flower dropped a petal in the hallway you could hear the hullabaloo of the dogs all over the island. At half-past five on Friday morning, Ivan Westray had said, he had to deliver provisions and oil to the Skerry lighthouse right out in the Atlantic, two miles west of Quoylay, an hour there and an hour back. If she wanted to come, good and well. But if she wasn't there, on Greenvoe pier, at half-past five in the morning, prompt, then that would be all right. It was up to her. No, there would be nobody else on board. He could give her breakfast. He had a little gas stove in the cabin. Coffee with condensed milk. Boiled eggs. Rolls a couple of days old. He had a bunk. There was nothing like lying on a bunk in swell after swell of the sea. He could assure her of that. It was all the same to him, whether she turned up or not. Good night.

Inga turned over and swam a few strokes till her feet touched the sand. Her body was livid with cold. Her shoulders and thighs shuddered. She turned and ran back along the beach, vaulting over the rocks till she reached the rock where her yellow dress was spread out. She lay on the flat stone once more, gasping and shivering. Little runnels seeped out of her and dried before they could reach the rock's edge. Her hair was plastered in black strands about her throat and shoulders, and her body was pearled with salt-drops. She hadn't brought a towel (she hadn't expected to bathe; she had just come to lie in the sun). The sun would have to dry her. She ached with coldness and lay still.

Inga lay and let the sun stream down over her. A warmth kindled in her breasts. She hesitated; then unhooked one scarlet slip and laid it aside. She offered two tender salt-dewed roses to the sun.

The radiance drenched her through and through.

If only she had the courage to be quite naked. She would be soaked in light like a honeycomb. Her fingers plucked at the single remaining shred of scarlet.

And at once her heart leapt and stampeded inside her – someone was coming! She could hear boots crunching among the loose stones. She could hear a voice cajoling and reasoning with itself. She hardly dared raise her head. The feet were silent now – whispers in the sand, slithers in the seaweed – but the quiet monologue went on, questioning, explaining, arguing. Inga peered over the edge of the rock. It was the man in the ragged coat who lived in the burnt house in the village. He was carrying a sack over his shoulder. Every now and again he stooped down and picked something up and admired it: a glass ball, a stick, a tin box. He either threw it away or stowed it carefully into the foot of his sack. And always as he trudged and stooped and shambled along the shore the monologue went on: 'Timmy had one nip of the ultra-violet today ...' 'Timmy should know better ...' 'Timmy won't come here again till there's been a westerly gale ...' 'That's lovely, a glass ball. The minister's mother, Mrs McKee, she'll give Timmy a shilling for this. She will ...' The voice was lost in the last gluts and mutterings of the ebb.

He had not even noticed her. Inga smiled. She turned over on her face. The flame enfolded her shoulders and ribs. It was not the time, yet, to be utterly naked.

She raised her head once more. The simpleton had vanished round the headland.

But why had Ivan Westray not kissed her last night at the crossroads, when he must have known her whole body was crying out for it? He did not behave like a D. H. Lawrence peasant at all. There was something cruel and cold and calculating about him.

The sun climbed higher. The pale tense body on the rock relaxed; the eyes closed; the fragile ribs rose and fell, gently; she became a part of the rhythm of the summer island. Inga, all honey and roses, slept in the sun.

A huge tremulous silence possessed the sea. The tide hung between slack and the beginning of the flood.

Through this silence the ferry crossed swiftly over from Greenvoe to Hrossey.

Samuel Whaness lifted his creels one by one, under the Red Head of Hellya. They were empty, there was not one lobster inside. From a dozen the mackerel bait was missing. Samuel stowed his score of black creels into the *Siloam*. Something was wrong.

A mile farther round the coast, between the Stack and the Taing, Bert Kerston was setting creels. That was also a good place for lobsters, though not any better than the fertile sea floor under the Red Head. Samuel Whaness turned the *Siloam* in the direction of the *Ellen*. The flood had set in half-an-hour before; the motorboat made slow progress among the glassy whorls. At last Samuel rounded the Stack and steered close in between the shore and the *Ellen*.

'How many lobsters did you get today?' said Samuel Whaness. His voice trembled across the water.

'A lot,' said Bert Kerston. He lifted up a box. It was heavy, with a slow audible scrithe of lobsters, a purple heave. Bert Kerston set them down again with a thump on the bottom of the boat.

'I got none,' said Samuel Whaness. 'Not one.'

'That's too bad,' said Bert Kerston grinning. 'That's the luck of the game.'

'I think,' said Samuel Whaness, 'many of the lobsters you have in that box are mine by right. You lifted the creels I had under the Red Head.'

'You're a goddam liar,' said Bert Kerston.

'I wouldn't add to the sin of thieving with the worse sin of blasphemy,' said Samuel Whaness. 'Watch your tongue.'

Bert Kerston lowered his last creel. The red cork marker bobbed about on the swell.

'Some Quoylay fishermen were out,' he said. 'I saw them from the middle of the Sound. They were working creels under the Red

Head. Two men in a boat. I couldn't see their faces right.'

Samuel Whaness shut off the engine and steered the *Siloam* right alongside the *Ellen*, till the boats scraped one another.

'Watch out,' said Bert Kerston. 'I painted this boat last month.'

The boats stoddered against each other.

'When we get back to Greenvoe, you and I,' said Samuel Whaness, 'we will divide the lobsters in your boat. I will be satisfied with that. I will take no further action.'

'Bugger off,' said Bert Kerston. 'Bugger off, you old fool.'

Samuel Whaness's face blanched. His great hands trembled and he seized Bert Kerston by the shoulders. The boats eddied apart. The men still clung to each other, making an arch of rage over the slowly widening sleeve of water.

Bert Kerston shook and beat himself free. He leapt at the engine, seized the handle, and swung the *Ellen* into stuttering quivering life.

Samuel Whaness hung over the side of the *Siloam*, his hands in the sea up to his wrists, his eyes wide and terrible.

'You bloody old fool,' cried Bert Kerston, 'you nearly had us both drowned.'

He stumbled to the tiller, eased the *Ellen* round in a wide circle, and made for the open sea.

Samuel Whaness stared into the fruitless water.

'You'll hear more about this,' cried Bert Kerston from mid-Sound. 'I'm going to phone the police as soon as I get back. Slander. Assault and battery.'

His voice came shivering and fragile across the water.

Samuel Whaness trembled. He took his fists out of the sea. His boat had drifted silently shoreward till she was nosing the weed. Samuel lifted an oar and pushed the *Siloam* off. His hand was still trembling as he inserted the handle. He twisted and wrenched for fully five minutes before he realized that the propeller was choked with seaweed. At last the engine coughed into life. He steered between the Stack and the Taing and turned for home, into long glories of light that came dazzling into his face from the slow glassy heave of the sea. He crinkled his eyes. The *Siloam* sped swift as a cormorant on the gathering strength of the flood.

Might God forgive him for losing control of himself.

Yet it was not the first nor the twenty-first time that his creels had been robbed by that Bert Kerston over the years. The man had deserved the fright he got. He deserved to be taken and thrashed. Yes, truly he deserved a long stretch in prison. Nevertheless God forgive Samuel Whaness.

He turned the boat into the bay.

That shameless hussy was still lying on the table rock. Samuel Whaness turned his eyes sternly. She was even more naked than before.

Timmy Folster, filling his sack with whelks from Sweyn Skerry, waved at him as the *Siloam* glided past, with shut-off engine.

Samuel took the rope and jumped on to the steps of the pier. It was the first day that summer that he hadn't returned with something, a gift of God, out of the boundless treasury of the sea.

It was the ecclesiastical division of the court, Mrs McKee decided at once. She had the feeling of Sabbath peace and gravestones; she could almost hear the rustling of bands and black gowns. The smell that comes off very old calf-bound books drifted across her nostrils. She could imagine very well this particular prosecutor; many and many a time she had listened to his voice, so careful in its phrasing and modulation, a young clever Scottish voice that trembled frequently (Mrs McKee thought) on the verge of sentimentality, yet was capable of sudden savagery, of a slow gathering wave of denunciation that broke out at last, bitter and lacerating, in *anathema sit*. Then the dramatic silence. Then again the coda of quiet clinching phrases; and one could imagine how deeply all the court had been impressed, and how the last doubter in the jury bowed his head in complete acquiescence as the reverend lawman gathered his black cloak about him and sat down at last.

Mrs McKee was always reminded of Simon's contemporary at university, Fergus Crichton, the clever boy from Dunoon who had won the gold medal, when she listened to that voice.

Indeed she felt rather important, sitting in her rocking-chair with the blue velvet cushion at her back. Fancy clever people going to all that trouble on her account. She felt – Oh, gracious! –

like one of the handmaidens of Mary Queen of Scots, beautiful and fated, while the speech lasted.

The prosecutor began:

In the year of Our Lord fifteen hundred and sixty an event happened in the annals of our church and nation of which we can, I think, be justly proud. I refer of course to the Reformation. In one brief heroic assembly the kirk purged itself of the accumulated error and superstition of many centuries. It returned to the only source of revealed truth, holy writ. The vision of all the people of Scotland was cleansed, as if the finger of the Lord had touched our eyes in passing. Henceforth we were a people acceptable to him. This goodly state of affairs continues, praise be, even unto the present day.

Yet eternal vigilance must be exercised. The house of God on earth is like other houses; it is subject to decay, to dry-rot, to fallen timbers, to withered stone, to the tempest and the lightning. Our adversary the devil goeth about his business often at the very threshold of it; this lewd obscene frightful creature that perhaps we Scots do wrong to call by half humorous names, such as Auld Nick, Sneckie, Prince of Darkness, Clootie, etcetera; the argument being that Satan cannot stand up to mockery; yet these same childish nick-names, known to every Scottish bairn from time immemorial, dilutes the stark horror of this being whose aim is and was and always will be to seduce us from allegiance to the faith of our fathers.

What would please the devil more than that our kirk, reestablished after so many centuries of popish error on the rock of scripture – what, I ask you, would please him better than that this same house of the Lord should be infected once more with ancient vain pomp and superstition? This same Satan is a master in the art of dazzling the eye and indeed all the senses. Think how the church of pre-Reformation Scotland was – to use a rather vulgar but descriptive phrase – tarted up with all manner of destructive tinsel: the statues and the stained glass, the fuming censers swung by acolytes at gilded altars, the grove of candles about the plaster feet of some saint. The wretched and the ignorant of the earth have always gone down on their knees before this mumbojumbo.

I do not need to tell you that Rome still flaunts these gauds and baubles in the face of mankind. And many there are who still hanker after these things, though nominally they are members of our kirk: not only the superstitious either, but people who are supposed to be clever, artistic, cultured. I say it with sorrow; year after year we lose a flock of such people to Rome.

Occasionally an innocent soul is ensnared.

It needs must be that offences come, but woe to her by whom the offences come.

I want you, brethren, to imagine a typical Scottish family of the present day; or rather, to be quite accurate, of a generation ago. This family lives in the respectable district of Marchmont in the city of Edinburgh, the capital of Scotland. The family at number two Marchmont Square consists of four persons, Mr and Mrs Alan McKee, Miss Flora Alder (younger sister of Mrs McKee), and a little boy of five, called Simon, the only child of the McKees. There is nothing remarkable in their circumstances. Mr McKee is not very robust, he has been badly wounded and shell-shocked during the First World War on the battlefields of France, but he is able to pursue his calling of chartered accountant's clerk in a respectable city firm, MacAndrew and Brae. They are all members of the Church of Scotland, and regular attenders on the Sabbath day. The child Simon is a pleasant little lad, a bit spoiled perhaps; but this is natural where there are two women folk in the house who dote on him. He says his prayers regularly, if a little hurriedly, every night before he goes to his crib, and he trots along to the Sunday School with Tommy MacIndoe his pal from downstairs, once the morning service is over. Once Aunt Flora heard Simon say a bad word - 'damn' - on the stair head, and she smacked him across the fingers and called him a naughty boy; whereupon Simon wept. But in her heart of hearts Aunt Flora knew that Simon hadn't known the meaning of the word, he had heard the older boys in the tenement say it and out of utter innocence repeated it; so immediately she bought him a bag of bon-bons from the newsagent's shop downstairs and presently Simon was quite happy once more and Aunt Flora gave him a kiss on his tear-stained cheek.

Well, such little storms are in every family: the cloud passes and the sun comes out again.

Today we are not primarily concerned with Simon – the sad case of Simon is due to come before you quite soon, tomorrow, I think, and an abler tongue than mine will present it. Today we have to consider how the prisoner has put in mortal peril the soul of another human being, a kinswoman of hers, and a child at that.

The very same day that Simon said the bad word, a letter came from Mr McKee's sister in Caithness. This letter brought the sun out with a vengeance; for Aunt Phillis in Caithness (she was married to a farmer, Walter Melville of Broad Mains) wanted to know if there would be room in the McKee household for Winifred her daughter, aged fourteen, for a few weeks. Winnie Melville had not been very well lately. She had had a tooth extracted in the spring and some kind of infection had got into her jaw. She had been off school for a month and more. The doctor had got the gum infection cleared up, but thought Winnie would be better of having a complete change before she returned to school. Therefore, asked Aunt Phillis, would it be a terrible burden for Alan and Elizabeth to have Winnie until she was quite well again? The girl was beside herself with excitement at the prospect of being in Edinburgh; she had never stayed in a city before; all she knew was the farms and the fishing boats of the north.

Of course it would be no trouble at all. All that would be required was a small turn-round of beds: Aunt Flora could sleep in Simon's room – the spare camp-bed fitted into the corner quite nicely. And Winnie would have Aunt Flora's bed for the duration of her stay.

They only dimly remembered Winnie from a holiday they had had in the north seven summers before; she had seemed a nice little lass then, perhaps too timid and impressionable to fit well into that stark rural background. They hoped she and Simon would get on well together. They were all quite excited.

Winnie arrived three days later. They met her at Waverley Station and took her home in a taxi. She was a thin freckled quiet girl. But she quickly thawed out under the kindness of the women. She turned out to have quite a sense of humour too, and while they were still all seated at the table after tea, replete with the Caithness cheese and chicken and rhubarb jam that Winnie had brought down from Broad Mains farm, the floodgates suddenly opened. She told them about all the funny things that happened in a rural community. About the neighbouring farmer who went up to Thurso Mart and was offered a second-hand car for sale. He had never driven before, but he had bought the car and drove it the eight miles home. Oh yes, he said, he had gone into the ditch twice, and he had bumped into a sheep, and a cat in Castletown was dead, but apart from that he had managed home fine, as they could all see. And that same farmer drove his car till he died ten years later, and he had never passed a test in his life. They were still laughing when Winnie started to tell them about Geordie the fisherman from the village who was very henpecked by his wife, but he got drunk every Saturday regularly and came home and raged about the house all weekend, sometimes smashing dishes and shouting that he (Geordie) would let the whole wide world know who was the boss in his circus, and *crash* would go another saucer against the wall ... Aunt Flora looked a bit shocked at the conclusion of that story.

Now there was no stopping the girl; she was caught up in the full flood of narrative. Her cheeks were flushed, her eyes shone, and she spoke with such enthusiasm that her tongue seemed to be too big for her mouth and she sprayed the table-cloth with a continual fine jet of spittle, until Aunt Flora prudently removed the jam dish and the cake-stand. And what stories! – about the fairies in the hills, the small green ones who loved music, and about the seal tribe down at the rocks who were selkies indeed when they were in the sea but human beings once they shed their pelts and danced on the moonlit sands. 'And what's more,' said Winnie, 'it's true, because I've seen them with my own two eyes ...' Her two wide blue eyes stared at them but it seemed as if the girl was looking beyond them into another world altogether. And Simon sat beside her, his eyes fixed on his cousin's face, utterly enraptured.

'Winnie dear,' said Mrs McKee, 'you've done us all a world of good. You're like a fresh breeze in the house. But you're tired, I know it, after that long train journey, and you should be in your bed Aunt Flora has put the hot bottle in.'

Simon said no. He plucked at his cousin's sleeve and begged her to go on, she must tell just one more story, then she could go to bed. But Mrs McKee was very firm. Winnie *must* get her rest, she had been unwell and she had had a long journey. She would tell Simon stories in the morning ... And the girl agreed. She was tired. She kissed Simon on his petulant rosebud of a mouth and was ushered into Aunt Flora's flower-papered bedroom, and under a flowery quilt.

Later that night the two women discussed Winnie. 'She is a nice child,' said Mrs McKee, 'I'm so glad she's come.' But Aunt Flora, though saying nothing against Winnie, was not so enthusiastic. 'She has far too much imagination,' she said. 'Seal people, indeed! Fairies! And all gospel truth – she's seen them with her own eyes! Phillis will need to keep her eye on that girl.'

In fact Winnie told no more stories; it semed she had emptied herself that first evening. And Simon, after asking for a story the next morning at breakfast-time, and getting for reply a slow grave headshake, promptly forgot about it too. When he plucked Winnie's sleeve afterwards, it was to get her to play Ludo with him, or Happy Families. And the girl would squat down on the fireside rug beside him after dinner and rattle dice, though she would much rather be looking into the shop windows along Princes Street.

Winnie was very patient and gentle with Simon – even Aunt Flora agreed about that – though there was such a difference, nine years, in their ages. Winnie was fourteen. Simon followed his cousin about everywhere, like a little dog, with eyes of utter devotion.

The best days of all were when they were taken out to explore the city. You may be sure they had a grand time, Winnie and Simon, as the summer brightened about them. They were shepherded everywhere, of course, by one or other of the ladies, Mrs McKee or Aunt Flora. They were taken to the zoo at Corstorphine, and to the beach at Portobello, and the Castle ramparts, and to the Leith docks. They attended a cinema matinée at the Regal one Saturday morning: Roy Rogers in a western epic. Every tea-time they climbed the stairs to the top flat at Marchmont demolishing ice-cream cones with hot languid tongues. And Winnie wrote postcards home every now and then, saying what a fine time she was having, and would Mother please send her at once her summer vests and knickers (for it had suddenly got hot) and her bathing costume, and please, another postal order ...

So the first week passed. And then, one Monday morning, Winnie disappeared. When she didn't come home for dinner at half-past twelve, Mrs McKee was almost beside herself with worry. Several times she was on the point of getting in touch with the police. But Aunt Flora restrained her. Good grief, the girl wasn't a baby, she was in all likelihood sitting in the Princes Street gardens listening to the band. They weren't exactly living in the days of Burke and Hare ... Two o'clock came. Mrs McKee spoke about phoning Alan at his office. Simon hung about the women's skirts, whimpering. Winnie had promised to bring him a comic from the shop, when she was getting white laces for her tennis shoes. That was the errand she had gone out for, to buy white laces in the wee shop across the road, a piece of business that should have taken her no more than ten minutes. She had run down the stairs with a shilling in her hand passing eleven o'clock, and now it was twenty-five past two. 'At three o'clock,' said Mrs McKee, 'I will phone.' At three minutes to three the bell rang. She opened the door to a white freckle-splashed face and large shocked eyes. It was the wanderer. It was Winnie.

Mrs McKee didn't know whether to rage at her or cover her cheek with kisses: but it wouldn't have made much difference to the girl, who sat down on the rocking-chair beside the fire and said over and over again in her sharp awkward Caithness tongue that she had seen a terrible thing, a terrible thing, a man with a blank face.

A plate of Scotch broth was put into her hands.

No, she didn't want it.

The man with the scabs for eyes.

'Now, young lady,' said Aunt Flora, 'just please tell us exactly where you've been. Your Aunt Elizabeth has been sick with worry.' Blindness. And rags. It was as if the scarecrow from the cornfield at Broad Mains had found its way down to Edinburgh and was following her. It was terrible, terrible.

'Where's my comic?' said Simon, and climbed on Winnie's knee. But she pushed him away, quite roughly.

The face she had seen was a bunch of thistles.

Then Winnie got up and went into her bedroom. When Mrs McKee looked in ten minutes later she was sprawled on top of the eiderdown fast asleep.

'This is too much,' said Aunt Flora. 'I would send the girl home. Of course this is not my house.'

But when Winnie appeared at five o'clock she was the same happy girl as always. The white mask had completely left her face. 'Gosh, Aunty Liz,' she said, 'I am hungry for my tea, I am the hungriest person for my tea in the whole hungry world.'

Simon opened the Ludo board on the rug and arranged the counters. Winnie squatted down beside him.

'Listen, pieman,' she said (she always called Simon pieman) 'listen to this. I'm going to tell you a true story. There was once a man who had two blue opals for eyes.'

'What's opals?' said Simon.

'Precious stones, silly,' said Winnie. 'He was a very rich man. Well, he must have been, to have such jewels in his face. Once he went hunting with his retainers, this duke – he was a duke, I forgot to tell you that – and his horse got separated from the other hunters, he rode it so fast. He wandered about on his horse for a long time, waiting for the hunt to catch up with him. Night came on. He got tired. He tied the horse to a branch and he lay down under a tree to sleep.'

'Was he lost?' said Simon.

'Pieman, I am trying to tell you,' said Winnie. 'He was utterly lost. Little did the duke know that there were robbers in the forest. The robber chief found him asleep under the oak tree. "It's the Duke," said the robber chief, "the lord with the opal eyes. Somebody give me a knife" . . .'

'He killed the duke,' said Simon.

'No he didn't,' said Winnie, 'he wasn't such a fool. He didn't want to be hanged. He was a clever bandit, all he wanted was the duke's eyes. He was just bending over the sleeping duke to cut out the opals when he heard a horn sounding deep in the forest, far far away, the horn of the hunters and the distant whinnying of horses. So then he knew they were out searching for the duke. He had no time to take both the eyes. The hunters would have caught him. He cut out one of the opal eyes and then he and all the robbers fled away to their cave under the mountain. When the hunters came to the oak tree they found their lord with blood running down one cheek. But that was all right, he still had one eye left, he could still rule over his domain and see that justice was done, which it was, for his soldiers trapped the robbers in their den next winter and hanged them in the forest. Then there was peace in the countryside. "What a happy contented people I rule over," said the one-eyed duke. Little did he know. One day he was out walking with his knights and ladies. It was a beautiful day in spring. They walked into the forest. The leaves were beginning to come out on the trees. A young nobleman played on a lute. Suddenly a lady held her nose. "Goodness," cried this lady, "whoever left these disgusting bundles of rags beside the path? They stink in the wind." . . . And they did stink too, like offal, these rag-bags. A retainer kicked one of the bundles to make way for all the silken folk to pass. And the bundle began to cry. The bundle stood up. It was a boy. It was very poor. It wept with hunger. The second bundle stood up. It was a girl, the sister of the first bundle. It cried. "Why are you weeping?" said the duke. "Because," said the ragged boy, "a wicked duke rules in this part of the country, and he has driven our father from his farm, and our father and mother could no longer feed us, and last night they left us in the forest while we were sleeping, and so we shall die of hunger and cold, because of that wicked duke." . . . The duke was a good man, as I said before. What did he know of the cruel things his courtiers were up to whenever his back was turned, robbing poor people of their land to line their own pockets? The duke didn't know, he was such an innocent good man. And so the lament of the two rag-bags filled his heart with sorrow. This is what he did, before any of the lords and ladies could stop him, he unscrewed the solitary opal from his face and gave it to the boy. "There," he said, "go and find your mother and father again. You will be able to buy a large farm with this precious opal, a farm with a mill and three pair of horse and a hundred silky cattle." . . . Then he lay down on the road, blind, and his heart nearly broke with grief. The lords and ladies left him and went back to the castle. What use was a blind duke to them? By and by they elected a new duke from among themselves, one who would wink at all their thievery and oppression. As for the real duke, the blind duke, he grew thinner and more ragged as the summer came on. He lay down in a ditch. The rain washed away his face. The sun burned his hands and turned them to dust. At last he was nothing but a stick with a few tatters clinging to it. A farmer found him lying there. "Well," said Wattie the farmer, "just what I'm looking for, a scarecrow." And he set the duke up in his oatfield to frighten the birds. And that's the end of the story.'

'That's a sad story,' said Simon.

'It isn't,' said Winnie. 'It's a very funny story. A rich man being changed into a scarecrow. I think it's very funny.'

And Winnie Melville began to laugh, sitting on the rug before the fire while Aunt Flora fried kippers and Mrs McKee set the table. Simon looked at her with wide eyes, and soon he was laughing too. They collapsed on top of each other across the Ludo board, scattering the counters, shrieking and gasping with laughter at the miracle of metamorphosis. Simon's eyes were wet with happy tears. He held his ribs. 'Oh,' he moaned, 'I'm sore with laughing.'

'That's enough now,' said Aunt Flora sharply. 'You're behaving like a pair of barbarians. The kippers are served.'

Afterwards, when Simon was in bed, Winnie explained what had happened. She was very sorry for upsetting everybody. It would never happen again. Please would they forgive her?

'Of course, dear,' said Mrs McKee. 'What else. Tell us.'

Winnie had come out of the wee shop after buying the white laces and the comic, and just at that moment a number 23 tram from Morningside rattled down the street and stopped immediately in front of her. Two old ladies climbed on board. And Winnie, on a sudden impulse, jumped on board too – it was a wonderful thrill, it was the very first time she had used the city transport unaided. She felt gay and free and independent, sitting on the upper deck, as Edinburgh swayed athwart her – the Meadows, Bristo Street, the Medical School, George IV Bridge, the Mound, and at last Princes Street itself. There she got off. She spent an hour looking in a hundred shop windows. She pressed her face against the railing of the Gardens, and saw the tulips and the statues. She wondered idly if they would be worried about her at home. She walked back up the Mound and into the High Street. She felt all of a sudden very hungry. And there she saw an old blind ragged man trying to get across the street, and losing himself at last among buses and taxis. Then she had taken the tram home. That was all. She was sorry.

'Well, dear, so long as you had a good day,' said Mrs McKee. 'But next time you do such a thing let us know beforehand. Then your Aunt Flora and I won't worry.'

'She is a very strange girl indeed,' said Aunt Flora when Winnie was safely tucked up in bed. And Aunt Flora shook her head.

Winnie Melville's holiday went on as before, after that one solitary adventure. They all went out to Cramond village on a beautiful morning and crossed the River Almond in a ferry-boat. They walked to the top of Calton Hill. They took a bus out to Swanston where Robert Louis Stevenson lived for a time. And then one tea-time, during Winnie's third and last week in Edinburgh, Mr Alan McKee dropped his happy bombshell.

'Get ready,' he said, 'pack your bags, choose a place where there's sea and sun, empty all the winter money out of your piggybanks.'

It transpired that he was on holiday. A week was owing to him from last summer when they had been so busy in the office in St Andrew's Square, and so Mr Minto had said, 'Alan, if you wouldn't mind, I think you should have that week now before the paper avalanche starts . . .' So, said Mr McKee, where were they to go? In such beautiful weather – and it looked settled too – they weren't going to stay in the city, that was one thing sure.

The women had no idea, Mr McKee had taken them completely by surprise. But it seemed that Mr McKee's asking for advice was only a conventional gambit; he had got the loan of Fingal MacRae's old Ford – 'Take it,' said Fingal MacRae from Inverness, his colleague in the office, 'take the old heap of rust. It's cost me a fortune in repairs this past winter. I don't care if I never see it again. Take it, man, by all means . . .' They would tour the west coast of Scotland in Fingal MacRae's heap of rust, said Mr McKee.

That was a busy night for the women, packing their cases, making sandwiches, filling thermos flasks. The sun set over the hills in a warm glow. 'A red sky at night is the shepherd's delight,' said Winnie. Simon hardly slept with excitement. Mr McKee hirpled across to the Golf Tavern on his stick, to be out of their way.

They had a big breakfast of ham and eggs and tomatoes, for, said Mrs McKee, goodness knows when they would get their next meal. Then down the sixty-two steps of the tenement they went, burdened, and out into the sunlight. And there, drawn in to the pavement, was the heap of rust. 'It's a perfectly respectable looking car,' said Mrs McKee. 'That Fingal MacRae!' Tommy MacIndoe waved good-bye from the door of the wee shop. Simon gave him a sixpence out of his savings. Then they were off.

I will not bother you, brethren, with a lengthy account of this week-long holiday, except to say that they enjoyed themselves very much in the west – as who wouldn't, among those seas and mountains? The weather wasn't uniformly good. They moved from sunshine into sudden rain, then back into sun again. 'It's like travelling across a chessboard,' said Winnie happily, as the sun glittered once more on the rain-beaded windscreen of the car ... This kind of chessboard weather is, as we all know, a characteristic of our western coast.

We are only really concerned with two characters: Mrs Elizabeth McKee and Winifred Melville, her niece by marriage. On them we are able to concentrate. I mention the weather, the mingled sun and rain, because it too is in a way one of the *dramatis personae*; as we shall presently see.

They arrived late one afternoon at a little village in Ross-shire. Mrs McKee declared she would die if she didn't get a cup of tea at once. Aunt Flora spied a hotel across the road. So Mr McKee stopped the car and out they all trooped, and they had a lovely high tea (but rather expensive) in the wee hotel: grilled trout and barley scones. There were several hours of daylight before them yet. Mr McKee shifted back plates and cruets and spread out his road map and pointed to another village twenty miles farther north. That would be a good place to stop for the night. While Mr McKee settled the bill with a waitress who spoke very softly – 'her throat is lined with silk and satin, and she has a tulip for a tongue,' Winnie assured Simon – while Mr McKee checked his change and then slid a shilling under his plate for a tip, the dining-room window was all of a sudden loud and blind and streaming. They had moved into a black square of the chessboard.

It didn't last of course. They crossed the street under the last weepings of the shower and settled themselves once more in the car. And presently, as they toiled in low gear up a steep mountain road, with the sea far below, the whole world glittered like a jewel. Anonymous islands littered the west. 'That's where the mermaids live,' said Winnie to Simon. They bored their way through a tremulous flock of sheep and a shepherd who kept lifting his bonnet to them very obsequiously. Then they reached the crest of the hill, and far below them, on the other side, lay enchantment: a bay of brilliant sand, a small mountain studded with rocks, and between mountain and sea, on the far horn of the bay, a wee village with a pier and a half-dozen fishing boats. This was the place Mr McKee had seen on the map.

'A bathe,' cried Simon. 'I want a bathe. Please.'

'Postcards and stamps,' said Mrs McKee. 'Do you know this, I haven't written one single postcard since we left Edinburgh? I must do it tonight.'

The car left the region of clouds and snow for the wet cornfields and the fishing boats. Mr McKee stopped the car in front of a shabby horned cow. Simon began to tug off his jersey.

'Come on, Winnie,' he yelled, 'see who gets wet first.'

But Winnie didn't want to bathe. She would walk with Aunt Liz into the village. Mr McKee said they were to get a *Scotsman* from the stationer's shop, if they could, when they were buying postcards. Simon, stark naked, burrowed in a carrier bag for his striped bathing suit. Mr McKee began to fill his pipe. It was a calm crystal evening. Aunt Flora smacked Simon on the rump for being so shameless; the folk in the village might be watching him through telescopes.

It was a mile and more to the village, far longer than it had seemed, but Mrs McKee and Winnie enjoyed their walk across the sand and among the bristling dunes. They passed the first cottages. Far behind them, fragile and purified by distance, they could hear the happy screams of Simon in the sea. The general merchant's shop was still open, thank goodness, but only just; the dark morose shopkeeper was putting up his first shutter. 'There is postcards,' he said, 'but the *Scotsmans* is sold, I only get three whatever, one for the minister and one for the schoolmaster and one for the priest. I do not sell stamps. Only the post office sells stamps. You will be needing penny stamps for postcards . . .'

While this melancholy man was speaking to them it grew dark, and the sweet bottles on the shelf dulled. They chose a dozen postcards. 'Ach now,' said the shopkeeper, 'I think it will come on to rain. That will be one shilling and sixpence . . .'

Rain spattered the paving stones between the hotel and the petrol pump. The brilliant bay became a drab streak. There was a hush-hushing between the hills. They hurried on. The paving stones shone like black mirrors. Then the deluge began. Mrs McKee pulled Winnie into an open doorway out of the torn sheets of water. They were standing in the porch of a church. Winnie's hair hung in a score of rat-tails among her freckles.

'Goodness,' said Mrs McKee, 'who on earth would have thought it was going to rain like this!'

But Winnie wasn't there.

Mrs McKee peered into the gloom, and her heart nearly missed a beat, for it was a Roman Catholic church. There were two plaster statues, one against each side wall, and at the feet of the larger one – probably the Virgin Mary – three candles were lighted. A little red flame shone like a ruby at the side of the altar. Along three of the walls ran a sequence of paintings showing the Lord on his way to Calvary. It was all very lurid, Mrs McKee thought, a bit distasteful, like a sideshow at a fair. Of course she knew one or two Catholics in Edinburgh – Pussy Brae had married one – and they were good sincere people, but looking at all this Mrs McKee was very glad that she was a Presbyterian. The house of God, she said firmly to herself, is not a theatre or an art gallery or a music-hall. The ghost of dead incense pricked her nostrils. The rain drummed on the roof of the church.

But where was Winnie? Mrs McKee peered into the dim interior.

Winnie was sitting in the back seat of the church, as if she was waiting for somebody.

Mrs McKee heard a shuffle in the door behind her. An old

126

woman in a shawl stood there, feeling her way in, her hand fluttering slowly over the font, probing in the direction of Mrs McKee herself, only a yard away. The face was blind. Mrs McKee hurriedly slipped into the interior. She sat down on a rush-bottomed seat on the opposite side of the aisle from Winnie. Those pads hanging on hooks from the chairs in front, they would be for kneeling on. There was nothing like that in their church, thank goodness. She hoped that the old blind woman would not want to sit where she was sitting.

But no: the shawled one had found her way into the church and was moving slowly but with confidence down the aisle, as if she had got her bearings now. Mrs McKee got a whiff of dampness from her shawl as she went past. Mrs McKee smiled across to Winnie at the other side, but Winnie's white face was intent on the person who had just come in.

The old blind woman stopped. She faced the altar. Her hidden legs seemed to collapse under her, slowly and painfully, and as she sank her right hand wavered across her face and breast. Half-way to the floor she pulled herself painfully to her feet again, and turned, and shuffled a few steps to the plaster statue with the candles flickering and dribbling before it. She bent down. She took a candle out of a wooden box at the side of the statue and fitted it carefully into the grove of candlesticks about the feet. Her hands saw everything. They were deft and sure and subtle. She had probably been weaving nets all her life, thought Mrs McKee, and spinning wool. Her hands remembered. She took a matchbox out of her apron pocket and lit one and applied the flame without hesitation to the wick of the new candle. The small flame lapped the wax and burned brighter and shone upon a great suffering and serenity. The old one went down on her knees. Her fingers were looped among beads from which a small silver crucifix dangled. Her mouth moved. The beads slid through her fingers.

One of the candles guttered and went out. The new flame burned steadily. The old woman sighed. The rosary slipped through warped and cunning fingers. She has seen much birth and death and love, thought Mrs McKee. That's certain. Well, if her religion was a comfort to her ... The flame lapped a joyous intent face.

Weak sunlight filtered through the north-west window of the church.

Mrs McKee got to her feet. Time to be going. She looked round for Winnie. The girl wasn't there. There was nobody in the church but the old blind woman and herself.

Mrs McKee hurried out into the late sunlight. Really, that girl – Flora was right, there was something quite strange about Winnie, though Mrs McKee liked her very much. And there Winnie was, standing among the sand dunes, a lonely figure against the primrose evening sky. The car was rattling along the shore road towards her. Simon stuck his head out of the window. 'Winnie,' he shouted, 'I caught a jelly-fish.'

Winnie made no answer.

They booked three quite nice rooms in the little hotel in the village. They had a nice dinner too: cockaleekie soup, cold roast venison, with turnips and potatoes and cauliflower, coffee with cheese and biscuits. Winnie said nothing all through the meal. Before the coffee came she excused herself; she had a headache, she thought she would lie down for an hour. If they didn't mind.

'You rest yourself,' said her Uncle Alan. 'That old tin lizzie would give anybody a headache.'

And Winnie, with her freckled serious face, climbed upstairs to the small attic bedroom that the landlord had allocated to her. They did not see her the rest of that night. Mrs McKee peeked in about ten o'clock. Winnie lay in a web of quiet summer shadows. Mrs McKee did not know whether she was asleep or not.

Winnie was quite her old self next morning at the breakfast table. Simon spattered the map with bits of egg-yolk and marmalade in his hurry to see where they would get to that day.

'Close the map,' said Mr McKee. 'I have to be back at my desk the day after tomorrow. We're bound home, my lad.'

At that Simon set up a thin high wail like a quivering bagpipe reed, and Mrs McKee tried to comfort him by saying they were going back a different way; they were taking the road through the Grampians, they would see deer and maybe mountain cats. Still, Simon refused to finish his piece of toast.

While Mr McKee was settling the bill at the reception desk,

they stowed their bags and then themselves into the car. It was another chessboard day. The village and the mountain were smitten with early light, but dark bruises lay on the sea, near and far. Then they heard an outcry down by the boats. At first they could see only a young fisherman with black curly hair. He was pleading in Gaelic at the open door of one of the cottages, turning and pointing occasionally to the rain-squalls in the west. Obviously, in his opinion, it was not a good day for setting lines. A fierce passionate voice answered him from the interior, in Gaelic also. The boy was upset. Certainly he was being addressed in no complimentary terms. He flushed, looked left and right, and his worst fears were confirmed; the whole village was enjoying the harangue. Every door had one or two listeners standing in it. Even the drinkers had come out of the hotel bar, their whisky glasses in their hands. The melancholy stationer peered through his rack of postcards. Every face was turned to this warring house. The young fisherman did the only thing he could do – he walked, pretending he had not a care in the world, down to the rocks where a net was spread. But there was no escape for him. The voice came louder and sharper from the cottage, a fierce enraptured music. Then the accuser herself appeared. Mrs McKee saw with a start that it was the old blind woman that she had seen in the Catholic church. Her shawl was thrown back. She shook her two clenched fists in the direction of the fishing boat. Her voice rose in a passion of scorn and denunciation.

All the men standing in the pub laughed and raised their glasses. It was obviously not the first time they had witnessed this performance. 'Ah, now, that old Seona,' said one of the men to Mr McKee who had just emerged from the hotel, 'she is the great one, though she has no sight. If it wasn't for that old woman not a fish would be caught between here and Ullapool . . .'

The car started up, and turned out of the square. Hands waved to them from every door, and faces smiled. Mrs McKee turned for a last look at this strange village. The handsome young fisherman was sitting on the rock pulling on a long rubber thigh-boot. The old blind woman stood in the cottage door. The rapture was out of her, there was nothing but peace on her face, and she was smoking a clay pipe. Curtains of rain moved in from the Minch. Mrs

McKee saw that Winnie was looking too. Then the car turned a corner and they took the road between the mountains.

They arrived back in Marchmont late that evening, sunburned and tired and happy. Simon was already asleep. They had to lift him out of the car and carry him up the three flights of stairs and lay him down on the couch. Winnie declared that she had never had such a happy time. Never, never, never. Wouldn't the girls in her class at home be envious when she told them all the places she had seen? They would and all.

Mr McKee jerked away on his stick to the Golf Tavern for a pint. He had to wash all that dust and petrol fumes out of his throat, he said. He still had one day's holiday left. He wanted to be away from women's tongues for an hour.

'We're all pleasantly tired,' said Aunt Flora. 'I'll make cups of cocoa and we'll sleep like tops.'

The following Monday morning they saw Winnie off at the Waverley station.

A letter came from her a few days later. 'Dear Uncle Alan and all, thank you for giving me that wonderful holiday. I got home safely. Daddy was standing at Wick station when the train drew in. Is Simon being good? Some day I will tell him the longest loveliest story in the world. Kiss the 23 tram for me. Daddy loved Aunt Flora's shortbread. Dear Aunt Liz, you are the nicest kindest person in this world. The west is full of secrets. The wounded stag will come to the well of healing at last. Love, Winifred.'

'She is a very strange girl,' said Aunt Flora.

And that was the last they ever heard from Winnie. The truth is that they were not very devout letter writers in that family. They exchanged cards at Christmas, of course, and holiday post-cards; but apart from that months went by without any news at all of the north. So, as the years passed, it was only random scraps of information they got about Winifred Melville, generally in notes from her mother.

Winnie was doing quite well at school – her best subjects were Latin and history ... Winnie had passed her school leaving certificate, in October she was going to Aberdeen University ... Winnie got the class medal for English, we are indeed proud of her ... Dear Alan and Elizabeth, you will hear anyway, it is better that you hear from myself. Winnie had a baby boy in April. She refuses to marry the man. We do not even know who he is. She is living with the child in Dumfries ... There is no news of Winnie for more than a year – Wattie and I are broken-hearted ...

'I knew something like that would happen,' said Aunt Flora. 'Poor Phillis. Poor Wattie.'

Ten years had passed since that memorable tour of the West Highlands.

They were seated at the breakfast table one Saturday morning. Alan McKee had been dead for eight years. Simon was in his second last year at the Royal High School, a tall awkward sweet-natured boy. There was little difference in the two ladies; they had a few more steel threads in their hair, a finer-spun reticulation about eyes and mouths. Aunt Flora opened the *Scotsman* and read here and there, her spectacles down near the point of her nose. Mrs McKee gathered all the kipper bones on to one plate.

'Well, I declare,' said Aunt Flora. 'Listen to this. Sit down, Liz. Cross my heart and hope to die. It *must* be her.'

'What on earth are you talking about?' said Mrs McKee.

'Listen,' said Aunt Flora. 'Sit down and listen. It's Winnie Melville.'

It was a book review. Three novels were being reviewed together. Aunt Flora muttered rapidly and inaudibly through the first two tepid notices ... 'I have left the best offering to the end. This is *The Stag at Bay*, by Winifred Melville. One trembles on opening any historical novel by a lady, especially a first novel. This one is different. True, it is about Prince Charles Edward Stuart, but thank the Lord it is not in glorious technicolour; it is woven of strange lights, grey and silver. The prince moves through the story like a spectre, only half-glimpsed; we feel that he is a symbol of all men who are reduced to gnawing the bone of poverty and danger. And yet the royal seal is on him as he stumbles from corrie to hovel. What the novelist wants us to realize is that all men, beside being harried and destitute, are heirs to a kingdom: *homo sapiens* is both immensely poor and immensely rich. Whether she has succeeded is more open to question; that is to say, good though the book is, she is not likely to find many attentive readers in a generation whose sights are firmly fixed on

Science and Progress. It should surprise no one that Miss Melville is a convert to Catholicism. The only treasures that declare themselves to this spectral prince as the danger closes about him he finds in a half-ruined chapel where he and his companions take refuge one sunset: the only water-drops, the altar flame, the hidden heavenly banquet. Yet he cannot feast here either – he has renounced his faith to gain an earthly kingdom. Outside, in the fog, drift the red-coated hunters . . . It is a strange disturbing first book. I look forward with more than the usual eagerness to Winifred Melville's next novel . . .'

'Good for Winnie,' said Mrs McKee.

'Become a Catholic,' said Aunt Flora. 'What's good about that? If you ask me, it's worse than the illegitimate child. Poor Wattie. Poor Phillis.'

I have finished. With these last words of Miss Flora Alder I come to a close. For hers is, thank God, the authentic affirming voice of religious Scotland. What of the other woman who sat that morning at the Marchmont breakfast table, and who now, twelve years later, sits before this tribunal of the elect in a distant island? You will not have failed to observe that during most of my speech she has had a smile about her lips. It was this same woman whose hand plucked an innocent girl out of a Highland rainstorm into – Lord have mercy on this poor Scotland of ours – the abode of The Scarlet Woman.

Timmy Folster lowered his sack of beachcombings against the outside wall and sat down on the window ledge, sweating. It was the hottest afternoon of the summer, so far. He eyed the sack with innocent joy. He longed to untie the string from the neck of the sack; his hands would wander among the sea plunder and he would set it out on the grass in different patterns. But not while Mrs Olive Evie was sitting at the shop door knitting, and all the other women were coming and going. They were all as inquisitive as gulls, the women of Greenvoe. Timmy raised the loaded sack and lowered it into his house through the charred window. He scrambled in after it. Now for it. First he took off his coat and threw it over the bed. He approached the sack shyly, as one might sidle up to a lover. He knelt down beside it. He caressed it for a while, then suddenly he jerked the string from the neck of the sack and peered into the dark hole. He inserted an arm. Two pieces of driftwood that the sea had gnawed blunt and bare; he threw them with a clatter on to the hearth. A book, the pages stuck together: *Lady Jasmine, a Romance,* by the author of *Vernal Lovers.* Timmy laid the sodden thing carefully on top of the range. A glass ball, hollow and green; there weren't many of them now since the fishing boats had stopped using them for floats. Mrs McKee said he was to be sure to bring her any glass balls he found, for her garden. Timmy laid the glass ball carefully on top of his bed. He drew out four great sweeps of tangle, sea phalluses, and set them in the rafters among a score of old shrivelled ones. When he had a hundredweight gathered he would get Mr Evie to send a postcard to the agent in Hamnavoe. Timmy could hardly believe it when the agent told him they made lipstick and table jellies and garters and false teeth and many other things out of these tangles. Such richness is in the sea. The sack rattled; Timmy reached far inside and pulled out handful after handful of whelks. They danced and stotted across his floor. 'Timmy's supper,' he said. The sack was nearly empty now. He burrowed into it like a rabbit and came out with a star fish. It wasn't of any value at all, still it made a bright splash on the dark blue stone of the floor. Timmy sat smiling at it for a while. He had kept the greatest treasure to the end: the sealed bottle. He brought it out and set it on the floor gently. He took his breadknife from the table and scraped away at the wax. Goodness, the cork was driven in tight! Should he ask the loan of a corkscrew from the hotel? No, it would make them all wonder. He attacked the buried cork with his knife, removing fragment after fragment, but very slowly, because the cork was almost as tough as rubber. At last he was through. He applied the bottle to his eye as though it was a telesceope and held it to the light, but the bottle was a deep opaque purple and he could see nothing. He shook it: there was something inside, a movement, a whisper. Carefully, with a bit of wire, Timmy coaxed the contents to the neck of the bottle, inserted his forefinger, and prised out a stained coiled envelope. He ripped it open. Inside was a ten-dollar bill and a letter. 'This bottle with contents was dropped into the North Atlantic Ocean on 12 April 1912 from s.s. *Titanic* on her maiden voyage westward by Cyrus K. Glockenberg 343 Spalding Avenue South, Salt Lake City, Utah, U.S.A. I would be pleased if the finder would send me a note saying when and where the bottle was picked up. It has been a great voyage. We are moving through cold seas now. Last night Mrs Glockenberg and Miss Harriet Glockenberg (daughter) saw the Aurora Borealis. The bill is to cover postage, etc. Thank you.' Timmy folded the ten-dollar bill carefully and put it in a tobacco tin behind the flue. The best one to ask would be Ben Budge, only Ben wasn't well, old Dr Silver from Quoylay had been with him all afternoon. Or maybe Mr McKee the minister. Or The Skarf might do. He didn't want everybody to know about the windfall, that was the thing. Greenvoe was an awful place for gossip. The minister was the most likely to keep it dark. Mr McKee would tell Timmy exactly what to do. He would see him when he went with the glass ball to the manse in the evening.

Timmy was rich and famous. He felt a necessity to celebrate. He fixed his eye on the bottle of methylated spirit. Just one small egg-cupful, what harm was in that? He drew the curtain. The star fish blazed from the floor. Timmy went over to the mantlepiece and took down his egg-cup.

The women stood about the shop door like statues in the early evening light. Time moved round them, a light wind, and occasionally shook a few trite words from their mouths. But mostly they existed within a huge horizon of silence; there, while the stone withers, souls with angels dark and bright negotiate.

'We close at six-thirty,' said Mrs Olive Evie. 'I have such things to do as make my husband's supper. Mr Evie has been away all day at the county council meeting in Kirkwall. He will be coming back at any moment. The ferry-boat will bring him. Something very important has been going on at the county council meeting. I know it. Mr Evie did not sleep all last night, hardly a wink.'

'A tin of syrup, and I have my purse,' said Mrs Ellen Kerston. 'Well, they can say what they like, and maybe he does take a drop too much at times, but Bert Kerston is a good enough fisherman when he puts his mind to it. A whole box of lobsters! There's twenty pounds' worth of lobster in that box if there's a penny. Well, we have our bits of quarrels, everybody knows that, but I was right proud of him today when he came staggering up from the pier not with a load of drink but with a load of sweet blue lobsters. I was that.'

'A packet of safety pins,' said Alice Voar. 'I'm sure as can be that the seed struck home. I know it. You can always tell. Every woman knows. "There are many many ways of doing this beautiful thing together," he said in the darkness, and then he carefully loosened my arms and legs and breasts as though he was a gardener on a fine April morning. He kissed me like rain falling. "Your body is a garden, I am the gardener of love," he said. And then in the cleared soil, deep down, the new root struck and quivered.'

'A half-pound of New Zealand butter,' said Rachel Whaness. 'I am very worried indeed about Samuel. "What does it matter," I told him, "whether you ever catch another fish, we have plenty of money in the bank at Hamnavoe, enough to see our time out, besides what we keep between the pages of *The Pilgrim's Progress*." He would not be comforted, no, and he never touched the warm flour bannocks and the rhubarb jam, though there's nothing he likes better than that for his tea. "It is an evil and a corrupt island," he kept saying, "and the Lord will not suffer Hellya to trouble the sea for long ..." The spirit of my Samuel is troubled with a black cloud.'

Through the still bright air the women could hear boxes and crates being unloaded on to the pier from the ferry-boat. A butterfly drifted into the shop and clung to Alice's finger for a moment before dallying out into the sun again. Mr Joseph Evie in his black Sabbath suit passed the shop window and entered the house by the front door.

'Do you want anything else? The shop shuts at half-past six,' said Mrs Olive Evie to the women. 'I have no New Zealand butter, only Danish. Mr Evie is just back from the county council meeting. He wants his tea. It's twenty to seven.'

Bella Budge stood in the shop door.

'I want two yards of grey flannel,' she said. 'The old doctor from

Quoylay, he's just off. He's going back now in the ferry-boat. I'll
be busy all night tonight at the sewing machine. Ben'll be needing
it before the week-end, I doubt. He's been off Cape Horn all morning, in a hurricane. He kept shouting that the mainmast was
down. Then old Dr Silver put the needle in his arm.'

The desks were littered with shells and wild flowers. Petals had
spilled over on to the floor and were scattered everywhere. It took
Miss Margaret Inverary more than an hour to tidy the classroom
in the evening after she had had her tea. There was only one item
of any interest in all this heaped treasure of sea and land. That
was the Orkney primula, a tiny blue flower that grows in a few
scattered sea hollows only; Johnny Corrigall of Skaill had found it
on top of the North Head. He had cut it out of the salty grass with
a knife, and put it in a matchbox with its root in a clod of the
native soil. Miss Inverary carried the matchbox out to the school
garden. With her trowel she scooped a little hole in the earth. She
fitted the loaded root into the hole and pressed the new soil round
it with her fingers. Johnny Corrigall had won the prize for finding
the primula – two apples from the bowl on the sitting-room sideboard.

Miss Inverary went into the kitchen. She rinsed her fingers
under the cold tap.

She took a book at random from the shelf and wandered slowly
upstairs. Her bedroom was full of luminous shadows, from sea and
sky. It was too early yet to light her tilley lamp. On the other
hand it was too dark to read. Korsfea encroached more and more
over the village, its shadow had fallen on the Budge house and the
hotel and the store. The sea-glitter still wavered on her ceiling and
walls. She took her pyjamas from under the pillow.

She wandered over to the window. Down below, in the village
street, all was quiet. The voice of Alice Voar could be heard, gently
chiding one of her children. 'Thu should been sleeping an hour
ago,' murmured Alice Voar. 'Close thee eyes.' Soon out of the Voar
house came only the muted flutters of several sleeping mouths.

Ben Budge roared once among whelming seas.

A finger of mist curled round the North Head, and the little sheep holm in the bay was suddenly indistinct. The sea fog was silently creeping back. Further out the Sound reflected, ever more brilliantly, the last glories of the day. Miss Inverary sat in the window seat and looked out.

The laird's car shattered the idyll. It careered round the corner of the Budges' house, scattering a cluster of white hens, and rattled to a stop in front of the general store. A light went out at once in the attic window of the hotel. Mr Joseph Evie, still in his dark suit, left his house by the front door and touched his cap in the direction of the driver. Discreetly he entered the back of the car. The laird pressed the rubber bulb of his horn – it was as if the village had farted. A hat and coat and scarf and brief-case – one thrusting fluent articulation – went from hotel to car and relaxed into the seat beside the laird. Then the laird backed the car into the school playground and swung it round. Bella Budge's hens went berserk again. Away the car lurched and rattled into the interior of the island.

The fog laid layer upon layer of gauze across the sea.

Ivan Westray came up the pier, manoeuvring a metal canister of beer towards the hotel, whirling it round and round until the cobbles shrieked; as if he was spinning some enormous top. He did not look in the direction of the schoolhouse. He whirled the great clanking cylinder through the open door of the public bar.

The Skarf crossed over from his cottage to the bar, carrying a long book with a marbled cover. A woollen muffler was wrapped round his neck.

In Quoylay a house was touched by the setting sun and its windows momentarily brimmed with fire; then again the glory passed and it was a small grey cube on a hillside.

Miss Inverary turned from the window towards her bed. She moved, a glimmer, in the wardrobe mirror. She went over to the tilley lamp and pumped it. She struck a match. The lamp hissed and filled her bedroom with hard metallic light: it drowned the sea-gleam on her wall. Miss Inverary abruptly turned the tilley lamp off, and beauty flowed back, muted and evanescent. The mirror was a dark pool now. She turned slowly once more to the bedroom window. She was just in time to see a small cocky figure turning the corner into the hotel: Bert Kerston.

The fog had descended swiftly in the last minute or so; Quoylay was utterly lost. Grey fronds and tentacles groped about the boats moored out in the Sound – the *Siloam*, the *Ellen*, the *Engels*.

A grave voice floated on the evening from the Whaness house. Samuel was reading, as every evening, a chapter from a pious book to Rachel.

On the window ledge stood a paraffin lamp with a green shade. Miss Inverary lit it with great care, and adjusted the wick till the quavering flame was a hard ruby. She did not draw the curtains.

Half-way through her undressing she remembered that of course she had locked the front door. She wrapped the dressing-gown round her and glided downstairs on bare feet. The faint delicious tang of apples had leaked into the hall from the parlour. She turned the snib.

From anywhere in the village it was possible now to see the green glow in the bedroom window of the schoolhouse, even through the drifts of fog.

The sheep holm was suddenly expunged from the sea.

'Simon,' said Mrs McKee, 'where on earth have you been?'

The Rev. Simon McKee stood in the door of the manse kitchen, his arms full of tall dewy spires, lupins. His fair hair was threaded through and through with tiny droplets of fog; even his eyelashes glittered.

'I went for a walk,' said Simon. 'I got stuck in the middle of that old sermon, so I went to the hill. I came on thousands and thousands of these in a hollow. So, says I, I'll bear an armful back to old Liz. Then the fog came down.'

'They're lovely,' said Mrs McKee. 'Two letters for you, one a holiday brochure.'

Mrs McKee ran to the cupboard and brought out a white earthenware pitcher. She half filled it with water from the tap and set it on the kitchen table. Blue petals rained on the floor.

'I was the only living thing in a lost world,' said Simon.

'They're just beautiful,' said Mrs McKee, smiling among the long lupin spears. 'There's plenty left over. We can have some for the church on Sunday. Dry your head with that towel.'

'Once I fell in a ditch,' said Simon, 'right on top of a sheep. You never heard such a mixture of curses and bleats.'

'Old Mr Budge the sailor is ill,' said Mrs McKee. 'Timmy Folster was here with a glass ball he found at the shore. "Don't send the minister round," said poor Timmy, "Ben's an atheist ..." Of course we've always known that. But I could go with a few flowers for Miss Budge.'

'I'm starving, matriarch,' said Simon. 'Have you got any of that stew left?'

Simon's forefinger probed and ripped through an envelope.

Mrs McKee found the green stew-pan at the bottom of the kitchen cupboard and put it on top of the cooker. She hung the flame of a match over the hissing gas.

'Winifred Melville,' she heard Simon say from the living-room. She almost dropped the plate she was carrying.

Simon wandered into the kitchen.

'A letter from Winifred Melville,' he said, 'the cousin that writes novels. Well, I never! She wonders if she can come to Hellya for a holiday with her two kids. She's just finished – let's see what she says – "a new novel and I really feel the need of a change. I'd do my stint in the house – I'm a good cook, I promise you – and I'd pay for the three of us. I remember you well, Simon, the nicest little boy in Scotland ..." Oh Lord, that's going a bit too far. I don't remember her at all. Two kids. Will we have them, madre?'

'She spent a holiday with us in Edinburgh once,' said Mrs McKee. 'In Edinburgh and the west. You were just a child. It was a happy time. Yes, of course they can come.'

Blue petals rained silently over sideboard and carpet.

'He's a writer,' said Mr William Scorradale the landlord. 'Nothing else. That typewriter of his clicks and clacks away from morning to night. He hardly takes time to eat. He must be writing a book about Orkney. That's why he's here.'

'A pint for everybody,' said Bert Kerston. He took a roll of pound notes out of his hip pocket and laid one on the bar counter.

The Skarf licked and thumbed among the pages of his manuscript. Occasionally he stroked out a word or a phrase and wrote something new in the margin. His lips moved silently, testing the euphony.

'Have a pint for yourself,' said Bert Kerston to Bill Scorradale.

Timmy Folster came in.

'How the hell,' said Ivan Westray, 'can a man write a book about a place if all he does is sit on his arse at a typewriter?'

'Give Timmy a pint,' said Bert Kerston. 'I had a good day at the creels.'

The beer tap snorted and drivelled and emitted foam into the empty jug.

'Timmy can wait,' said Timmy Folster. 'Timmy is in no hurry. Timmy would like to show you something, gentlemen.'

'It's the new barrel,' said Bill Scorradale. 'It takes a while for the beer to settle. He went out tonight. The laird came for him in his car. They picked up old Evie. Then they drove off in the direction of the Hall.'

The tap began to vomit tawny gouts into the jug.

'It's coming now,' said Bert Kerston.

'A fat lot he'll learn from two scarecrows like that,' said Ivan Westray. 'If he wants good stuff to put in his book he should go to the likes of Ben Budge.'

The beer began to flow out of the tap in a smooth brown stream.

'Have you ever read a book,' said Timmy Folster, 'called *Lady Jasmine, a Romance*? It's a very good book.'

The Skarf put an asterisk at the end of his day's work and cleared his throat.

'What have you got for us tonight, Skarf?' said Bill Scorradale.

Ivan Westray put down his empty tumbler and made for the door.

'You're not waiting?' said Bill Scorradale. 'The Skarf is just going to read.'

'I have to be up at five in the morning,' said Ivan Westray. 'The lighthouse.'

Ivan Westray walked out, was transfigured to a ghost, was dissolved utterly in the pearly air, though his footsteps echoed more loudly than usual over the cobbles, all the way down to the *Skua*.

Fog eddied and spun and shredded about the door. The bar window was blind.

There was an inch of muddy beer at the bottom of the Skarf's tumbler. He threw it about till it seethed feebly.

'My throat is dry,' he said.

'Give a pint of beer to The Skarf with my compliments,' said Timmy Folster, and laid the ten-dollar bill on the counter. 'The Skarf has always been a good friend to Timmy.'

'What in God's name is this?' said Bill Scorradale. 'Where did you get hold of this?'

But The Skarf had already begun to read:

'Mansie Hellyaman, what news of him, how does he fare now in his quest for light? In the days of Earl Patrick Stewart he fell on evil times, he was humiliated and scourged, he dragged his plough through alien acres like an ox. Yet a flame had been kindled in him that could never go out. Sometimes the flame sank to a glim, to the merest bud of light.

'See him then, see Mansie Hellyaman standing, with a thousand others, round a stake outside St Magnus Kirk in Kirkwall. Tied to the stake is a girl he knows well, Sigrid Tomson; her father is the Hellya blacksmith. A huge masked bare-chested man comes with a torch and kindles the logs round Sigrid Tomson's feet. The crowd screeches with a terrible joy as the flames climb up to her thighs, to her heart, to her throat, to her terrified praying mouth. Her hair is consumed in one russet second. And Mansie Hellyaman, he adds his screech to that dreadful chorus. He believes, with the others — with the sheriff and the minister and the merchants and the fishermen – that the girl is a witch. He believes everything the clerk has read out in the indictment: that she spirited her lover into the darkness; that she blighted the young corn; that she put a curse on cow and stallion; that she lured ships upon the Hellya rocks ... No court today would accept the flimsy evidence on which this girl was convicted. Even in her own day she was reported to be of a rare modesty and innocence – "the lewdest ale-house whispers do not call her maidenhood in doubt" to quote one contemporary letter.

'Mansie Hellyaman shouted with bestial glee as the long smirched skeleton slumped at last among the whispering ashes.

'The flame burned high in him when he sat time and again throughout the eighteenth century on the stool of penitence in the crowded kirk, to be publicly rebuked for, it might be, fornication, or playing football on the Sabbath, or getting drunk at the Hellya horse market, "to the disturbance of the peace and the outraging of the lieges ..." In this way those gloomy men, the minister and the elders, sought to constrict him and restrain him. But Mansie Hellyaman, hemmed in by bigotry, was true in this also to the light; for the man of reason is not an enemy of natural joy. The earth is his and all the goodness thereof. Our mouths are made for kisses and honey and song.

'The flame guttered very low the day that Mansie Hellyaman was seized among his furrows by the press-gang. He knew that there was a state of war between England and France; it seemed there had been for a long time and probably there always would be; but he did not see how it concerned him; he had no quarrel with anyone. Yet the laird and the minister urged him to volunteer; they offered him bounty money, good golden guineas; they described to him the wonders of Africa and the Low Countries. He went back from their cajolings and threatenings to his plough. One winter day a voice summoned him from the end of his rig. He turned. Six uniformed strangers stood all about him, and one held a pistol. He ran from them, he stumbled across the furrows he had just made, he made for the sea caves. All too soon the ropes were round his elbows and he was in the small boat. Voices lamented for a while from the shore; then all he heard was the noise and tumult of the sea. From the deck of the man-of-war he saw Hellya, a distant whale-shape against the sunset.

'How did he manage to keep the precious flame burning in the years that followed? One winter he lay below, listless with scurvy ... He found himself, some time later, in a place of terrible fire and clamour, the sea burning purple and red about the shuddering ships. An iron ball bounced on the deck of the *Imperial* and threw up a fountain of wood splinters. He saw them pouring rum into Lowrie Shetlander; then they held Lowrie down while old Sawbones the surgeon separated the screaming lad from his shattered leg, and a man stood by with a bubbling tar-pot. Then the hellish noise faded. The fleet floated idly, with tattered sails. Body after body, sewn in canvas, was dumped into the North Sea. The chaplain thanked God for a victory on the Glorious First of June.

'The flame all but went out, one summer morning as the great ship dipped idly through Caribbean islands. He had seen the backs of many a sailor scored and furrowed from the lash. The thing they accused Mansie Hellyaman of was an accident; he had turned suddenly to reply to a mate and his elbow knocked the jar of grog out of the bo'sun's hands. A quick accusation, a quick sentence, the stripping and the tricing and the roll of the drums. Did he think of Sigrid Tomson as the lash lapped his body in flame? ... "22 – 23 – 24" ... Branding could not have seared him more terribly. It was finished. The chanted numbers ceased. The drum-roll ceased. They brought to his wounds then a new coarse white flame – salt.

'Peace was signed. Mansie Hellyaman stumbled home again: a bitter-tongued man with a taste for rum. Young women did not care to meet him on the lonely roads. His hand was clumsy with the plough. He refused to set foot in the lobster boats. He lay about the smithy forge winter after winter, telling lies, quick to take offence, cadging a sup of whisky or a plug of tobacco. He was more broken than an otter released from a trap. But, in spite of everything, the flame endured.

'Mansie Hellyaman, grown poor in his over-populated island, decided upon emigration. He herded great tremulous flocks of sheep in Queensland. In the stations at Hudson's Bay he traded for pelts with the Indians. He stood on the verge of a diamond mine near Johannesburg and organized a descent: black men went down into that rich blackness; and went down; and went down; and rose again, and were poor always. He came home again, Mansie Hellyaman, with shares and securities that he gave into the keeping of the Bank at Hamnavoe. It is now the middle of the nineteenth century. He is not a wealthy man, no; but for the first time he knows that there will be bread and cheese in his cupboard the next morning, and every morning till he dies, and his children will not lack a sark to their backs, and he will not lie in a pauper's grave.

'He was caught up in the great dream of agriculture. New methods of farming were being tried out everywhere: enclosures, root crops, the renewal and sweetening of the land with clover. The laird had retired to his Hall, he was not interested in his lands any more, the government had fixed the crofters' rent too low for him, he was glad to sell out wherever he could. Mansie Hellyaman bought up three old crofts cheap – three crofts that had been worked brutishly for a thousand years to keep a piece of bread and a bowl of ale on the table – and he knocked them into one decent-sized farm. He had a pair of horses, a dozen cows, a hundred sheep, a servant man, a boat and a cart. And besides that he owned two houses, one in Kirkwall and one in Hamnavoe, that he rented out to townsfolk. And he had a share in a smack that traded as far as Newcastle. And every year the banker sent him a statement that assured him he had more money than the year before. Mansie Hellyaman was a capitalist now. The crude lamp of feudalism was broken at last. He lived according to another light ...'

'Time, gentlemen,' said Bill Scorradale.

The stable at the Bu farm.

> *The Lord of the Harvest. The Master Horsemen. The Novice who has attained the degree of Reaper. He is blindfolded. He wears a yellow shirt; one shoulder is bare and livid. The sacred sign of agriculture, the horse-shoe, is in his hand.*

THE LORD OF THE HARVEST: We have come to the station of THE YELLOW CORN. What are you seeking here, Reaper among the master horsemen?

REAPER: A kingdom.

THE LORD OF THE HARVEST: The crofter with wife and son and daughters – gleaners, they stoop after his scythings – what does such a poor man know of a kingdom? Were it not good for him indeed to bide in the humble station whereunto he had been called – to labour awhile under the sun and then to die?

REAPER: Our arms overflow with barley and oats, earth treasure, a rich abundant surety.

THE LORD OF THE HARVEST: What hinders you from the place?

REAPER: Blindness. Wounds. But I have heard an utterance of

wind in the corn. I have half understood that word. Tell me what I must thole now?

(Silence)

THE LORD OF THE HARVEST: Death.

(Silence)

THE LORD OF THE HARVEST: Not the kindly death of candles. Thy bones must be broken with flails in the barn.

REAPER: No.

THE LORD OF THE HARVEST: I speak of the death of circling millstones.

REAPER: No.

THE LORD OF THE HARVEST: And of the death of twisting flames.

REAPER: No.

THE LORD OF THE HARVEST: Through these gates your road goes. I do not know what is at the end of it. Are you willing to thole it?

REAPER: *(Does not answer.)*

THE MASTER HORSEMEN: Answer. Answer, Answer.

REAPER: *(whispering)* I am willing.

> *(The Master Horsemen stand about the Reaper with flails and querns and burnt stones. The lantern is put out at the wall. There is a long silence, then a single cry in the darkness.)*

THE LORD OF THE HARVEST: It is finished. He is gone from the trampling of hooves. He has entered into the stone and the fire.

FIVE

Sometimes the fog thinned out and then Inga could see the loom of the lighthouse. The fog-horn blared from its base at half-minute intervals, like a bull in passion. Hellya was buried behind them in wet shifting silent masses, but the sea under the Black Head of Quoylay shone like scraped pewter. The lighthouse vanished again. Ivan Westray turned the wheel.

'Don't fret,' he said, 'I know this sea like the back of my hand.'

There was a different sound in the sea now, a plangent wash, a scurry of wave-drawn pebbles. A blackbird sang out of a bush.

'That rock is called The Widow,' said Ivan Westray. 'You can ask yourself why.'

The Widow emerged athwart them, a black bowed mass. Ivan Westray shut off the engine. The *Skua* glided through a quiet stretch of water. He picked up a coil of rope and flung it into the blind morning. A hidden voice shouted, 'Got her.' A rubber-tyre fender on the *Skua* bumped against a wall of concrete. A young man stooped over them, lowered a knotted tattooed arm, swung first Ivan Westray on to the pier and then – with more difficulty, as if he was manoeuvring a heavy butterfly – Inga. She stood on the pier, gasping and laughing. Another older lighthouse-keeper joined them.

'I didn't think we'd see you today, Westray,' he said. 'Come up for a mug of coffee. Who's the young lady?'

The lighthouse towered above them. How small it seemed from Hellya, like a stick of new chalk on the horizon. It was immense. It was a bit frightening.

The fog-horn blorted. It blocked out chunks of their conversation. A gull swung in a long plane athwart them, then its flight collapsed in screams over the lap of The Widow.

'Better get the stuff unloaded first,' said Ivan Westray. 'I don't want to wait too long. The fog might thicken. Where iss Tonald?'

'In his bunk,' said the principal keeper. 'He was on watch all night.'

Ivan Westray lowered himself down into the boat again and began to shift boxes and drums.

'You come up to the kitchen,' said the light-keeper with the tattooed arms to Inga. 'You're bound to be cold. There's a cup of coffee.'

The fog-horn enveloped them in its blare.

At half-past eight, as every morning, a sudden hullabaloo broke out simultaneously in two Greenvoe houses: the Kerstons' and the Voars'. The children were being got ready for school. There were smacks, screams, choruses of laughter, one aria of passionate rage.

'You little bitch,' cried Ellen Kerston, 'that's the second plate of porridge you've knocked over this week. Tom, you wash first – Judy, wash his knees for him. Ernie, you run round and ask Rachel can she spare a cup of milk. I told you the porridge was hot. Your sock's inside out, Judy . . .'

Ellen stirred the black porridge pot with a wooden spoon.

'Now then, Sidney,' said Alice Voar, 'button your coat up to the neck, it's a damp day. No, it isn't a ghost at the window at all, it's fog – you bide in, peedie Skarf. Put your jotter under your coat, Sophie. No lollipops, mind, Sander, that shilling's for the school milk.'

Alice cut three more slices from the loaf on the table. Their washed faces were barred already with syrup and crumbs. Alice dipped the cloth in the soapy water once more, over another grimy sleepy whining face, and sighed.

The two cottages wailed, murmured, screamed, chortled.

Bert Kerston emerged from the hubbub into the silver blind silent morning, and crossed the road to the pier.

Some children from the farms lingered idly about the school playground. Miss Inverary appeared at the door and agitated her bell. The country children turned in the direction of the sounding bronze. They seemed like creatures summoned out of a dream. Miss Inverary disappeared inside. A hubbub broke out in the village. The dream-walkers were overtaken by a rout of berserkers, the village children. They swirled together in the threshold, a loud tight knot.

'Please, miss,' whispered Judy Kerston at the teacher's desk.

'Well, Judy,' said Miss Inverary.

'Please miss,' said Judy, 'Mary broke her porridge bowl.'

Nobody knew yet.

Bella Budge scattered the last handful of oats to the hens. They strutted and glared and scavenged among the grass blades and between the flagstones. Their feathers were damp.

Nobody knew but Bella.

What did you do with a dead man? What were the duties of the living towards the dead? It was a long time, twenty years since Bella had performed these black ceremonies. Half an hour before, when Ben had gagged on his last breath, she had been uncertain.

'You get strength from somewhere,' the old women had wailed in every death-house when Bella was a girl (and that wasn't yesterday) – 'the Lord gives you strength to bear it.' Then they would set about the shrouding, while the widow sat, important and weeping and black and useless, in the high chair beside the fire.

Bella would do it all herself. She didn't want them interfering: that wicked Evie woman, and Alice Voar with her overflowing face and heart, and Rachel with her harps and fires, and that loud Ellen Kerston. Thank goodness they didn't know yet. She had comforted Ben when he was a peedie boy – he was five years younger than Bella – the times he fell and cut his knees on the road, or had toothache, or his pigeon flew away. So she alone would give him this last comfort.

She bent over the shape in the bed.

Ben had been five years younger than Bella but now this very ancient wisdom was graven on his face; she felt like a girl in the presence of a stone idol. Ben lay there very old, very remote, very strange.

An ancient answering wisdom rose through her as she looked at him. Of course she knew what to do. The voice of the first elegaic woman in the island, a dweller in a stone place, murmured to her mildly.

She took the zinc bucket from the corner of the lobby and went out to the pump, and filled the bucket with water. Fog rolled heavily through the hills.

Yes, and the times Ben came home from sea and he hadn't a ha'penny because he had spent it all in Glasgow or in South Shields on drink, Bella had taken out her stone jar of egg-money and given him a shilling or two to get tobacco; because Ben was her brother and also because he was the only man she had ever greatly cared for. She had liked Ben better than she had liked her father Aaron Budge the miller. She had liked Ben better even than her sister Aggie's boy Tom in Vancouver, though she liked Tom very much too. Ben had cursed and sworn a lot, but still she had liked him, if that was possible, better than herself.

She set the clanking pail on the stone floor beside the bed, and cut a piece of flannel out of a remnant from the shroud.

She got the mortal clothes off Ben without too much trouble – the shirt and semmit and woollen drawers – because he was light and the suppleness of life had not yet gone out of him. Then she began to wash the body. It was not the first time she had washed Ben. Every Christmas Eve when he was a small boy she and her mother would wash him all over in front of the open peat fire: so that if the Lord came to the byre next the Mill House that night to be born, Ben would be clean to welcome him. And in the hot summer days, when they both had the task of keeping the Hall cattle out of the corn, and the sun burned through their thick woollen shirts, Bella would take Ben's clothes off and he would jump up and down in the cold burn, laughing half in panic and half in joy, till she coaxed him out again and let him run about in the sun to dry.

Bella put the water of death on Ben, and she dried him with a new towel. A small boy, a very ancient stone idol, and here between the rum-smelling corpse of Ben.

Bella put the death shirt on him then.

Ben was utterly amazed at his new state; he stared back into time with wide eyes and his jaw fallen open. Bella had taken him once to the Lammas Market at Hamnavoe, when Ben was six years old. Their mother had given them a shilling each to spend. And Ben had been enraptured by everything he saw: by the coconut shies, by the swing-boats, by the shooting galleries, by the fruit stall with its oranges and apples and pears and sweetie-jars, by the goldfish, by the blind fiddler who wandered through the crowd making a path for himself with his flashing music. Then they had stopped at the tent of the Prince of the Congo. An immense Negro draped in a leopard skin stood on a box; he chuckled to himself like a pot of boiling tar. A small man with a waxed moustache and a cigar was urging the people to enter the booth, one shilling a time, to see the imminent performance by the Black Prince. A brazier of coals burned beside the tent flap, with a poker stuck in it. All at once the little man plucked the poker out of the fire and handed it to the masker. He seized it, rolled his eyes round the crowd, and licked the white-hot poker twice with his tongue. 'Sugar,' he said, 'sugar.' . . . And peedie Ben had stood there and gaped at him as if he could never take his eyes away.

Now he looked into a much greater mystery.

'That's enough, Ben,' said Bella. She pressed his eyes shut. She bound up his jaw with a strip of flannel. Then Ben seemed to be more at ease with his new state.

He seemed to be almost complacent, like a Kirkwall merchant on a market day, when she folded his hands across his chest. The corners of his mouth turned up in a slow acquiescent smile.

The blessing of peace was on Ben's mouth. There would be no more of that cursing and swearing out of it – all the oaths he had picked up on every waterfront of the world – Shanghai, Bombay, Liverpool, Boston. Bella remembered the first bad word of all. That was when their father and mother were still alive and Ben had come home after his first trip to Australia. Ben was seventeen at the time. (Aggie had been away from home a year, married to Rob Groat the servant man at the Hall.) He was a different Ben altogether from the shy boy they had seen off from Hamnavoe pier – for he had black hairs on his lip now and he spoke in a queer rolling accent. And when he tucked up his sleeve to sup his porridge they saw a blue drawing on his wrist – a winged heart with

'Mother' scrolled inside it in scarlet. The trouble flared up that first evening. Ben said he was going trout-fishing in the loch next morning. Was the rod still where it used to be, lying across the rafters of the mill? Yes, said his father mildly, but it would be a bright day – he could tell by the look of the sunset clouds and the airt of the wind – not much of a day for fishing with all that dazzle on the surface. 'I don't give a bugger,' Ben said, 'I'm going to have a try.' Aaron Budge struck Ben on the mouth. 'You will not use language like that in this house,' he said. Ben had fallen on the floor, as much with shock as with the force of the blow. The old rheumaticky miller seized his stick that hung by the crook from his chair. He struck Ben over the shoulders. 'Never. Never. Never,' he said, 'such language, so long as I am the master in this house.' The mother stood motionless and speechless with terror beside the door. The daughter came between the father and the son; she beseeched; she seized the descending stick till it hung quivering in the air six inches above Ben's cowering shoulder. Ben picked himself up and went outside. The miller hobbled back to his chair and filled his pipe. The women moved between hearth and cupboard and table, mutely preparing the supper. There was not a word spoken in the house that night. Ben returned from the village an hour before midnight. 'I am sorry for using bad language in this house,' he said. The mother crept away silently to her room; she was too old for such rage and violence. Bella lingered behind, in case things should flare up again. 'Sit down, boy,' said the old man. Ben laid a full bottle of rum on the table and sat down on the opposite side of the fire. 'This is a present for thee, Daddo,' he said. He spoke in the old island way, and all the coarse slang of the fo'c'sle was absent from his voice. 'Bring two glasses, lass,' said the miller. Bella went off to her bed as soon as he had laid the glasses on the table, for now she knew there would be no more fighting. When her father drank he was a happy man. Next morning the empty bottle stood on the table, and two sticky sweet-smelling glasses. And Ben went to the loch after breakfast, but he caught no trout.

Two winters later their father was dead. They had to move out of the Mill House, to make room for a new miller. The mother and the daughter found a cottage called Biggings to rent in the village, with a little field in front of it where their hens could run and their geese march. They were happy enough there. One night of March there came a passionate thundering at the door, just when they were getting ready for bed, and a wild outlandish cry. Bella went to the window and peered out. It was a stranger with a black beard and a canvas bag over his shoulder. But the stance was familiar, and the tilt of the head. She opened the door for Ben the sailor.

He folded first the sister and then the mother in his arms. He sat down on top of the bed for five minutes without saying anything. Bella ran to hang the kettle over the peat-fire, and set the teapot on the hearth to warm.

'I went to the mill,' said Ben. 'I went to the goddam mill. Who opened the door but Cheesy Spence of Rambister? He told me. It was like he had taken a goddam baton and smashed it down on my skull. He told me about Daddo. Then he told me where you were living.'

His eyes glittered and his cheeks were wet.

The old woman motioned him over to the deep straw chair beside the fire where Aaron Budge the miller had always sat. Ben – though he came home only once in a while – was master of the house now.

'Some goddam landfall,' said Ben.

There was no one to reprove him for cursing and swearing that night, or ever after. But now the blessing of silence was on his lips.

Bella felt the need of light. There should be candles set about the house. Ben was at the beginning of a long journey: and everything was strange to him: and he was groping in the first darkness of death. There should be one candle at least, set on the bedside table.

She turned and there in the door stood Timmy Folster. 'Timmy is sorry about Ben,' he said.

Two or three others came in quietly. Bella roofed her eyes with the edge of her hand and peered out at the intruders – it was Joseph Evie and William Scorradale from the hotel. They looked foolish and embarrassed. They muttered things that Bella couldn't understand. She wished they would go away. She and Ben had been quite happy together these past two hours.

More shapes loomed through the door, carrying a dampness with them: Rachel Whaness, Alice Voar, Ellen Kerston. Rachel had a bunch of bluebells. She filled the stone jar on the mantelpiece with some death-water from the bucket and arranged the bluebells in it.

'He looks that bonny,' said Alice Voar.

Ellen Kerston did nothing but shake. She laid her head in her hands and every now and then a quake went through her. She lifted her head from her hands and her face quivered and brimmed over. It was too much. She returned her mourning head into the keeping of her hands.

A face appeared at the window. It was The Skarf. He raised his clenched fist in a silent salute towards the dead worker on the bed and went away.

'If only we had known,' wailed Ellen Kerston at last, 'we would have sat up with him last night. If only we had known he was going to be taken so soon.'

'I managed fine,' said Bella calmly. 'Ben and me, we managed fine by ourselves.'

Mr Joseph Evie cleared his throat.

'Bella,' he said, 'one or two things will have to be attended to. The death certificate will have to be signed by Dr Silver. He was here yesterday, so that'll be all right. I'll see to everything, don't you worry. I'm the registrar myself so there'll be no difficulty about that. Could you say just exactly when Ben, eh, passed away? That needs to be entered. Oh well, it doesn't matter. His date of birth 'll be in the big Bible. Then there's the undertaker, that's Andrew Hoy of Rossiter. And the gravedigger, of course, that's Samuel Whaness. I'll fix all that. There's also the matter of his Old Age Pension. Now, I'm sure you'd like me to send a cablegram to Tom in Vancouver, if you let me have his address.'

'If you like,' said Bella. 'Ben's just done writing to him.'

People moved from the door, making way for a new arrival. It was the minister, the Rev. Simon McKee. He made his way through the sobs and the lugubriousness.

'Good for Ben,' he said. 'Good for Ben. He's off on his last voyage. He'll be all right, old Ben.'

'It's dark for him,' said Bella.

Simon McKee kissed her withered cheek.

'Dark, yes,' he said. 'For a watch or two. But he's sailing into the sunrise, old Ben.'

He turned towards the quiet shape on the bed.

'Go in peace, old sailor,' said Simon McKee. 'The anchor's up.'

Samuel Whaness shut off the engine and let the *Siloam* drift blindly. The ebb-tide was taking them in a westerly direction, that was all he knew. It was a piece of nonsense ever to put out in such a fog, but he was determined to raise the score of creels he had under the Red Head before that thief Kerston got to them. The sea swirled rapidly about the boat – not an easy careless toss of waters but the slumbrous silence of the ebb in full spate, glazed and pitted with whorls, emptying itself into the open Atlantic like a great river, and taking the *Siloam* with it.

At times Samuel could see nothing at all outside the grey dome in which he was confined, and the rapid floor to it, the Sound of Hellya. Then a corner of the dome would silently collapse, and a muted brightness filter through, and shift about before the solid wall of the dome was rebuilt. For one fleeting second that morning the veil of the temple was torn, and through the dazzling rent Samuel saw the Skerries lighthouse three miles away, and the sun hurrying across a shredded tissue of fog. Then the dome reestablished itself more solidly than ever.

The *Siloam* began to rock and plunge. The slow ponderous swell from the west, the Atlantic beat, was meshed here with the rapid ebb, and the floor of the dome was all echo and confusion. Samuel steadied himself against the thwart. He bent down and jerked his shoulder and swung the engine into life. The Red Head lay a mile and a half to port. The *Siloam* lurched out of the tumultuous meeting of the waters. A deluge of spray burst over the straining hull and slashed into Samuel's face. He blinked and turned the tiller away from him. In half a minute the boat was out of the tide, and was shouldering into the open sea, the slow ponderous onset of the Atlantic. Far off, beyond the dome that imprisoned him, Samuel could hear a confused thunder, the waves breaking on the crags.

He opened the throttle. The *Siloam* rode the sea well, ettling and champing and flinging the spray from her; and it was centred always in that small confining igloo of fog. 'There is no confinement,' said Samuel, 'we are enclosed in the mercy and providence of the Lord.' And long thrills of joy went through the *Siloam* as she opposed the eastward march of the waves.

A segment of the dome collapsed on the port side. Out of the pearly light loomed, all at once, immense and threatening, the western crags. Then the mist washed again across their faces. But Samuel saw, dancing now in the double gloom of crags and fog, the first of his markers. He circled it slowly and hauled the creel aboard. A huge lobster, a two-pounder, scrabbled inside the net. Samuel drew it out and tied the clashing pincers with elastic. Carefully he stowed it into the lobster box.

He had a good catch this morning. Nearly every creel had its lobster. In one creel two, barnacled and blue-armoured, were locked in a death grapple. Samuel disentangled them and stowed them away, one after the other, in the box. He turned the *Siloam* in the direction of his last creel of the score he had set here five days previously; it was right at the base of the Head. Samuel could see the kittiwakes sitting on the cliff edges in vigilant rows. They watched him with utter indifference

The inshore waves were huge. They gathered themselves in curling crested ranks along the shallow floor before flinging themselves against the rocks and cliff bases in diagonal dazzling thunderous prolonged death.

Samuel located his red float in two fathoms. He hauled the creel in. He had trouble keeping his feet in all that turbulence. There was a small lobster inside, a half-pounder.

Then the sea flung the *Siloam* at the crags.

Samuel, the small lobster still in his hand, was looking into the cold eye of a kittiwake. He saw a clump of seapinks in an interstice of the crag; he could have reached out his other hand and plucked one. He was falling now, the boat still under him, and it was all curious and dreamlike. Boat and man fell in a slow parabola against the cliff. From a ledge the bones of a sheep rose to meet him. Samuel considered that the sheep must have fallen over the cliff the previous winter, but perhaps the skeleton was very ancient. He heard, among the sea noises, a crunching and splintering of wood.

The grey dome collapsed utterly. Samuel was resting instead under a dome of crystal, of purest light. Joy flooded all his veins. Why had he held back so long? He rose to his feet. From near and far, through all the aisles and bays of the temple, came sweet sacred music. When Samuel tried to walk his feet moved in a solemn dance. Silent presences came and ministered to him in that place. They pointed with silver hands the way that he should go. Surrounded by these he set out, smiling, to discover the habitations of the saints.

Judy Kerston clapped her hands. She screwed up her face till her eyes were little slits of delight. She whispered to Phyllis Anderson who shared the desk with her, 'A story!' Phyllis Anderson smiled back at her. For Miss Inverary was going to tell them a story. Instead of that horrible geography that they had expected – the map of Scotland unrolled and hung over the blackboard, and all the towns with the names that made you laugh in a way, they sounded so funny (Motherwell, Wishaw, Airdrie, Coatbridge) – Miss Inverary said that instead of that she was going to tell them a story. 'Charles Brown, take that chewing gum out of your mouth, come out to the floor, put it in the waste-paper basket, now return to your seat. Chewing gum is a very filthy habit ... Gino, put more coal on the fire ... Judy Kerston, when you have quite stopped whispering to Phyllis Anderson, I'll begin ...' A score of hostile eyes looked round at Judy Kerston ... 'Yes, Sidney Voar, you may leave the room if you have to, but you'll miss the beginning of the story ...

'Once upon a time there was a little princess in Norway. Her name was Margaret. One day her father the king said to Margaret, "Margaret, messengers have come to Norway from the King of Scotland. The King of Scotland has a son. You must go to Scotland and marry that prince. Then some day you will be Queen of Scotland ..." The little princess wept because she didn't want to leave the palace in Norway where she was so happy with her swans and her little reindeer. But the king said, "Here is a picture of the prince, look at it, the King of Scotland sent it to me so that you could see his face." Margaret had never seen such a handsome prince, with his long fair hair and blue eyes and red mouth, and his suit of golden armour that shone on him as bright as the sun. Then she was very eager to sail to Scotland and become the wife of that handsome prince. A ship was got ready to carry her across the North Sea. The little princess put the picture of the prince in her bosom. She went aboard to the sound of trumpets. The ship weighed anchor and the silken sails were hoisted. The king waved her farewell from the castle battlements.

'Now that King of Norway had a great enemy, a wicked witch who had power over sea and wind. The witch's name was Inga. This witch decided that she could hurt the king most by destroying his daughter, the Princess Margaret. She was such a very cruel witch that, though she could have drowned Margaret in the sea at once, she plotted to make the death of the princess long and hard. So in her hovel on the side of the mountain she stirred a pot of water in all directions with a wooden spoon, and as soon as she did that the North Sea became very rough and Margaret was seasick. Then the witch Inga blew with her bellows into the pot of water till it frothed and boiled, and when she did that the ship was tossed here and there with terrible gales, so that the poor little princess lay in her bunk and could neither eat nor sleep. She grew pale as a candle. Day after day the terrible storm continued. When the storm grew calm at last, this witch flung a live peat into the cauldron of water till it hissed and was full of steam, and then the ship was lost for a whole week in dense fogs. At last the fog lifted. The captain of the ship sighted islands in the west. "Thank God," he said, "we will reach land soon. These are the Orkney Islands ..." Word was brought to the cabin where the princess lay that a harbour was in sight. But it was too late. Margaret lay dying on her silk pillow. They carried her ashore to a little fishing village beside the sea. "I am very hungry," she said, "I would love to eat an apple." But when her handmaid came with a bowl of apples to her she could not eat one. "I hope my prince will come soon and we will be married," she said. These were her last words. It was not the prince that came but first a doctor and then a priest and finally the gravedigger.

'The Prince of Scotland stood in his golden armour on a high cliff watching the sea. He was waiting for the ship to come from the east with his bride. But it never came. Never never never.

'They call the village where the little princess died "Saint Margaret's Hope" to this day. It is in the island of South Ronaldsay.'

Shirley Voar began to sob bitterly.

'There there,' said Miss Inverary. 'It was only a story. There. I've wiped your eyes. Smile.'

'Please, miss,' said Judy Kerston, 'did they live happy ever after?'

'The princess was drowned,' said Johnny Corrigall.

'Please, miss,' said Mary Brown, 'maybe she only pretended to be drowned.'

'Maybe, please miss,' said Phyllis Anderson, 'the prince kissed her and then she came back to life.'

'Please, miss,' said Sidney Voar, 'I know the name of the prince.'

'Do you?' said Miss Inverary. 'John Corrigall, drape the map of Scotland over the blackboard.'

'Please, miss, Ivan,' said Sidney Voar.

Inga followed the young light-keeper up the endless stone spiral, round and round. Radiance showered on them from above. They climbed towards it; the light-keeper a few steps ahead of her.

Inga looked up at a transfigured creature. Light blazed all about him. He stood looking down at her, holding on to an iron rail, beaten about with splendour. She stood beside him at last, panting.

They moved in a brilliant glass bubble.

Inga looked around. The sun beat down on them from a cloudless sky. It was very hot in the dome. Below lay an infinity of wool, dense and shining.

Here and there the fog opened in frightening chasms; Inga's head swam looking into them. Once it split completely open, and she could see for a moment the western cliffs of Hellya in diffused sunlight, and a little fishing boat under the Red Head. It was the silence of it all that was so unnerving. Her head swam again; she had to take a firm grip of the green-painted railing.

The fog washed silently against the base of the lighthouse.

'Look here,' said the young light-keeper.

At the core of the tower he pointed out the lamp: an oil lamp with a mantle and burner. How on earth could such an insignificant thing – that might do all right for a farm kitchen – keep ships off the rocks, and guide them the way they were going winter after winter?

The horn blorted beneath them.

'In a westerly gale,' the light-keeper said, 'the tower sways like a tulip.'

Inga looked down on the scrap of skerry below them, and the grey cube of the pier. The fog had withdrawn a bit. A tarnish of sun licked the rock. Two small figures were busy about a scatter of boxes and cylinders on the pier. Ivan Westray was helping the principal keeper to load boxes on to a hand-barrow. A cauldron of mist boiled over the scene. The two men were ghosts once more.

The horn roared like a bull in torment.

They left the brilliant bubble and descended into a slotted twilight, going round and round. Half-way down he put his thick blue-scrawled arm round her shoulder. He stopped, and his breath came unevenly.

Inga offered him a cold cheek.

Then they went on down, round and round, into the well of darkness, one after the other. A marvellous smell of frying bacon rose to meet them.

The horn blorted.

On the last turn of the spiral the light-keeper turned to Inga and said, 'I suppose you think you're too good for the likes of me, you with a posh accent like that.'

They moved towards a sudden clatter of plates, and the sound of men's voices, and the deep bass laughter of Ivan Westray.

They had all gone, except Mrs Olive Evie, to the house of mourning. 'What hypocrisy,' thought Mrs Olive Evie, 'a filthy-tongued old man like that.' All pretending they were sorry. Well, she wasn't sorry, except she didn't see how she was to get rid of the pound box of bogey roll that he alone in the island used to smoke at the rate of two ounces a week. Maybe the wholesaler in Kirkwall would take the tin back. She hoped so.

Mrs Olive Evie sat behind the counter, and pondered.

Mrs Olive Evie took down a new writing pad from the pile of writing pads on the shelf. (And that was another thing, old Budge had used up a writing pad every week to write to that waster of a nephew of theirs in Canada. Bella Budge would come in for a writing pad every Monday morning, when she drew the Old Age Pension for them both. But there was only fourpence profit on a cheap writing pad like that.) Mrs Olive Evie considered that it was a good opportunity, when they were all away parading their grief in Biggings, to write some letters that she had been meaning to write for some time.

Fog bowed over the threshold, touched a card of clothes-pegs with a spectral finger, withdrew.

Mrs Olive Evie wrote the first letter: 'To the Director of Education.

'Dear Sir – It will be of some interest to you that your teacher in Greenvoe, Hellya, Miss Inverary, is carrying on to a scandalous extent with the island boatman, a person of bad character. He was seen leaving the schoolhouse in the early hours of one morning. Is this a fit person to be in charge of the innocent children of Greenvoe? Yours faithfully, A Friend.'

Mrs Olive Evie folded the letter and slid it into an envelope and addressed the envelope in block letters.

Mrs Olive Evie then wrote her second letter: 'To the Moderator, Orkney Presbytery, Church of Scotland.

'Rev. Sir – I am sorry to say that your incumbent in Greenvoe, Hellya, is drinking to such an extent that it is bringing the cloth into disrepute. He is drinking whisky in his study in secret under the pretext of curing an imaginary cold sustained by his mother. Is this a fit person to have the cure of souls in this island? Yours faithfully, A Shepherdless Sheep.'

Mrs Olive Evie folded the letter and slid it into an envelope and addressed the envelope in block capitals.

Mrs Olive Evie then wrote her third letter: 'To the Manager, National Assistance.

'Dear Sir – To one like yourself who has the disbursing of public funds for the relief of poverty, it may be of interest that one of your beneficiaries Timothy John Folster of Greenvoe spends most of his relief money on methylated spirit for purposes of refreshment. Keir Hardie and Lloyd George did not intend this. Yours faithfully, Pro Bono Publico.'

Mrs Olive Evie folded the letter and slid it into an envelope and addressed the envelope in block capitals.

Mrs Olive Evie then wrote her fourth letter 'To the Lord-Lieutenant.

'Sir, I wish to bring to your notice a crying shame, the case of a man devoting his whole life to the service of the people of the island where he resides and never receiving recognition in the Queen's honours. A man like that is entitled to the O.B.E., the C.B.E., or the B.E.M. Others of far less account have been summoned to Holyrood Palace. He is county councillor, church elder, registrar, justice of the peace, in short, a pillar of society and a good friend to the needy, and a person of the highest integrity. He wears out his life for the people here. I refer to Joseph Evie, General Merchant, Greenvoe, Hellya, Orkney. I think I am only speaking for the entire community in beseeching you to bring this letter to the notice of whom it may concern. Yours faithfully, Housewife.'

Mrs Olive Evie folded the letter and slid it into an envelope and addressed it in block capitals.

There were shouts and cries from across the road, then a stern muted admonition, *Be quiet, old Mr Budge has passed away*, then a scatter of feet. A troop of ghosts ran past the door of the shop. School was out; it was the dinner hour.

Mrs Olive Evie wet the inside flaps of the envelopes, four hot lollops of her tongue, and banged them shut with her fist on the counter, one after the other.

She searched inside Mr Joseph Evie's desk – the post-office compartment – for the sheet of stamps.

Judy Kerston came in for a lollipop.

The prosecutor stirred at the edge of the shadows. He stood up and shuffled his papers. Mrs McKee knew him; he was the one she disliked most of all. He was the one she could imagine most clearly (though his figure was always in shadow): the hunch of shoulders, the bull-neck thrust forward, the thick brutish mobile mouth. What made him even more distasteful to her was his knack of imitating all these dear voices out of the past; he had every little shade and lilt and intonation off to perfection. 'He should have been an actor, not an advocate at all,' Mrs McKee thought resentfully. He began.

'The lady has kept the court waiting again today. So be it. We are in no hurry. The gravity of the case is not altered thereby. It will and it must be answered in full, however long it takes. All this shameful and dolorous business will be sieved to the last grain.

'I want you to imagine a little boy, ten years old, in a sick-bed. He is just recovering from that rather serious disease of childhood, measles. He has always been a delicate boy, and so the symptoms – the fever, the sickness, the insomnia – are particularly marked in his case. Also he is taking longer to recover than the other boys in the tenement who have been smitten about the same time – for example, Tommy MacIndoe. His eyesight is affected; he cannot bear the light coming through the window; he will have to live in a world of shadows for a week or two yet, until he is more or less fully recovered. Also he has been troubled these past two days with an agonizing earache. But he is a brave child. He only whimpers into his pillow when his nurses are out of the room. When they sit at his bedside, reading *Coral Island* and *Eric, or, Little by Little* to him, he listens attentively, his white strained face propped up by pillows. In the street, far below, the traffic of Edinburgh ebbs and flows, and the recovered children call to each other.

'More than the inevitable ills of childhood is troubling this small boy. He has not yet recovered from a severe psychological shock, the death of his father six months before. True, in the family in general this death was not wholly unexpected. The father had been severely wounded in the First World War, at the Battle of the Somme. He had returned home at the end of hostilities; he had taken up his duties (he was a clerk in a firm of chartered accountants) at the same desk which he had vacated for sake of his country three years previously. The wounds were in his thigh and hip; he had been left with a permanent limp; and frequently he had to undergo hospitalization in the Royal Infirmary of Edinburgh for the alleviation (always temporary, alas) of the recurring pain and discomfort. Yet, in spite of all that, he was able to do a good day's work at the office. He enjoyed his life: his home and family, his friends, his club, his few holes of golf on Bruntsfield Links on a summer evening, a glass of beer afterwards in the adjacent Gold Tavern. Especially, perhaps, he was devoted to his only son: this clever, nervous, delicate child. They played chess together in the winter evenings. The boy listened open-mouthed to the stories he told of the western front; until his mother would come in and say, "Now, now Alan, that's enough. The boy won't sleep a wink tonight, with all this excitement. I believe you British were quite as bad as the Germans, anyway. It's time for your bath, Simon . . ." And the boy would go, with one last adoring look at his wounded father, the hero. Suddenly one Saturday morning when Simon was just ten, his father collapsed and died on the street, coming back from the newspaper shop with his copy of the *Scotsman*. The boy, standing at the wellhead of the tenement, saw a shape covered with a coat being manoeuvred and jerked up the angles of the stair by Mr McIndoe from the ground floor, and the postman, and Mr Blair the stationer. His mother took him by the shoulder and led him, sobbing wildly and distractedly, to his bedroom. He knew, without being told, that his father had gone from him for ever. He had followed all the other Somme heroes into the darkness.

'And now this same boy lies here, slowly recuperating from measles. What can they do, his mother and aunt, to make him better quickly, so that he can get back to his school, the Royal High, and catch up on his studies? They try him with fruit – oranges and grapes and apples; he peels them listlessly, takes a few bites, throws the half-finished pulp into the waste-paper basket. "Mother, please will you and Aunty Flora not speak so loud, my ears are sore today, it's like needles going through them when you laugh like that . . ." When they come back from the shops in the Bridges they can see from his stained cheeks and exhausted eyes that he has been crying in their absence. "See what we've brought you, Simon – malt with halibut oil in it! You'll be a big strong boy by the time this jar is empty." They hold a heaped teaspoon of brown stickiness to his lips. His mouth closes on it, his throat swallows; then he runs to the toilet and retches violently. The jar of malt is put away in the back of the cupboard and never touched again. And when they bath him at night they can see how pitifully thin his body is – the birdlike shoulder-blades, the torso that is all ribs and spine. "No," says Dr Aitchison, "the boy isn't fit yet for the hurly-burly of school. Give him another fortnight. The spring sun will do wonders for him."

'One day the mother reads an advertisement in the morning paper. Spread over a half page a certain tonic wine is lauded to the skies. Above and around and below a huge drawing of a bottle of this panacea is printed a score of testimonials – unsolicited letters – from satisfied customers, expressing heartfelt gratitude for the wonder that this particular tonic wine has wrought in their lives; how it has helped them to recover, with almost miraculous speed, from depression, insomnia, lack of appetite, listlessness, debility, the after-effects of childbirth, shingles, measles, flu, gastritis, etc., etc. The mother rises from the breakfast table. She takes her purse from the sideboard. Simon is still asleep. There is a licensed grocer shop at the foot of the stairs. Yes, Mr Jarvey has a stock of this tonic wine. One bottle, Mrs McKee? Much obliged . . .

'Simon is given his first glass of wine after breakfast.

' "Whatever is that you're giving him?" cries the aunt. "Oh Elizabeth, should you really? Is it wise? A boy of that age . . ."

'Simon however drinks the tonic wine without complaint. Yes, he says, he quite likes it. Four times a day the bottle and the wineglass are brought from the cupboard. More than once Simon asks, looking up from his jigsaw puzzle, if it isn't time to be given his medicine yet.

'It was wonderful, the way it seemed to help him, that tonic wine. Day by day he grew stronger. They could draw the curtains and let in the sun. Aunt Flora could laugh as loud as she pleased without hurting his ears. One fine afternoon in late March they went for quite a long walk through the Meadows: his first day out. The next morning – a Saturday – Simon was playing hopscotch in the back yard with Billy and Tommy MacIndoe from the ground floor. He never looked back after that. He ate his porridge and egg and toast every morning, to the last crumb. He would come in at half-past twelve, shouting wasn't his dinner ready yet, he was hungry. It did their hearts good to see how quickly he was borne along on the tide of recovery. Another week, and Simon was rigged out in his uniform and seen on to the tram that stopped at the gate of the Royal High School.

'The mother attributed it all to the tonic wine. She blessed the day she had opened that paper and read the advertisement. She thought of writing to the manufacturers and telling them what their product had done for her ailing boy.

'But Aunt Flora reminded her that Dr Aitchison had said Simon would improve in any case with the fine sunny spring weather.

'In view of the later history of this Simon, I want you to know who was the person who first put alcoholic drink into his mouth. It was none other than the woman who is sitting in the dock before you today: Mrs Elizabeth McKee, his mother.

'I must ask you to have patience with me. It is rather a long story that I have to tell. I promise that I shall be as brief as possible.

'Simon McKee is a clever boy at school; he is what is called in Scotland, approvingly, "a lad o' pairts". The school work is no trouble to him at all. What other boys agonize over at the kitchen table at home when they would a thousand times rather be playing football – the writing of the weekly essay, the Latin and Greek paradigms, the memorizing of lyrics by Wordsworth or R. L. Stevenson – all this Simon takes in his stride. His eye goes down the page a little contemptuously, as if this was child's play, almost beneath his notice. Perhaps mathematical problems give him a little trouble. And he is no great shakes at cricket and swimming. But the school terms pass happily enough for him. Regularly he bears home, at the end of the session, a Greek prize or a composition prize. I must not give you the impression that he is a bookworm and a prig. He is popular with his fellow pupils, and even – which is more significant – with the rather rough boys in the tenement, those who are not particular about their language or the places where they urinate, those who fight and squabble at the street corners (like Billy MacIndoe and Sandy Vallance with their regular black eyes and bloody noses), those who attend the grim prison-like school in the nearby square. Simon McKee is a thoroughly pleasant boy, without a trace of snobbishness or intellectual arrogance. The charwoman looks up at him smilingly from her bucket and cloth as he passes her on the landing on his way to school.

'The years pass uneventfully. Simon is seventeen. He has obtained his school leaving certificate with six passes on the higher level. The next stage is the university: he must make up his mind pretty soon as to a career. The trouble is, he seems not to have a vocation for anything in particular. His mother and his aunt prompt him from time to time. "Simon, you would make a first-rate doctor. Think how you could help handicapped people like your father. It's rather a long course, that's true ..." Simon wrinkles his nose; his affections do not that way tend. They suggest the law to him. No, he shakes his head resolutely. "The church?" says Aunt Flora, but without much hope, for she knows Simon is not a particularly religious boy. He goes to church at St Kentigern's every Sunday, and to the Bible Class afterwards, but over and above that he evinces no particular religious enthusiasm. No, again. Aunt Flora's hopes of one day seeing Simon in the ruff and buckles of the Moderator of the General Assembly are dashed. Well, there was only one thing for it, Simon must be a teacher. Simon acquiesces, though half-heartedly, more to silence the women of the house than out of any sense of vocation. He enrols at Edinburgh University in the arts faculty.

'The story of his school days is almost, but not quite, paralleled. Simon does well at the university; well enough, that is, to pass all his degree exams at the first go; not like those mediocrities who, having spent the summer term rowing and playing football by day, and dancing and pub-crawling along Rose Street by night, and taking girls up Arthur's Seat, sit squirming miserably in the examination hall in June, and then have to return in September for another go; a ruined book-fretted summer behind them. Simon passes all his exams with moderate ease, but he no longer takes home any prizes. "Well, mother," he says, "what do you expect? I'm not a genius, I'm competing with the very best brains of Scotland. I'm doing well enough." But Aunt Flora turns down her mouth and looks just a wee bit disappointed.

'At last, after three years, the university course is finished. Simon has passed in all seven specified subjects. In the great drum-shaped MacEwan Hall, seated with serried ranks of black-gowned contemporaries – and while his mother and aunt, in flowered hats, watch from the gallery – Simon steps forward when his name is called, is lightly tapped on the head by the dean, and given a scroll in a red cylindrical box. He has received the blessing of his Alma Mater. He is a Master of Arts. Aunt Flora up in the gallery is all sunshine and storm; she dabs her smiling welling eyes with a frilly handkerchief.

'They have a little celebration dinner that evening in the Ochil Restaurant, all three of them: so nice – asparagus soup, plaice, chicken and mushroom and potatoes, raspberry trifle with cream. They are seated almost in the centre of the restaurant, and Simon is wearing his graduation gown; he hasn't wanted to, but Aunt Flora has pleaded and nagged him into acquiescence. From time to time some diner turns and looks approvingly at the young man, and whispers to his table, and all look round. The people of Scotland dearly love a successful student: education, "getting on", is part of their religion. Aunt Flora's heart is fit to burst with pride.

'Before the coffee, however, Simon tells them that he must be off; he hopes they won't mind if he just slips away. He has arranged to meet certain of his fellow-graduates, they are to have a little get-together, to celebrate. They have been planning it since before the finals. Aunt Flora looks disappointed, but his mother quite understands. "Shoo," she says, "be off with you, Simon. Your aunt and I are seeing to the bill. Have a nice evening." Simon slips out of his gown. His mother folds it carefully and stows it in Simon's briefcase: it is on hire, it must be returned to the shop in George Street tomorrow. Simon waves bye-bye from the door (his long university scarf trailing almost to his knees). The waiter arrives with the coffee, the caerphilly, the bill. Would the ladies like a liqueur with their coffee, a Benedictine, a Drambuie? Aunt Alora looks at Mrs McKee. Mrs McKee says they would like a Drambuie indeed, for, you see, it is a special occasion . . .

'That night as the mother and aunt are preparing for bed –

winding the clock, putting the guard over the fire, setting out the breakfast cups and plates – they hear a scuffling outside the main door. It is as if some dog were padding and scratching on the woodwork to get in (but they have no dog, only Twopence the cat). They look at each other nervously. At last Mrs McKee, always the bolder and more practical of the sisters, sets her mouth in a firm line and walks out into the hallway and eases open the door. A kind of sack falls in at her feet – she cannot see very well in the dim gas-light. But the sack is alive, it wheezes and rolls over on the linoleum. It is a man – a foot slides out and fingers clutch at the wall. Mrs McKee screams. The man rolls over on his back and the grotesque mask of a loved face stares blindly up at her. It is her son Simon. He is helplessly drunk. His scarf is missing. The front of his new raincoat is fouled with vomit. He groans twice, then begins to snort loudly like an animal. Aunt Flora, appalled, stands in the sitting-room door, a poker in her hand. From the foot of the stair comes the muffled laughter of the graduates who have taken Simon McKee, M.A., home after their celebration. "You beasts!" cries Aunt Flora down the immense lighted well, "Sh-h-h," says Mrs McKee, "the neighbours." The laughter passes out into the summer street. The mother and the aunt turn back to their paragon.

'Of course it is all forgiven. After a few days of sighs and silence and hurt expressions – and, I might add, of real throbbing remorse on the part of Simon – they return to their normal routine, just as if nothing had happened. Simon says he is sorry. They almost fall over themselves to put kisses of forgiveness on his cheek.

'And so the summer passes. Simon goes for long lonely walks over the Pentland Hills. If the day is very hot he takes the bus out to Cramond with Kim Somerville or Tommy MacIndoe; they spend the day bathing and boating. More than once he has the smell of beer on his breath when he comes in, tanned as a tinker and hungry as a hawk, for his supper. Aunt Flora sniffs the air discreetly. The two women never mention the beer drinking to one another; as if it was tacitly agreed between them that a glass of good beer never hurt any young man, and surely it is a natural and a pleasant thing to end a day in the open air with a refreshment. But often Aunt Flora looks troubled and preoccupied as

Simon, over his cheese and toast and cocoa, talks more lavishly than usual and sketches an extravagant gesture with his hand. "Now, then, Simon," says the mother, "you've talked enough for one night, you've rattled away there like a Newhaven fishwife. Off to bed with you."

'The ladies of the house have assumed all along that in September Simon will enrol at Moray House, the teachers' training college. It comes as rather a shock to them – but, goodness gracious, a pleasant enough shock – when Simon one day announces to them over the tea-time kippers that after all he will not be going to Moray House – he has been accepted for Divinity Hall. He will study for the ministry of the Church of Scotland. Aunt Flora claps her hands with delight. Nothing makes a Scotswoman so proud as to see a kinsman of hers "wagging his pow in the pulpit". They note with satisfaction that after three more years' study Simon will have another degree; he will be a Bachelor of Divinity. Just imagine that – Rev. Simon McKee, M.A., B.D. They smile. They acquiesce.

'Simon, then, betakes himself at the beginning of October to the college on the Mound, a marvellously sited place looking out over the new town of Edinburgh to the Firth of Forth and, beyond that, to the turquoise evanescent coast of Fife.

'I will not strain the patience of this court by describing in great detail the graph of Simon McKee's progress at Divinity College. The truth is that there is very little to describe. He proved to be a student of average ability, no more. There was one occasion, in his second year, when he failed a degree exam in June – the subject was Old Testament History – and had to re-sit in September. There was gloom in the top flat of the tenement in Marchmont when one morning the postman delivered the green envelope of failure. This had never happened to Simon before. Aunt Flora's lip quivered and she had to leave her toast and marmalade half finished.

' "Shucks," said Simon, "I'll pass the thing in September."

'There was gloom quite frequently now in the top flat, especially at the week-ends; indeed, invariably at the week-ends. Friday and Saturday nights Simon devoted to drinking with his friends in the pubs of Leith Walk and the High Street. The mother and the aunt would hear the key in the lock after eleven o'clock, then Simon's feet blundering, ashamed and supperless, into his own room. They would hear the toilet being flushed two or three times during the night. Once at least they heard him being violently sick at four o'clock in the morning. Most Sundays he refused his food; at best he might eat a half-slice of toast in the evening, with a cup of milk. Their Simon was a white miserable face hanging over the sitting-room fire all that day. Invariably on Monday morning, smiling in that pleasant open way he had, he would ask their forgiveness. Invariably it was granted, with fading ardour as the weeks passed by Aunt Flora. Once Aunt Flora uttered a taboo name to Mrs McKee: John Dunbar. John Dunbar had been their maternal grandfather. John Dunbar's life, after the age of thirty, had been completely centred in the bottle. John Dunbar, timber merchant, went bankrupt at the age of thirty-seven. John Dunbar died aged forty-one, leaving five children, and, to quote Aunt Flora, he "filled a drunkard's grave" in the Grange cemetery. A taint like that, said Aunt Flora tearfully, could be inherited. It might slip a generation or two, then inexplicably in this member of the family or that the fatal pattern might re-establish itself.

' "Don't be silly," said Mrs McKee to Aunt Flora. "Divinity students are a wild lot, everybody knows that, they've had that reputation since the university was founded, goodness knows how long ago. They sow their wild oats. You can't blame them. They get a church when they're finished, they marry, and they have to be as solemn as rooks for the rest of their time. Simon's just like the rest of them."

'But Aunt Flora refused to be comforted.

'She refused very much to be comforted the night of the Welsh rugby international at Murrayfield when Simon didn't come home at all. Ten minutes before midnight they heard a knock at the door.

' "It's Simon," said Mrs McKee. "He's forgotten his key. Open the door."

'A tall blue tower, a policeman, stood on the doormat. He was sorry to disturb them. Was a Mr Simon McKee, who had given his occupation as a student, normally resident here? It was just to say that the said Simon McKee and five other persons describing themselves as students had been mixed up in a brawl with some Welsh rugby supporters in a public transport bus proceeding towards the Dean Bridge. After the pubs had closed, always a bad time. No, Ma'am, nobody had been injured. They had all been too intoxicated to do each other much harm. But the people on the bus had been very much alarmed. The ringleaders had been arrested and duly lodged in the cells – red bonnets and university scarves in about equal numbers. Drunk and disorderly, that was the charge. He was her son, was he? The lady could stand bail if she so desired, but he would strongly advise her to let him cool off for the night in the cells like the others. He would be all right in the morning. It was his opinion that a night in the cells did them young chaps no harm at all, it gave them a good fright, it knocked a lot of the uppishness out of them. Oh ay, bail or no bail, he would have to appear in court. Yes, Ma'am, good night, don't worry, he's safe – "just wan o thae things . . ."

'Simon appeared at home after breakfast-time on Sunday morning, white-faced and racked with hangover. And appeared on Monday morning, with ten others, in the magistrates' court. And was admonished, this being his first offence. And asked forgiveness of his mother and Aunt Flora in the taxi coming home. His mother had kissed him, as always. But Aunt Flora had pursed her mouth and looked fixedly out of the taxi window. When they got home she went straight to her own room, and only emerged in the afternoon when Simon left to attend a lecture.

'After that Simon really seemed to pull himself together. He stayed at home at nights and devoted himself to his books. He even missed a few week-ends in the High Street howffs. He was cheerful and considerate, just like the boy they used to know. Aunt Flora was released by degrees from her gloom. He sat his exams before the Easter vacation and was confident he had done well. As a reward the mother and the aunt sent him on a seven-day cruise from Leith to the Orkneys and Shetlands. Aunt Flora put an extra five-pound note into his hand on the gangway. "But remember, dear," she said, "no drinking. For your mother's sake. Please."

'Simon came back delighted with his trip. The voyagers had

experienced gales and blizzard and two days of halcyon calm. "That old ship," said Simon, "sailed through the entire weather spectrum." He had been sick just once, in the Sumburgh Roost south of the Shetlands. In Kirkwall he had spent a whole morning in the roseate gloom of the Cathedral of Saint Magnus. He had taken a bus to Hamnavoe; he had never seen such a queer quaint cluster of houses, a grey helter-skelter flung down between a blue tongue of sea and a hill. "Oh, it was right fine, the northern isles," he said to Aunt Flora. "I would go back there again like a shot."

'They observed with pleasure his clear eyes and steady hands as he unpacked his case. He had not been drinking. Fergus Crichton, Simon's fellow-student, came galloping up the stairs, breathless. The exam results were on the notice board – Simon had a beta plus, in Hebrew.

'The summer term began on the Tuesday following. An afternoon or two that term would be devoted to practice preaching, Simon told the women. "Well," said he, "you're a gey poor minister if you can't raise the stoor from the pulpit rail." Yet they could see he was a bit worried about it. Public speaking set him shaking with nerves. At the class-room debates in the Royal High he had hung his head and looked fixedly at the floor whenever the eye of the teacher roamed the class-room searching for a speaker. Then there was the occasion the Bible Class appointed him their spokesman; that was seven years ago; Miss Pritchard the organist was leaving to get married. Simon had fretted himself sick about the presentation speech for days and days beforehand. On the afternoon of the day he was actually sick. In the end Tommy MacIndoe had had to do it.

'Simon came home for tea one day in late April, very pale and confused. No, he would be all right, he assured them. He had had to preach an impromptu sermon before the entire class; it had come at him out of the blue – "McKee, do us the honour of preaching for fifteen minutes on this text"; he had not done very well at all. "My tongue was shrivelled to the root," he told them. "O God, it was awful." And to tell the truth he looked awful, as if a white star of shock had burst upon his face. His mother was seriously concerned. "Simon dear," she said, "we know you're near the end of your course, but there's absolutely no need for you to go on if you don't feel up to it. I'm serious, dear. We're not bare-handed, you know – your father and your grandfather left a little money. You could do a bit of tutoring – something like that – to help out, something that won't be a strain on you. Your health comes before everything."

'Simon said he would be all right. It just took a bit of getting used to. Next time he would do much better, he knew it. And when would he have to preach a sermon again? Next Tuesday afternoon said Simon, but this would be a prepared sermon; at least he would have notes to refer to. At tea-time on Tuesday they waited anxiously at the table. Simon came in, smiling, and threw his books on the couch. It had gone well. Mr Graham the lecturer in systematic theology had congratulated him at the end of his discourse. The other students had had to criticize him – his style, delivery, subject-matter. He had made short work of one or two of them in his replies, especially that Andrew Baillie from the Borders who saw himself as the future Archbishop of Glasgow once the Presbyterians and the Piskies were united – he had taken the wind out of his sails all right. He had had a most successful day. He had chosen as the subject of his sermon St Paul's great text on charity.

' "All right, dear," said his mother, "don't excite yourself. I'm so pleased. Sit down at the table. There's a lovely piece of smoked cod in the oven for you."

'Simon chattered away all through the meal. All three of them were pleased and excited. They felt that Simon had crossed a formidable frontier; he had broken out of his prostrating nervousness.

'Indeed he had. Three more sermons he was required to preach in the college that term, before the final examinations; and the prospect didn't worry him one little bit. Well, he was excited when he came home, and more loquacious, but that was only because he was still riding the crest of his afternoon eloquence. Professor Wylie had taken him aside on the last occasion; he had told Simon privately that it was extraordinarily good, a rare mixture of simplicity and erudition. "I was most impressed, McKee," Professor Wylie had said. "Archbishop Baillie" had been pretty sick about it all; they had torn his sermon to shreds the week before. Simon laughed and banged his fist down on the tea-table till his poached eggs shivered. He looked from one to the other with a kind of waifish slovenly joy.

' "You're over-exciting yourself, dear," said Mrs McKee.

'The week of the finals came. Simon returned home each evening quiet and confident, his middle and index fingers furrowed from the hard driving of a pen. He thought he had done quite well, he told the women – in fact he was sure of it. So, it seemed, thought the examiners, for when the results were announced in late June Simon had passed *magna cum laude*. A kiss was stamped on each side of his face that morning when the postman brought the news. Simon smiled gently. He was pleased, he told them, for their sakes. They had been so good to him. He kissed them in return, one after the other, silently and sincerely.

'The next morning Simon and two of his friends – Fergus Crichton from Dunoon and a boy from the Orkneys called Flett, both divinity students – left for a week's climbing and camping in Glencoe. They returned the day before the graduation ceremony; Simon's teeth and his eyes flashing out of the tinker tan of his face. They were just a wee bit worried, the mother and the aunt, that there might be a repeat performance of that other graduation. But no: Simon did not go out at all that evening. Instead he sat in his room; he had one or two letters to write, he told them. Of course at six o'clock they had had a nice celebration dinner in a hotel in the Pentland hills, a place they had never been to before, but it had been recommended to them by Pussy Brae. Mrs McKee and Aunt Flora, while Simon was away hanging up his coat, had a whispered conference over the oak table. Dared they? Was it safe? Well, only this once. Simon returned. A waiter ballet-danced round them with tomato juice; and returned, bowing; and pirouetted in again with grilled plaice and – "just to wish you the very best, dearest Simon" – a bottle of Sauterne . . . It had been a lovely meal. Towards the end of it Simon had appeared a trifle impatient – no, no coffee and cheese for him – he really was in a great hurry to get those letters written, applications to this presbytery and that – if they didn't mind. A taxi was summoned, it whirled them back to Marchmont. And Simon sat in his room all evening with – as he said – his letters.

'Next morning he was rather ill. "It's the reaction of it all," said his mother. "You don't feel the strain at the actual time, it comes a fortnight or three weeks later ..." Aunt Flora, however, had seen that blanched stricken look before, only this time there was a new light in it: loneliness. This sufferer seemed to be marked and set apart.

'Two days later Simon, quite recovered, departed again, this time with a group of young people, lay and missionary, who were conducting an evangelical campaign in the West Highlands. He kissed Mrs McKee and Aunt Flora in the door. It was still high summer. He was wearing an open-necked khaki shirt and a kilt of the MacGregor tartan, and he had a laden rucksack on his back. He was in good spirits. The little indisposition had passed away like a cloud.

'Simon had been gone a week when Fergus Crichton, his fellow-student from Dunoon, called. Simon had borrowed two books from Fergus in the middle of last term, and now Fergus had called to collect them, as he was going home for good the very next morning. Fergus was bidden to come in. While Aunt Flora made him a cup of coffee in the kitchen Mrs McKee combed through Simon's books in his bedroom. And goodness, it was quite a search, for there were piles of books everywhere, on top of the cupboard and on the window ledge and even piled in a cairn in one corner of the room, as well as in the large open bookcase against the wall. But there was no sign whatever of Fergus' books. Where on earth had Simon put them? Mrs McKee looked under the bed. That must be it – they were in the large wooden brass-bound trunk that had belonged to Simon's great-grandfather, the unmentionable John Dunbar, bankrupt timber merchant. Mrs McKee had some trouble prising off the latch with a spoon – it was so tight – it squealed like a nest of rats. The genteel murmurs of Aunt Flora and Fergus Crichton drifted through from the kitchen. At last the latch was off. Mrs McKee threw back the lid. The trunk was crammed with empty spirit bottles of every shape and size; round, squat, dimpled; miniatures and gills and flagons and even a tregnum. Most of them had contained whisky, but there was a gin bottle and a vodka bottle here and there. From this squandered treasury Simon McKee had drawn his summer-time eloquence.

'Fergus' books were found at last on the sewing-machine in the sitting-room . . .

'The court has been very patient with me in my protracted presentation of this case. I must ask you to bear with me for a short while yet. The sun has set. From now on twilight deepens fast into night.

'Simon McKee was ordained into the ministry of the Church of Scotland later that year, and inducted the same day as assistant minister of the church of St Kenneth in the city of Glasgow. He came to the large congregation with many glowing testimonials from his teachers and professors in Edinburgh; from his parish minister; and from Aeneas Bell the greengrocer at the end of the street who was the McKee's district elder. He preached at the morning service the following Sunday in St Kenneth's. A critical middle-class congregation was impressed by the quiet searching eloquence of the sermon, the balanced phrasing, the restrained beautiful delivery. A few of the spiritual connoisseurs were struck by the expression on the face of their young minister – the pallor of one who had knelt long in solitary meditation, a twentieth-century anchorite. It seemed as if a star of holiness had burst upon that brow.

'Mrs McKee, proud and inwardly quaking, sat in the gallery. Aunt Flora, even with the sedative Dr Aitchison prescribed for her, just couldn't bring herself to travel through from Edinburgh. She would have broken down in her pew, she told Simon, and ruined everything for him.

'Mrs McKee, having seen that Simon was settled down in good digs with a kindly Irish landlady, returned to Edinburgh the next morning by train.

'They saw Simon often that winter. Of course his busy times were the week-ends, but always some day in mid-week – usually a Wednesday – he would visit them, taking the train from Glasgow. He was gentle and affectionate, as always, but, they thought, more withdrawn, more immured within himself than ever, as if his real existence was taking place inside a mirror. Yes, he liked the work of the parish very much, he told them. Dr Fordyce, the minister, could not be kinder or more considerate. Yes, Mrs O'Donnell was a good cook – her Scotch broth on a cold winter afternoon was something to be marvelled at. And yes, she aired his woollen underwear on her oven door the whole evening on his bath-night, which was generally a Monday. He could not have been more fortunate. "I have landed on my feet," said Simon, putting his shy lonely smile on one after the other.

'And preaching? they pressed him anxiously. Oh, he managed quite well. Some of the older folk thought his sermons a bit too intellectual. "What they want," said Simon, "is for me to shout and rage and stamp up and down in the pulpit. That's a grand sermon, whatever gibberish comes out. I refuse to surrender to holy barbarians. I have read John Donne – my grapes are out of the same vineyard."

'They would fuss about him the whole evening. He was to be sure to take one halibut oil capsule every morning until the end of April. Had he plenty of socks? – he must change them if ever his feet got the teeniest bit wet – they would get him three new pairs from the wool shop in the morning, just to be sure. And Aunt Flora said slyly to him one evening, "And what about the future Mrs McKee, Simon? Some day you'll have a kirk of your own. A manse is a lonely place without a wife in it." Simon said he wouldn't mind a week-end in the Cairngorms with Miss Drawbell who sang soprano in the kirk choir. And "Oh Simon!" they cried, shocked, and the next moment rolled back in their chairs laughing. "You're a terrible boy," said Aunt Flora, "you don't improve. Go to bed now. You have to catch that early train in the morning." And Simon would kiss them both good night and go to bed in his old room – lapped in excessive warmth from gas-fire and electric blanket and hot-water bottles – and be up in good time to catch an early train to Glasgow.

'The word alcohol was never mentioned. There was no trace of it on the boy whenever he visited them; they would sniff about him delicately like two horticulturalists in a threatened rose-garden. The worm had been driven out. They assured each other that Simon was all right now. Dr Fordyce was like a father to him; that was what he had missed all along, a father. Simon's wild oats were sown – now he had put his hand to the plough of the spirit. Dear good Simon.

'One Wednesday in the month of May Simon didn't come

home, nor did he come on Thursday or Friday or Saturday. They were mildly anxious. If Mrs O'Donnell had had a phone they would have rung to inquire. Of course they could have rung Dr Fordyce at the manse, but they didn't want to bother that busy man with trifles. They didn't have a phone themselves; the Anguses did, downstairs, but Aunt Flora had fallen out with Mrs Angus about the washing of the stairhead; and Simon knew it; so he wouldn't have rung there to summon them. The least he could have done was send them a postcard to explain why he couldn't come. They were a little displeased with him. It was inconsiderate.

'When Simon didn't turn up the following Wednesday they were seriously upset. The boy must be ill. He always caught a bad cold in the spring. There he was, no doubt about it, lying in his bed in the guest-house coughing and sweating, and how could Mrs O'Donnell look after him properly when she had a dozen other lodgers coming and going? . . .

'Greatly daring, Mrs McKee slipped out to the phone box across the street and dialled Dr Fordyce's number. Growlings filled her ear. Who was speaking? Who? He couldn't quite make out. Oh, Mrs McKee. What Mrs McKee? From Edinburgh? Ah, Simon's mother. Ah. Yes. Mrs McKee was not to panic. She must listen carefully – it was necessary for her to come through to Glasgow as soon as ever she could. Dr Fordyce had to talk to her. Yes, about Simon. No, it was impossible over the phone. No, Simon was not ill, at least not in the normal sense of the word. Now if she were to take the three o'clock train from Waverley, he, Dr Fordyce, would meet her with his car at the station. He would recognize her all right from seeing her at Simon's ordination. Things would work out for the best, he was sure. God bless her.

'However Mrs McKee endured the next three hours she could not have said – she got strength from somewhere to go through with it. In the train she sat like a prisoner being hurried to execution over some vast Siberian expanse. Dr Fordyce met her at the station – a tall silver melancholy presence. She waited dumbly for him to drive her to the mortuary where Simon lay sheeted on a slab.

' "My dear woman," said Dr Fordyce. "Come over with me to

the coffee-bar. We will have a cup of tea together. You need it, by the look of you.'

' "I won't go another step," said Mrs McKee. "Please tell me now."

' "Simon is safe," said Dr Fordyce. "He has turned up again. We were worried about him. He went missing, you know. He simply disappeared. He didn't turn up at church the Sunday morning before last. There was the organ pealing and the congregation seated and an empty pulpit. Finally they had to send for me, all unprepared as I was."

' "But he's safe," said Mrs McKee. "Thank God."

' "You'll see him in half an hour," said Dr Fordyce. "I will not tell you any more, not one word, till we're seated at that coffee table. My dear woman, you're absolutely done in."

'He told her, breaking a piece of shortbread, of the Sunday search for Simon. He had not been in all Saturday night, said Mrs O'Donnell. On the bedroom mantelpiece stood an empty whisky bottle, and a glass, and a jug half full of water. There was a further clue to go on: his tweed coat was missing from the peg, his walking brogues weren't in the cupboard. There was no doubt about it. Simon had gone with his drink into the hills.

' "I was in a quandary, I can tell you," said Dr Fordyce. "What was I to do – contact the police? They would have set up a hue-and-cry, and found him at the end of the day in some Loch Lomond hotel, absolutely plastered. I trembled when I thought of the newspaper headlines next morning. No. I was sure Simon was safe. You see, dear woman, I have known for some time that Simon is an alcoholic. And it grieves me to the heart, for I love the boy."

' "Yes," said Mrs McKee. "Much love has been squandered on him. Too much love, I feel."

' "We'll visit him as soon as you've drunk your tea," said Dr Fordyce. "I see you haven't touched your cake. (It has to be paid for, you know, whether you eat it or not.) He's up at the manse. He's very tired, of course, exhausted. No wonder. But there's still a lick or two of flame under the ashes."

'Dr Fordyce told Mrs McKee he had not been deceived for long. Before Simon had been at St Kenneth's a fortnight the minister knew he had a rare bird in his hand – for this gifted sweet-natured assistant of his would close himself in the vestry and emerge an hour later with a slack white smile on his face; and then climb with ceremony into the pulpit, and conduct a flawless service.

'"His sermons were great," said Dr Fordyce. "I was as green as the tree in the manse garden with envy. But to deliver them at all he had to make himself simple and heroic with whisky. I am hurting you very much."

'"I have known it longer than you," said Mrs McKee.

'This was not the first time Simon had disappeared, by any means. He would simply walk out of Mrs O'Donnell's and disappear for anything up to thirty-six hours: from Friday morning to Saturday evening, that was the pattern. And Mrs O'Donnell would bring his supper into his room, when he got home at last. And there he sat in the armchair reeking of drink, and trembling like some mad musical instrument between hilarity and melancholy. And Mrs O'Donnell would loosen his tie and take off his muddy brogues and coax him into eating a sandwich or two.

'"A good woman that," said Dr Fordyce. "A Catholic and everything. But I have no hesitation in sending my assistants to her ... To return to the sad business. Until this last time the lad never failed to turn up for his duties on Sunday morning. Never. But even so he put me in a fine pickle, once I knew for certain how matters stood with him. It was best to confront him right out. *Look here, McKee, I said, I know you drink. It won't do in a busy parish like this, you know. You're not an eighteenth-century minister now. What the devil's wrong with you, man? You're well-liked. There should be music put to some of the sermons you preach. I find no fault in you. Then why do you have to tilt the bottle, eh?* ... He stood there before me, grey in the face, and said nothing. *And anyway, I said, where do you go on Fridays and Saturdays? Where's your boozer? I'm not being nosey – I just want to know in case anything happens* ... Then he came out with it. It seems there's a shepherd's hut half-way up a mountain in Perthshire. He first came across it in his student days, rambling through the Highlands with a couple of other divinity students. He told me that's where he went, with a bottle of whisky and bread and cheese in his knapsack ... Mrs McKee, I would have got rid of him at once. I would have kicked him out. No good at all in the kirk, that kind of thing. But I couldn't bring myself to do it. I couldn't drive Simon into the wilderness. My dear woman, I love the lad like my own son."

' "I understand that," said Mrs McKee.

' "Well then," said Dr Fordyce, "this last mammoth disappearance of his, I drove in my car, alone, that same Sunday afternoon, up to Perthshire. I left my car in the village. I nearly killed myself climbing that mountain: an old fool like me, sixty years old. And when I got to the shepherd's hut after an hour and more it was empty. But it hadn't been empty long. There was the whisky bottle and a crust beside it and a few hot embers on the hearth. But the bird had flown. Half-way down the sheep-path I fell in with this old man. *Oh now, says he, the young fellow that comes here most week-ends, your reverence, is he not in the old ruin? That's a wonder now. Let me see. Oh no, he wouldn't be, for didn't I see him making over that ridge three hours ago and more, as urgent as a deer* ... And the old chap pointed north. I climbed back to the hut and waited for a while in case he might come back. But no, he didn't. The fire went black out. I came down before night trapped me in the gullies. Simon was lost in the trackless wastes of the Highlands.

' "What was I to do, woman? I thought of getting in touch with you, but it would have wounded you, the whole wretched business would have come out and you would have been desperately hurt. I thought again, but only for a moment, of going to the police. As it happened, the police came to me when Simon had been away for six days – they had got an anonymous phone call. *We have received information, said the sergeant, that Mr McKee your assistant is missing.* God forgive me for telling them a lie. *Missing? I said. Good gracious no. McKee is having a few days' holiday. He is hill-walking in the Highlands. I was up at his cottage on Sunday afternoon ... Just checking sir, said the sergeant. Thank you. We have to follow up these things. You know the way people are – they'll say anything but their prayers* ... We had a good hollow laugh about it, standing there in the manse door.

' "With every day that passed my fears grew. *I'll give him another week*, I thought – *maybe the lad is seeking his own cure among the burns and the clouds. It is possible. But if he isn't back in another week, everybody will have to be told: the mother, the congregation, the presbytery, the police, the reporters. The great mouths of the press will shout the slander and disgrace all over Britain* ... So I reasoned. It was a matter of the utmost delicacy, between a sick man and his God. The less interference from other folk, the better, I thought. Mrs O'Donnell set a knife and fork at Simon's place every morning. The following Sunday came. Still no Simon; I had to do all the preaching myself, but that wasn't too much trouble – I have a suitcase with a stack of old sermons in it, fiery stuff from the days of my youth. Monday, Tuesday, Wednesday passed. On Thursday morning I went downstairs to answer a knock at the door. If it wasn't the old Perthshire shepherd! *Your reverence will forgive me now*, says he, removing his bonnet, *for troubling you at all. But the young man you was looking for the Sabbath before last, he has turned up. I thought now your reverence would want to know. He has given me your name whatever. Didn't he come back to the hut the day before yesterday*, says he, *with a grey look on him, and sodden with the rain and the dew, and hardly able to speak at all. He had been on a boat with fishermen, he kept repeating over and over again, in deep wide waters, westward* ... *But he looked to me more like a deer with the wounds of the pack on him. So I made him lie down and put a couple of blankets over him. He ate an oatcake and cheese and some milk. Then he went to sleep, and he looks to me as if he'll sleep for a month. So now, the gamekeeper from beyond the river, he was coming down to Glasgow today about some business, he says, but it's more likely to see the Rangers playing against St Johnstone, and I met him in the Mason Arms that afternoon and arranged for him to give me a lift into the city in the morning, in his shooting-brake. For I was sure you would be anxious, and I have the visiting card you was so kind as to give me that Sabbath afternoon on the mountain. Oh no*, says he, *I'm not seeking any reward whatever, it's just that I'm a bit nervous with being in the great noise of Glasgow, and if you have such a thing as a dram in your cupboard, that will be all the reward I am wanting* ... No, he couldn't bide long. The hills and the sheep would be missing him. He drank down his dram, and then another. I got out the car. In two hours he was back among his silences, and I was sitting beside Simon in that stony draughty hut. The poor lad was broken with grief and exhaustion; yes, and with something spiritual and ineffable, a wrestle with angels. He's up at the manse now. I've made him as comfortable as an old widower can. But I'm sure he'd be much better at home with you, Mrs McKee, for the next month or two . . . Would you say, now, there was another cup of tea in that pot? . . ."

'Thus Dr Andrew Fordyce to Mrs Elizabeth McKee, sitting in the railway restaurant over tea and cakes and shortbread.

' "What will become of him?" said Mrs McKee.

' "I must be brutal with you," said Dr Fordyce. "Simon is no good to St Kenneth's or any other busy parish in Scotland. He could go to the mission fields. He could do administrative work, but that means staying in a city. The best thing for him would be some quiet place in the country, some place preferably with no pub and no licensed grocer. There Simon must work out his salvation."

'She took Simon back to Edinburgh that same evening. He was at home for a month, slowly recovering his strength and serenity. He had only the vaguest knowledge of where he had been that fortnight of his disappearance; twelve days had been ripped out of the calendar of his life. He thought he had been on a seine-net fishing boat for a while, out of Mallaig. He remembered being sick, and a dark heave of water. He remembered the kindness of coarse-speaking men in yellow oilskins . . . The mother and the aunt did not press him too much.

'Dr Fordyce could not have been kinder. He moved heaven and earth to find a suitable place for Simon. At last he was successful. There was an island in the Orkneys called Hellya. The population had dwindled alarmingly in the past generation, but still the remaining folk had souls to be saved and stood in need of a pastor. For the past six years they had had to make do with a lay missionary. But now the missionary had been called to Nigeria, and the lovely old eighteenth-century manse stood vacant. Would Simon not consider Hellya?

'Aunt Flora was simply livid with fury. What, Simon wasting

his life on some skerry in the Atlantic – Simon who everybody knew was a brilliant preacher and would go on to occupy a great position in the kirk some day! Just because he had been ill through overwork and overstudy. She was more than surprised at Dr Fordyce! One thing she was sure of, she wasn't going to live in a wilderness like that. Elizabeth could go if she wished; in Marchmont she would live and die ... They had never seen Aunt Flora so inflexible.

'But Simon said with great humility that he would go if he received a call from the islanders.

'The call came a week later, and the Rev. Simon McKee and his mother set off by aeroplane from Turnhouse airport. Two hours later, after brief stops at Aberdeen and Wick, they found themselves in the islands. There was a brief taxi journey; a brief ferry crossing with a young Norse god standing morosely in the wheelhouse; and there at the pier of Greenvoe to conduct them to the manse were Colonel Fortin-Bell and Mr Joseph Evie.

'That was just over four years ago. Since then nothing sensational has happened – nothing like that blank fortnight among the mountains and the fishing nets. It has been rather the slow insidious rotting of the remainder of a great promise – a smouldering away – a spreading mildew – a relentless devouring by moth and rust.

'For Simon did not settle down in a drinkless parish, as Dr Fordyce had hoped he might. These places, though they can be found in Scotland, are very rare. The island of Hellya is cursed with a hotel. And so it happens that, once every six or seven weeks, the minister of Hellya sets out at the behest of his dark angel to fulfil his destiny. He covers his quest with every kind of subterfuge (for since the evangelical and temperance movements of the nineteenth century it is almost unheard of for a Presbyterian minister to touch alcohol). He slips out from the manse suddenly one evening and meanders in the direction of the beach; he is doubtless out for an evening walk, a breath of fresh air after being shut up in the study all day. Good evening, Alice Voar, and how are all the kids? Oh, that was good. He trusted she was well. He hadn't seen her in the pew for one or two Sundays ... Nice Laddie, nice dog, down now, nice Laddie Kerston ... Well now, Timmy, and when are we going to get that door of yours sorted, eh? Another winter and it'll be rusted completely away ... So he drifts, this man of God, between the general store and the pier. He pauses just outside the door of the public bar. He half turns away, he appraises the fall of the waves on the beach, he studies the dappled evening sky. Then suddenly he whirls about and with one mindless stride is in through the door with Wm. Scorradale, Licd. to Sell Ales, Wines, Spirits, Tobacco painted over the lintel. A cousin of his in Australia – he tells the landlord – he has had a letter from him, this cousin has read in some article somewhere about the Orkney malt whisky and would be most obliged if he would send him a couple of bottles. What, Mr Scorradale would pack the whisky and wrap it himself at no extra cost, apart from postage? Oh no, that wouldn't be necessary – you see he would be enclosing a letter to his cousin with the parcel. How much? Six pounds. Thank you. Yes. It was a bonny evening ...

'Or it might be that he was expecting visitors in a week or two. Yes, trout fishers, they wouldn't be too pleased if there wasn't a dram for them when they came back tired from a day's casting in the loch. Now would they? These trout-fishing guests of his said that that was the most exquisite moment of the day: to sit down beside a peat fire with a glass of malt whisky in your hand, and the light going, and the music of the waters still in your ears. He himself wouldn't know. Yes, three bottles, Mr Scorradale, if you please ...

'Or it might be the feeblest and most pathetic lie of all; that his mother has a bad cold, and the only thing that seemed to help was a drop of hot toddy before she went to bed. A gill? Oh, a full bottle while they were at it, it was always handy to have in the house, in case of emergencies ...

'These are some of the subterfuges by which Simon McKee appeases the dark angel that stands over him always. Then, when the supply is exhausted, usually within two days, and he dare not go back to Scorradale for more, and he is on the rack of a hangover, he mounts his pushbike and makes for the farms; especially the farms where they brew the rich heavy ale of the north.

'And the whole island laughs at these pathetic little charades. And well he knows that they laugh. And sometimes he smiles himself, sitting at his desk and wondering, as the six-week period of abstinence draws to an end, what new lie he can tell across the public bar. His invention is almost exhausted. Would Westray the ferryman bring him drink over from the town, and not blaze the fact all over the island? It might be worth considering. That might be the best way of all.

'I have finished. I have gone on far longer than I intended. But it was necessary, I think, to put the complete picture before you.

'Where does this torrent have its quiet tainted beginning?

'I will put one last image before you, then I will trouble you no more. It is this: a pale ailing lad, fretted with earache and the dazzle of the spring light, lying listless on a Marchmont couch. A woman holds out a glass of red wine to him. The traffic ebbs and flows outside, and the shouts of children come from the back gardens. The boy drinks.'

The fog heaved and groaned and shuddered. A monster with glaring eyes leapt out of the dissolving heraldry and trembled to a halt at the gable-end of the general store. It was the car from the Hall. Miss Agatha Fortin-Bell switched off the headlamps and got out. From the back seat she heaved a square wickerwork basket and set it down on the road.

'Mrs Evie,' she shouted, 'a word with you. I want the loan of your barrow. Hello there.'

Mrs Olive Evie knitted away at a Fair Isle cardigan behind the counter. She let on not to hear (though, as The Skarf said, when Miss Fortin-Bell called you could hear the echoes at John o'Groats). Mrs Evie knew perfectly well what was in the wind. This was the day for the summer distribution of the welfare clothes. She didn't see why she should lend any assistance.

'I say, Mrs Evie,' cried Miss Fortin-Bell, 'your hand-barrow.'

Mrs Olive Evie knitted away silently. She didn't see why there was any need in Hellya for welfare clothes at all. They could all afford to smoke, yes and drink too when the notion took them. She didn't see why she should hurt her own shop by assisting in the handing-out of woollens, drapery, and footwear. She fixed her mouth in a firm line.

Miss Fortin-Bell, without more ado, seized the barrow from under the window of the shop and wheeled it over to the basket. She manoeuvred the scoop of the barrow under the edge of the basket and with one heave and totter settled the basket squarely and securely on the slatted seat of the barrow. Miss Fortin-Bell was a very strong woman.

Which door was which? She always got them mixed up. Well, it didn't really matter. Start anywhere. Her hair was a bed of seed-pearls. Her kilt swung damply against her calves. She set down the loaded barrow at the first door she came to. She opened the door.

'Hello there,' she said.

Mrs Ellen Kerston rolled out of the kitchen.

Mrs Ellen Kerston was very sorry. Her husband had forbidden her to accept any welfare clothes. Her husband was a very proud person. He would kill her if it came to his ears that she had accepted one stitch. He was a terrible man in his rages. No, she was sorry, but there it was. She would have Miss Fortin-Bell know that her father had been one of the biggest farmers in the island of Quoylay. Pride had been bred in her bone. She could not but agree with her husband. Good afternoon.

The dialogue of whale and horse.

Miss Fortin-Bell wheeled the barrow to the other end of the village. The old woman who kept the hens came out in answer to two thunderous knocks. The old woman's face has the very pure look on it that is left briefly by birth or love or death.

Who was it? The laird's sister, Miss Fortin-Bell? Oh, she was expecting somebody else, Andrew Hoy of Rossiter with his measuring-tape. No, she had enough clothes to see her time out. Yes, Ben was inside, but he wasn't needing anything either. Would the laird like a few hen eggs for his supper? She was expecting Andrew Hoy from Rossiter with his tape measure. That's who she thought was at the door.

Bella Budge retreated slowly before the imperious presence.

Miss Fortin-Bell stalked Bella Budge step by step into the centre of the room. Then she looked sideways and saw the waxen face on the pillow. Then she was out in the fog, shaking. She had to sit down on a shaft of the barrow for a minute. A band of sweat silvered her brow.

The colloquy of horse and hen and skull.

Enough of this nonsense. Why hadn't the silly old woman told her in the first place that her brother was dead? Over there was the beachcomber fellow smashing up jetsam wood with an axe at the end of his house. Miss Fortin-Bell rose to her feet. She trundled the barrow towards Timmy Folster. Sounds mingled, splintering wood with pealing iron.

The dialogue of horse and otter.

Timmy was most grateful. Yes, Timmy was badly in need of a pair of boots. Did they have tackets on the soles? That was fine, he wouldn't slide and break a leg in the seaweed. Oh; trousers too. What generosity. Timmy had one pair of trousers, the pair he had on, and as the lady could see his shirt – such as it was – was sticking out of the arse of it. Would the lady not deign to enter his humble abode? Oh well. Timmy was most grateful anyway.

Timmy went joyfully in at his scorched window bearing the gifts of the rich and the mighty. Miss Fortin-Bell raised the shafts of her barrow and veered away from that patchwork of smells: piss and meth and mildew.

There was one house she didn't want to go to – the one where the communist lived – where she had been so insulted at Christmas. Now where on earth did that terrible person live? He should have been horsewhipped for the things he had said. She trundled the barrow past a window.

'Get to hell away from here, you faggot,' said a voice from the interior. 'Horse-face, bugger off. Don't relieve your conscience at this door. Away, you centaur.'

A pale oval with huge glinting circles in it squinnied at her through the window. A red ellipse widened and roundened and pursed, The Skarf's radical mouth. A rigid cylinder jerked slowly and deliberately upward, twice, The Skarf's insulting thumb.

Horse rampant and tarnished sun.

Miss Fortin-Bell found herself, breathing fire, outside a door that seemed to hide a cot of doves. Of course it was the woman with all the bastard children. She ought to have known, by the rose-bush. Her basket was always well lightened in this house. Her thumb depressed the sneck.

'Hello there,' she called.

The dialogue of pigeon and horse.

Oh, it was the lady from the Hall. Come in, come in, she must pardon the mess, it was all them kids, what a stir-up they made. Wait till she took that nappy off the chair, peedie Skarf still wet himself sometimes. Oh yes, there was a new one since last summer, over there in the pram look, sleeping, the angel. Sigrid. Sigrid Voar? Oh no, just Sigrid. You see, she didn't know who the father was. It was that dark she never saw him. It was the Saturday night of the Hamnavoe Carnival, the next wildest night of the year after Hogmanay. Whoever he was, he kissed her in the cattle-shed at the pier. So she didn't know what to call this precious in the pram. This peedie one clinging to her apron, that was Skarf. Skarf. Yes, Skarf was the father. She liked Skarf. Maybe he was lazy, a bit, but nobody could deny he was right clever. Well, let her think, she had, let her see, yes, seven bairns now. Yes, she called them all by their fathers' names, it kept them from being jealous of one another. Only in the school Miss Inverary insisted on calling them all Voar, she said it made it simpler for her with the school register and everything. The one older than Skarf Skarf was Sam Westray, that was him out there chasing rags of mist, he was home from the school with a cold in the head. The boatman was his father, Ivan Westray. She didn't like Ivan Westray very much, he had never paid so much as one black penny for the bairn. Oh yes – ha ha –the lady was right, steps and stairs. The next biggest one after Sam Westray was Shirley Whaness. Yes, that was right, the religious fisherman. Rachel was good to Shirley. Rachel had no bairns of her own. Rachel wanted Shirley to stay in her house all the time. But Rachel wasn't getting Shirley, it would break her heart to let Shirley or any of the bairns go. Shirley was seven. After Shirley came Sander Scorradale. Sander would be nine come Lammas. She got two bottles of guinness every week-end from the hotel and a half-bottle of gin at New Year. Yes, as the lady said, that was something. Then there was Sophie Kerston. Sophie was like her father, very small. A wicked temper the thing had too, when she was roused. Sophie was eleven. How many was that? Six. The oldest one was Sidney, a right clever boy at school, so Miss Inverary said, and in August he would be going to the senior school in Kirkwall. She would like Sidney to go on to the college and pass out for a minister, only he had brown nicotine stains on his fingers already, so it wasn't likely he was kirk-inclined. Oh yes, she was indeed very proud of Sidney, and so should the lady be too. Sidney what? Sidney Fortin-Bell. Some mistake? Oh no, there was no mistake about it at all. It happened when she was a kitchen maid up at the Hall – oh, that wasn't yesterday, it was when old Mrs Fortin-Bell was still alive but poorly, before the lady came to be with her uncle the laird. The laird had come to her in the Hall kitchen one Saturday afternoon. A nice old gentleman. He had wanted her to light him down to the cellar with a candle – he was going to look for some particular bottle of wine to entertain the Hamnavoe provost that evening at dinner. Half-way down the stairs he had blown the candle out ... She hoped there was nothing amiss. The lady was looking pale. Would she put on the kettle for a cup of tea? Oh well, if the lady was sure she must be off so soon. And what about the basket of clothes – was the whole lot for her? It was all right, really, the laird sent her a ten-pound cheque every quarter regular, and he let her live rent-free in the cottage. It was the very worst fog they had had that summer so far. And poor Ben Budge was dead. Sam Westray, come out of that fog and try on this jersey at once. Good-bye. Thank you kindly.

The soliloquy of the horse, proud plumes of fire, a passion of hooves, on the metalled road outside.

'I will thank you,' said Mrs Olive Evie from the door of the shop, 'not to take away Mr Evie's barrow without permission in future.'

Miss Fortin-Bell swung the starting handle. The car shuddered into life. The fog received them.

The parley of beasts on the heraldic shield of Greenvoe was over. They re-entered the stone and the silence.

Now were the feet of Samuel grown heavy and stained with travel, for after that first pure access of joy in the temple the keeper of the gate thereof revealed to him by fair words that he was by no means come yet to the City of God but he must fare on alone for many a mile before he arrived at the place. And he put a staff and a lanthorn into Samuel's hand for to help him on his journey, and fastened stout sandals upon his feet.

Samuel bade farewell to that angel porter and the other bright presences that thronged the gate, and addressed himself to the pilgrimage. He walked all the middle part of the day with the sun above his head and his feet in the dust. After a time, being weary, he sat himself down at the wayside to rest. He heard, very far and faint under the horizon, the sea, as it were a thread of surf, and was glad that his face was set towards the interior of that country, where those ancient sorrows of salt would be all overpast and forgot.

As he thought on these things, it seemed to him that shawled women came about him in the twilight and ministered comforts unto him. They brought him to a house that was nearby the road, where a fire of coals was burning in a hearth. And they poured water into a basin and set his feet in that coolness and light, and afterwards dried him with woven napkins. And they brought to him cakes of the best wheat, and they begged that he should bide with them awhile until he had further refreshed himself with sleep. And one kissed him on the cheek, and her mouth smelled of roses. Another lit a candle and set it on a shelf so that it gave light to all the house. And then the man of holiness looked upon the women of the household, and in the candlelight he knew their faces, for their faces were the faces of the women in the island from which he had set out upon the first stage of his pilgrimage that same morning. An unquietness came upon him. He looked closer at them and could not discover the face of her whom he loved (but fruitlessly) with the love that is due from husband unto wife. But Samuel knew these other women for sinners and daughters of seduction, and he bade them sternly begone, and they shrank from him like wraiths of mist from the cliffs, and the last to vanish was the woman that had kissed him with lascivious lips, whose name was Alice.

Then Samuel came and stood at the lattice window of the House of the Women and looked out into a garden that had rose trees in it, and lilies, and lilacs, and many another fair plant, and in this grove beside a fountain was the stone image of a woman that (it seemed to him) had been carven in the likeness of his wife Rachel. Many sorrows were graven on the face of that statue, the grief of childlessness and the new pain of widowhood, so that tears ran down her stone face and dropped slowly into the bowl of the fountain. An answering commiseration rose in Samuel, yet when he sought for the door that led out into the garden he could by no means find it. In the taste of that grief he awoke, and found himself where he had fallen asleep at the wayside.

The pilgrim woke to a great babble of voices and musical instruments and random cries, and he looked about him, and behold on either side of the road a fair had been set up, with people in holiday garments coming and going among the booths. And Samuel sought to avoid that vanity by taking another path, but he could not, for the only road ran right through the merry hulla-baloo. Then Samuel took his staff in his hand and hardened himself to pass among the revellers. There was a booth in that place for the sale of ardent liquors, and many red-faced reeling folk made a clamour about the barrels and flagons. And Samuel considered awhile the face of the man who was purveying that which in the end stingeth like a serpent, and it was the man he had known in the time of his mortality in that fair island, the same that kept the hostelry there, whose name was called Scorradale. And while he looked, a man lurched from the place of tankards and retched violently on the road, and again and again his belly heaved into his throat. And Samuel looked, and behold the man was a great toper and thief called Kerston that likewise he had known form-erly. The drunkard clung momently to Samuel's coat as he passed, but Samuel shook him off, and passed on. He discovered to his amazement a frond of seaweed on his sleeve, and in his hand a limpet shell, and it was as if a sign had passed between those two fishermen in their encounter. Samuel cast these worthless un-wanted things among the stones.

At the next booth sat a man whose face brimmed with crafty secret smiles, and when this one or that in the carnival approached they whispered in his ear, and it seemed none could go nor come nor perform any office whatsoever nor acquire any favour in the fair except by leave of this subtle councillor. And he listened to their petitions and fed upon them as one would feast on honey and figs. And Samuel looked, and it was a face he had known otherwhere, and the features wrote themselves as the man Evie that had been a petty merchant and potentate in that island that he had shaken from him like a burden that very morning.

'Why then am I not quit of these faces?' said Samuel within himself.

He passed deeper into the fair.

And Samuel stopped before a booth where there was much pointing and rib-poking and ridicule among those who stood to behold the spectacle, but others stood still with awed mouths. For this was a gorgeous tent, with a gilded pole in the centre and hangings of scarlet; yet the glory had long since vanished from it, and our pilgrim saw that the gilt was peeling and the silk had many a hole in it from the moth's devouring. On the crest of the booth was a stone in form of a shield, quartered, with ancient devices cut on it. And behold in the midst of this tarnished pomp a tableau of three: an old man with a palsy in his hands, and a monster that was half a woman and half a horse, and a young naked woman. The old man uttered in a hollow voice over and over again, *I am the master of this fair, I am the father and protector of you all. I pass in my chariot. I trouble the dust.* And while Samuel looked, the proud stone that crowned this tableau seemed to crumble and to run out in dust, like time from a loaded hourglass, till all was emptiness.

And Samuel passed through the thickening throng, and there against a blackened stone a man squatted and begged alms from the passers-by. His clothes were a ravelment of scorched rags. Now and again a coin was flung into the dust beside him, but mostly ridicule and contempt were put upon him, to which mockery he responded with unoffended smiles. And one reveller to amuse his fellows spat at him, but he let the insult run down his cheek as if it had been a fleck of shining sea-water. And (though he reeked indeed of debauchery) he looked on all men as if he loved them.

Still Samuel made a way for himself through the tumult with his staff.

Soon Samuel beheld a booth that was a great abomination unto him, for that it had a text of holy writ inscribed upon the portal, concerning the bush that burned always but was never consumed by the fire, the same which Moses beheld on Mount Sinai; which is taken to be a figure of THE CHURCH; but this booth Samuel considered to be a simulacrum and a delusion unto the people. For he which purported to be shepherd to all souls in the fair sat by himself apart within the darkness of the booth and brooded over a bottle, whilst the seven wolves of sin loped ever unregarded about the fair, a spectral pack. And further in sat an old woman who with shears cut from a bale of dark cloth the shapes of monsters, and the floor about her was strewn with cuttings, and at times she smiled and at times was troubled by the forms she herself created out of the web.

Now Samuel longed to shake the dust of this place from his feet. Yea, his soul panted for the City of God, even as the hart panteth for the water-springs. Set it is among quiet pastures and still waters. And there is no night there, nor winter, nor death, nor rage of seas: but all is such opulence and splendour that the very pebbles of the streets are solid sapphires and diamonds, which the children cast at each other in holy and innocent games, and the dust that their feet disturbs lieth about the pavements in drifts of purest gold. But what with the throng and the jostling and the thrusting of many bodies in every direction, Samuel could make but small progress through the fair.

Presently he came to a place where a man stood upon a wooden box and harangued the people with promises of worldly felicity. There is nothing, cried he, beyond this fair and the infinite stars over it – yea, and our five witty senses and the inborn lamp of the intellect – these alone exist. Needful it is, cried the man, that we look upon this fair to reform it, yea and to make it a place where men might walk with dignity, and their children after them, a city signed with the sun. In the new light men will see how wretched and bestial and dark their condition has hitherto been. Yea, in that glorious morning they will burn down the booths of privilege, oppression, superstition ... But in truth only a few folk stood about this preacher, for the multitude did not receive from him what they all so ardently sought – instant sensation, the foul delights of the pig-sty. And indeed Samuel agreed with the speaker thus far, that the fair seemed full of Gaderene scrithings and foetors and squealings and grunts.

Still Samuel made a way for himself with his staff and lanthorn, and presently the press of people slackened, and thinned out, and were a few isolated drunken stragglers coming and going, until at last he was alone on the road. Behind him the fair kept for a time a confused diminished murmuring, like a beehive. Now Samuel's feet were strong and urgent upon the road. On either side stretched fair shining fields, for the countryside was white towards harvest. A gladness came upon the pilgrim as he progressed. Yet it seemed strange to him that there were no labourers in the fields. Samuel examined more closely the heads of corn that hung their quiet bronze across the ditch, and plucked one, and it was bursting with ripeness. Yet when he looked upon the farm houses, he saw that in this one the door hung warped and useless from its hinge, and sheep drifted through that one, and the roof of another had fallen in, and all the hearth-stones were black. And the glebe, that had seemed so richly burdened, in truth stood rotting at the door of winter.

Then Samuel heard again as it were the turning of a wave.

Now shadows began to gather like pools among the hills, and one star shone in the west. Wherefore Samuel struck a flame in his lanthorn, and walked on, for he considered that in all likelihood he must now endure another night in the wilds before he could see at last the towers of the City of God on the horizon, like opal and agate and beryl and purest crystal, a myriad shining, the dwelling places of the saints.

The wash of the sea came to him again, wave upon wave falling among stones, and this (together with the familiar ravaged faces he had encountered earlier) disturbed Samuel greatly; yet he considered within himself that the shadows of a man's former life must needs cling about him for a space of time, until the memory withers away utterly at last in the dawn of eternal life.

As Samuel walked on through the deepening night, a footstep fell in with his, and a figure kept pace beside him, and conversed with him. And this man's talk was all of foreign lands, of bazaars and icebergs and albatrosses, for he had been (he said) a sailor.

Now, however, he was grown tired of adventuring, and was bound home. And truly his conversation might have been a pleasant diversion unto Samuel, but that it was plentifully studded with profane and blasphemous words, so that Samuel upbraided him concerning his language, and furthermore he warned him that unless he purified his tongue he would in no wise pass through the portals of the City of God. To which the seafarer replied that they would have to take him as they found him, he had a berth booked there and not hog, dog, or devil would keep it from him, for now he had the promise of a long rest. The manner of speech was as familiar to Samuel as flecks of spindrift on the face. Then Samuel in the darkness raised the lanthorn as high as his shoulder, and peered into the face of this reckless one, and behold the man had pennies for eyes and a gravecloth was tied about his jaw; and a terror came upon Samuel, and he stood stockstill on the road. *Attend me with spade and shuttering three days hence,* said the corpse, and left Samuel and fared on alone into the deeper darkness; as a man might vanish into the maw of a great wave.

Samuel heard indeed the bruit of the ocean on his right hand not far off, so loud and insistent that now he considered within himself whether he had not mistook the road entirely.

A weariness and a sorrow fell upon this pilgrim, and he sat down by the roadside to compose himself with prayer and reflection. How can any man ever be sure that he will gain entrance into the City of God? Dismal forever the soul that is turned away from that gate by the swords of angels, however good the man might have been in the time of his mortal life, however resplendent his gifts and works and benefactions. Samuel indeed believed that he was one of the chosen, a sprig of the burning bush, one of the true sheep of the fold, but now, betwixt sea and city, doubts gnawed at his soul like worms. This much was certain, that unless the mysterious hieroglyph of charity was graven deep in a man's heart, he would not enter, he could not enter, he could not endure for a day or an hour the love of God that was the light and the life and whole commerce of the city towards which he travelled – yea, he would shrivel in the air of paradise, as a jellyfish melts in the sun, such was the ardency of the fire of God's charity.

The sounds of the sea ran ceaselessly now through the sluice of his skull, so that he could hardly pursue within himself the holy argument.

Nay, but he had faith, and by faith alone a man is justified.

And then Samuel heard, mingling with the hush and crash of waves, a single lost dolorous cry.

His whole being quickened with rage and unbelief. There was no sea in this place, God had hung up the seas like tapestries that had the shapes of fish and bird and ship woven upon them, on the walls of his city, to be a diversion to the elect, and what mortal men call the sea is but a wavering reflection of that heavenly artistry. He was being plagued with delusions of the devil: first the hostelry of the women; then the fair; then the rotting fields; now these ancient sea sorrows. He rebuked himself sternly. He had been summoned. He was late. He might yet reach the city before daybreak. He trimmed his lanthorn. His staff and sandals beat forward upon the road that narrowed here to the width of a sheep-track.

He lengthened his stride. Then once more, through the collapse and wash of surf, he heard the cry of drowning.

Samuel turned back. He left the sheep-path. He found himself on a wide moor of whins and heather. He stumbled down a slope towards the hidden centre of pain. The wind was rising. A fog-horn moaned at him from far away. The moor dipped and dipped ever more steeply, then stopped abruptly, then flung itself upon sea noise and emptiness. Samuel swayed on the verge of the cliff. He crouched down. He peered over the edge. He seemed to know the place; still it was hard to see, fog fumbled and tore in every fissure, and the cliff base was completely hidden. It seemed as though, from one noise among the tumult of noises, a boat was being pounded on the rocks far below. The sea sent cold breath after cold breath up at him. A fleck of spindrift stung his lip. 'I am too old for this', said Samuel. He hesitated, then turned and yielded himself reluctantly to the perpendicular. His knuckles shone white among the heather tufts till he found a first foothold; then he began to climb down with care from ledge to fissure to crack. It was slow precarious work, especially without a rope or a helper; he drew his crag-skill from old almost-forgotten experience.

It was broad daylight, he noted with surprise, except that the crags were blurred with the shifts and shrouds of fog. He groped and felt his way down the sheer face. The sea sucked and stretched and echoed and whitened beneath him, and he heard now clearly enough the irregular rasp of wood on stone. He knew this broken ladder of rock all right, many a time he had climbed down and up again after gulls' eggs on the Red Head of Hellya when he was a young man. His rubber boots – what had become of his sandals, stick, lantern? – hindered him; he eased them off, one after the other, and let them go; they thudded softly from the face. The foghorn sounded regularly from the Skerries. His feet clung and paused, found niches, narrow bases, felt down, probed, hesitated. It was a poised skilful unhurried descent. He must have been sprawled for a half-hour now on the crag face, he reckoned, jerking himself slowly down. His feet and his hands read the rock like a blind man at a page from a massive familiar stone book. He thrust his knee into a crevice. The next buttress was the Kist where you had to ease your weight over to the left, first the left foot and then the right hand and then the right foot, and feel with the left foot down to a ledge carpeted with campion and guillemots' droppings; there they had plundered for days when they were boys in the summer holidays. Samuel smiled to remember it; the three best cragsmen in his boyhood were himself and Ben Budge and Mansie Anderson. The immensity and indifference of the sea came up at him in cold breath after cold breath. He paused and looked down; the half-destroyed boat was maybe twenty feet under him now; and the sight of it disconcerted him, for it had a familiar curve to it. He swung himself across the Kist. All the way down from here you belonged utterly to the sea. Its vastness heaved up at you and fell away in cold yawns and chokings. His hand clung to a wet spur. His foot probed down, and was deluged to the knee, and again to the thigh. His toes touched vibrant wood, a thwart, rowlocks, then he lost the boat again in a rising souse of sea. Samuel waited for the next swell to come and then he let go. He fell into the bottom of the boat, among creels and an empty can and what seemed a writhe of wool and rubber. A man's body was lying in the stern, so saturated that it seemed to be pumping water out of itself. Samuel got to his feet and stooped over the corpse. It was? Yes, it was Kerston, it was the drunkard and the blasphemer and the thief. And in a flash he recognized the strewn untidy intact interior of the *Ellen* (he had made some mistake – this was not the boat he had seen from the Kist being systematically smashed apart). Was the man dead? No sound out of him. A thin green stream oozed from his mouth, the spew of drowning. The boat seemed now to be well clear of the base of the crag, free and whole and buoyant. Samuel bent lower over Kerston. He must try to save this man. He put his mouth to the cold mouth and emptied his lungs unto it. The kiss transformed everything; for the body seemed to mingle with his, to rise up and through him, to stand high above him; and his own body fell through the drowning with an amazed cry. He was a slobbered face laid obliquely on the bottom of the boat. He was an eye gazing into an empty limpet shell that slipped back and fore with the movement of the boat – this shell was the most beautiful thing the new eye of Samuel had ever seen. He was a shoulder racked up and down and across with barbs and burning wires. He was ribs contracting and opening like bellows with a slow rhythmic pulsation. He was a gutted heart that flushed and glowed and flamed into coughings and retchings and chokings. Green bile flowed out of Samuel's mouth. Samuel thought that the tassel of bladderwort stuck in the flank of the *Ellen* was the loveliest creation of God; and the shifting limpet shell was an emerald of the sea, a piece of the original slime shot through with a throb of divine wonderment. He had come to the place. Out of gratitude Samuel tried to say a word or two. A groan burst from his mouth.

'So you're alive,' said Bert Kerston above him. 'By God, Whaness, you nearly had it today. The sea nearly got you. You'll never be closer.'

Bella Budge sat in the window between the fog and the cold shape on the bed.

The door shook and Andrew Hoy of Rossiter, the undertaker, came in dankly.

'Where is he?' said Andrew Hoy.

'Over there on the bed,' said Bella. 'Where else?'

Andrew Hoy took a tape measure out of his coat pocket and measured Ben as if he was a plank of wood, and indeed it was in terms of planks of wood that he now viewed the stillness on the bed. (Ben had been outraged at the price of the new coat Bella had bought for him from Joseph Evie three harvests ago. 'My next goddam coat,' he said, 'will be a wooden coat' ... Now he was being measured for his wooden coat.)

'Standard size, that's good,' said Andrew Hoy. 'Funeral's on Monday. Half-past two. I've seen Evie. I've seen the minister. I have still to see Whaness the gravedigger – I expect his boat'll be in now. Who do you want to carry the coffin?'

'The Best kens,' said Bella.

'There's not that many to choose from,' said Andrew Hoy. 'There were a hundred men in this island when I was a boy. I'll speak to a few. You'll need to have a bottle of whisky for them, maybe two.'

'Rum,' said Bella. 'That's what Ben always drank.'

'Whisky's more usual,' said Andrew Hoy.

'Rum,' said Bella firmly.

'I'll order two bottles then from Scorradale. That'll come to nearly six pounds. Drink was half-a-crown a bottle when I first drank.'

'Well, well,' said Bella. 'Tell me this, how much will the funeral come to?'

'Forty pounds odds,' said Andrew Hoy.

'Forty pounds!' cried Bella. 'It's dearer to die than to live.'

'There's a death grant,' said Andrew Hoy. 'That comes out of his national insurance. Ask Evie about it. It covers about half the cost. Do you want a wreath?'

'I suppose so,' said Bella. 'Forty pounds!'

'I'll see to that too,' said Andrew Hoy. 'Lilies is best. Now if you'll excuse me. I have a meeting tonight in The Bu stable. I'm late as it is. I have the coffin lashed to my bike outside. An oak coffin. I hope you don't want pine.'

'Anything,' said Bella. 'I don't know about wreaths. *Flowers for the living,* Ben always said. *The dead can't smell . . .*'

Andrew Hoy went out for the coffin. Bella crossed over to have a look at Ben. His face was as remote as a star. She returned to the window seat. The grey hosts of the fog trekked silently past the window. They flowed round hidden Korsfea and deluged peatbog and grass and corn on their passage out to sea. One could think of them as all the island dead from the beginning of time.

A dank hen entered. It cocked at her a mad cold glittering eye. It had never had a scrap to eat since early morning.

Andrew Hoy pushed the door open with his shoulder. He entered awkwardly, his delicate white hands clutched round the slanting coffin.

'I don't know where we are,' said Ivan Westray. 'That's the truth.'

There was a man in the island of Hellya called Ivan. He was the son of William who was at home in the farm called Anders in Hellya. William was the son of Thomas who went mad one winter; ward was put upon him in the town of Edinburgh in Scotland; he was there till he died. His father also was called Thomas. He came from the island of Norday. Ivan had a boat called *Skua*. He ferried men and beasts between Hellya and the island of Hrossey. There was a tall stone tower built on a skerry west of Hellya. This tower had a fire at its highest part. It burned by night to warn sailors from the rocks that were dangerous in that part of the sea. Men kept perpetual watch and ward over the fire. Ivan sailed often to the tower; he bore food and other comforts to the guardians of the flame.

They could see nothing. Half an hour earlier, when they had set out from the lighthouse, the fog had thinned to a fine tissue. Through tossed soundlessly tearing unrolling bales of thinnest muslin they could glimpse Hellya. The veils tore and shredded. Another veil was withdrawn. A window in the manse glittered.

The red crags of Hrossey glowed with the late sun. But Quoylay on the other side of the Sound was utterly obliterated.

'It may come down thicker than ever just before sunset,' the principal keeper had said, adding some torn tissue from his pipe to the silent grey undulations sweeping out to sea. 'I've noticed that happening often.'

The horn blared.

'Miss Bell could stay the night,' said the young light-keeper. 'It isn't often we have the pleasure of entertaining a grand lady. I'm on watch. I'll put clean sheets on my bed.'

Ivan Westray, standing in the doorway, said he thought the fog was lifting. This was the clearest it had been all day. He tilted a half-finished can of beer. The metal tinkled against his teeth.

The principal keeper took the pipe from his mouth and shook his head.

'If the noon sun doesn't burn it up,' he said, 'it's here for another day. Just look at those lumps. The wind's blown it away northward, for the moment anyway. Maybe if you were to make a dash for it now.'

Ivan Westray sent the empty beer can clattering over the skerry.

'Come on then,' he said to Inga. And he strode down to the boat.

There was a man in the island of Hellya called Alisdair. He was the chief man in the island at that time, and bode at the Hall there. He was the son of Fingal who stayed mostly at Aberdeenshire in Scotland till his death. He was the son of Hamish who was killed in the fighting against those blacks in Africa who were called Fuzzy-Wuzzies; he was mostly at home in Hellya. He was the son of Colin who bought the island for ten thousand gold pieces in the year of the potato famine. Many of the island people sailed overseas, to Canada and New Zealand; later Colin turned over the crofts to be pastures for sheep. Alisdair's son was Robin. He married, a woman called Helen who was at home in Berkshire in England; her father had got his wealth from the manufacture of horns for mechanical carriages. Robin and Helen had one child, a daughter called Inga. She was at school in England, at a place called St Albert's. Always in summer she betook herself north to her grandfather's estate in the Orkneys. She was said to be a beautiful young woman, though rather lascivious.

The principal keeper was very solicitous. What had Inga been thinking of, to leave home without a coat? It was never safe to venture far in Orkney, even on the likeliest day, without a coat. He could lend her his duffle jacket. He sent the young light-keeper to bring his duffle jacket from the hook. It had been a great pleasure indeed to have Miss Fortin-Bell on their rock. He trusted she would not be long in coming back. Oh, he had almost forgot, she hadn't put her name in the visitors' book.

The horn roared.

The third lighthouse-keeper, a dark silent Highlander called Donald McAra, stood at the lighthouse wall and said nothing.

'Hurry up,' shouted Ivan Westray from the pier. He stood there with the painter coiled in his hand.

The red glow faded from the crags of Hrossey. The wind made a melancholy sough about the white tower.

The principal with the visitors' book and the young light-keeper with the duffle arrived simultaneously at the door. Inga was thrust into the jacket and buttoned up. The sleeves came down below her finger-tips. She had to pull the right sleeve back to sign the visitors' book.

'It iss thickening,' said Donald McAra gloomily from the sea-ward wall.

'For hell's sake,' cried Ivan Westray from the concrete steps, 'I can't wait for you all day.' The engine jugged gently.

How man seeketh to know woman: how with many subtle stratagems and with tremblings of the spirit and with alternate dolours and delights he seeketh to find out a way into the core of that mystery – this, gentle listeners, is the theme of our romance. Brake stirreth; hart rouseth; the horns sound near and far.

'Thank you for everything,' said Inga. 'It's been a marvellous day. Super. I'll never forget it.'

She ran down the pier and stepped into the ettling boat. Ivan Westray pushed off with a pole. Flutters of hands from the pier and from the circling boat, cries of farewell. Ivan Westray set her bow for the squat cone of Korsfea.

The Widow held one unstable shroud over her knees. Then the sea was suddenly dense with shrouds. The swathings fell on them, clustered coldly, gave way to yet thicker layers. In two minutes they were swaddled in a blind cocoon. Korsfea had vanished. One roseate outcrop of crag was touched by an ashen finger; it crumbled. Ivan Westray lit a cigarette. Inga looked behind her. An orange glowed high through the fog; the newly lit tower. Then the orange faded.

The rock voice shouted its warning.

'This is the worst it's been all day,' said Inga.

Ivan Westray said nothing. He held the boat on a steady course. He hummed tunelessly through pursed lips.

'It's like a journey into the land of the dead,' said Inga lightly. 'The first ghosts are all round us.'

'It's just a fog,' said Ivan Westray. 'I assure you. All that fancy talk will get us nowhere.' He left the wheel for a moment to reach for his yellow oilskin. He tossed the end of his cigarette into the sea. Then he pushed his head and arms into the oilskin, and pulled it down over him. He tilted his cap. He touched the wheel. He put furrowed brows on the sea. He looked very handsome in his yellow oilskin.

'Where are we, knight of the sun?' said Inga.

'Ask some bloody sensible question,' said Ivan Westray. 'The boat's headed for Hellya. I haven't altered course. We'll hit the island somewhere.'

'There are reefs,' said Inga, 'rocks.'

'Well,' said Ivan Westray, 'one thing sure, you can't live for ever. I would rather die in the sea than in the eventide home. Now shut your mouth till I concentrate on the steering.'

The blort of the foghorn shook them; as if from a few yards' distance.

'The fog,' said Ivan Westray, 'it twists everything. Sights, sounds, feelings. We're all right so far.'

The wind was rising from the north, a thin keep, and the grey hosts pressed on more urgently over the heave of the sea. Ivan Westray lit another cigarette. He tossed the cigarette packet to Inga. He bent across and held the flame of his lighter out. Her cheeks hollowed. She puffed and coughed, but the cigarette went out. Her hand was shaking a little.

The cry of a hidden bird entered the music of the sea, and faded.

Ivan Westray looked at Inga intently. He left the wheel. He sat down beside her. He took the cold cigarette out of her mouth and lit it from his own, then put it back into her mouth in a tangle of blue threads. Then he undid the top toggle of her jacket.

'Oughtn't you to be steering?' said Inga.

Ivan Westray undid the centre toggle, then the bottom toggle.

He pressed the thick cloth back over her shoulders. The cigarette fell out of her hand. A twelve-foot wave rose against the *Skua*.

'It's cold,' said Inga.

They fell against each other as the boat swooned down into the trough.

It was thicker than ever. The foghorn belched again, distantly.

A gull fell slowly out of the fog, hovered, settled on the stern of the boat, furled its wings. It turned a cold eye on the man and the woman in the cabin.

When it cometh at last to love, wild fowls and beasts, look not for man nor woman to have pity upon your hunger in a cold season; no, for then their thighs are loosened and a great host passes between them, all the hungry and piteous and naked that ever shall be on earth; nor can they spare a thought then for you, sea fowls, nor utter bread upon the waters for to staunch your hungers.

The bird stretched on tiptoe from the stern and unfurled and let go, a quick wing-flutter, a long plane and glide over the surface of the sea, and vanished into piercing plangent fog.

Ivan Westray took Inga by the arm and threw her down on the floor of the cabin. The boat, lying broadside now to the waves, lurched violently twice. He knelt across her. She clobbered his head with her muffled hands. Then her fingers shot out of one sleeve and flicked at him. A long pale fissure appeared on his face and grew livid. One drop of blood gathered and fell on her throat, a small warm spatter.

'No,' said Inga.

The boat ettled and fell away before a tumult of waves. Flecks of spindrift sifted over. They stung Inga on the bare shoulder.

'No,' she said.

And I would not have you think either that love is all sweet desire and gratification, and thereafter peace. The essence of love is pain; deep in the heart of love is a terrible wound. Yes, and though a man should grow wise and quiet at last, yet if he hath trafficked in love but once, he shall be borne to his grave with the stigma of suffering on him. His monument shall bleed.

Ivan Westray turned Inga over on her face. He lifted her by the slack of the coat and shook her out of it. She staggered and sprawled on the deck on her knees and forearms and fists.

She tried to get to her feet. A tumult of sea threw her against the cabin door. A plate slid off the rack and spun over the floor and slithered away into a corner. The two books fell off the shelf together. *The Orkneyinga Saga. On Love Carnal and Divine: Seventeenth Century Sermons.*

Ivan Westray lifted Inga up again and carried her over to the bunk. Drops of blood fell from his torn cheek on to hers. He laid her down. The last breath had been driven out of her. She lay like a throttled fish. Her shirt came away in two quick rents.

Blades of coldness passed into her body.

She opened her eyes at last. Up above, a scrape of sky. It brightened. It became a blue circle. Round this serene pole swept all the cold hosts of the fog.

Inga kissed the torn face beside her.

There was a rasping of wood on stone, a heave and stotter and prolonged rasp and rent.

Inga was free. She looked up. Ivan Westray was prodding the Greenvoe pier with the pole. The boat lay quiet. Little waves slipper-slapped on the concrete. Ivan Westray guided the boat to the steps. He leapt on the lowest step and tied her up. One side of his face was a scarlet map.

When he came back Inga wrapped the duffle round her nude shoulders. The coat was foul with sand and soil and blood and gull droppings.

'I'll tell you something,' said Ivan Westray. 'I don't fancy you at all. You're too thin. You're too full of bullshit out of books. I like women to know what it's all about. Did you get what you wanted? Try again next year. Now get away home. I don't want you on this boat all night. My reputation in this island is bad enough as it is.'

Inga huddled into the corner of the cabin and drew the blanket up over her mouth. She watched while he rounded off his day's work. He carried the empty containers and boxes up the steps of the pier, taking two or three at a time until the *Skua* was unloaded.

He examined for a while the long gouge on the side of his boat.

He climbed down into his boat. He washed his hands in the sea and dried them. From the cabin cupboard he took out a fold of silk. He wrapped it carefully in a square of brown paper; then he put it in his oilskin pocket.

And moreover who knoweth where the one jewel of love is to be found? For let a man travel far in search of it, and trade in every bazaar and market, and bear off the best treasures that are offered there; yet receiveth his soul no satisfaction therefrom; and many there be that after a lifetime of lust and liking and amorous dalliance descend disappointed to the dust. Yet on a day set apart and hallowed it may chance, once in many generations, that a knight cometh to a certain place, a tower or a chancel or a stone in the desert, and knoweth of a surety that there, guarded by ghost or dragon, abideth his heart's desire, the one pearl that all his life he hath sought.

Ivan Westray put the kettle on the gas-ring and cut slices of bread and stabbed a tin of corned beef with an opener.

Inga watched in silence.

The granddaughter of the chief man in Hellya asked a certain boatman to take her to the sea tower. There was much fog on the way back. The boatman whose name was Ivan forced Inga to lie with him in the cabin of the boat called *Skua*. Inga said he had done her a great wrong that day and that he would suffer for it. Ivan laughed. He said they would see about that.

Mr Joseph Evie put the letters and packets into the mail-bag to be ready for the ferry-boat in the morning; all but four letters with identical familiar writing on the envelopes. He put these four letters into his hip pocket. He came round the counter and tested the shop door from the inside to see that it was secure. He passed his eyes round the interior of the shop. Everything was in order. He moved into the living-room.

Mrs Olive Evie was sitting in her nightgown beside the fire, drinking cocoa.

'That man is still in the hotel,' said Mrs Olive Evie.

'Yes, I think the fog will clear by tomorrow,' said Mr Joseph Evie.

'The Skarf came in for an ounce packet of shag, and a biro. I marked it down in the book,' said Mrs Olive Evie.

' "Terms Cash",' said Mr Joseph Evie. 'Whenever they come in wanting tick just point to the notice above the desk, TERMS CASH. No need to say anything. Just point. When will you ever learn?'

'Old Budge,' said Mrs Olive Evie. 'How much would he have left now?'

'Go to bed,' said Mr Joseph Evie.

'I've mixed your cocoa in the cup,' said Mrs Olive Evie. 'The sugar is damp with all this fog. The kettle's singing.'

The kettle sang on the range. Presently it purred, the lid rattled, and a grey plume snorted out of the spout. Mrs Olive Evie was in her bedroom now, shuffling about and opening drawers. The kettle ramped on like a warhorse. Mr Joseph Evie did not empty boiling water into the cocoa cup. He waited until he heard a dull thud and a sigh: Mrs Olive Evie in bed. Then he took the four letters with the identical script on the envelopes and, one by one, held them to the steam until the flaps curled back. He withdrew the letters from the envelopes. He read them seriously, twice through. He considered for a long time, swaying in the rocking chair. Three of the letters he stuffed between the ribs of the fire until they fell back among the ashes in black whispering flakes. The fourth, addressed to the Lord-Lieutenant, he carefully resealed, adding a line of saliva from the grey tip of his tongue to the dead saliva of his wife. Mrs Olive Evie began to snore in the bedroom. Mr Joseph Evie tiptoed into the dark shop and opened the mail-bag and added the letter. Then he secured the neck of the mail-bag with string and pressed the lead seal flat.

The kettle was heaving on the range like a thing possessed, throwing out a jet of steam and boiling spittles, when he got back into the kitchen.

'I'm coming, I'm coming,' said Mr Joseph Evie.

He lifted the throbbing kettle and hung a colourless column upon the mixed cocoa and sugar and milk in the clay hollow.

'Is his boat completely wrecked?' said Bill Scorradale, pulling on the lever. 'The *Siloam*.'

'Smithereens,' said Bert Kerston. 'I saved his oars and a few of his creels. Rachel gave me a five-pound note when I took him home. I didn't want to take it but she pressed it in my hand. Took it out of that book in the window. It smelt sort of damp, mildewy. A fiver. So we better have a whisky all round.'

'Ben Budge died early this morning,' said Bill Scorradale.

He measured out two tots.

'So Rachel told me,' said Bert Kerston. '*The angel of death hovered over this island today*, she said. *He took Benjamin Budge. Samuel he spared.* A funny way to talk, that.'

'Ivan Westray's late tonight,' said The Skarf.

'He went up to the schoolhouse half an hour ago,' said Bill Scorradale.' He must have been in a fight in one of the Kirkwall pubs. There was sticking plaster on his face. He had something in his hand he was carrying up to the schoolhouse, a sort of small parcel.'

'Struggling like a shot seal in the water,' said Bert Kerston. 'Old Whaness. When I found him. Another minute and he'd have been a gonner. I pumped him for half an hour before his pulse started up. His very tongue was blue. And do you know what he had the bloody impudence to say, coming in to the pier?'

Timmy Folster came in.

'Well, Skarf,' said Bill Scorradale, 'and when are you going to start reading, eh? The bar shuts in twenty minutes.'

'Timmy always likes when The Skarf reads,' said Timmy Folster.

'I'm not going to read,' said The Skarf. 'Not tonight. Never again. I've written all I know. What's coming to this island is beyond prose. It will be poetry and music. The Song of the Children of the Sun. We'll all be dead, I expect. But the folk of Hellya will know it when they experience it.'

'The Skarf is right clever,' said Timmy.

'There he sat in the stern,' said Bert Kerston, 'shivering and shaking. Blue as bloody lead. And as we were passing the Taing he looks accusing-like at me and he says, *What were you doing there anyway, Kerston, at the place where my creels are?* To me, the chap that saved his life. I didn't bother to answer. Give Timmy a pint. Shivering and shaking and snatched from the jaws of death, teeth clashing together, to talk that way.'

The front door of the hotel opened. There was a slight displacement of fog. Someone passed out into the village. The fog settled.

'The guest,' said Bill Scorradale reverently.

Timmy Folster raised his pint of beer.

'Timmy is drinking,' he said, 'to the memory of Ben Budge. We must all be pall-bearers at the funeral on Monday. Andrew Hoy came to tell Timmy about it.'

The guest moved through the village just as night came down. The fog was thicker than ever. A purplish clot engulfed Greenvoe, except where a light from window or open door sank a crepuscular shaft into it.

The guest stood at Timmy Folster's burnt door. The sheet of corrugated iron swayed in the wind and twanged against the stonework. Timmy was not at home. Fog distorts all sights, sounds, touch, tastes, smells: unutterable stench brimmed out of the window. What seemed to be a half-filled blue lamp stood on the mantelpiece – the meth bottle.

The guest made a mark in his notebook.

The guest stood at the door of Alice Voar's house. The house fluttered like a dovecot. Deep within her Alice nourished the root of love. Alice cherished it with all the slumberous warmth of her body. Alice curled languorously about the exotic seed. The rose in the jam-jar in the window was a bare thorn and twenty shrivelled curls.

The guest made a mark in his notebook.

The guest stood at the door of the Whanesses. A man slept in utter exhaustion; he had travelled far, he had trespassed for a fleeting second into the land of the dead, and that is a long, hard, forbidden journey. A woman lit a lamp on the table. She came and held it over the sleeper. She uttered shapeless sounds over him. A few tears ran down her face on to the blue flagstones of the floor.

The guest opened his notebook and wrote.

The guest stood at the door of the Kerstons. Dreams threaded through the faces of strewn children. A woman sewed beside a lamp. A youth pushed past the stranger, not noticing him, and entered the house, and said good night to his mother, guiltily, and began to take his tie off beside the fire. The woman smiled. All her folk were safe, even Bert who was having a pint or two in the pub after his two lucky days on the sea. He too would soon be home, gathered to her, enwrapped safe at last, her entire man.

The guest wrote a sign on the white paper.

The guest stood at The Skarf's window. Pale sheets of paper scattered on the table inside, every sheet a scarred and clotted battlefield; and the cocoa-lid beside the ball-point pen overflowing with cigarette ends; and six warping creels in the rafters. Books in tea-boxes all over the room, hundreds of them, a few lying open and marked beside the manuscript where The Children of the Sun with many a glorious wound on them held a hard-worn ridge of history against trolls and priests and lairds; until the day come. A war on paper.

The guest made a sign of cancellation with his pen.

The guest stood at the drawn curtains of the manse. Silence possessed the sitting-room. Shadows humped here and there. A bowl of tall wild lupins stood on the sideboard; tongues of blue flame in the darkness and silence. Two petals fell off the sideboard, one after the other. The deprived lupin shivered ever so slightly. These tiniest of muffled thuds, that minute tinkle of water in the bowl, startled the shadows. The lupins had known the wind on the hill.

The guest considered, wrote, deleted, wrote.

The guest stood under the tall school window. Inside a woman stood among her scattered apples. This was her dream. She stood among bruised apples. A statue lay among the windfall, with a loose fold of Paisley pattern about it. The woman was shaken and a plucked tree. Some of the apples were withered: not all. The blossom had drifted away on a late spring wind. She dreamed. The blossom-time had been beautiful. An apple here and there was rotten. It was not before time. She put her arms about the statue. The cheek of the statue was broken. She opened the silk at the torso of the statue. She put her mouth to the nipple on its cold white chest.

The guest's pen sank deep in the soft white paper.

The guest stood at the door of the general store. Inside was a bottle of Scotch mixture, three shillings a pound. Inside hung a jersey with a Fair Isle yoke, four guineas. Inside was a sheet of fourpenny stamps. Inside was a letter concerning the worthiness of a certain one to be made an Officer of the Order of the British Empire. Further in was a cold kettle. Further in was a bed; on it reposed Mr Joseph Evie and Mrs Olive Evie; they slept; between them a great gulf was fixed.

The guest wrote.

The guest stood at the door of the house of death. A wooden hexagon lay upon wooden trestles. A lamp burned on the mantelpiece. A face shone out of the hexagon towards the rafters. Three white strangled hens depended from the rafters by their feet: meat for the mourners. Three bottles stood on the table. Two people moved here and there. The bright face was covered. Then the man put his hammer and screwdriver into a canvas bag. The woman opened the door: light split the purple sea of mist for a moment. The man walked out. Andrew Hoy of Rossiter did not notice the guest. He mounted his cycle at the end of the house and set out for the stable of The Bu. The guest followed, walking among blue and yellow and crimson gouts of fog.

What he had written, he had written.

The guest stood outside the locked stable of The Bu.

Inside proceeded the initiation ceremony of The Horsemen. The guest could hear nothing: a night wind surged among the surrounding cornfields and filled all Hellya with the sound of ripeness.

> *The Lord of the Harvest. The Master Horsemen. The dead man lying blindfolded and bandaged; the horse-shoe on his chest. The lantern is extinguished. The Master Horsemen light candles and stand about the fallen Harvester.*

THE LORD OF THE HARVEST: This is the end of the sufferings of the hungry and the poor. Now art thou cancelled, crossed out. Thou art nothing. Thou hast no part in the estate of man any more, nor ever can have, being dead, having suffered the pain beyond death, being now ashes and cinders and dust; departed out of the sweetness of the sun and the knowledge of men, a thing of darkness and silence. I take from thee the sign of the horse.

(*He takes the horse-shoe from the Harvester and hangs it on the nail in the east wall.*)

With thee it is everlasting winter. Men will come soon with a stone to set upon thee.

(*The Master Horsemen spread a shroud over the Harvester. They bring a stone and lay it at the head of the victim.*)

SIX

The cone of Korsfea was shorn off. The loch of Warston was drained; red-throated divers and eiders and swans had to seek other waters. Hellya was probed and tunnelled to the roots.

The operation began one day when a gang of a dozen men with enormous baggage landed on the pier from the *Skua*. The strangers pitched tents in the field beyond Bella Budge's. A score of men crossed over from Hrossey the following day, and occupied the tents. All that week the *Skua* ferried more and more workers across; within a week they outnumbered the island people. Their vivid faces were everywhere in the island. Their feet beat on the roads with a different rhythm. Consignments of picks and shovels arrived. A first wooden hut was erected in a field under Korsfea; after a fortnight a few clerks occupied it.

Joseph Evie and William Scorradale achieved wealth in one wild month. The new inhabitants of Hellya had to be fed and refreshed like other men. At the end of every day Bill Scorradale secreted sheaves of banknotes in his mattress. The workmen trudged into the village every nightfall. Queer Irish quarrels broke out in the bar one week-end. Bill Scorradale didn't care. Let them fight. Tolerantly he rubbed his hands on his shiny apron. The longed-for harvest had come. He sweated up from the cellar with bottles a score of times a day. Ivan Westray assisted him behind the bar for two pounds a night.

Mrs Olive Evie stood behind her counter and could have sold her Fair Isle jerseys – suddenly raised in price to seven guineas – over and over again, and her melons and her tins of corn-beef and herring. The labouring work, which seemed to be taking place where the pasture of The Glebe met the heather of Korsfea, made the navvies very hungry; also they were paid high wages. Mrs Olive Evie sent her retail prices rocketing. Mr Joseph Evie was in the town most of the time; he was said to be finalising plans for the future of Greenvoe and its inhabitants.

Ivan Westray shuttled back and fore between the town and the island all day, week after week. He raised his fare from fifteen shillings to a pound per crossing, then to twenty-five shillings. Nobody queried it. Men with drawing-boards and theodolites and briefcases crossed over to the island; security officers with Alsatian dogs; clerks, cooks, cable-men, crane-drivers, pier-builders, more and still more labourers. Ivan Westray would cross over in the morning with bunches of picks and shovels piled here and there about the *Skua* – in the afternoon with a watchman's hut lashed to the cabin roof – in the evening with a sextet of cement-mixers.

The temporary camp was uprooted. The labourers moved into huts adjacent to the work-site. A wooden town sprang up overnight, with cook-house, laboratory, laundry, canteens, sick bay, offices, a hall, a detention centre. The Irishmen began to beat out a hard black ribbon between the pier and the site. Work started on a perimeter fence.

The island began to be full of noises – a roar and a clangour from morning to night. A thin shifting veil of dust hung between the island and the sun. The sea birds made wider and wider circuits about the cliffs. Rabbits dug new warrens at the very edge of the crags.

A phrase – 'black star' – was uttered by one of the engineers over pints in Scorradale's one Friday night. It went from mouth to mouth in the following days, whispered, as if it was a piece of magic, a very secret codeword. Even the villagers used it – to them it stood for the new music that had taken possession of Hellya. In fact there was nothing mysterious about it. 'Operation Black Star' – that was how the word was openly described in advertisements for workers that appeared in *The Orcadian* and in the window of Mr Joseph Evie's store.

After six weeks of pile-driving and crane-swinging, the pier got a temporary wooden extension. After that larger boats could approach and tie up. Great cargoes of cement were unloaded, lorries, more hut sections, cranes, bulldozers, transformers.

What exactly was happening up there between the Glebe and

Korsfea? It was impossible for any villager or islander to find out – the almost completed fence was too well guarded by men and dogs and barbed wire – but it seemed, from things the labourers said in drink, that a system of tunnels was being dug into the heart of the island, five of them in all (said Jock MacIntosh the foreman from Glasgow) radiating out from one central underground chamber. So it was indeed a kind of black star that was being burned and blasted under the roots of Korsfea and Ernefea and The Knap. What it was for, of course none of the navvies could say. It could be for oil or silver, though they didn't think so. All that mattered to them was that they were being paid large wages, with plenty of overtime and bonuses. The beer in their new canteen up at the site was passable, and there was bingo twice a week and a film show every Friday evening. It could be some kind of atomic work, they could not say . . . *See us six more pints of heavy, Scorrie.*

It soon became apparent that a kind of tension existed between Black Star and Greenvoe. For one thing, Greenvoe lay athwart Black Star's daily supply lines. Hens, sheep, children were forever wandering in front of the urgent lorries that thundered hourly between pier and site. The track between the huddle of houses was too narrow and eccentric to admit the larger vehicles; it was dust after a week of sun; and a quagmire when it had rained for an hour or two, a necklace of pools. *Greenvoe will have to go,* the engineers said in the hotel when they were flushed and omniscient with 'Claymore' whisky at the week-ends . . . The Welfare Officer up at Black Star had, however, more compassion. People lived in Greenvoe (he said); they had tied up their boats there for centuries; they could not be set destitute on the hills and shores. Ours is a compassionate as well as a questing age. The poor must be fed, housed, protected. The authorities – that is what everybody called the unseen anonymous men who had set Black Star pulsing – decided to solve the problem in the only way possible nowadays, by the generous distribution of money. Most of the villagers brooded uneasily over the forms they had to fill up and sign, but Mr Joseph Evie explained everything to them with tact and patience. The first cheques began to flow through the post office into Greenvoe.

Piecemeal thereafter the village died.

Bulldozers turned one day on the hotel, after Bill Scorradale had been paid extravagant compensation. The bar gaped briefly at the sky; then attic was mingled with cellar, and by night Bill Scorradale's castle was a stir of dust and a wide strewment of stones. Bill Scorradale looked at the ruin with dazed joy. Next morning the metal monsters attacked the store from three sides. But by that time Mr Joseph Evie and Mrs Olive Evie were safely in their Kirkwall bungalow with their windfall; though Mr Joseph Evie travelled frequently back and fore to smooth out the difficulties that cropped up from time to time between the two communities.

Once the wooden extension to the pier was finished the services of the *Skua* were no longer in such demand. A helicopter pad was built at the Glebe and the engineers and technicians flew in from Aberdeen. One day in August a very important man arrived, the controller. Ivan Westray hit an Aberdeen navvy and toppled him into the sea because the man asked him, sneeringly, where the palais-de-danse and the casino were. Too late he began to love his island.

Greenvoe shrivelled slowly in the radiance of Black Star. It was obvious, of course – even the Welfare Officer admitted that – that the village was moribund in any case, a place given over almost wholly to the elderly, the fatuous, the physically inept. Black Star merely accelerated the process.

The houses of the village went down, one after the other, as they were bought up by the authorities. They collapsed before clashing jaws and blank battering foreheads.

One after another the householders bore their extravagant cheques over to the banks at Kirkwall and Hamnavoe.

Alice Voar resisted for a month all blandishments and bribery. After all, any compensation she could expect would be on the small side, for all she owned was a garden shed and a rose bush (her house belonged to the laird). She had never seen so many men before. She was bewildered. She smiled here and there and everywhere, to begin with, till her face was set in a rigid rictal mask. These men behaved very strangely. One twilight two men knocked her down into the ditch, beyond Rossiter. She smiled. She scratched and kicked and flowed out of the clutching hands. She ran home like a hare before a diminishing darkling thud of hob-nailed boots ... A week later, at the pier head, a man from Tyne-side slowly crackled a five-pound note in front of her face. A signal had been made, but she did not understand it. She smiled and turned away ... There were random knockings at her door after the new wet canteen at the site closed for the night, so that she had to get Samuel Whaness to put a bolt on the inside. The knockings came louder and oftener. The door rattled at four and five o'clock in the morning. She smiled and comforted peedie Skarf, and turned over again to sleep. One night her rosebush was ripped out of the ground. It was more than she could bear. The mask broke. Alice tremblingly accepted her small cheque. She gathered her flock round her (all except Sidney, who had got a well-paid labouring job at the site) and fled to her sister's house in Ham-navoe. Her sister saw from her kitchen window the tribe chat-tering and clattering up the steps of the close, laden with gear; she turned the key in her lock. Door after door closed against her. Alice's flock wandered the street of Hamnavoe that night in a deepening silence. Finally they were given accommodation in an old second-war army hut on the side of the granite hill above Hamnavoe, and the bairns ran happily among swarming faces and a closer weave of stone, and were soon gathered into the new community. In April, Alice brought forth a tiny sun-kissed idol, and called him Singh Voar.

Timmy Folster had one glorious month among the dustbins of the site – paper-back novels, half-eaten pies, old cups, broken false teeth, pick shafts, bottles now and then with a good dram in the heel of them. He moved in on the debris of the hotel and found, among such treasures as an old sewing machine and a gramo-phone with a horn, a scattering of charred and smudged cards that seemed to refer to almost everybody in the island, including him-self. There were a good number of erasures and queries and cor-rections, as if they were only working drafts. He spent an hour that night reading brief cryptic biographies.

FOLSTER, Timothy John. b. 21/7/17. 5′ 4″ 104lb. Eyes blue. Hair dark brown. Bachelor. Third (only surviving) issue of John and Mary-Ann (*née* Linklater) Folster, Greenvoe: both deceased. No distinguishing physical characteristics. A casual harvester on farms, a casual beachcomber (we find that he has never declared any flotsam or jetsam to the relevant authorities). In receipt of state assistance. Education: Greenvoe Primary School ad age 14. Property—one house 'Sea View,' village of Greenvoe; in poor condition consequent on a fire 1/12/65; value approx. £10. Relatives: one first cousin (male) once removed, believed to be in Queensland, Australia, emigrated 6/7/23. Medical note: occasional methylated spirit drinker. Winter bronchitis. General health surprisingly good all things considered, possibly on account of a sufficient diet of greens, fish, seaweed, and an open-air life. Black Star potential (ex ten) Nil.

VOAR, Veronica Ann Alice. b. 3/9/39. 5′ 3″ 112lb. Eyes grey. Hair blond. Mole, rose-coloured, on right breast; mole, honey-coloured, on left buttock. Spinster. Fifth child, second daughter, of Thorfinn and Jessie (née Coubister) Voar, Wester Swinnasay: both deceased. Housewife. In receipt of state assistance. Irregular payments, in cash or kind, from putative fathers of some of her seven children. Education: Greenvoe P.S. ad age 15. Property: one shed, one rosebush, one garden spade. Resides rent-free in cottage 'Tangbreck' in Greenvoe, property of Colonel Alasdair Fortin-Bell—two habitable rooms in moderate state of repair. Relatives: numerous, in other parts of Orkney, a few in Glasgow and Aberdeen, cousins in New Zealand, Canada, South Africa. Children: seven (illegitimate) age range 11 months—15 years. Health: excellent. Character: see note on children; otherwise not vicious or abandoned. Black Star potential—9.

WHANESS, Samuel Ezra. b. 1/3/05. 5′ 11½″ 183lb. Eyes pale blue. Hair blond, interspersed w. white and grey. Distinguishing marks: harpoon wound, a transverse three-inch silvery scar along right ribs. Recently-sustained cuts to both hands; bruises right temple, l. shoulder (but temporary). Fisherman. M. Rachel (née Tomison) Whaness 22/9/40: no issue. One illeg. daughter (reputed, tacitly acknowledged) by Veronica Alice Voar (q.v.) Elder son Ebenezer and Peterina (née Spence) Whaness (both deceased). Address: 'Bethel', Greenvoe, a two-room cottage in good repair, property of subject, inherited fr. father. Education: Greenvoe P.S. ad 14. Property (cash): £3,228: 9: 7 in notes of several denominations and scattered silver coin variously deposited about the cottage 'Bethel', esp. as interleavings of a copy (1793) of *Pilgrim's Progress* on shelf over bed; and (in coin) in iron chest under bed—deposit acct. Bank of Scotland, Hamnavoe, £6,221: 2: 1—various articles fishing gear: lobster creels,

oars, sail, spars, fishing lines, hooks. No fishing boat at present.
Health: a setback (temporary) consequent on recent swallowing and
inhalation of a quantity of sea water, and exposure. Black Star
potential—4 (?labourer).

WESTRAY, Ivan. b. 27/12/43. 6′ 1″ 189lb. Eyes blue, hair bronze.
Bachelor. Only son of William Albert and Catherine (*née* Manson)
Westray, both recently deceased. Owner-operator of ferryboat *Skua*
—mail carrier—goods, livestock, passengers. Education: Greenvoe P.S.
ad. 12, Kirkwall Grammar ad 17, Aberdeen University (only one year
medical studies completed; 3 months' rustication for violent disorderly
conduct; renewal of grant queried by Ork. Ed. Comm.; thereafter refused to resume). Address: cabin-cruiser *Skua*, Greenvoe Pier. Other
assets: the abandoned croft Anders with 12.5 acres arable and bog,
value approx. £200; £25: 4: 8 P.O. Savings Bank. Relatives nil. Prison
record: held overnight and subsequently admonished Aberdeen
Sheriff Court 9/6/61, drunk and disorderly; held one week-end Kirkwall, subsequently fined £3, Kirkwall Sheriff Court, drunk and
disorderly at Hamnavoe Carnival, 23/7/67. Health: (1) Physical—
excellent (2) Mental—hereditary instability, 'morbus orcadensis'
(grandfather, sister, cousin underwent mental treatment). Issue: (1)
illegit. son by Agnes Carroway, Aberdeen (2) illegit. daughter by
Deborah Auk, Kirkwall (3) illegit. son by Veronica Ann Alice Voar,
Greenvoe (q.v.) Black Star potential—9 (knowledge of adjacent waters,
reefs, etc, wd. be invaluable).

Timmy read till his eyes were sore. There seemed to be a card for
every single person – man, woman, and child – in the island; and
besides that every place in the island (pasture, ploughland, knoll,
quarry, croft, pig-stye, sheep shelter, ancient monument, farm,
burn, waterfall, elevation, inland water, marsh, cliff, foreshore)
was described on its own separate card. Timmy got bored; the fire
sank in the stove. He emptied the grey drove on to the dying
embers. The stove roared and was a white blaze for twenty
minutes, and Timmy fell asleep in that warmth.

Mr Joseph Evie stepped in through his window the very next
afternoon and told Timmy he was going to take him for an outing,
seeing it was such a fine day. Timmy was delighted. He spat on his
shoes and wiped them with the sleeve of his jacket. He spat on a
sea-bleached comb and drew it through his fell of hair. He stepped
after Mr Joseph Evie into the *Skua*. On the Hrossey shore a large

blue van with a red cross on it was waiting. Councillor smiled, driver smiled, beachcomber smiled. Beachcomber followed councillor into the van. The van drove to Kirkwall. They passed a fine big house on the outskirts. 'Goodness,' Mr Joseph Evie, 'what a fine big house! I think we'll just go in and pay our respects, Timmy.' Timmy said that in his opinion that would be a good idea. Mr Joseph Evie knocked at the door. A lady with a white head-dress and starched cuffs received them; she seemed indeed to be expecting them. She took Timmy and Mr Joseph Evie to a room where half a dozen old men were smoking and grumbling and dozing. Timmy had never seen so many clean white beds, nor such high glittering windows. He turned to tell Mr Joseph Evie so, but Mr Joseph Evie was not there. Instead, the kind severe lady and a girl with bright eyes were standing beside him. 'This will be your bed, Timothy,' said the lady. It was a white rectangle topped with snowy pillows. But first they took him to a small room full of steam and jets of water and began gently to take his clothes off.

One nudge of the bulldozer and Timmy's house in Greenvoe was a rickle of stones. They found ninety-seven empty bottles in the closet.

The church stood among crashing seas of masonry.

The court was in recess once more, but behind the scenes the case against Mrs Elizabeth McKee proceeded inexorably. It was building up to the verdict and the judgement. She knew it; they were anxious now to be done with this case and this tedious old woman.

House after house collapsed round the manse. Mrs McKee drew her curtains closer against the dust and the raped skyline. It occurred to her that the engines of destruction were only waiting for the court's final sentence to bring the manse about her ears. She heard strange voices in her garden. *Simon*, she called. Simon did not come. He had gone to the site to play darts with the labourers; he had said that, she remembered, at tea-time. A long darkness lay on her. She awoke in broad daylight. They were breaking up a tombstone in the cemetery. *Simon*, she called in terror. They were summoning up the island dead to testify against her. It was terrible. Simon came, but he was changed – she saw him for what he was, a creature imprisoned in his own selfishness, a gleam in a mirror; he spoke but his speech was a sequence of bright false noises. Her womb had uttered a vain thing upon the world. She turned from him resentfully. The gable end of Timmy Folster's house went down in a long slither and clatter; a little dust sifted into the room, it writhed and settled on the sideboard. Again it was dark. She dreamed of Millicent and Pussy and Alan and a lovely summer picnic on the sand at North Berwick. *Simon*, she said, her voice trembling with laughter. It was morning. Simon did not come. She wandered round the house. They had taken Simon from her. A new bitterness cut lines about her mouth. That was a cruel thing, to take her boy away from her. On the other hand, she was better without him: drunkard that he was. What ingratitude, after all that she had done for him. She felt much more free when she was alone. The clock ticked and chimed, but time was a slow sequence of glooms and gleams. *You must eat,* said a voice from the kitchen. It sounded like Flora's voice but it couldn't be, Flora (the lucky thing) was lying dead (of cancer) in the Grange cemetery of Edinburgh. *Stop them interfering with the dead people in the churchyard,* she cried angrily in the lobby. The machines were not in the village; they had retreated, she heard a distant roar from the far side of Korsfea. It was dark again. A woman bent over her with a plate. *You must try to eat, dear,* said a voice. Who was this person? It was of course Mrs Whaness, flickering among the solid blocks of shadow, and her tray heaped with haddock and tea and rhubarb jam and buttered bannock. She rejected the woman and her food. Who had taken her into the house anyway? She fell asleep again. Two boys she had never seen before woke her with shouts. Wide smiling faces, fair flaunting fells of hair. They were not real, of course, they must be witnesses summoned for some case or other that she could not for the moment remember. Simon stooped into the tarnished mirror, burdened with cases. A figure stood behind Simon. Mrs McKee sighed on the mirror and rubbed her hand across the stain. It was a face from thirty years ago. It was Winnie Melville. She knew the freckles, the wide grey eyes, the slowly gathering smile. And Winnie too was a prisoner of the mirror. She exchanged a cold kiss with this stranger. Diminished laughter: the boys were running among the tombstones. *Tell them not to interfere with the graves,* she said sharply. *Soon there will be nothing in Hellya but skeletons and shadows.* Winnie brought gifts, a set of Wedgewood cups and saucers. Her fingers went over these brilliant shadows – one fell in the hearth and broke – then it was time to sleep again. *I have brought ruin to everything I have touched and known,* she said to Winnie when she woke. *Millicent. Alan. Simon. Now I am bringing ruin to this whole island. This is happening because I live here.* She ate to please them, a few slices of banana on a piece of bread, a cup of milk. These boys, they were worse than the machines, the clatter of their feet on the stair and their selfishness and their real voices. They flashed in and out of the mirror all day long. She slept. She woke. She slept. Simon and Winnie were whispering together in the depths of the dark mirror. They were conspiring against her. Winnie's voice brightened; it cajoled. Simon went away. Winnie and she were alone together, drinking tea beside the fire. Winnie was in the middle of a monologue. She listened dully. *Colm. Hamish. My latest novel 'Down the Nights and Down the Days'. Colm's father. My Festival play, 'Oysters', a success really. Hamish and his clarinet. Colm's father. Colm going to the university, medicine. His father a doctor too. Hamish set on the sea. Colm's father the dearest sweetest handsomest. The precious burden in the womb, bearing it off twice, into secrecy, silence. 'Down the Nights', amber all was preserved in. Colm. Colm's father. Colm. Colm ...* Winnie's voice flashed. It dazed her. It was more intolerable than the sun in the mirror. She writhed with annoyance in her chair. She clicked her tongue against her teeth several times. What did she care about this woman and her fancy-men and her silly books? Such vanity, egotism. *I am going to bed,* she said suddenly – *hand me my stick, please.* The long twisting stair. The cold bedroom. She took the cairngorm from her throat, the heavy silver drops from her ear-lobes. She sank her little tired face among the pillows. *God pity me,* she said. *God pity us all ...* She woke. She put on her clothes. She came downstairs. The sitting-room was a dazzle of light. That woman had drawn back the curtains. *Please,* she said angrily, *I cannot live in this glare.* Winnie came in from the garden carrying an armful of tulips. *All these lorries and cement-mixers! Just look at the dust on the blossoms, Aunty Liz* ... The island throbbed and clanged. The workmen were digging a tunnel into The Knap, Simon had said. She turned from Winnie. She drowsed in her chair. She woke. The tulips, yellow and red, swung from long fluent necks. Simon and Winnie whispering together again in the mirror. *Aunty Liz, you'd be the better of some fresh air. I'm going down to the beach. It's quiet there. Please come, dear.* If only they would mind their own business. She was too weary to argue. If it would stop them conspiring against her, even for an hour. *I need my stick,* she said, *and my coat.* Across the threshold the sun scraped at her eyes like new sandpaper. Should she turn back? The sun was hurting her eyes. She saw now how the village was half demolished. She walked across the scar where the hotel had been. Her feet encountered grass, boulders, seaweed. She refused Winnie's arm. They were on the beach. The slow regular peal of the waves. Terns calling and curving above. She was under the cliff. Her feet moved in the dry sand. A day of sunbursts and showers. The sky darkened. She walked nearer to the waves. The sand sucked and gleamed. Winnie spoke. *I think it won't rain till we get back. It's a checkerboard day. We're in the middle of a bright square.* Winnie was silent again. Grey wedges, a shifting gleam on the horizon. A gap in the crags here. Clatter, screech, boom-oom-m. Goodness, she had almost forgotten the construction work. The island she had known for four years was dying. There were new throbbing pulses all over Hellya. What was the name of this place now, Keelyfaa. The loom of another cliff. Caves and rocks. She stood in the shadow of the cliff. She was enfolded in the sea silence once more. *I am very tired. It is going to rain. I should not have come out with you in the first place. The sun is hurting my eyes.* She sat down on a rock. The cliff yielded its glow to a cloud. The cloud surged on. The cliff kindled to red again. Drops of rain fell. Her thighs were cold. She felt as if the stone was entering into her. Rain and sun on her face, wearing it away. She was very old. An age of sun and rain had washed her features away and her face was a blank. She was part of the rock she sat on. The rain had scoured her eyes smooth. The rain had

224

obliterated her mouth. She could not speak any more. The rain surged through the bones of her face. The rain stopped. Her stone eyes kindled to red. She opened her eyes. Simon stood there, Winnie, two boys at the edge of the gleaming sand. Beyond them the sea, shot with wavering sequences of light and darkness. *You're all right Mother. It was maybe a bit too far for you. We're going home now. Take her arm, Winnie* ... In the house she made them draw the curtain. *Please, I am very tired. I cannot have all this noise and disturbance. Simon, I am too old to entertain visitors. I would be glad of some peace now.* They left her. She breathed the balm of old shadows. That rain! That sun. She shivered with dread. She had looked beyond the mirror into the sun and it had changed her into stone. The light had all but entombed her in its perdurable diamond. The shadows came about her. They surged softly out of the most ancient places of the house. The mirror had now power over them. They bore salves and unguents. Flora came, smiling, and went away again (perhaps she dreamed that about Flora). They put poppies on the stark erosions that sun and rain had made on her flesh. She slept. It was morning again. Winnie's voice from the garden, telling Colm to make less noise, Aunty Liz was not very well, please stop at once ringing that bicycle bell. As if she cared. An immoral woman like her, yes and a traitor to her faith, that such a one should be living under the roof of a manse. Winnie flowed into the mirror, carrying a tray. It was time to speak to her plainly. *There is something that you should know. Simon is an alcoholic. I am accused of very grave crimes which I have not committed. As for you, I forbid you to worship your images in this house.* She slept again. The kindly dead came about her with urns and opiates. They came with herbs. She did not know sometimes whether she was awake or asleep. Once she heard Simon's voice. *A problem, we must be out of the manse by the end of the month, must be, and with the old one this way.* Winnie had gone, she had taken her boys with her. They had vanished into the sun and the rain. The island rang day after day like a spasmodic gong. Soon now. The shadows ministered to her with all reverence and love. She awoke. She had no awareness of Simon any more. She slept. Occasionally a querulous or a bullying or a hypocritical voice beat about her peace, urging her to take a cup of tea, and she would be sure to feel much more comfortable after a good wash; and she would be the better of a thick cardigan, there was snow in the ditches this morning. She ignored their hectoring. Her communion with the shadows was almost perfect now. A very pure thing it was. She returned their visits sometimes, averting her face from the mirror to stand at last in a host of shadows in the hallway. She returned to the rocking-chair comforted. Writhen stems sprawled out of the vase on the china cabinet. It was morning. She drowsed in her chair. The room was a hollow drum, all the furniture was gone, only the tall mirror remained. That was cruel. She wept. She slept again, a long dark unquiet drowse. She woke. The garden clanged. The wall whispered. The wall shrieked and split, a fissure appeared in the plaster, bricks grinned like rotten teeth and collapsed. Torrents of light and cold poured in. A clanging monster entered the breach, like some undersea creature. Her mouth was sour with dust. She choked and coughed. Brilliance eddied and washed about her, it swept her off her feet. The mirror fell across her. She covered her eyes. Beyond gleams and splinters the terrible silver trumpet of the sun summoned her.

'I'll just draw the blind a little,' said the visitor. 'The light's in your eyes.'

She knew at once where she was, from the sounds on the stone outside – she was in her own city, Edinburgh. It was a beautiful day in spring; she knew it was spring from the slant of the light on her face. Among Edinburgh silences, birds sang in the trees. All her senses were quickened. It was morning. She could almost feel the dew-flight from the grass-blades on Arthur's Seat.

And it was a hospital. Echoes. Brisk distant voices. The tang of disinfectant. She knew from the week of her appendicitis, and a very long time ago that was, that she was lying in a hospital ward. The muted sun lay on her eyelids.

The visitor spread gifts on the locker and over the foot of her bed. Apples, roses, bedsocks, barley sugar, a *Scotsman*. He enumerated each item as he unfolded it. She saw nothing. Her eyes were sealed yet. She had been too long at the assize of shadows.

It was spring. She felt very tired. Of course she was tired. Her whole life, everything she had known and loved, had fallen on her and all but buried her alive, like an undermined house. Beams and stones had all but crushed her. Was this the judgement upon her – 'for that thy days have been wicked and perverse and desperately deceitful' – forever to sit in a fallen house, an old bereaved exiled loveless woman, crouched over a cold hearth, in a white air of winter.

'Yesterday, when I came, you were asleep,' said the nice visitor.

Time built itself up again, not as an ancient storied house, but as a drift of butterflies. A delicate light lay upon her branching quickened veins; she was young again; she was Liz Alder on the day before she met Alan McKee. She remembered that this happened to her April after April, this feeling of reprieve that was so rare and evanescent that it came and vanished like a silent tumble of butterflies. She kept her eyes closed; the stranger at her bedside must not spoil with look or speech or kindness the host of Aprils that wavered slowly and delicately through her renewed being – Simon awash with lupins and dew; Simon's head in lamplight, bent over his theology books; Simon constellated with measles; a girl whispering to Simon of jewels and blindness on the fireside rug at Marchmont; Simon quiet as apples in his cradle; the slow throb and curve and quest of the foetus in her womb; Alan and Elizabeth in their rented flat at Marchmont, the new heavy bridal furniture gleaming about them; swoon of seed between rapt loins, the chosen lonely one, pilgrim, escaped from the sweats and toils and raptures, entering in at the dark door of woman, predestined, ushered, accepted; Alan home on leave from France, shy and smiling, so handsome in his uniform, swinging himself on crutches towards the barrier at Waverley station; Alan's first kiss; Millicent whispering and pointing across Mackie's restaurant in Princes Street to a table in a corner where sat, unsmiling and alone, drinking chocolate, Messrs MacAndrew and Brae's new clerk . . .

Simon – of course the visitor was Simon – sat down on the hard hospital bed. 'Well, old Liz,' he said, 'you're looking a bit better today.' A mouth on her cheek, a finger tucking a curl of hair under her bedcap.

The sweet burden of the sun lay on her eyelids. She was young in the ruins of her body. She touched his wrists with lyrical withered fingers.

The Skarf became a clerk in the office. He had applied for a watchman's job at the site, with full board and laundry and accommodation, after his house was knocked down, but the interviewer – Mr Aloysius the chief clerk – saw at once that a desk rather than a charcoal fire was the place for such a literate wellinformed man. The Skarf wore a blue suit and a grey tie. The work was not hard. He got on well with everybody, especially Mr Aloysius. He was allowed to keep his favourite books in boxes under his bed. Every evening he had a few jars of beer in the canteen, and he had amiable arguments on politics and religion with construction workers and truck drivers and labourers, anyone who would listen and talk. He spoke of starting a debating society. There were film shows and sing-songs. Mr Aloysius once, over a noggin of whisky in the office canteen, expressed regret to The Skarf that the whole life and economy of the island should be so abruptly and radically altered. But no, said The Skarf, they were not to look at it in that way. Industrial man, bureaucratic man, was a superior creature to agricultural man; he could bear a greater infusion of the light; just as the farmer's cycle was a stage beyond the dark blunderings and intuitions of the hunter. Hellya was a microcosm; this was how it must happen, inevitably, all over the universe.

'An interesting fellow, that,' said the controller to Mr Aloysius.

Mr Aloysius was flicking through a file in the office one sunny afternoon. The file was marked secret, and was labelled 'HELLYA, INHABITANTS of'. There was nothing much to do; there were many idle days in the office. The Skarf and the other two clerks were playing rummy over by the window. Mr Aloysius found a card headed 'SKARF, Jeremias Jonathan'. He read idly to begin with, then with growing interest:

b. 22/6/21. 6' ½" 154lb. Eyes light blue. Hair auburn, thin at crown and temples. Bachelor. Only child of Rolf Skarf and Rina (*née* Williamson), both deceased. Fisherman. Health: Severe astigmatism. Incipient multiple sclerosis (hands, left leg involved). Education: Greenvoe P.S. ad age 15. Property: one fishing boat *Engels* (fit for sea? in urgent need of painting and caulking), together with forty-five (45) creels; one house of two apartments in Greenvoe, 'Dayspring,' with uncultivated garden in front— value approx. £150. Relatives: cousins of various degrees scattered throughout Britain and Commonwealth but not intercommunication. Pastimes (1) beer-drinking to an innocuous extent (2) intensive study of the theory of socialism; calls himself a Marxist—Leninist—Maoist; an active and tireless propagandist; but his ideas much tinged with mysticism. *This man is a high security risk. He should on no account be offered employment at Black Star or any other envisaged site, in Hellya or elsewhere, in any capacity whatsoever.*

Mr Aloysius extracted this card from the file and slipped quietly out of the office. He knocked at the controller's door; entered; and laid the card on the controller's desk. 'Sir,' he said, 'someone has blundered.'

An hour later, just before the office closed for the day, The Skarf was summoned to the holy of holies. He emerged ten minutes later carrying his employment and insurance cards and an envelope containing a fortnight's salary. His spectacles glinted with bewilderment. He was at once escorted to the main gate of the site by two security men and an alsatian; and was abandoned to time and chance. 'The Irish papists can have my books,' he shouted back from the end of the road.

He limped down to the village (he was, he noticed, increasingly troubled by this weakness in his left leg). His house was a cavity in the ground, between Timmy Folster's cavity and Alice Voar's cavity. He sat for a while on the charred stone that had been his hearth, and smoked a cigarette.

He heard after a while the glut-glut of the sea retreating from the caves at Keelyfaa. The ebb tide was building up to full power.

The withdrawing waters keened from the distant headland of the Taing.

The Skarf laughed quietly to himself. He rose. He walked, trailing his left foot a little, across the links to the beach. He put into his jacket and trouser pockets several heavy round stones.

He noticed a cormorant lying on the wet sand. It fluttered and yearned away from him, but it could not move further; its wing was broken. The next flood tide would drown it.

The Skarf untied the *Engels* at the pier and tried to push her into the water. He fell in swathes of slippery seaweed and had trouble getting to his feet again. He thought for a moment that he and the cormorant might drown together, when the high tide covered the beach in seven or eight hours' time. But in the end he managed to balance himself against the hull and heave his body inside, in a slow crazy cartwheel. He grabbed an oar and levered himself to his feet.

He prodded the rock with the oar, through sand and seaweed and slowly diminishing water, until the *Engels* was free and buoyant. The engine was old, dry, corroded. He fitted oars into rowlocks, dug the blades into the water, and slowly increased his stretch, and pulled strongly towards mid-Sound.

He saw that a small pool of water was weeping into the boat, through one of the warped seams. He knew exactly where the leakage was occurring; he could see the little muscular worm of water working between the breach and the surface, and rippling there, and spreading a wider ellipse of sea-water. After a quarter of an hour his fine black office shoes were awash. The Skarf rowed strongly until he reached the first dimples and whorls and bottle-ends of the ebb; then with one tug at the starboard oar he swung the bow of the *Engels* westward.

He noted that there was a moderate wind from the west, so that air and tide were opposed to each other. That always whipped up a big broken area of water where the Sound of Hellya and the Atlantic Ocean intermeshed. From mid-Sound he could see the jagged saw-edge of the horizon. He would come to a place, in twenty minutes or so, where the sea was all mountains and chasms.

By now the *Engels* was a sixth full of water. The salt spring was bubbling up faster than ever from the warped boards. The Skarf's trouser bottoms were soaking. The bailing tin bobbed about in the increasing inundation. The Skarf bent down and picked it up and threw it into the tide-rip. By now the boat was well and truly in the power of the ebb. The Skarf had pulled in his oars some time before. He sat with folded arms looking back at Hellya. His spectacles glimmered. Even from this distance he could hear, very faintly through the increasing hush and boom of the sea, the whine of pneumatic drills and a single volley of blasting between the Knap and Korsfea: the music of The Children of the Sun.

Water sloshed over his knee. The *Engels* creaked. They were nearing the turbulent gate of the ocean.

There was pollution in the sea. Bert Kerston hauled his creels in the rocky sheltered bay beyond the Taing, and four of the seven lobsters were inert.

The burn of Hellya rises in the central hills. Ernefea and Korsfea and the Knap seem to bear up in their brown and purple hands a brimming chalice; it is the tiny Loch of Ernefea. Above Rossiter the loch spills and splashes over; it becomes a burn, falling from level to level; it squanders opals and sapphires and emeralds among the shallow stones, is all torn lace in the waterfall below Blinkbonny, and a swatch of green silk among the reeds at Skaill; before it gathers itself for a final rush among the immense round boulders that belong half to the sea and half to the fields.

Bert Kerston noted that on this particular day the burn, as far as he could see, was all khaki-coloured scum, and the filth fumed out over the water of the bay for half a mile and more. A haddock floated on the surface, belly up. He turned for home.

He tied the *Ellen* up at the pier. His house was cocooned in silence. Even to look at the door from this distance he knew that it was stricken; piteous unwanted fertility. The children hung about the end of the house with huge eyes. Bert Kerston could not bear to go inside, to experience once more that creature on the bed tearing herself in two. He took Judy by the arm and whispered to her, 'Listen carefully. Tell Rachel Whaness. Your mam'll be all right. I can't go in. I'm too busy.'

Judy, with one last flutter of eyes into the moaning interior of the house, ran off to Rachel's door, and Laddie the collie bounded silently after her.

Bert Kerston re-crossed the Sound in the direction of the Sutbreck Hotel. He sold the three live lobsters to Mr Selfridge and at once began to convert the money into whisky. He got drunk fairly quickly, and maudlin with it. Did Mr Selfridge realize that he had to leave his house in a week's time? There was this compulsory order on it, it was needed for the site. No, he didn't know where to go. And him with a newborn child, another mouth to feed: Ellen had begun her labour that morning, the midwife was with her. Besides, worst of all, the sea was rotten, dead haddocks drifting through the Sound. This had never been known before. There would soon be no work for him or any other fisherman out of Hellya or Quoylay; and just at the time too when the chief cook at the site would pay any money for a good lobster.

Mr Selfridge was sympathetic. It was no use looking on the black side of things. It just so happened that they could help one another, Bert Kerston and Mr Selfridge. Fraser the ghillie had gone and broken his arm at the week-end, and now there was no one at the hotel to instruct the summer visitors in the art of fly-fishing, nor to row them out to the likeliest places in the loch. No, he wasn't taking Sandy Fraser back, he was an unsuitable ghillie for other reasons. He couldn't offer much in the way of wages, seven pounds a week, but there was the wee cottage at the head of the loch rent-free; dinner in the hotel kitchen every day except Sunday; perks galore. 'And besides, man,' said Mr Selfridge, flicking a middle finger at the palm of his other hand as if counting notes, 'the tips, the *tips*.'

He and Bert Kerston pledged each other with double whiskies.

Bert Kerston had a somnavigant return across the Sound to Greenvoe; the night was blue velvet, the waves were shifting starlit hulks of peace. He walked up the pier to his house, as if it was he that had got rid of a great burden; the window was a peaceful square of lamplight. He rattled the latch cheerfully, and crossed the threshold into a tiger's cage – a batter of fists against his face, a wrench at his hair, his mouth full of the warmth of new blood. He saw the white passionate appalled face of Willie and the amazed faces of the younger children; then sideboard and lamp and mirror and all the faces spun slowly round. He was crouched on his side on the floor and a boot sank again and again into his ribs, a dreamlike battering. A voice pleaded. Dark cold air rushed over him; he was outside, crouched against the gable-end of his cottage, his mouth struggling with blood and breath, and his torso a map of smoulderings and numbnesses.

'They should not have done that,' he said.

He was sitting before a huge fire, in a dancing net of light and shadow. There was a woven text on the wall, GOD IS LOVE. The tea scalded his mouth. 'It died, the infant,' said the voice of Rachel Whaness. 'It died almost as soon as it was born. It is God's will ...' He swooned into brief sleep. He heard a voice reading slowly and ritually. The flame was lowered in the lamp. 'Ellen is fine,' Rachel's voice came out of the darkness. He woke up in the deep chair, and the fire was out. It was morning. Two masks lay awry on the pillow. 'My son meant to kill me,' he mumbled through a thick leather mouth. When he tried to get to his feet he almost screamed; it was as if a red-hot poker was being raked through his rib-cage.

He dragged his body down to the boat, trying to avoid the poker that sank into him again and again, waking sears and spurts of agony. He fell into the *Ellen* and pushed off, and almost broke himself apart starting up the engine. Every heave and toss of the boat touched the quick of him. He shuddered from agony into agony. In certain positions the pain guttered and sank; it was then, turning in relief, that the pokers glinted into him, raked him from throat to navel, stabbed him to the very heart. He groaned and clung to the tiller.

'Ellen told Willie to do this,' he whimpered.

The *Ellen* studdered against the wooden jetty at Sutbreck. He managed to manoeuvre the painter. He crawled up the wooden steps and gasped slowly through another assault of pokers – watched indifferently by swans – to the vestibule of the hotel; and spread head and arms along the bar counter; and groaned aloud.

'If it isn't my new ghillie,' and Mr Selfridge. 'Been fighting, then. One of them Irish navvies, was it? Well, you're in no state to start work today, my boy. I'll get Millie to make up a bed in the attic. Best have a drink first, eh?'

After Bert Kerston had had a few whiskies he felt better able to control the pain. A few farm workers came in. He told them about

Ellen and the dead baby. He did not, however, mention the son who had raised his hand against the father. He wept a little; tears mingled with the whisky and the dry blood at the corner of his moustache. A few more glasses were passed to him. 'Bloody Irishman,' he said. 'I'd have killed the Mick if they hadn't dragged me off him.' He was drunk again by the time Millie and Moira hustled him upstairs and and under the blankets.

The doctor came that afternoon, and strapped him up, and prescribed sleeping tablets.

He lay in the attic reading westerns while his two cracked ribs slowly mended. It was a calm, bereaved, beautiful existence now. One afternoon a week later he heard flutters of laughter in the corridor below; a familiar barking; the thud of heavy objects; and presently a wheezing and a deliberation of feet on the attic ladder. He knew before the huge red face could rise into view that it was Ellen. The attic quaked with her emotion. He was engulfed in bosom; the voice above him soothed and stormed and pleaded: 'Never again . . . never will he darken my door . . . no son of mine, to do a thing like that to his own father . . . Dear love, Bert, are thu better then? . . . And has gotten a fine job and a cottage for us all at Sutbreck, the clever Bert that he is . . . No more lobsters, and a good thing too . . . And nobody to nurse thee but them two trollops of chamber-maids . . . Never mind . . . Yes, we're all well, and Westray took all our stuff over today, every last stick of furniture . . . And what's this on thee chest, strapping? Good lord, it must have been right sore . . . That Willie . . . Dear Bert, I've missed thee terrible, terrible, terrible.'

Then Laddie leapt on to the bed and began to lick his ear.

Bella Budge presided over a diminishing republic of hens. Fewer wings beat at her skirt with every morning that passed. It became obvious to her that they were being stolen by the workmen at the site. 'Poor men,' said Bella, 'they'll be half starved up there, no doubt, and all that noise and gutter too.' She took Kitty inside and abandoned the rest to their fate. One by one, after nightfall, the hens were strangled or riddled with shotgun pellets. Bella appeared above the *Skua* one morning, when Ivan Westray was getting ready to cross over with the official mail. Ivan Westray lifted her aboard – she was as light as a hare. A fierce clucking came from under her shawl. Bella gave the ferryman a pound note, but said nothing. It was the first time she had ever left the island. From the middle of the Sound Ivan Westray could see the door of Biggings standing open. 'You've left your door open,' he said. 'Yes,' said Bella. Her bosom clucked. Bella broke a biscuit and chewed the pieces and put the salivated crumbs inside her shawl. At Kirkwall pier Ivan Westray lifted her ashore. She disappeared among a crowd of seamen and dockers and lorry-drivers. There was one last diminished squawk from the region of the harbour office.

A bulldozer nudged the wall of Biggings next day. A rat rushed out. Dazzled spiders pirouetted briefly from the rafters. Cupboard and box-beds crumbled like matchwood. The bulldozer passed over and through Biggings till it was as flat as a field; and this is what Tom Groat in Vancouver would come home to, if he ever came home.

Samuel Whaness, now that he had no boat, was employed as a hut tender up at the site. The day before his roof beam lay across his cornerstone, he and Rachel went to live in a small wooden hut near the south gate. Their duties were to keep the workmen's huts clean, to sweep the floors, to make the beds, to keep the bogey stoves alight, to wash the dishes. There was one large hut in the centre of the camp that was used mostly for film shows and bingo. One Thursday night a man from the office ordered Samuel to arrange wooden forms down the centre of the hall (after sweeping up the bingo cards and cigarette debris) and to set up a table against the gable wall. 'It must be some kind of a meeting,' said Samuel to himself, 'a debate or something.' He was just giving the windows a final flick with his duster when a stranger came in with a suitcase. The man opened the case and spread an immaculate linen cover over the table; then he slid something underneath the cloth with great care. Samuel watched from the summit of his step-ladder. The man delved deeper in his case and came out with a crucifix and a silver cup and glittering green vestments. He leaned a large open book against the wall; at the top of the page was printed in red, *Feast of the Assumption of the* B.V.M. It was to be a Roman Mass. Samuel set the step-ladder to his shoulder and rushed outside. He appeared breathless at the door of his own hut. 'Get ready, woman,' he said to Rachel, 'we must leave this place at once.' After midnight, having wakened Ivan Westray, they sailed in the *Skua* to Hamnavoe; and stayed that night at the house of an evangelist above a butcher shop; and next day, after the gospel meeting, crossed over to Hoy, where Rachel's brother, a widower, lived in a four-roomed cottage. Willie Tomison was a crofter-fisherman. 'You're welcome to stay for as long as you like,' he said to Samuel and Rachel, 'so long as you don't preach at me, nor pray over me when I have the cold, no nor read that *Pilgrim's Progress* out loud when I'm having a smoke in the chair after my day's work . . .' And later that night Willie offered Samuel a partnership in his fishing boat, the *White Owl.* 'No,' said Samuel vehemently, 'I will never bait another line. That's all finished . . .' In a few days' time the interior of Willie's croft, called Meadows, began to twinkle and glint and glow with Rachel's labour (up to then it had been rather dirty and untidy, like the houses of most bachelors and widowers). She opened the window for the first time since Eve Tomison had died; tides of clean sweet air began to flow round the house. She left religious tracts in Willie's chair, just before Willie was due in from the sea or the fields; Willie lit his pipe with them. She planted daffodil bulbs in Willie's garden patch, and sowed sweet-william seeds around the door. She made the first bannocks and rhubarb jam that Willie had eaten since Eve's time. 'Could thu no make a drop of ale too?' said Willie. But Rachel refused to make that devil's brew.

Rachel was busy and contented, but something irked Samuel. The huge solemn man hung about the house all day like a sick dog. Willie didn't want him in the fields or the byre; he was a nuisance there, he knew nothing about the rhythms of the earth. 'Smoke, or do something, man,' said Willie.

One morning Samuel put on his coat and walked over the hills. 'He's gone to the pub at Longhope for a drink,' said Willie to Rachel, 'and quite right.' Rachel's mouth was too full of clothespegs to make any kind of answer; the rope between stable and byre fluttered and flaunted with immaculate shapes in the big wind. It was washing day at Meadows.

Samuel did not come back all day. After tea Rachel was ironing and Willie sat smoking beside the fire. They heard a faint shout from the beach. They went outside, not too quickly (for time is not a conflagration; it is a slow grave sequence of grassblade, fish, apple, star, snowflake). Wood scraped on stone. Rachel lingered in the threshold, her cheeks flushed from the flat-iron. Willie discovered Samuel trying to drag a strange yawl up the noust. The name painted on the boat was *Maggie-Anne*. Willie went to the stern and pushed. They laboured and hauled together till the boat was well out of reach of the waves. Rachel stood in the door, her face turning slowly to stone.

Samuel changed the name of the boat to *Sion*.

Within a week he was fishing again; but he always took his yawl in the opposite direction to the *White Owl*; nor did he come home, every Friday night, with a bottle of whisky and two ounces of bogey roll, like his brother-in-law.

Miss Margaret Inverary, clad in Paisley pattern pyjamas several sizes too large for her, sat at the kitchen table of her mother's house in Morningside having breakfast of toast and marmalade and coffee. Toby, the grey kitten, lapped milk under the sink. A letter rattled in through the letter-box. Her mother was listening to the nine o'clock news in her bedroom. The letter was postmarked 'Orkney'. She ripped the flap of the envelope with a long urgent forefinger. It was from the Education Committee. It said that, owing to unforeseen but imperative circumstances, the Greenvoe school would not re-open after the summer vacation; but that there was a post available for her in the secondary department of Hamnavoe Academy, as assistant teacher of modern languages; and it was very much hoped that she would be able to accept, as her services had been greatly appreciated in the island of Hellya, and the last report of the Inspector of Schools had been an excellent one in every respect.

Margaret folded the letter and put it in her handbag. She went into her bedroom to dress.

The Edinburgh Festival was in its second week. The weather was good. Lovers lay on the green slopes under the Castle, among the fountains and the trees. Two mini-kilted Greeks with profiles like gods strode along George Street. A huge van full of students stopped outside a church hall in the Canongate; they at once began to unload a nude plaster statue, a mounted eagle, a rolled-up back-cloth, two hampers, a life-size gondola. A hound leapt softly out after the props and the players. The lid of one of the hampers opened and a girl in a yellow robe looked out of it and laughed. Another fringe play was about to begin.

Margaret sat in a café at Tollcross. Two foreign gentlemen came in; one was half-blind. They ordered bacon omelettes. They began to argue about a certain trombone player, in stony awkward English that gave great vehemence to their pronouncements. The man, he should not be allowed to perform on a tin whistle, said one in bitter scorn. But no, said the other, he had this intimacy of understanding, a knowledge that comes from the soul, of Mozart, Bloch, Kodaly. They forgot their argument. They turned their impatience elsewhere, the chef, the waitress, where were their omelettes, they were late, they were required in the theatre, please (plucking passionately at the apron of a pretty rushed-off-her-feet waitress) their meal ... They were like withered petulant boys. Margaret recognized the faces of two very famous musicians.

At Cramond the bay was all white swaying triangles. A young man and a girl picnicked on the beach, eating sandwiches and pouring white wine into cardboard cups. Their bodies were brown with long weeks of sunshine. A jet plane, too remote to be visible, spun a long slender white thread across the blue. A bather rushed up out of the sea and fell among the baskets and bottles, scattering salt drops everywhere. The picnicking couple remonstrated with her, between laughter and anger. The intruder was a magnificent-looking girl, even shivering and salt-beaded. A triangle of sandwich hung out of her mouth. The boy began to rub the sea from her shoulders with a towel.

It was a week of sunshine. Margaret trundled back and fore across the city with her season bus-ticket. She was tired, after the noise and heat of the Princes Street super-market (her mother was not too well that day, and she was getting the provisions) and she went down steps into a Rose Street pub for a lager and a sandwich. A tableful of poets sat next to her; she recognized this face and that; they were arguing over their beer as to whether a Scots poet should write in English or Lallans. Two black men moved past the drinkers to a table in the far corner; they had sinuous grace and balance, their progress was a slow fluent dance. (We white folk go in spasms and jerks, Margaret thought.) A lonely girl against the bar wore an immense round hat like a cartwheel, and she tinkled when she moved (there was a chain of bells round her left ankle); she drank tomato juice with voluptuous melancholy. A north-east voice as hard as granite spoke from the poets' table: 'We're finished, poetry is finished, we don't mean a thing any more to the people who matter, I mean the men in the factories and farms. We don't break our holy bread among them any more, like Burns and the ballad-makers.' The table was loud with rage and denial. A fist beat on the wood; the tumblers shivered and slopped beer over. A few silent men in overalls smiled over at the table of violent language. A barman stretched over the counter and gave the poets an anxious look. Students surged in from the hot street, and after them a very old smelly woman with a broken feather in her hat.

The late summer evening came down. Margaret walked up the Mound, carrying her shopping basket. Her mother would be extremely cross and worried; she should have been home hours ago. The music of mountains came from the Castle esplanade, cadences of piercing melancholy and valour: a bagpipe. She turned at the bus stop. The city was all jewelled. Bracelets and necklaces and tiaras of light had fallen here and there: emerald, onyx, diamond, sapphire, opal. It was marvellous. Her bus clanged to a halt. She climbed on board. She was borne away into more sedate regions of the city, where people worried about cancer and the rates.

At home, while she waited for the tea to infuse, Margaret opened her handbag and took out the letter she had received that morning. She tore it up and threw the pieces into the fire.

It was as if she knew that the school and schoolhouse of Greenvoe had been battered into rubble that same day.

*

The black star exploded slowly under the hills and at last drew the whole of Hellya into its mystery and passion.

The bulldozers, having flattened the village, turned inland to the farms.

The Glebe went down in a brief clatter of stones. Nothing stood there by nightfall but the wooden box-bed where generations of Browns had loved and died and been born. Then the navvies broke it up and carried it to the bogey stoves in their huts; for the nights were growing chilly.

The farm of Isbister shuddered some days later. The two gable-ends tottered and leaned towards one another and embraced for the first and the last time. The black hearth-stone stood among the ruins. The smell of living lingered for an hour, then mingled with a wind blowing out to sea, and was lost.

The destruction of Skaill down by the shore caused some excitement. When an inner wall fell one workman heard a dull clangour under the roar of the bulldozer; another saw a faded gleam. The Viking sword and shield and helmet – a death hoard – were flown to Edinburgh and caused a brief wonderment among archae-ologists and historians, before they were coffined at last in a museum case, far from Hellya.

Rossiter died in a cloud of dust. The labourers had never seen such quantities of stour as rose from the disordered stones, as if the finest purest grains of sand had been used to cement them. The men in the bulldozers covered noses and mouths with handker-chiefs. Rossiter died in cold dry whispers. The ghost of the house drifted seawards.

Blinkbonny had, for five centuries, put its reflection in the loch: pellucid and quivering on summer mornings, bleak and broken when the east wind came snarling across the reeded waters. The bulldozers raged for an hour, then the mirror lacked that faithful image for ever. (The mirror itself was smashed – that is to say, the loch was drained – one month later.)

A most disagreeable scene occurred at the farm of The Bu, when the bulldozers converged there early one evening. The demolition men had been led to expect that the farm buildings would be vacated, like others, when they came. Nothing of the kind – a hundred hens meandered about the field at the end of the house, ducks quacked in the milldam, cows sauntered and swung heavy udders among the silken grass. Jock MacIntosh the foreman looked in at the curtained window. Mansie Anderson and his wife, nine children, and two servant-men were having their supper of cold tongue, tomatoes, bere bannocks and tea at the long table. Jock MacIntosh knocked at the door. Nobody answered. He knocked again, louder. Mrs Thomasina Anderson came out and said that they didn't want to buy any bargains today, thank you, and shut the door in his face. Jock MacIntosh and his twelve mates returned among the silent bulldozers to debate the matter. They decided to begin work immediately on the old mill further down the burn; it was not used any longer; nobody lived there but rabbits. The two bulldozers advanced down the field, Jock MacIntosh in front, the other labourers behind. The bulldozers halted. Jock MacIntosh raised his pick to strike the first blow. A black-and-white fury rose out of the ditch and struck him on the chest and knocked him over on the grass; teeth raged among forearms folded over throat. Two Irishmen killed the dog of The Bu before the dog of The Bu could tear the gullet out of Jock MacIntosh; they broke Rover's back with a heavy stone from the burn. The assault was called off for that day. Jock MacIntosh, trembling with fright and rage, knocked once more at the door of The Bu, violently. Nobody answered. He peered in at the window. The supper table had been cleared and they were all sitting round the fire talking mildly. Willag the old servant-man was filling his pipe in the corner. Simon Anderson and Hector Anderson were playing draughts on the sideboard. The old mother was knitting a pair of long woollen drawers. They behaved as if the ancient ceremonies of life were going on for ever in The Bu farm of Hellya. That is what came out of the day's incidents; Magnus Anderson refused simply and absolutely and steadfastly to leave his farm. The compensation originally offered had been generous, as it had been to all the Hellya farmers – sufficient to set them up in new farms in other parts of Orkney, or to retire in comfort. The authorities now offered to increase The Bu's compensation by twenty-five per cent; Mansie put the official letter in the fire. After a month of stale-mate the position became serious.

One morning the controller himself, accompanied by Mr

Aloysius and Mr Joseph Evie, B.E.M., came out to The Bu to explain the position to Mansie Anderson. There were handshakes, the men were courteously invited inside. Mansie Anderson cleared cats and children out of the kitchen. Mr Aloysius spread a blueprint on the scrubbed table. The controller spoke. His English was delivered in heavy impressive chunks (he was, it was said, a German). *Black Star. I am from Black Star. You understand? I am, so to speak, the boss. The underground work, soon it will be completed. These tunnels, they were of importance. Yes. Much money was spending on them, many millions of pounds. Two men had been killed in the shafts, one drowned. In two years it would be finished, the construction work. All the shafts would be useless as rabbit warrens then. Yes, but the proper work of Black Star, that would only be commencing. Necessary then to have one permanent entrance in Black Star. You see? A gateway, an orifice. The engineers, they were convinced that this so vital opening, (yes, you follow?) it should be sunk through the cornfield of The Bu, nowhere else in Hellya was suitable: underground springs, deposits of schist, granite. Was very technical. Also, you understand, this gateway into Black Star, it was to be no mere hole in the ground. O no. Certainly not. A complex of buildings – reinforced concrete – about a central dome, you see, here on the plan . . .*

Mansie Anderson studied the blueprint with great interest.

The wooden camp, it was very temporary. Like a patch of mushrooms, yes? Yes. The huts would vanish, so. Well, then, the dome. In the buildings round the dome would live, reside, operate, the executives, the engineers. Here, at The Bu, here will be Black Star HQ.

What went on in the dome itself, that would be most secret, most beautiful – a pure rite of science.

Mansie Anderson said it was a good harvest day. He thought he might cut a lane in the oatfield before dinner time. It was good of the gentlemen to call.

The controller turned his back on Mr Aloysius and Mr Joseph Evie. The negotiation from now on was to be between himself and Mansie Anderson alone. He lowered his voice. He laid his hand earnestly on Mansie Anderson's shoulder. His thick spectacles shimmered. He expressed himself in intense half-whispers, hewn boulders.

The very great importance of Black Star. How should it be explained? Great secrecy was involved. I shall be frank. This Black Star, it was utterly essential to the security of the western world. The fate of nations, it could depend on this one little cornfield. Indeed. That was so. We ask for your entire co-operation. Let me be quite frank, perhaps brutal. If you refuse to sell it, the cornfield, then, you understand, the matter is out of my hands . . .

The pendulum of the old grandfather clock swung and racketed through more than a bronze minute.

Mansie Anderson went over to the mantelpiece. He brought down his pipe and black twist. He scraped away at the inside of the bowl with a knife.

He said that he intended to sow turnips in that particular field next year. He would like very much if the gentlemen would drink a jug of home-brewed ale before they left.

Finally, and regrettably, the most extreme measure had to be resorted to: eviction. One day in early autumn the sheriff's officers, armed with a warrant, moved against the place. The labourers came in behind them. There was a brief disgraceful fight inside the house itself; then old Mansie was thrust out, with a purple bruise on his forehead. A child came out and sat in the byre door and began to pluck daisies. Thomasina and Hector and Marilyn and the younger servant-man came out and stood about in the yard. The old man turned his back and looked out over the burnished sea; behind him the harvest-field heaved its burnish. After the inhabitants, the furniture. Tables, chairs, books, ale-kirn, grandfather clock, gramophone, TV set, beds, pictures in heavy frames, blankets, chests, tea-caddies, crockery, were strewn about the yard like the passage of a defeated army. Great wheels trundled to and fro, flattening the ripe corn. Then the workmen began to round up the animals. They had got the bull safely hobbled and were lifting the last raging hen-coop on to a lorry when there was a violent explosion from the door of the barn. A Dundee labourer fell, bleeding. They saw the smoking barrel of a shotgun sticking awry out of the door slit. Geordie Simison the young servant-man was rushed and overpowered and arrested before he could do any more mischief. The younger children yelled with rage and pity; their mother hushed them. The labourer had only one or two pellets in his shoulder. Through all this uproar old Mansie stood like a flushed statue at the end of his house, in the setting sun ... After sunset they worked by arc lamps. At dawn The Bu, built by Thorkeld Harvest-Happy in the year 1006, was a cavity and a scatter on the side of the hill.

It took three days to demolish the baronial hall, with its turrets and battlements and coat-of-arms. The Fortin-Bells, grown rich once more with compensation, stalked deer in the west. Agatha and Inga rode their horses with style across the strath. The colonel pulled great lithe leaping sklinters of bronze out of Highland rivers; the salmon fishing was good that year. In Hellya the skyline flowed on uninterrupted by the hall. Among the heather a sandstone shield crumbled slowly; one could still discern, after a winter, a faintly sculpted stylized horse and half obliterated words WE FALL TO RISE. The rain fell. The sun shone. The horse melted into the stone. A blank shard lay in the heather.

Two Indians – an elderly man with a limp and a young man – stood on the Black Head of Quoylay and looked towards Hellya. A penumbra hung over the island, as if it was being slowly pulverized. Muffled hammer-thuds from the heart of Korsfea echoed faintly across the Sound. A half-finished dome gleamed out of The Bu's cornfield. The old man shook his head. They picked up their heavy cases and turned away.

After fifteen months – as suddenly as they had begun – all operations ceased in the island. The order came within an hour of the controller receiving an urgent secret message by telephone. He in turn phoned this point and that in the island. Everyone stopped working. It was as if an armistice had been declared. An uncanny silence fell. Evacuation began within a week, and proceeded with smooth efficiency. The engineers and consultants left first by heli-

copters; then the office staff, on the *Skua* to Kirkwall, bearing files
and charts and blueprints; then the labourers, gang after gang of
them, on the cargo boats to Aberdeen and Leith, sharing the space
with cattle and eggs and hogsheads of whisky, the exports of
Orkney. A month later a government ship called at the enlarged
pier of Greenvoe and took away the heavy stuff – lorries, bulldozers, cement-mixers, transformers, cranes, fire-engines. The huge
radii of tunnels into Korsfea and The Knap and Ernefea petered
out, a black blasted star. The H.Q. complex itself, facing the west,
remained a truncated battlement. (Every material of man grows at
last mellow and beautiful, except concrete – as the years passed
the site stared out of the heather like scabs of blindness. A concrete foundation is never sweetened by weeds and grass. It looks
hot and hurt in sunlight; it resents the gentle or the resounding
kisses of the rain.) The watchmen abandoned the gates. The camp,
a score of wooden huts of various sizes, was left to warp and
wither. The three telephones in the office were dumb and deaf. In
the canteen a dartboard fell from a wall. Dust sifted into the piles
of crockery in the cookhouse. The covers of a hymn book in the
community hall began to curl. The rats and the birds and the
spiders returned delicately and secretly. Grass sprouted through
floorboards.

The island was empty all the following winter.

In spring another invasion took place, but this was only a small
temporary holding operation. A score of labourers, a clerk, a cook,
and an overseer returned; their task was to enlarge the perimeter
fence so that it took in the whole island. It was a powerful deter-
rent – ten-feet-high concrete posts set at intervals of a yard, sunk
deep into the soil, and strung through and across with a dense
warp of barbed wire. NO ADMITTANCE notices appeared at four-
hundred-yard intervals, red lettering on a white enamel ground.
Hellya was to be sealed forever from the rest of the world.

The last labourer shouldered his pick and departed. The only
people left were the dead in the kirkyard. The disturbed dust
settled on a seedless island.

Deep in the heart of Hellya the Black Star froze.

*

One midsummer evening, ten years after Hellya had been finally evacuated, a rowing-boat dipped under the Red Head. From that immense cliff the gathered warmth of the day fell on the crew. The seven men on board seemed anxious to make as little noise as possible; they whispered to one another; that oarsman dipped his blades with a slow lingering plangency. The sun has set but still the northern sky was a glow of crimson and saffron and jet, and the Atlantic caught the luminous riot with still greater brilliance. The boat smashed soundlessly through the stained glass of the sea. She dipped past Thorkel's Hole in growing twilight. Occasionally one of the men would look up; the skyline of Hellya was scored with concrete posts and five-fold strands; a blank music that forbade any entry. The rower raised his oars; salt drops rained back into the sea, a small lessening tinkle. The boat drifted towards the caves of Keelyfa. It was high tide.

The bow was made fast to a spur of rock. They waited till the last croft lights were out in Quoylay and Sutbreck; then a young man began to climb up the shallow cliff face from the boat – here it was no more than thirty feet high – but in the deceptive light he had to be careful, for what seemed a deep secure foothold might be a mere crack in the rock wall. He levered himself up awkwardly. Another man stepped from the boat on to the crag; an unlit lantern was slung over his shoulder; up the erratic stone ladder he went with sure, seeing hands. From the hidden west side of the island came a muted thunder of surf. The third man to leave the boat was very old; he clawed anxiously at the rock as soon as the boat vibrated off under his feet; the others stood under with raised hands. But this time the leading climber had got to the top, and the second man, half-way there, was having some trouble with the lantern he carried; he cursed softly. The old man wedged his feet in a fissure; he snickered down at the glimmering faces below; and began to lever himself upwards even more quickly than his two precursors. A fourth man sought and found a handhold from the fluent thwart, and heaved himself on to the lowest buttress. A disturbed kittiwake chided the old man and flew far out into the Sound. The climber with the lantern was dragged on to the cliff head. A fifth climber left the boat with a bulky canvas bag roped to his shoulder. A star shimmered northward in the primrose sky, and was a needle-point of brilliance in the sea's molten glass. The old man turned on a wider ledge near the top and took from his jacket pocket a pipe. The struck match illuminated for a moment his withered face. The kittiwake, all complaints still, swung in and alighted on another part of the crag, not too far off. The young man with the seaman's bag surged up the face like a cat. The sixth man began to hesitate upwards from boat to ledge to crack. Sparks fell from the old man's pipe as, with muted gasps and laughter, he was hauled by the first two climbers on to the forbidden island. The oarsman exchanged boat for cliff; he was the seventh and last climber. The fourth and the burdened fifth climbers arrived at the top simultaneously; the fourth climber showed a bleeding hand to the others. The sixth climber called softly up to them, he was in difficulties, his knees had somehow got locked. They opened the canvas bag and lowered a rope down to him; he made a panicky clutch at it and held on for a while before tying it round his waist. By the time they had dragged him up over the edge the last to leave, the oarsman, was sitting in a grass hollow finishing his cigarette.

All the colours had drained from the north. They sat in a web of shadow.

'Yes,' said the old man, 'this is the place all right.'

On the very edge of the cliff was the ruin of a building, a low irregular broken circle of wall; only a few stones showed through the encroaching turf. The recent fence-builders had by-passed this broch. Over the centuries, parts of the cliff had fallen away and carried some of the masonry with it, for only an arc of the original keep was left. From this place the early people of Hellya had defended themselves from sea-borne enemies and from the shadowy aboriginals who dwelt in the interior bogs, those who slipped out with noose and knife after sunset. Round here they had sown Hellya's first grain and reaped its first harvests; this was where they had made their music and laws and myths. This navel had attached many generations of Hellyamen to the nourishing earth.

'We'll begin,' said Mansie Anderson of The Bu.

He took a horse-shoe out of the canvas bag. He kissed the horse-shoe and laid it in a niche of the wall and covered it with a black cloth. Tom Kerston lit the lantern. They hastened to put on their sackcloth, all except young Skarf who stripped to the waist and knelt down in the centre of the broch; he shivered a little in the night air. Sidney Fortin-Bell and Johnny Corrigall tied a cloth round his eyes. Gino Manson set the glimmering lantern on the highest stone of the truncated wall.

'Lie down,' said Mansie Anderson to the novice. With great care they laid him flat on his back. He was dead; the Harvester had been trampled and broken to death by the horse-shoe he had borne so faithfully and so long. They tied a grave-cloth round his jaw. They bound his wrists in front of his body. They set a stone at his head.

The Lord of the Harvest said solemnly, 'This is the Station of Stones. For thee, Harvester, the road goes no further. It is winter. Thou wast long in search of a kingdom. Thou hast come to thy kingdom. It is the kingdom of the dead. Thy heart is a few grains of cold dust. What does it hold now, thy heart, in the way of hope?'

There was a long silence. The Master Horsemen, standing round the dead Harvester, bowed their heads.

A slow shiver went through the corpse. He whispered. He uttered four syllables – 'Rain. Share. Yoke. Sun.'

A breath of night moved over the priests and victim in the broch ruins. It fretted the lingering gleam on the sea. After a time one of the Master Horsemen said, 'It is a wind that moves in the dust. His mouth is ashes. The wind shakes a sound from the dust that was his mouth.'

The other Master Horsemen nodded solemnly. 'It was the wind in the dust.'

There was another long silence.

Then the Lord of the Harvest intoned, 'But what did the dust seem to say? He was looking for a word. Unless he has found the word we ourselves are locked in the stone. We belong to the kingdom of death.'

The Master Horsemen consulted together. One bent down and put his ear to the mouth of the dead man. He rose and shook his head.

The sky was a broken net of stars above them.

At last one of the Master Horsemen said, 'I will make bold to speak. It ill becomes me. You will call it foolishness. Yet I will say what I heard. The dust seemed to utter this word, *Resurrection*. It was indeed a blank squandering of breath.'

The Lord of the Harvest rose up. He clapped his hands together with great joy. He cried, 'The dust that was his foot has stumbled on a new stone. He is dead, but the dust that was his tongue has uttered a new word. Take the shroud from the dust that was his eyes.'

Three of the Master Horsemen hastened to take the bandages from the eyes and the jaw and the wrists of the dead word-man. They lifted the shroud from his nakedness. The body lay grey and inert.

'There is nothing,' said the leader of the Master Horsemen. 'There is darkness. There is silence. There is a silence beyond silence.'

A long low wail trembled on their lips.

In the north-east a little colour seeped along the grey of the horizon – a tarnish of yellow, jet, a flush of rose. The sea made instant flawless response. The colours multiplied.

The Lord of the Harvest took the black cloth from the niche where the horse-shoe had been secreted. The horse-shoe had vanished. In its place was a loaf and a bottle.

The Master Horsemen raised the Harvester to his feet. They put a white cloak over his shoulders. They brought him over to the niche where the whisky and the bread stood.

Slowly the sun heaved itself clear of the sea. The cliff below was alive with the stir and cry of birds. The sea moved and flung glories of light over Quoylay and Hrossey and Hellya, and all the skerries and rocks around. The smell of the earth came to them in the first wind of morning, from the imprisoned fields of the island; and the fence could not keep it back.

The Lord of the Harvest raised his hands. 'We have brought light and blessing to the kingdom of winter,' he said, 'however long it endures, that kingdom, a night or a season or a thousand ages. The word has been found. Now we will eat and drink together and be glad.'

The sun rose. The stones were warm. They broke the bread.

More about Penguins
and Pelicans

Penguinews, which appears every month, contains details of all the new books issued by Penguins as they are published. From time to time it is supplemented by *Penguins in Print*, which is our complete list of almost 5,000 titles.

A specimen copy of *Penguinews* will be sent to you free on request. Please write to Dept EP, Penguin Books Ltd, Harmondsworth, Middlesex, for your copy.

In the U.S.A.: For a complete list of books available from Penguins in the United States write to Dept CS, Penguin Books, 625 Madison Avenue, New York, New York 10022.

In Canada: For a complete list of books available from Penguins in Canada write to Penguin Books Canada Ltd, 41 Steelcase Road West, Markham, Ontario.

Penguin Modern Classics

Mastro-Don Gesualdo

Giovanni Verga

Translated by D. H. Lawrence

On the face of things, Mastro-Don Gesualdo is a success.
Born a peasant but a man 'with an eye for everything
going', he becomes one of the richest men in Sicily,
marrying an aristocrat with his daughter destined, in time,
to wed a duke.

But Gesualdo falls foul of the rigid class structure in
mid-19th-century Sicily. His title 'Mastro-Don',
'Worker-Gentleman', is ironic in itself. Peasants and gentry
alike resent his extraordinary success. And when the
pattern of society is threatened by revolt, Gesualdo is the
rebels' first target ...

Published in 1888, Verga's classic was first introduced to
this country in 1925 by D. H. Lawrence in his own superb
translation. Although broad in scope, with a large cast and
covering over twenty years, *Mastro-Don Gesualdo* is exact
and concentrated: it cuts from set-piece to set-piece – from
feast-day to funeral to sun-white stubble field – anticipating
the narrative techniques of the cinema.

Penguin Modern Classics

Little Novels of Sicily

Giovanni Verga

Twelve scorching stories of Sicilian life
translated by D. H. Lawrence

Little Novels of Sicily shows a nineteenth-century society
fighting to survive against prejudice and a feudal system;
against drought, heat, malaria; a society which travels by
train yet still sees men condemned to the galleys for minor
crimes; a society ripe for revolution but unprepared for
change.

Against a 'solemn and changeless landscape', Verga's
characters slide dramatically up or down the social scale:
Don Piddu, suddenly dispossessed, becomes a mere field
overseer, his daughter falling prey to a seductive stable-boy;
while Massaro, an ascetic peasant, becomes owner of
'possessions as far as his eye could reach'.

D. H. Lawrence, who translated the sketches, believes them
to be drawn from Verga's own village. Certainly, each one
is a genuine cry of pain, despair and anger against brutal
conditions.

The Fox in the Attic

Richard Hughes

The Fox in the Attic is the first volume in Richard Hughes's historical novel sequence, *The Human Predicament*. Combining both the historian's and the novelist's brand of truth he brilliantly recreates the period between the two World Wars.

'This magnificent, authoritative, compassionate, ironic, funny and tragic book . . . vivid both in the evocation of character and in the unfolding of action' – *The Times Literary Supplement*

'An extraordinary creation – extraordinary for its originality of viewpoint, its mixture of the sinister and frolicsome, its audacity in mingling fictional and historical characters' – Kenneth Allsop

'There are few living writers of whom one would say that they had genius; but somehow it seems the most natural thing in the world to say of Richard Hughes' – Goronwy Rees

The Wooden Shepherdess

Richard Hughes

The Wooden Shepherdess is the second instalment of
Richard Hughes's long historical novel sequence, *The
Human Predicament*, of which the first volume, *The Fox
in the Attic* was published in 1961.

This new volume opens with Augustine a fugitive from the
law in Prohibition America; Mitzi in her Carmelite cell;
Mary in a wheeled chair; and Hitler in prison.

'An extraordinarily vivid recreation of the inter-war
years ... the two volumes we already have of *The Human
Predicament* are in themselves enough to make the novel
a major and a unique contribution to the century's
fiction' – *Daily Telegraph*

'Mr Hughes's inventiveness is still formidable, his scope and
range enormous; he is still writing with undiminished
verve, economy and delicacy' – *Sunday Times*

Also published in Penguins:

A High Wind in Jamaica